More Lik
Than

ROBERT CRAIG

PHOENIX

A PHOENIX PAPERBACK

First published in Great Britain in 2004
by Weidenfeld & Nicolson
This paperback edition published in 2005
by Phoenix,
an imprint of Orion Books Ltd,
Orion House, 5 Upper St Martin's Lane,
London WC2H 9EA

This is a work of fiction. Names, characters, places and incidents are either the product of the author's imagination or are used fictitiously. Any resemblance to actual events or locales or persons living or dead, is entirely coincidental.

A CIP catalogue record for this book
is available from the British Library.

ISBN 0 75381 846 9

Printed and bound in Great Britain by
Clays Ltd, St Ives plc

www.orionbooks.co.uk

For Nicola

With thanks to:
Alice Chasey, Emma Finnigan, Richard Milner;
and also to Susy Behr and Charles Buchan,
with the biggest thanks, every time, going to Laura Susijn.

ONE

Everyone who lives in the city knows that the *Apollo* is Bradford's roughest nightclub: bouncers outnumber bar staff and frisk down the patrons not only as they enter but also as they leave. Statistically, *Apollo* customers are more likely to be seriously wounded on a night out than a soldier on active service.

The toilets were in the entrance lobby of the club, placed to service both sections of the *Apollo*: a bar and the club itself, which had an entrance fee. Anna and Natasha would routinely enter the bar, wait a few moments, then walk back into the entrance lobby, use the toilets then walk past the bouncers and into the club, without paying, as if they were returning.

Anna asked Natasha the same question they asked each other at this time every Saturday night, after they had found somewhere to stand which gave them the best possible view of the place.

'What do we come here for?'

The *Apollo* is the type of nightclub where lads tell their mates, 'If you can't pull in here then you might as well give up,' and women come knowing they will be propositioned several times – even if, to save having to buy them a drink, most men won't make an approach until ten to two.

As always, the memory of previous Saturday nights returned once the girls were inside, trapped, and saw the usual specimens: leering, sweating, swaying.

Anna had already made eye contact with one lad. He had grinned. She then made eye contact with another, who raised his pint to acknowledge her. She pulled off the trick of having both know she was interested without either being aware of the other.

Anna's ex-boyfriends had described her with words such as slobbish, stoutish and shabby. Those who had disliked her were more brutal. They thought her shorter and larger than Natasha, though in fact the girls were the same height and a similar weight. Natasha's exes had described her as fussy, easy-going, complicated, difficult, each ex giving contradictory accounts because with each she had acted differently. Her hair was such a light brown colour that in some lights it seemed grey. She changed the style so frequently that few people ever commented on it. Anna had kept the same style all through her adult life: short, loose curls, a brown so dark most people would have said it was black. Their smiles showed the real difference in their characters: Anna smiled broadly, sneakily when she was verging on laughter. Natasha's smile was permanent but slight, but when she was having fun the smile changed her eyes, the shape of her face and the heart of anyone who might have disliked her. Natasha's exes invariably wanted her back; Anna's exes invariably wanted her deported.

Natasha answered Anna's question with the same reply they gave each other every week at the *Apollo*.

'We come here because we're skint and it's cheap and we can never agree where else to go.'

They were approached by a man. 'Did you know it's closing down?' he asked. He was shorter than both of them. He had a red dot on the tip of his nose – a scab from a burst spot. His hair had grown carelessly and had been given no guidance, lying on his head as if it were drawn on. He wore a black jacket and blue trousers. There was a strong possibility that he lived his life unaware of the invention of mirrors.

'*Here?* The *Apollo* is closing down?' Anna asked.

'No it isn't,' Natasha insisted.

The two of them stood closer to the man. This was the nearest he had got to female contact in years, and he tried not to smile, to demonstrate that he shared their concern. He stood on tiptoe yet still had to crane his neck. He wished they would stand slightly further back so that he wouldn't feel so dominated.

'They can't afford the insurance since the riots.'

They quizzed him for more information, which he gave sparingly, conscious that once this subject was exhausted they would have no further interest in him.

'It's closing!' Natasha told Anna.

'Good.'

'Yeah, good,' Natasha agreed. Each girl took a drink of her lager. Then another, then another.

'Can I get you a drink?' the man asked, hoping to prolong their need of him.

'No, thank you,' Anna told him.

'Neither of you are . . . interested?' he asked. 'Interested' was a word chosen with a care rarely found at the *Apollo*.

'Of course we are,' Anna answered, viciously. 'You're gorgeous – how could we not be interested? We're both dripping like broken cisterns.'

He left.

'Oi,' Natasha remonstrated with her friend, 'that was a bit nasty.'

Natasha was careful not to sound too annoyed. Saturday remained the one night of the week that the girls still enjoyed each other's company, the one night when their past fondness for each other instantly returned.

'Imagine,' Anna offered by way of explanation for her bad temper. 'The *Apollo* closing!'

'Good, though, we said,' Natasha reminded her.

Natasha and Anna had been told – though their earliest memories are from long after this date – that they had met at infant school. At the very end of their school life, to avoid receiving poor exam results, they hit upon the genius scam of simply not taking their exams. They left school the same way most other girls from their estate did, as quickly and as unqualified as possible, educated only to pram-pushing level. They didn't care: all they knew for certain was that they each had one true friend, someone who had been there all their life and would always be there, the most important person in their world. When they acquired passports and had to fill in the back page with two names to contact in case of an emergency, each girl defied its purpose and put one name only – each other's.

Natasha and Anna shared a comfortable, modern Housing Association flat, a sanctuary against the outside world. They understood their situation was unusual and would not stay the same for ever. Everyone they knew who was their age had suffered a stream of serious partners and was now entrenched permanently in a stultifying relationship. It had to be their turn soon. In their world it was conscription. But by moving in together they hoped they had found a loophole. Until they had lived together each had believed that there was nothing they didn't know about the other. They were very wrong. To avoid their growing resentment showing, they would make a joke out of each other's bad habits. Natasha made fun of Anna's scruffiness, her lack of organisation, her tendency to leave the bathroom partially demolished. Anna, in turn, mocked Natasha for her terrible ironing. Natasha regularly ruined clothes by making the material shiny or adding creases which should not have been there. There were hundreds of smaller incidents which annoyed them both: washing-up not done, bills not paid on time by the person responsible, fundamental items of food, such as milk, used up and not replaced.

To begin with the agreement was that Natasha would clean and Anna would cook. This arrangement failed as Anna's cooking became worse, and her definition of cooking became broader. 'Toast is not cooking,' Natasha had told her.

Their first-ever real argument was after Natasha ruined a silver wine rack. The rack had been all Anna had kept of her mother's possessions. Natasha, unaware the silver was only plating, washed the rack with a pan scourer, removing significant sections of the silver plate.

The second time they fell out was when Anna had an abortion.

Natasha was never anything less than supportive, but Anna had the operation, then returned to work less troubled than if she had returned from the dentist. They argued after Anna made a silly, distasteful joke to Natasha: 'Well, that's one way to lose weight quickly.'

There had been a truce in recent months, in spite of money becoming a greater worry. There was a period of severe hardship when they had to replace their washing machine and were forced to save to buy another. They had to set off earlier for work, walking instead of taking the bus.

Having to stay in on Saturday night was Anna's greatest test. She began a jigsaw but became bored before she had collected all the straight edges. Natasha had taken a very long bath. She dressed in her pyjamas, made herself something unhealthy to eat, then crashed out on their settee and watched junk. Anna began to pace around, pestering Natasha by reminding her of the time, and which pub they would normally be in if they had gone out. The next day, the conclusion of a week of poor diet, Anna accompanied Natasha to her mother's for Sunday dinner. They returned home from that ordeal reminded of why they were such good friends and were temporarily happy not to be in a settled relationship with a man.

TWO

For Natasha and Anna the determining factor in taking the job in the shoe shop was that there had been two vacancies, and they could work together. Years later, both girls had realised how depressingly long their futures were going to be and had independently reached the same conclusion: 'I want change.'

The shop was always busy in spite of being expensive, and even with their thirty per cent staff discount Natasha and Anna still bought their shoes elsewhere. On Saturdays, in snatched moments, they would anticipate the night ahead, the clothes they might wear, who they hoped to see, any new bar they could visit for a change.

After leaving work they grabbed a hamburger, fries and a shake to eat on their bus ride home, flirting with the driver if he attempted to forbid them boarding with food.

At home they would burst into the flat and put the CD player on, the volume up as high as they dared, audible over the sound of showers and hair-dryers. They plucked or shaved, applied make-up, fixed hair, dressed, re-dressed, dressed again. On Friday night Natasha would always ensure that whatever clothes she had decided to wear were cleaned, ironed and laid out ready. Each Saturday, at the last minute, Anna would go through her whole wardrobe – then look through Natasha's. In desperation she would often revert to rummaging through the washing basket.

Finally ready, they braced themselves for the walk to the bus stop. Before they had set off this particular Saturday night, Natasha had called Anna into the kitchen. She'd pointed to a couple on the street, play fighting, the girl hitting the boy for having made some teasing remark. Then they embraced before the boy gave the girl a piggyback, him running so as to scare her, she screaming hysterically.

Natasha wondered if the couple were faking their fun, then she wondered if all those other couples she knew, the wretched, bickering, defeated couples, had also played those games, though they had long since accepted that their fate was miserable.

Natasha checked the *Radio Times* and set the video for the programmes she didn't want to miss; Anna checked that her sheets were reasonably fresh. Just in case. They left for their night out, catching the bus back into town, self-conscious in their showy clothes and thick perfume.

When they jumped off the bus, Anna told Natasha: 'A girl just can't have the same fun with a bloke she can with her mate.'

'I suppose we'll settle down. Everyone I know says it's bound to happen.'

'It's Saturday night. Let's forget everything other people think.'

Natasha had been going out with Derek for three weeks. She had stayed with him this long as a result of no one else asking her out. Through all these three weeks the only occasion she believed anything he said was when he had told her his name.

'Did Derek tell you where he was going tonight?' Anna asked. Anna had seen Derek: he was at the edge of the *Apollo*'s dance floor, tormenting some girl's tonsils with his tongue.

'His mum's in hospital. He's broke anyway, I had to lend him money so he could take her some Lucozade.'

'How much did he borrow?'

'Twenty quid.'

'Twenty quid? Where the hell does he buy his Lucozade?' Anna knew that if she told Natasha of Derek's infidelity Natasha would confront him and there would be trouble. Being thrown out of the *Apollo* came easily: the bouncers hated everyone, to cover all eventualities.

Anna bought fresh drinks. When she returned, Natasha was having fun: she was giving out a phone number.

'A false number,' Natasha clarified after the boy had left. 'You've seen him before, haven't you? Every time I come in here he pesters me for my phone number. I had to get rid of him.'

'Whose number did you give him?'

'I just made up some numbers.'

Another boy made his approach. 'I've seen you in here before,' he informed Natasha.

'I think I can account for that – I have been in here before,' she answered, smiling to confuse him. Not able to judge whether this was encouraging or dismissive, he abandoned foreplay and spoke his mind.

'Can I bash your gash?'

Natasha had been coming here too long to be so easily shocked. 'It's sweet of you to ask, but I'll pass if you don't mind.'

He left. Another came along. By *Apollo* standards this one was a catch – at least he made an attempt at charm; some didn't even attempt standing.

'Now then, ladies, I was wondering what you were drinking.'

Until now Natasha and Anna had both been drinking lager. Anna told him, 'Smirnoff Ice.'

He constructed an equation around the formula of the cost of the drinks against the chance of either of these two girls consequently sleeping with him. 'Well, thanks for telling me. Now I know.' He left.

'I'm glad this place is closing down,' Anna told her friend. 'I don't want to get involved with any more men from here. I can't afford to take any more time off work appearing in court as a witness.'

Anna decided to point out Derek. Natasha, for want of any better entertainment, was over by him within seconds. He pathetically moved away from the girl he was with and said a feeble 'Hello' to Natasha, as if nothing was untoward.

'Where's my twenty quid?' she shouted. The raised voice alerted the bouncers. They were standing behind her before she had finished the question. They allowed her enough time to collect her money before escorting her away. The club was still quiet so they took the risk of not expelling her.

'Why did you even go out with him in the first place?' Anna asked.

'Because he has nice hands . . . I'm really going to have to tighten up my vetting procedure. You know, I'm finally beginning to come to a conclusion about men, at least the men I've met . . . What it is, I think . . . What I need to do is find a better prospect. I need to find myself a man with money.'

Anna might have believed the sincerity of this statement if Natasha had not immediately begun smiling at a thug. Anna knew he was a thug, because the tattoo on his neck said so, in gothic lettering. To her amazement and horror she saw Natasha walk up to the thug, flirt, touch and talk. A moment later she was back.

'Let's go,' Natasha said, 'before the fight starts.'

'There's not usually any fighting till much later.' Anna was distracted by the noise of the thug fitting Derek with a buffet-shaped hat.

'Come on,' Natasha said. 'I've got twenty quid – let's get a kebab and a taxi home.'

In its beginning, the early rumours about the *Apollo*, like most new clubs, were that it was busy and exciting. Situated outside the city centre, on the route towards the estate where they had been born and grown up, Anna and Natasha, on their first ever visit, expected to see lots of people they knew.

Inside, their first impression of the place was aided by arriving knee-bendingly drunk, each needing the support of the other to keep upright as they collapsed through drink, then laughter. In some clubs this spectacle might have singled them out, but at the *Apollo* everyone was paralytic. The bouncers preferred drunks; they fought less harmfully. A cross-section of Bradford's drinkers – ranging from the casual drinker to the career drinker – had all found a home in the club. Within the first hour, Natasha and Anna, in equal measure, were both approached by many men, each with a story to tell.

'It's like a club for divorcees,' Anna told Natasha. 'Every bloke who's spoken to me has just come out of a long-term relationship with a woman who – according to them – was an absolute *bitch*.'

'It makes you wonder why they're so keen to find another,' Natasha replied. Anna was grinning, enjoying herself. After two hours Anna and Natasha had met up with people they knew from their old school; the estate; friends of friends; ex-girlfriends and boyfriends of friends, and people who knew their brothers and sister.

At midnight a fight broke out. This didn't ruin the night; it was simply another item on the entertainment agenda. The DJ had played U2's *Sunday Bloody Sunday,* which had encouraged gangs of lads to gather into circles and jump up and down, eventually falling onto people and tables. When apologies were not forthcoming, glasses and tables were launched. When the gangs were evicted the DJ chose to follow U2 with House Of Pain's *Jump Around*, which encouraged more jumping – which vibrated the dance floor so much that the DJ's turntable was knocked and *Jump Around* came to an abrupt end. The DJ responded with, 'Keep away from my decks, you wankers,' then played the record from the beginning.

Anna danced with some lad, then later they kissed for twenty minutes while Natasha listened to some manic depressive explain to her why he could never make his former wife happy, no matter how hard he had worked, or how much attention he had paid to her. Natasha kept the thought to herself, but would have loved to tell him that perhaps all he had to do was clean his teeth.

'His teeth looked like he had a mouth full of Sugar Puffs,' she told Anna as they later made their way from the *Apollo* to a nearby curry house. Anna was exercising her jaw, trying to regain some feeling.

They didn't go to the *Apollo* the following Saturday. And for the first year they only went occasionally, when they were exceptionally short of money. In the last year or so, after the two girls had moved into their flat together, money became even tighter, so the *Apollo* became the only club they ever went to. On some nights they didn't even go to the pub first, but got drunk at home and made their way to the *Apollo* at ten.

Some months back Anna had been barred from the *Apollo*. She had met a boy and gone out with him several times. In the club she met an ex-girlfriend of his and they compared notes. It turned out that everything he had told Anna – about his job, his history, where he lived – was a lie. When he came in the club she attacked him, and was barred for a month.

'I don't like being lied to,' she needlessly explained to Natasha. 'It's like they're saying I'm stupid, or gullible – or not worth telling the truth to. You know?'

For four Saturdays the girls had to go once more to other nightclubs but found that they were unable to relax there; they knew few people and were conscious of their dress and their age. They seemed to receive very little attention from the opposite sex, and the music they played was designed for serious dancing, rather than as a background to chatting and having a good time.

It got to the point where even Natasha was looking forward to returning to the *Apollo*. After this, they went almost every Saturday. Natasha's only qualm was that going so frequently was like an acceptance of the fact that they fitted in there and were happy to do so.

'But we don't fit in,' Anna argued. 'We have fun because we take the piss out of everyone.' And some Saturdays were still good; they still got drunk, they still danced, they still got chatted up by imbeciles, which was fun, or by nice lads – which was even more fun.

One night, they asked each other for the first time why they still went to the *Apollo*. They had had a sober night during which they talked about the future, the inevitable future that creeps up on everyone, when you stop going to nightclubs without realising you've stopped.

Though neither girl was that drunk, the harsh lights of the kebab shop sobered them up completely. The maxim of the shop was printed on a sheet of A4, now stained from grease and heat:

IF YOU DON'T EAT YOU DON'T SHIT; AND IF YOU DON'T SHIT YOU DIE.

'I can't get my head round it – the *Apollo* closing down.'

'The odd thing is, I thought I wanted it to close down.'

The climax of their week had been – as all too often – a disappointment. To strengthen their resolve to find themselves better men, they reminded each other of the boys they'd met at the *Apollo*. The list was a horrific litany. Of the two, Natasha was the one who didn't easily recover from these men, each time taking their offences too personally. Natasha's fault was that she was too trusting, Anna's that she always saw the best in people. Both conceded this.

'But hold on,' Natasha said. 'Since when did those things become faults? It's not us who are in the wrong. It's good to trust people, it's good to see the best in people.'

Though it wasn't their turn to be served, the lad in front of them was so blathered, barely standing, his head on his chest, that they pushed past him to place their order – belligerent with a new sense of ruthlessness.

Outside they continued talking, holding their kebabs in front of them with one hand, like hymn books, picking at the soggy salad. Anna was giving Natasha a description of her ideal man.

'I'd like someone who doesn't think that making a phone call is the greatest romantic gesture imaginable. A male equivalent of you, and a relationship like I have with you. And honesty. Honesty is important. None of that is unreasonable, is it?'

They passed an alley; at the opening a couple were arguing, the boy attempting to persuade the girl to have sex with him in the alley.

'It's already being used,' she told him. Through drunk-blind eyes he saw nothing.

'Come on, I'll be quick.'

She relented. 'Have you got a johnny?' He shook his head; she walked away. 'Forget it, I'm not using a crisp packet again.'

Natasha tasted a slither of the lamb: the grease had already congealed and it tasted of snotty salt.

'I want someone who's down to earth but isn't an arse. Not cocky or full of himself,' Natasha replied. 'And – you're right – it has to be like it is between us. I don't want confusions or misunderstandings. He has to *get* me. So if I want the impossible, I might as well be ambitious. I'm bored of having boyfriends who borrow my money. Or steal my money,' she told Anna. 'From now on I am going to have nothing to do with a man unless he has money.'

'Mercenary bitch.'

'That's me. Day one.' Natasha was finally deterred from picking at any more of her kebab as they passed a lad on all fours, spewing as if cheering a football team. He wiped his chin, flicking the remnants across the pavement.

They heard a vicious shout behind them. 'Oi! You! You owe me a shag – it was a deal!' They turned and saw the thug Natasha had conned into beating up Derek. She threw her kebab towards him, even though he was hundreds of yards away. By good fortune a taxi was passing – and was persuaded to stop by Natasha's good looks and by Anna stepping out into the road, flapping her arms.

When they arrived home they quickly changed into their night-clothes, and settled together on the settee to watch the trashy romantic film Natasha had taped: happiness, tragedy, complications, triumphant love against the odds. They turned all the lights off so the only illumination was the blue cast of the TV screen.

Derek phoned. Natasha had expected he might and had planned a suitable response. She put the phone to her arse, farted, then hung up. Anna was crippled with hysterics, then moved off the settee for a few moments.

THREE

Anna had two brothers, both violent drunks. They were always together – inseparable so as to provide mutual protection against all the enemies they had nurtured over the years. Being quick to fight and as ferocious as all imbeciles, if they entered a pub, everyone would acknowledge them, then be on their guard for the rest of the night. As ugly and stupid and violent as both were, both had girlfriends they lived with. Both cheerfully cheated on these girls whenever a chance arose.

Anna never saw her brothers except by accident; she was kept up to date on their lives by gossip, rumour and reading *Court File* in the local paper.

The last conversation she had held with them both had, as always, been basic.

'All right?' one had asked.

'Yeah. You?' she returned.

'All right, aye.'

'All right then?' the other asked.

'Yeah, fine. What about you?'

'Yeah.'

'See ya then. See you both.'

Their parents, both drunks, had died within two years of each other, the last to go, her mother, dying when Anna was fourteen. Her father had frequently cheated on her mother, always attributing his infidelities to drink. She always forgave him and took him back, attributing this weakness in her to drink. Anna went to live with an aunt and uncle, who later moved to Scarborough, freeing

Anna from the burden of regular visits except when she fancied a trip to the seaside. Faced with the prospect of living alone, Anna suggested to Natasha that they found a place to share. Natasha eagerly agreed. She had remained at home after her younger sister, Brenda, had moved in with her fiancé. Natasha's parents rarely spoke to each other, except when her mother insulted her father. By default Natasha was landed with the job of peace negotiator, failing in her role when the only sensible advice she could think of to pass on to her parents was to get divorced. Though both Anna's parents were dead, people said Natasha was prettier than Anna, so their good fortune was equal.

Natasha envied Anna her Sundays. Without parents to visit, Anna could stay in bed, recovering if she had a hangover, simply doing nothing and taking all day to do so.

The Sunday bus service was so poor that Natasha often walked the three miles to her parents' house, the length of the walk joyously delaying her arrival. During Sunday dinner Natasha sat with two women in unhappy relationships and would be quizzed on her own love life. Under this duress Natasha, last week, had told them about Derek, inventing a better job and a better character for him. Now, this Sunday, after last night, she would have to tell the truth; that Derek had a crap job, a crap character – and, thank God, he was history.

An imagined conversation ran through her mind, with her taking both roles, imitating Anna's speech mannerisms and her bluntness. These days Natasha imagined conversations with the Anna she had known before they lived together – that Anna was nicer.

'Cheer up, matey,' Anna was saying, 'it could be worse.'

'How? The Sunday ritual of witnessing two couples who are miserable giving me a hard time for not also being in a couple?'

'Tell them we're lesbians.' Natasha wasn't sure if she had said this aloud, and checked around to make sure no one was near, then carried on putting words into Anna's mouth. 'It's what everyone thinks anyway.'

When she had first moved in with Anna, she would enter the old estate with some sense of satisfaction. At least she had moved away; she had not, as most of her contemporaries had done, moved into an estate house with an estate boy, had estate children, stayed for ever. Today she walked on for a while without thought, then the imagined conversation resumed itself. 'The hard time they give me, I sometimes think it would be easier just to surrender and marry the first dummy from the *Apollo* who asked me.'

There was no sun to be seen this Sunday morning, but Geno's ice-cream van drove past nevertheless. She knew where the van would stop, even though there were no customers to hail it. The van waited, and she waited – she knew this was where the van turned, to tour the estate again. The same driver, conceivably the same van, had been doing the same turn in the same place since she was a child.

Natasha continued now, speaking in her mind, but only to herself, not to an imagined Anna. 'I've fought against them and their attitudes, all my life. I'm not going to surrender now. My mum and dad are miserable: they fucked up their lives by hitching themselves to someone they didn't connect with, yet they're happy to see Brenda heading towards the same mistake and want me to do no different.'

Her parents' house was easy to distinguish from their near neighbours. They had bought the house and were keen to advertise this: brickwork had been painted glossy crimson, the path ended at an arbour, and the front garden was cluttered with amateur landscaping.

Brenda, her younger sister, and Keith her fiancé were already inside, sitting together on the settee – something they never did at home. Natasha's father was sanding wood; remnants and off-cuts of timber littered the living room. He was making wall units with his usual impeccable precision. Everything he had made during the course of their twenty-eight-year-old marriage, he had re-built, then re-built again. He had a productive hobby, but no new projects. The joy of having a handy husband had long since faded. Natasha's mother entered the living room holding a tray with four cups of tea, which she distributed.

She told her husband, 'If you want a cup of tea, make one yourself, you fucking idle, fat bastard.'

Brenda made a protest about swearing in front of Keith, though Keith – as ever – appeared not to register anything that happened. The time was seven minutes past twelve. He tapped the face of his watch, hoping it was running slow.

'What?' her mother replied defensively. 'Oh, I'm sure Keith's heard language a lot worse than that.'

He had. Last Sunday.

'Couldn't you get a Saturday off work, Nat?' Brenda asked. She asked the same question regularly.

'What for?'

'To go shopping. I'm stuck in all day – then all night. I hate weekends!'

'They'd never give us a Saturday off. We're too busy.' Natasha was waiting for Derek to be mentioned. How long now?

'You should have brought Derek with you,' her mother said. Two seconds.

Natasha dived straight in, admitting that Derek was another mistake and was now consigned to history. She attempted to sound casual. She didn't need to try that hard.

'You'll never find someone even half-decent at the *Apollo*,' her sister told her.

'How do you know?' Keith asked. 'When did you ever go to the *Apollo*?'

Brenda answered, 'Before I met you. In the days when I used to have a life.'

Keith and Brenda began a row, throwing insults at each other, which continued until they were sitting at the table and dinner was being served. Natasha's father had prepared the meal, as he did every Sunday, yet her mother took the glory of serving. She served everyone except her husband. As her father helped himself to food and Brenda and Keith continued their conflict by other methods – namely fierce, venomous silence – her mother whispered to Natasha:

'You do need someone, love. It's not good to be so independent. Imagine if you don't get yourself a man before you're too old, think how you'll regret wasting your life.'

Natasha knew better than to comment, yet she could not resist. 'Wasting my life?'

'You've been away from home for a year now. A year this week.'

It seemed longer. Maybe as recently as six months ago Natasha might have argued with her mum, putting forward the reasons why living away from home, with her lifelong friend, was an excellent idea which had led to happiness. But now Natasha couldn't help agreeing with her mother. Which was intolerable. By the end of dinner Natasha had decided to confront her sister and mother on the irony of their positions.

'You all want me to settle down, yet your relationships are both miserable,' Natasha found herself blurting out as she loaded plates into the sink. She found herself being ganged up on by four people. They told her she knew nothing about serious relationships. It wasn't all lovey-dovey; no one knew what went on behind closed doors; you had to take the rough with the smooth; it was a question of give and take.

Bludgeoned by cliché, Natasha left for home at four o'clock, far happier. Life would be different from now on. The imminent closure of the *Apollo* had made the decision for her, given her the kick up the arse she needed. From now on she would be mercenary and cold; calculating and manipulative. That type of person was smart.

FOUR

When Natasha returned home she made no comment on the messy state of the flat. While they watched TV that Sunday evening she even made cheese on toast and poured two glasses of wine – finally finishing off the bottle which had languished in their fridge for months.

'Ta,' Anna said, looking down from the TV to her toenails, which she was painting green. If she was at all suspicious of her friend's good humour she made no comment. Some hospital drama was on.

'How's your day been?' Natasha asked.

'Excellent. I've done fuck all.'

Anna brought a slice of cheese on toast towards her mouth using the same hand she was holding the brush with, and then had to wipe green nail varnish from her cheek.

'Is it all off?' she asked. Natasha nodded yes, then began to write out a plan. She had begun scheming, the intended victim being her best friend and flatmate.

'What is it we're looking for in a man?'

'Are you writing this down?'

'No no, this is something else,' Natasha told her. 'Come on, what do you look for in a man?'

'Like?'

'Personality,' Natasha clarified.

'That would be nice. A man with a personality. All I want a man for is sex. Everything else is a bonus.' Anna had long since learnt to expect nothing from men. She had learnt that no man was 'different' – except that they each had different flaws. Anna often wished – keeping this easily misconstrued wish a secret even from Natasha – that she didn't fancy men, didn't like sex, didn't desire the company of interesting and funny men. The glimpses she had had of interesting and funny men suggested that they were like that *in the beginning*, for a week or so, sometimes only days, often only hours. It's how they were when they were chasing her, quickly dispensing with funny and interesting once they had her, replacing them with boring and possessive.

Natasha attempted to keep the discussion focused. 'So, accepting that we like sex, and will eventually settle down, we're agreed that'll we'll give up the impossible search for compatibility and simply look for someone who will free us of the burden of work and the worry of having no money?'

'So we don't have to go to that bloody shop ever again?'

'Sounds good, doesn't it? So we're definitely agreed?'

If the *Apollo* was closing, and both girls were tired of the idiots they met there anyway, Natasha knew the club she wanted to go to. It was called *Bartok*, but everyone, including its staff, called it *Bartok's* for reasons the Hungarian owner could never comprehend. The entrance fee was an outrageous twenty-five pounds, fifteen if you arrived before ten o'clock. The entrance fee at the *Apollo* was two pounds, and Anna resented paying even that much.

Natasha had written a 'Schedule of Persuasion'. *MONDAY – say nothing to Anna so she will not suspect you are planning.* Throughout Monday Natasha stayed strong and silent and did not mention the next weekend. *TUESDAY – mention the weekend only in passing.* Natasha was still calculating how best to do this when by good fortune Anna commented that she could not believe that it was still only Tuesday.

'I know,' Natasha replied, seizing the chance. 'Another four days until Saturday.' Anna made no comment. 'We'll have to start thinking about where we're going on Saturday night.' Natasha cursed herself for being ahead of schedule. Anna, however, simply nodded in agreement and the subject was dropped.

WEDNESDAY – mention Bartok's in an unrelated context. When she actually had to think how best to contrive a way of mentioning the club without being specific, nothing came to mind.

Alone in the stock room, after dinner, Natasha thought through the conversation she might have with Anna, playing it out in her mind.

'If we go to *Bartok's* before ten it's only fifteen quid in, Anna.'

'Fifteen quid is a joke!' She had Anna's voice wrong in sound, but perfect in her choice of words and delivery.

'It'll be a different experience. It will be fun. It's a one-off.'

'You say one-off, I say fuck off.'

As they left work on Wednesday evening and waited for their bus, Natasha finally gave up the quest for subtlety.

'If we go to *Bartok's* before ten it's only fifteen quid in.'

After recovering from the shock just of the suggestion of paying so much money, Anna regained some of her senses. '*Bartok's* . . . fifteen . . . *ONLY*?'

'But –'

'But nothing. I'm not going to *Bartok's*. What do you want to go there for?'

'A change,' Natasha offered.

'Change is all we'll have left. I'm not paying all that money to get into a nightclub unless it's inclusive of booze, the taxi home and the definite offer of an acceptable shag.'

Natasha knew her friend well enough not to pursue this argument; she would only force her into an intractable position.

THURSDAY – diplomatically mention Bartok's as a specific destination. DO IT CAREFULLY! With her plan now so thoroughly wrecked, Natasha instead solicited Anna for a better idea.

'I don't have any, but I'm not forking out fifteen quid,

especially when the only reason you want to go to *Bartok's* is to get off with some rich guy.'

'You might get yourself one, too.'

For a fraction of a second Anna was convinced. But then: 'Fifteen quid?'

'It's an investment,' Natasha added feebly.

FRIDAY – if she's not convinced, offer to pay for her. Natasha's gamble was that this offer would demonstrate the strength of her desire, and so Anna would obligingly reject the offer, yet still agree to go. Natasha again improvised.

'Come on. Please. It'll be a change. It'll be fun. It'll be a laugh. Come on. Us two – in *Bartok's*! It's just a one-off. Come on, Anna. Please. If it's crap I won't ask again.'

Friday afternoon. Suddenly, with Anna's consent, they were already excited about Saturday night. They began speculating about the club, how they should behave, the music that might be played and whether they should dance at all, yet never forgetting their reason for going, even though Anna still maintained that ideally she would choose to find a man she actually enjoyed being with.

'Impossible, Anna,' Natasha lectured with the casual cynicism Anna knew to be a lie. 'There are no people we know who are together and happy.'

'My aunty and uncle.'

'They're *dull*. It's easy to be compatible when you're not interested in anything, have no opinions, no ambitions or hopes. Of all the boyfriends you've had, how many have you been compatible with, compatible in a real, permanent way?'

'None,' Anna conceded. 'But I haven't really been trying.'

'So you think if you'd have been trying one of them might have been Mr Right?'

'Not a fucking chance. They've all been divvies. That might be the difference between us, Nat. I accept that men aren't my type. They're never going to understand me like you understand me. We've known each other since we were embryos, it seems like. So

I agree with you – if compatibility is not an option, let's look for someone with cash. But if I did meet someone who was nice, I'd prefer him to someone who was well-off.'

' "Nice"?' Natasha scoffed.

'You know what I mean. Someone who wasn't a doylum.'

On its busiest days the shop quickly degenerated into chaos, the staff dodging each other as they ran back and forth from the stock room, jumping the hurdles of opened shoeboxes and scattered shoes which grew in number as the day progressed and they had no opportunity to clear away the rejects of one customer before another grabbed their attention. Often, at the end of a day, staff would survey the shop and, like after a malicious burglary, the carpet could barely be seen for wreckage.

On this Friday, as hard and as fast as they worked, customers were given wider smiles than was necessary, Anna and Natasha suddenly flush with anticipation.

Gerard Peters, the shop manager, their boss, was merely four years their senior yet had perfected a method of being condescending to everyone in the world. His shirt, ironed by his mother, was always accompanied by a jokey tie – motifs from *The Simpsons* or *South Park* – to compensate for a startling lack of personality. Fifteen minutes before the shop closed, Gerard gathered the staff, his hands above his head to gain a silence which already existed. He smoothed down his hair, shining the grease. Before Gerard handed over their wage slips he sometimes used these weekly occasions as an excuse to lecture on customer complaints, the untidiness of the shop, or the lack of any coherent organisation in the stock room.

'No wage slips today. There's been a problem.'

The amount of their earnings never altered.

'But the money has still gone into our bank accounts?' Natasha asked, the first to anticipate this problem. Anna was the first to read Gerard's expression.

'Oh shit. You're joking?'

'It'll be in first thing on Monday. It's a computer thing. You'll have to dip into your savings for the weekend.'

Even if the two girls emptied both their accounts – inconvenient as this would be – their pooled resources would total sixteen pounds.

'That way at least *I* could still get into *Bartok's*,' Natasha joked on their otherwise silent bus ride home.

FIVE

One autumn, at middle school, aged ten, Anna and another girl asked if Natasha wanted to go to the park, to sweep leaves. The girls' idea was to make piles of leaves to jump into, run through and make into dens. Natasha couldn't see the fun in this, and resented Anna for being with another friend, and so declined. In the park, a photographer from the local paper snapped the girls up to their necks in leaves. The photograph was printed in the paper, to herald the arrival of autumn. At school the following day Anna and the other girl were celebrities; no one was remotely impressed by Natasha's protest that she had *nearly* gone with them.

One way or the other, Natasha was determined to go to *Bartok's* tomorrow night. She had set such store by the place she felt that any revision to her plans would result in her missing out on something. She did not want to have to wonder how the night might have been. A fortnight would pass before the girls enjoyed another Saturday night out; and in that time they would – she knew this – have forgiven the *Apollo* for its *Apollo*-ness and return.

She phoned Brenda's and spoke to Keith.

'You know those ceramic hair straighteners of mine that Brenda's always wanted?' Anna heard Natasha ask Keith. Then: 'And you said you were thinking about getting a portable CD player for when you're in your garage? I want to sell mine.'

The deal was done. Even though Anna had understood

Natasha's sacrifice, she had not spoken out for fear of accidentally dissuading her friend from the sale.

When she came off the phone, Natasha told Anna the new plan.

'He's bringing the money and collecting the straighteners and CD player tomorrow night, about seven. He's loaded – I know that because he's always bragging that he has so much money that he doesn't know what to do with it – yet he haggled with me for every penny. Anyway, tomorrow night, I say we rush home from work and be ready to go out as soon as he gets here. We drink as much as we can, in the cheapest pub we can find, then get to *Bartok's* at nine forty-five. We can take it easy in there, drinks are bound to be expensive.'

The plan was agreed. Natasha slept well while Anna lay awake speculating on the benefits of having a rich boyfriend; or even one who wasn't necessarily rich, just well-off; or even one who was poor but not tight either; or even just a bum who would be nice to her. To entertain herself whilst she waited for sleep, she had a conversation with Natasha, with her taking both roles, imitating Natasha's mannerisms and pseudo-cynicism.

'Do you really think *Bartok's* will be the answer?' she asked Natasha.

'Not unless the question is, "Where can we go to pay shitloads of money and feel awkward and out of place?" '

'It was your idea to go!' Anna exclaimed. Actually, Natasha would have answered with something cautious, like 'We'll see what it's like.'

'We hope for too much,' Anna would have told her.

'Nothing wrong with that, seeing as we've always expected too little.'

'We can't expect to find the man of our dreams in a club. I have doubts about finding him on this continent,' Anna might have said. She then thought about this answer, and revoked it. She was truly excited about tomorrow night. There was nothing to lose.

Imagine if she met a man who remained interesting and

enjoyed trying to make her laugh. Someone who was charming and funny as well as genuine. That type of man did not go to the *Apollo*. *Bartok's* might be different . . .

Saturday morning. Natasha woke Anna up a little earlier than was necessary. She had brought her breakfast in bed: scrambled eggs and fresh orange juice. She had never done this before.

'Tonight's the night!'

'I'm glad you persuaded me now,' Anna said. 'It's been a long time since we've been this excited about going out.'

'I'll tell you when it was – Corrine Slater's hen night.'

Corrine Nichols, née Slater, used to live just a few houses down from Anna's family home. Brenda had assured Natasha that she would not be going, and so Anna and Natasha had been free to anticipate the hen night with great excitement. Then Brenda arrived, and latched onto Anna and Natasha and set about ruining their evening by complaining over everything: pubs were too quiet or too busy, drinks were too expensive or else it took too long to be served. Eventually, sick of her sister, Natasha went along with Anna's plan to ditch her. They enjoyed a couple of hours of fun before Brenda caught up with them at the nightclub, where she ruined the remainder of the evening complaining about the earlier desertion.

'Let's hope tonight at *Bartok's* ends better than *that* evening,' Natasha said to Anna as they got ready for work.

'It'll be fine so long as your miserable fucking sister doesn't show up!'

'Tonight's the night' remained Anna and Natasha's most dominant thought all through Saturday. They were so thrilled that they did not discuss their excitement at work, just grinning at each other instead, and giggling. Only once did Natasha let slip an 'I can't wait!'

It wasn't until they were on the bus home that they released all their verbal excitement, talking without pause so that their burgers and fries became cold and had to be thrown away.

*

Preparing to go out had been easier when life was more innocent, when they only had to worry about attracting men, rather than the possibility of physical contact. When they were fourteen, the local Youth Club was open on Tuesdays and Thursdays, and on each of these days Anna would call at Natasha's house after tea, bringing a change of clothes and her make-up in a carrier bag. In Natasha's bedroom the girls would experiment with make-up and try to decide which clothes were sexy without being tarty. In those days, Anna would help Natasha construct a cleavage.

'Cotton wool can't make up the deficit,' Anna would tell her. 'We'd need two sheep for that.' Then Natasha would tuck in, then pull out, Anna's T-shirt so that the hang of her belly would appear to be the sag of her clothes.

'I'm a fat bitch,' Anna moaned.

'No you're not,' Natasha reassured her. 'Well, you're not fat, anyway.'

These days, as adults, the girls didn't need each other's help, but sought each other's advice simply for fun.

With good humour they now reserved only for Saturday nights, Natasha showered, while Anna rested her foot on the toilet to shave her legs, stopping only to flick the peppered foam at Natasha, who retaliated by aiming the shower nozzle at Anna and consequently drenching the bathroom.

A hangover from their past, they still got dressed in Natasha's room, never Anna's. They had made the attempt once, but Anna's room was such a mess that Natasha lost her hairdryer and Anna lost a shoe.

At Natasha's dressing table, they squeezed up together and applied their make-up in unison, first foundation, then doing their eyes, cheeks and lips.

'I wonder how many times a woman applies make-up in her life?' Natasha asked.

'Must be thousands,' Anna guessed. 'Except in your sister's case – then it's millions.'

They then dressed, helping each other with zips, brushing down clothes, drying hair, Anna rushing, stopping only to check the mirror to make sure nothing was too amiss; Natasha looking in the mirror constantly, stopping only when forced. Music played seamlessly in the background, to kick-start their mood.

Keith arrived and suspended proceedings, each girl flirting with him simply because they were in the mood. Natasha objected to his broad, teeth-revealing smile, his attempts at humour and his eagerness to chat. These were pleasantries he should reserve for his fiancée.

'Smarmy bastard,' Natasha thought about him.

'Smarmy bastard,' Anna said to him.

So finally, armed with the money and with the buzz which comes before all new adventures, they took a taxi into town; tonight they deserved no less.

As they trawled the pubs their new disdain made them attractive to the more selective boys. They were chatted up constantly, rarely having a moment to speak to each other as they instead parried the remarks of the many men who tried their luck. There were those whose comments they could not respond to, yet still took as flattery, such as 'Cor, you're fucking lovely.' Then *Apollo* types whose idea of a conversation starter was 'Hello, sweetheart, are you up for it or what?' There were those who tried bona-fide chat-up lines – the girls could have fun with these if the boys delivered them with irony. Then there were those few, the significant minority, who might only say 'Hello' and hope you would say hello back.

On this night, this special, spectacular night, Anna and Natasha had them all, every kind. Tonight was the night.

'If I don't get a jump tonight,' Anna told her friend, 'I'm going to sew it up.'

'I can't imagine that.'

'You think I'll definitely get laid?'

'I just can't imagine you sewing.'

Tonight, as they moved from one bar to the next, they talked to girls, too; never having realised before how many they knew. After going out in town on Saturday night for so many years, they recognised lots of faces. They might never learn these girls' names, yet they knew where they would be at certain times; they knew which ones had boyfriends, who was loud, who was shy; they knew some of their stories about divorces or run-ins with exes, or rivalries with other girls; they knew which were easy-going and fun and which girls were bitches.

They met two girls who worked with them in the shop, Stephanie and Nicola, both many years younger than them, out tonight with their boyfriends. The four of them stood together straining for conversation until Natasha and Anna appeared, and were lavished with attention.

Usually when they went out, they would see girls they knew from school, and run the gauntlet of those predictable, standard questions: 'Are you still working at . . . ?', 'Are you still seeing . . . ?', 'Have you seen . . . from school?' They would then have to listen to their boasts about better jobs and serious relationships. Each time they'd question why they still had the obligation to speak to people they knew only by misfortune.

Tonight Anna and Natasha were cheered by bumping into a gang of lasses they knew from their old estate, out celebrating one of their birthdays. These girls didn't care if Natasha and Anna were single. They were all too familiar with the cost of having someone. Their Saturday nights out were rare, requiring the organisation and preparation of D-Day: negotiations with partners, arranging baby-sitters, acquiring money. The gang passed around an illicit bottle of Bacardi to spice up their drinks; Natasha and Anna accepted a splash in their lagers. Not a cocktail sold to order, though fun all the same. The women laughed in full voice: for them fun – normally in such short supply – was snatched greedily.

The girls moved on, to drink their booze in the next pub. Natasha confided in Anna. 'I wonder what that lot would think of me if they knew I was looking for a man just because he has money.'

Anna drained her glass. 'They'd wish you good luck. They know money's more important than love.'

The time had come to walk to *Bartok's*, and Natasha was quickly sober at the thought.

'What if they think we're common in *Bartok's*?'

'*Common?* Fuck 'em! You're not ashamed of who you are or where you come from, are you?'

'Of course not. Fuck 'em,' she said, with none of Anna's conviction.

Natasha worried that *Bartok's* patrons would see that the elegance of her dress was phoney, bought as a second, needing a minor repair which Natasha had made. They would soon judge that her dull, unrewarding job had scarred her with its bitter mundanity. She should learn to settle down, remember her place, accept everything everyone else accepted. If she wanted status she should be modern and smart and earn the money herself. To mortgage herself by opting to find a knight in shining armour was little short of prostitution. And everyone would know this . . .

'I don't want to go to *Bartok's*. Let's go to the *Apollo*,' she told Anna. They continued walking.

'Are you serious? After all this messing about I'm going to *Bartok's* even if I have to go on my own.'

Natasha linked arms with her friend. 'Would you really leave me, Anna?'

'Of course not. Don't worry about anything. We're nice, smart people. We aren't petty or hateful or vindictive. Which makes us the equal of anyone in the world. And if anyone thinks or acts differently to us, we'll batter them senseless.'

'So you don't think I'm a money-grabber?'

'Of course I do. Big time.'

Anna could tease Natasha for her mercenary attitude because she felt the same. If being with a man just for his money meant being with someone she didn't love – so what? Who *was* with someone they loved? If her ambition meant being deceitful and dishonest, then that was no different from any other sexual relationship. And if ultimately she lived a life without trust, or honesty, or love, then this was nothing short of everything she had been taught to expect.

'What would you do if you met a millionaire?'

'Marry him.'
'What if he was very, very old?'
'Marry him quickly.'

SIX

The man Natasha was destined to meet that night, Geoffrey, had been sitting in an outskirts pub, sipping at a Coke, trying, and failing, to look nonchalant. He shuffled on his seat, crossed then uncrossed his legs. The purpose of wearing the expensive suit and driving the Jag was to boost his confidence. By taking the Jag, however, Geoffrey had condemned himself to staying clear of any alcohol, and without alcohol his mind could never quite be diverted from concentrating on the person he was: his inadequacies, his failings, his shortcomings. Self-confidence had no chance of battling its way through these monoliths. Only Geoffrey could make drinking a glass of Coke look complicated. He tipped the glass before it had reached his mouth, his reactions still quick enough to avoid staining the suit.

You could tell it was Saturday by looking round the pub; its customers had made an effort with their clothes and drank much faster. The landlord had fewer lights on and had turned the volume of the jukebox up by a notch. Everyone there had someone to talk to, someone who listened and responded to them. Geoffrey thought about Janette, his ex. Sort-of ex. There was no dispute that it was over; the only dispute was whether she had ever been his in the first place. He thought about her the way he did in any given moment of self-pity. He imagined her sitting on the stool next to him. Under these miserable circumstances he could not dream up the conversation they might have had, yet he knew that if she were here then their talk, as always, would start and flow naturally. Possibly she would be laughing at the way he had spilt his drink. Here was another warning he had ignored: her readiness to laugh at him.

He ordered another Coke rather than go to some other pub and have to face the chagrin of walking in alone again.

Geoffrey watched a middle-aged woman stand up and begin to dance. There was no dance floor and she had to work her routine in between the jukebox and the tables. She momentarily returned to the man she had left sitting down, grabbing his hand and pulling him to his feet. She danced close to him, forcing his moves. He made a gallant attempt to join in, having to concentrate too hard on maintaining the grin on his face to be able to keep in beat with the record. Such awkwardness was the price he was prepared to pay to be with her.

Geoffrey was too much of a romantic. Janette was on his mind constantly; he had permitted her to shame him with regret. This was the price he had been prepared to pay to be with her. It had never been love – not if subjected to even the most basic tests for that over-rated emotion. If he could only remember this then he could laugh at the stupidity of his behaviour, and hopefully be more sensible in the future.

Having reached the same conclusion he always did whenever he thought through his time with Janette, he decided to leave the pub and make his way towards the nightclub his friend's wife, Melanie, had told him about. He had no doubt his misery would continue there. He would order a fresh orange with ice. No – fresh *pineapple* with ice, let's live. As he tried to leave the pub he made three attempts to push open the door, which opened inwards.

As the blue neon sign for *Bartok's* came into readable view, Natasha again wanted to turn and run away. Anna purposefully began to chat, a dissection of their so far fantastic night.

'I'm glad the *Apollo* is shutting. I reckon that tonight has been so brilliant because we knew it was going to be different.'

Natasha listened and made suitable responses; she was even capable of laughter. All the time, though, she was preparing herself for disappointment. She had set too much store by tonight, attributing too many life-changing qualities to *Bartok's*.

Not far now, they only had to concentrate on crossing the road. While they waited for a gap in the traffic, other people gathered around them, some on their way to *Bartok's*; girls with their arms folded as protection against an unexpected cold breeze, boys with their hands in pockets and smiles cracking their faces.

A Jag stopped to let them cross.

As Geoffrey had got older, though he was still not yet thirty, he had grown into a man who wanted the most substantial part of his attraction to a woman to be compatibility; to hear her speak intelligently, a real intelligence which came from knowing of the falsehood of the world and of men, and making her subsequent bitterness a charm. Nevertheless, this thought did not prevent Geoffrey staring in awe at the girls who passed in front of his Jag, shooting the car, then him, admiring glances.

Then he saw the eyes of a, at first sight, perfect woman.

Geoffrey usually met women by knowing them first, often for years, skilfully turning flirty remarks into open suggestions. If their response over this prolonged period was positive, only then would he – probably still not ask them out.

Geoffrey thought that she was perfect. Perfect because he saw imperfections. Here was somebody who wouldn't trust him implicitly; he would have to earn everything. He saw in her the desire to submit fully to love, without being aware of this herself. He saw someone full of hope.

And if none of this was true, even if he was entirely wrong, she was still damn perfect.

Take the chance, he told himself: step out of the car and speak to her. If she is as you think she is, then you have to talk to her.

At first sight, Natasha thought Geoffrey was perfect too. He had flaws, which helped her idea of perfection. He was certainly looking at her, and she was aware that this look was a reflection of the look she was giving him.

She said nothing about this to Anna.

Instead she said, 'Anna, what if, by some miracle, I meet a man who has money but is also everything I have ever been looking for? A man I get along with, connect with in the same way I do with you. Can you imagine?'

'You're talking bollocks, you know.'

Natasha continued walking in the flow of people, meaning that any contact between their eyes was entirely fleeting, yet she saw him fully.

She saw her hope reflected back. He had warmth and humour. She saw into a character which was solid and generous, a spirit which was vulnerable without being broken. She saw tenderness and passion. She saw everything she could want, which was why she saw it. She didn't question these beliefs – such a doubt never occurred to her. She knew how rarely people's real souls fail to influence their eyes. She had connected with him in an unguarded moment, so he was not faking or designing it. He was the man she saw.

Natasha answered Anna: 'I know, but it's nice to dream.'

'It's nice to drink, too – so let's get a move on.'

As eye contact broke she considered returning to speak to him, and risk perfection being shattered. She could not think of anything she might say which would sound like anything other than lust or drunken stupidity.

'I wonder if there's any way we can sneak in?' Anna asked as the bouncers came into view, solid as supporting pillars, grinding gum.

After parting with fifteen pounds, as painful for Anna as passing a cricket ball through her rectum, the girls went straight to the toilet to repair wind damage.

Anna said to Natasha, 'I can't believe the way those bouncers treated us.'

Natasha replaced strands of loose hair and made a manic grin into the mirror to check her teeth for lipstick. 'I thought they were polite.'

'Exactly. This is a different world.'

Holding each other's hands to prepare for the big game, the girls grinned in anticipation.

Anna said, 'I dread to think how much a drink will cost in this place.'

'We'll have to drink slowly, then.'

'How's that done?'

Their hands separated as they left the toilet, then found each other again as they entered the main body of the club – so dark their eyes could not adjust fast enough, though this didn't prevent Anna's first question:

'Seen anyone you fancy yet?'

They walked around the club. It had no theme, nor any novel idea of how to look expensive. It was large, well-lit around the dance floor with mirrors everywhere, then further back there were booths and low ceilings, with simple, well-shaded lamps for discretion. The illusion of exclusivity was left to the patrons. They were better dressed, calmer, more upright than those who went to the *Apollo,* but otherwise Natasha and Anna were very unimpressed. Only now did each tell herself, silently so as not to spoil the expectations of the other, 'Of course everyone looks normal. What did you really expect?'

'You get the drinks, I'll find somewhere to sit.'

'The oldest trick in the book!' Anna joked. Natasha handed over money.

Anna was unaware that someone had seen her; and as he watched Natasha disappear he walked towards Anna, not making the common male mistake of first working out an opening line.

Richard was dark-haired, brown-eyed, taller than her and a real smiler. Anna was about to fall.

The chance passed. Geoffrey had failed: this perfect woman remained lost in passing crowds.

He drove the Jag towards the club, hoping the bouncers would see him in the car so that when he tried to enter in all his inadequacy they would have already formed a more impressed opinion and admit him.

No smiles for Geoffrey. The bouncers judged him too slight to be a threat and too sober to dare enjoy himself.

'Evening, sir,' one told him.

He was in the queue three customers away from paying when he saw the sign.

FIFTEEN POUNDS BEFORE TEN
TWENTY-FIVE POUNDS AFTER.

He checked his watch, relieved by the time. Then he disregarded this relief. This was fifteen pounds he did not wish to blow on a nightclub. There were only three customers before he had to face the dilemma of paying up or leaving. He tried to think of a plausible pretext for leaving which would not have the bouncers sneering.

The three customers were all together; they paid and entered. Geoffrey hovered. A bouncer turned to check the hold-up.

Geoffrey walked, paid, entered. At the bar he managed not to flinch when he was told the price of his drink. Then he sat down, away from view on the long seat which ran the length of the back wall, one hand holding his glass, the other on the seat.

The long seat had been the only free space Natasha, still adjusting to the dark, had seen. Not certain whether she could sit safely, she had put her hand down to make sure. She withdrew her hand when she felt someone else's.

'Sorry,' she told him. Then she recognised him, the man in the Jag, the man perfect for her.

He recognised her, too: the perfect woman. A nice voice.

'Are you going to sit down?' he heard himself asking, smooth bastard that he was. This had been a question which had slipped out unruined by fear. He kept his eyes on her and tried to put his glass on the table, swiping down three times until the glass reached.

She sat. Nice beginning. Natasha was about to fall. She looked over towards the bar, but couldn't see Anna for the crowd. Anna would have described Geoffrey as a bit dorkish, but so as not to offend Natasha would have added that he also looked sweet, and sincere.

Natasha smiled at Geoffrey. Geoffrey smiled back, nervously, as if he was under suspicion. Natasha waited for Geoffrey to speak. He didn't. The dork.

Anna immediately knew, from his first words to her, that she liked this man, that he was her type.

She had ordered drinks; two bottles of Bacardi Breezer, watermelon flavour. In glasses with ice – for show.

'Seven pounds,' the barmaid told her.

'Three pounds fifty each?' Anna queried. In the *Apollo* they were two pounds.

'I'll get these,' Richard told Anna – his first words. He repeated himself for the barmaid, handing over a twenty-pound note. 'And a Jack Daniels with Coke, please.'

The barmaid took the note and went to pour his drink.

Richard added to Anna, to break the short silence: 'I hope you don't mind?'

Anna was nervous. Afraid. Was this the posh variation of chatting up? Anna was more used to a slap on the arse and a slurred, 'I will if you will.'

'No. No. Great!' she told Richard. She figured he must be married, or at the very least up to his neck in some woman. The men in nightclubs who were the best-looking, the most charming and the funniest were invariably in a relationship. The ones who made a strained effort, with severe and obvious defects, were single. The *Apollo* patrons were invariably single.

Natasha collected her drink from Anna. No words were exchanged, only grins and eye movements, their shorthand.

Richard took his first sip of Jack Daniels, then smiled; Anna returned the smile before she had chance to consider if she might be wiser playing him differently, with less blatant interest.

'Jack Daniels and Coke. There's no better drink.'

'I like it, but it gets me drunk too quickly, then I get a hangover.'

'If you're worrying about hangovers then you can't be having a good time.'

'I'm having a great time,' she told him. 'I'm not worried about anything.'

'I don't often suffer from hangovers,' he said.

'Me neither. I spew buckets – end of suffering.' Even though he laughed, Anna wished she had not said this.

Richard stood close, without being discomfiting or intimidating. His smile was charming, without arrogance or lewdness. His confidence was assured without cockiness. Richard was certainly superior to her usual type. The type Anna normally landed were those with flaws and imperfections which made them circus attractions.

'So, come on, confess, which one is it?' she challenged. 'Are you engaged, living with someone or are you actually married?'

He was a little surprised and there was a pause before he answered. 'Married. How did you guess?'

It was a miracle of restraint that Anna didn't speak her first thought, 'Fucking typical!'

If she walked away she would have to join Natasha, and Anna would not be welcome there.

If she poured her drink over his head she would have to buy another. The drinks were too expensive to waste on gestures. Such indignation would be a gesture. They were only talking, his marriage was no obstacle. Even if they kissed, no real harm would be done. Even if they slept together, it would be him in the wrong, not her.

'I didn't guess,' Anna told him. 'I've just learnt that it's never simple.'

SEVEN

They were as young as six when they compared notes on how their mothers prepared for nights out. Anna's parents went out regularly, so she was more familiar with the process. Her mother's procedure was routine and hurried, and usually only basic: make-up slapped on as if buttering bread, clothes chosen by how clean they were, and her definition of fixing her hair was to wash it, and perhaps brush it if she had the time.

Natasha's mother went out rarely. Natasha watched in fascination when she did, asking lots of questions, whose replies inspired more questions. To avoid these interrogations she learnt not to tell Natasha if she was going out.

'What's that stuff that they put on their eyes?' six-year-old Anna asked Natasha. They were sitting in Natasha's mother's bedroom. Natasha searched for the eyeliner.

'This?'

'Don't know.'

Natasha searched for the mascara.

'This?'

'Yeah. What's that called?'

'Eye make-up,' the expert said. Natasha pretended to put the mascara on.

'Put some on me,' Anna said. 'We can wash it off after.'

Carried away with the enjoyment and the effect, they made each other up, the eyes and lips as exaggerated as cartoons, and washed it off so badly that Natasha's mother wasn't furious when she saw her because she couldn't contain her laughter.

A year later the girls were sitting at the same dressing table, and having learnt the lesson about make-up they now talked about clothes. Natasha told Anna that her favourite item of clothing belonging to her mother was a long leather coat she no longer wore.

'What about her knickers?' Anna asked. 'Has she got any special knickers?'

'What do you mean?' Natasha asked. They searched through her mother's underwear drawer and found nothing but ordinary, very normal knickers.

'My mum wears special underwear,' Anna boasted. She took Natasha home and they sneaked up to Anna's parents' room, where Anna showed Natasha the underwear drawer.

'This is what I like best of my mum's,' Anna said, holding up a basque she had seen her mother in once, after coming into the room unexpectedly. Natasha couldn't understand what it was, or how it was worn. To demonstrate Anna held it against herself.

'Oooh – I am so sexy! Come and kiss me!'

Natasha laughed, then listened in astonishment as Anna explained her theory that the basque had something to do with sex, which was – she knew for definite – something to do with how babies were made. Though completely confused and totally unenlightened, Natasha asked no questions.

A year later, nearly eight years old, Anna expanded on her theory.

'They kiss, and they hold each other, and they haven't to have any clothes on.'

'So what about the special underwear?' Natasha asked, the image of the basque still very much engraved in her psyche.

'It's like make-up – it's just a signal that you want to do it.'

'Oh,' Natasha said. Before this her confusion had only been abstract, like attempting to comprehend the size of the universe – now it was absolute. She had no idea what sex was, or how holding each other could make babies, or how wearing make-up could be a signal that women wanted a baby. Following this, everywhere Natasha looked she saw women very heavily made-up. Even Mrs Numan, her headmistress, who was very, very old, wore make-up. Natasha imagined her in the basque. It was horrible.

The girls never played at Mummies and Daddies. They preferred simply pretending they had their own home, where each could be the mother and have children to look after. When other girls intruded and explained that these homes were an imitation of how things were in their own families, the game lost its appeal; they had no wish to imitate that life. When they were older still, eleven and twelve, they were happy to make each other laugh by satirising their home life. Anna would imitate both her mother and her father being drunk; she did both voices in a psychotic burlesque which had Natasha in stitches. When it was Natasha's turn she did one voice only: her mother's constant whining, never taking a breath. Then she would do her father's response: a silent, blank zombie stare.

Other girls told Anna and Natasha that it was odd that they should both wish to be mothers living in the same house.

'Why?' Natasha asked.

There was never any full explanation of why their behaviour – pretending to be living together – was considered strange.

Not until middle school did they begin to understand. Their gym teacher, Miss Wheeler, was called a dyke. They asked someone what it meant and they explained about lesbianism. Some of the older girls said Anna and Natasha's closeness was dykish. Natasha and Anna both thought they should now be less open about their close friendship, but it never really happened. They still held their heads close together when they talked; they linked arms automatically when they walked; they even held each other's hands when they were really having fun. When one slept at the other's house, they never gave it a second thought but slept in the same bed, with their arms around each other.

They each had their first kiss within weeks of beginning their second year at middle school. Each kiss was with the same boy, Dominic Newsholme. He had kissed Natasha; then Natasha had told Anna about him. Natasha had asked Dominic – at Anna's request – to kiss her too. Anna and Dominic held their mouths together for a long time, and moved their heads around in circular movements.

'Did you like it?' Natasha asked Anna.

'I didn't think it was . . . I didn't *not* like it, or anything,' Anna replied, still trying to analyse the effect. The physical experience was negligible, neither was there a change emotionally: as before, she thought Dominic was a prat.

Natasha had liked the kiss, so let Dominic kiss her again. Then he put his hand between her legs. Horrified, but unable to think how she could retaliate, she told Anna, wondering if she should tell anyone else. Anna told her not to.

Anna told her brothers that a boy had touched her between her legs but that she was too ashamed to tell the teachers. Aged fourteen and fifteen, her brothers went to Dominic's home, called for him and, when he came to the door, thumped him in the face, then kicked him several times when he was collapsed on the floor.

'Touch our sister again, you fucking little pervert, and we'll set you on fire.'

When Dominic's mother found him, bruised and bleeding, she pestered him constantly, refusing to believe his feeble story that he had slipped on the doormat.

At upper school, the girls' schoolwork deteriorated. Anna had only ever worked hard because Natasha had. Natasha's favourite subjects had been Art, History and English, but the way the schedules were structured, with a compulsory language and a compulsory science, she had been forced to drop History. It was a minor loss, but Natasha remained resentful. Though uninterested and easily distracted, they had never been in any serious trouble until Mrs Combier, their French teacher, separated them for talking too much in her class. The girls went on strike, refusing even to pick up a pen until they were allowed to sit together again. They were sent to their head of year, then the headmaster. The compromise was detention, lines, and they were allowed to sit next to each other again provided they agreed to talk less.

This was a significant change; they cared less and less about the teachers, work, lessons. And by contrast, during this period, the respect they had for their own friendship was strengthened when they saw how so many of the friendships of their contemporaries were transient; how they ended easily over silly trivialities like boys. To them, falling out because of a boy was as foolish as amputating your legs to remove your shoes.

Both girls liked boys; they liked teasing, flirting, having a laugh, the intrigues of wondering who fancied them and whom they fancied back. But this couldn't ever be as important as a solid friendship built up over years.

Armed with the conviction that no boy could ever be as important as their friendship, they were appalled by the hurt and humiliation that so many girls were willing to go through in the quest for a boyfriend. It bemused them to think that so much importance was vested in a relationship built on the flimsiest of foundations. It's easy to fancy someone, they told each other, so why complicate this by fancying one person more than another? There is no such thing as a boy who is special.

When they lost their virginity, they told each other straight away: Natasha losing hers to Brian Huskisson while she was baby-sitting for an aunt; Anna losing hers on a golf course to a boy named Daz (or maybe Baz or Gaz), who only hours earlier had introduced himself by throwing popcorn at her in a cinema.

They had moved in together believing this a better alternative to living alone or living with someone who made you miserable. A year ago they had no reason to believe their friendship would ever make them miserable. Now, they needed new best friends.

As Anna talked to Richard and Natasha sat next to Geoffrey, both girls had the same thought at the same moment: that coming here, getting ready, the sacrifice to get the money, had all been worth the effort.

'I don't care that you're married,' Anna told Richard. 'So long as she's not here.'

EIGHT

Say something. Say something to her, you wanker, you ponce. She's waiting for you to begin a conversation – oh, for fuck's sake! Geoffrey told himself. To Natasha, he said nothing.

'I saw you earlier,' Natasha began, tougher and braver than Geoffrey.

'Yeah, I saw you, too.'

'You were in a car. Lovely car.'

'Right.' *Oh, for fuck's sake! Say something!*

'It must be expensive to run.'

'I suppose.'

She wasn't certain if these short answers were over-confidence, him making her do the work, or whether he was nervous – which would be sweet and encouraging. She was attracted to him, and he was the moneyed type she was here for. He had a flash car and so much money that the cost was an irrelevance to him; small change.

Geoffrey was so nervous his eyes itched. He didn't dare blink.

'Can I ask, what is it you do?'

'What have you got in mind?' he smirked, alluding to sex. Then grimaced, in case his smutty remark might offend.

'For a living!' she qualified, relieved that he had some interest in sex and was, after all, a little down to earth.

He risked honesty. 'I'm not working.'

She misunderstood. 'Wow. I envy you that sort of money, that's real freedom.'

Geoffrey wanted to know if the sparkle in her eyes, the

enthusiasm in her voice, was a happiness caused solely by her attraction to him. If he confessed about not owning the Jag and how little money he had, she might leave. At the moment he held her firm interest, had her company. Without her he was just a guy sitting alone, staring wildly, looking ill.

Fortunately, Natasha did most of the talking, telling him of her family, her upbringing, her work, Anna and the *Apollo.* He listened, laughing and questioning, offering no details of his own life in return and deflecting questions whenever she asked. He only realised how relaxed he had become when he tried to drink from his drained glass, tilting it so steeply the ice slid down and hit him on the nose.

While Natasha talked on, Janette crept into his thoughts and was immediately ejected. At this moment he could not explain why he had ever spent any time thinking about her; she was really not interesting enough.

'By the way, I don't know your name.'

'Natasha.'

He could safely judge Natasha to be less selfish, more considerate, more interesting. As he watched her talk, with her hand touching his to emphasise a point, he pictured himself making love to her. He hoped he could summon up the courage to ask her home, but feared otherwise. Geoffrey was too familiar with his own cowardice. If he had ever been in the Parachute Regiment he would have been the soldier complimented on his meticulous parachute-folding, but then discharged for always accompanying the pilot home.

In that split-personality thinking that women have to employ to match the duplicity of men, Natasha was telling Geoffrey that she had not been paid this weekend, while simultaneously considering her response should he ask her home.

If she had liked him a little less, she had no doubt she would sleep with him. This one, though, she wanted to make a better impression on. She had no one to compare him to, she didn't know this type. Maybe his attention and his subtle humour were all part of the orchestrations he used here every week, bemusing and conning a succession of gullible gold-diggers. *Best not to reach a decision. Act on instinct. He might not ask.*

Because his drink was finished, he would have to offer to buy her another one and she might accept. While still sitting, he reached into his trouser pockets to see if he could judge how much money he had left. She saw his hand moving around his groin and he quickly pulled it free, embarrassed.

He might not ask. If he asks, I'll say no. I'll tell him I'm flattered, that I like him and would want to see him again but don't think it would be a good idea to go home with him, Natasha told herself.

'Do you fancy coming back for a coffee?' he asked.

'Love to,' she said.

The answer took him by surprise. He elaborated: 'It's very noisy in here. I want to carry on talking to you.'

'OK,' she added. She felt like a slut even before she had stood up to leave, even if coffee didn't automatically mean sex, only the *attempt* at sex. 'No' was still an option.

Richard needed to say no more. Anna knew that she would, if asked now, willingly sleep with him, even though he was married. And if he didn't ask her, she would ask him. And if he smiled at her once more like that, she would demand.

'Where's the girl you came in with?'

Anna struggled to remember that anyone else existed. Richard filled the silence.

'Do you want to find somewhere to sit and talk?'

'OK.' She knew she should add more, so he would not think her entirely passive. Such unreserved interest was like showing your cards in poker, or buying a used car at the first price the salesman asked for.

He told her, 'Look, I guess I can't just expect you to dump your friend just like that, but . . . If you tell her how much I want the chance to talk with you, that I want to see if I like you as much as I fancy you.'

'Don't worry about it, I'll dump her!' Anna beamed. 'My friend's OK, she's talking to some bloke.'

Richard was holding their drinks. He handed them to Anna, who instinctively took them both. With her hands incapable of defending herself, Richard kissed her, quickly, to keep the kiss a joke.

'A cheap trick, I admit, but I wanted to get a kiss out of the way so we could have a first subject to talk about.'

'It's OK, but ask first, in future,' Anna told him as she leaned towards him, puckering. They kissed passionately, with Anna still holding the drinks, the cold liquid spilling down her fingers as the glasses tilted. He kept his hands on her hips and kissed tenderly, slowly.

'I'll bet you don't kiss your wife like that,' Anna told him when they broke from the kiss. 'If you did she'd handcuff herself to you. So who are you out with?'

Richard pointed to his friends. He was out with the same three friends he was out with every weekend – Raymond, Daniel and Malcolm. Richard referred to himself and his friends as 'the lads', Daniel referred to them as 'the gang', Malcolm as 'the pack'. Raymond, the dumbest, referred to them as 'the three musketeers'.

Anna saw a woman stand in front of Malcolm. Though too far away to hear, she could see that, in spite of Malcolm's grin, he was receiving a roasting. With one hand the woman held onto her drink, with the other she pointed, jabbing at Malcolm, words flying out without pause.

'What's that about?' Anna asked Richard. 'Is she his girlfriend?'

The girl's abuse made no impact on Malcolm's grin, so – to the delight of Raymond and Daniel – she poured her drink, red wine, over Malcolm's head.

'His *ex*-girlfriend, by the looks of it,' Richard predicted.

'What's he done, do you know?'

'Malcolm's also married,' Richard told Anna. 'But she didn't know he was married. My guess is she's found out.'

'Well, at least you've been honest with me.'

Even in the reddish lighting of the club Anna could detect the colour of Richard's blush. She commented on how noisy the club was. A hint. Twenty-five minutes later and Anna was grateful to herself for having checked her sheets before she went out. They were in her bedroom, undressing each other. The only pause was when the kettle boiled – filled only minutes earlier, when they were both still going along with the facade of coffee meaning coffee. When she returned to the bedroom after turning the gas off, she straightaway asked: 'Did you think that coffee would definitely mean sex?'

'That's why I asked for mine with cream and honey.'

She finished undressing. Though a bit late for this thought, she said anyway, 'We hardly know each other.'

'I know.'

'I'll feel cheap,' she joked.

'Me too.'

'Lights on or off?'

'Let's try both.'

'I really shouldn't be doing this,' Anna told herself as she gripped Richard. 'I wonder if Natasha is behaving.'

NINE

In his desperation to impress Natasha with his good driving, Geoffrey drove appallingly, stopping too suddenly, changing gears clumsily, driving too fast or too slowly. In his mind he projected this inadequacy out into the near future, if they should have sex and the possible consequences if he should, again, try and impress Natasha: sudden stops, speeding, misuse of the clutch.

'I can't drive,' Natasha told him, with a nervous smile on her face. Conversation which had flowed naturally and easily in the club now stalled into obtrusive silence. At the same time, Geoffrey stalled the Jag as the traffic lights turned green. In his panic to start the car he had trouble with the gearstick and momentarily lost his temper.

'Shit. Bollocks. Wank.' Then he remembered Natasha. 'Sorry.'

'Do you live far?' Natasha asked.

'No, not at all,' he told her as they drove past the street leading towards his bedsit. Ten minutes later and they were still driving, nearer now to his friends' home, which he was looking after for them, with Natasha believing Geoffrey had a terrible sense of distance.

'I can't drive,' she repeated. In desperation to break the silence, then from a real curiosity, she began to ask questions.

'Do you drink a lot?'

'I have done.'

'But you broke the habit?'

'It wasn't a habit,' Geoffrey protested. 'I mean there've

been occasions, not frequent occasions, when I have been drunk.'

'Have you ever been in trouble with the police?'

'Are you kidding?'

'Not *any* trouble?' Natasha persisted.

'None. That's not so rare, is it?'

'Among the men I've been out with it's unique.' Natasha regretted this confession the moment it was made. She had been asking him the wrong questions. He would guess her background and believe they had nothing in common.

'What kind of men have you been out with?'

'Oh . . . All kinds,' Natasha answered, then desperately attempted to amend the answer so she wouldn't sound like a trollop. 'Not many, really. One or two idiots, but other than them . . . '

Natasha worried that this new silence would convince him that any connection there had been between them was gone now they had left the noise of the club. She couldn't think of anything to say to remedy the situation.

'You must love this car,' she said in desperation.

'It's a dream to drive,' he answered, thinking, 'It's the car, it's the car again – she's only coming home with me because she thinks I own a flash car.'

'This car probably costs more than my parents' home,' she said, smiling in the hope of making this banal comment into a joke.

He struggled to think of a reply. 'They do cost . . . they're a lot of money.'

She stroked the dashboard.

'You live around here? Are we there yet?' she asked as they drove past large, detached houses.

'Here we are,' he told her as he pulled into the drive. She would be even more impressed by the house than the car; and therefore be more impressed by him. All he could do to console himself was remember he had not deliberately deceived her.

They stepped out of the Jag. He unlocked the house door, went in, dug out a slip of paper from his wallet, with the code for the burglar alarm, turned on the house lights and brought her in. Neither of them said a word.

'Come into the kitchen,' he told her at last. 'I'll put the kettle on.'

'This is a wonderful house. Do you live here alone?'

'I've never lived with anyone. Why do you ask?' He used her question as an excuse to halt making coffee. He had to think which of the cupboards the coffee was kept in. He tried one – not there, though by good fortune he had found the cups.

'It just has a feel about it, like a woman lives here,' Natasha said, then continued: 'It's clean, for a start. I'll bet you have a cleaner, right?'

This girl believed he was rich. They might be about to make love – possibly as a consequence.

'Do you want to take your jacket off?' he asked. It wasn't a decoy answer. She could tell he wasn't married: he wasn't so pleased with himself for persuading her here. As he spooned coffee into the cups, the shaking of his hand scattered granules over the unit top.

The decorations had a natural, easy elegance which she admired and believed she could, with similar funds, equal. He had managed to employ both modernity and comfort. The house was tidy without being too orderly.

He calmed his hand from shaking and ploughed the spilt coffee granules into his palm.

Each carrying their own cup, Geoffrey led Natasha into the living room. Rather than let her choose to sit on one of the armchairs he indicated for her to sit on the settee. Yet he did not sit next to her; instead he sat on the floor, at her feet, leaning against the settee and her legs. They sipped at their coffee.

'You have nice legs,' Geoffrey told her.

'Do men still look at legs? I thought it was just breasts and bums.'

'It's faces first. Everything else is after that. When I saw you from my car I noticed only your face.'

Without looking up to her, he patted her knee. She asked about his ex-girlfriends, asking who had been his most recent big love.

'That's a long story,' he told her, hanging his head.

'That's OK. We're not going anywhere, are we? Besides, I yattered on when we were in *Bartok's*, and you listened without telling me anything about yourself.'

'It's not exactly a flattering story. If I tell you everything, how ludicrously I acted, you're probably going to end up thinking you're here with an idiot.'

'I bet I don't,' she told him, now genuinely intrigued. 'If you sincerely liked someone and maybe got hurt or acted foolishly, don't you think I'll like you more for that?'

So he told her the full story of him and Janette. Not the glossed-over version he was using as the basis of his novel, but rather the honest, and therefore inexplicable, true story. As he told her the part where Janette returned to the husband she had divorced, he got up from the floor, not interrupting the story, and sat on the settee next to her, so he could look at her. He told the story with a smile, understanding his own foolishness. Then he began to tell her selected stories of his other failings with women. For the first time that night, Natasha was able to relax completely.

'There have only been two occasions in my life when I've attempted to chat up women I didn't already know. The first time – insignificant, yet this doesn't mean I've ever forgotten it – I was in a nightclub when I was seventeen. I walked up to a girl who was laughing and smiling and clearly having a great time. I said "Hi" to her and asked if she was having a good time. Do you know what her answer was? She said, "I was. Until now." So I walked away. The second time – again insignificant, but still no less painful – the same nightclub, one week later. Encouraged by my friends, who assured me rejection was all part and parcel of the fun, I walked up to a girl I had first ensured had seen me; she even smiled. I said "Hi" to her, then asked if she'd like to dance, or have a drink. She asked for a drink. The bar was very busy.

Seven valuable minutes later I returned to find her kissing a guy who had his hands on her bum and hadn't even paid the price of a drink.'

'And you've never tried to chat up a woman since?'

'I only talk to a woman if I already know her.'

'Maybe I've come into your life just in time to save you dying alone and miserable,' Natasha told him. Geoffrey laughed along with her so she wouldn't understand that this was the fate he had long since accepted as inevitable. She touched his legs to console him, and he put his hand in hers, gently, like an embrace. His story had come to an end. He should have used the moment, that interlude after one story ended and before another could begin, to kiss her, to let her know he was over the past and anticipating the future, even if the future was only the next few hours. He slightly tightened his grip on her hand, and she reciprocated. He looked into her eyes, and she held his look, the corners of her lips curling into a smile. He didn't kiss her.

Kiss her. Kiss her, you wanker, you ponce. She's waiting for you to kiss her – oh, for fuck's sake! Geoffrey told himself. He didn't kiss her.

She didn't understand why. She had given him the right signals, and he had reciprocated, yet he still hadn't followed it up with a kiss. Natasha worried in case all that talk of his ex-girlfriend had made him wish that she were here now. His blushing, the shaking of his head and his melancholy gaze into the middle distance all seemed to her to be clear signs of regret and embarrassment.

She considered how she could kiss him. She levered off her shoes and pulled her legs up onto the settee. Her feet were in contact with his legs. She considered which moment would be most favourable for her to lean forward to kiss him.

'Here. Take this,' she told him, handing over her cup.

'You haven't finished.'

'Take it, though.'

She hoped that after he had put the cup on the coffee table, he might resume his position and use the movement to sit closer to her. Instead he put the cup down, returned to exactly the same spot and held her hand in exactly the same way.

Geoffrey did not speak for several minutes, and Natasha did not attempt to fill the void. Afraid he had bored her, his courage came from panic. He leaned forward and touched her cheek with the tips of his fingers. She didn't smile. He kissed her, and then kept his lips on hers. Natasha was forced to adjust herself as she became uncomfortable. She was now firmly in the company of Geoffrey's true personality – his most vulnerable self. Not flash or cocky, but gullible and over-sensitive. Geoffrey asked if she would like another coffee.

While he was in the kitchen, she took the opportunity to use the bathroom, to check that her face bore no signs of punishment, to gargle with water, then to rid herself of stomach cramp caused by held-in wind. She clenched her buttocks to ease the fart out in steady, small doses, spraying the air with deodorant to cover her tracks.

When she came out, though he had finished making the coffee, he stayed in the kitchen. He handed her the fresh cup.

She sipped at the coffee, about to suggest they return to the living room, when Geoffrey excused himself and went into the bathroom.

He checked his breath and smelt beneath his arms. In a sudden realisation of panic, he checked the room in case any of Melanie's toiletries were on display. He buried everything slightly feminine in the airing cupboard, beneath towels. While Natasha had been in the bathroom he had done a hurried reconnoitre of the entire house to check for and search out any telltale signs of a woman's presence. He had even checked in the bedroom, just in case. While he was in there he allowed himself to consider the real possibility of sex, with all the pressures it might entail, all the possible problems which might arise. There were the usual worries about premature ejaculation, or impotence, or being too demanding or being horrified by demands made. Greater than the sum of these was the tremendous fear of simply not satisfying her, of failing to arouse her to any degree. All these potential problems outweighed the possible delights.

TEN

Natasha waited directly outside the bathroom door. When he finally emerged she presented him with his cup.

'It might be cold. What were you doing in there all this time? No, don't answer! Drink up, then give me a tour.'

Geoffrey looked behind him, into the bathroom.

'Of the whole house,' she told him.

'OK,' he told her. He took the cup into the kitchen and poured the cold coffee away. She had not followed.

'Shall we start with the kitchen?' he called back.

'Seen it. And the living room.'

He went back out to her. 'That only leaves the bedrooms.'

She smiled, hoping to be saucy and provocative, showing him she was neither passive nor afraid of her sexuality.

'Take me into the bedroom,' she told him, then wished she hadn't. She worried that he had never suffered a shortage of elegant women; women with that well-bred self-respect that lets the man do the persuading and pursuing. If he took Natasha into the bedroom she could hardly back down, yet she would know she was nothing but just another. Yet if he did not accept such a direct offer, it would be an insult. His long silence was an insult in itself, as if he wanted to run away.

He stepped forward and took both her hands.

'Let's go back into the living room, get comfortable on the couch, kiss, and talk some more – unless you're sick of talking?'

She did not speak or move.

He knew enough to add: 'I'm so flattered that you are prepared to, er, that you were thinking . . . It's just that I'm sort of nervous. I haven't had sex for so long I'm not sure if my licence is still valid. Is that too much of a pathetic confession?'

'No,' she said, relieved.

They didn't speak much for the next hour. They lay together on the settee in passion and intimacy, a demonstration of the movements of sex without either of them removing any of their clothes and nothing more penetrating than tongues into mouths.

Then they held each other comfortably and eased into a relaxed state where Geoffrey slept soundly, thinking only, 'Wow, that was nice,' and Natasha lay awake, her brain whirring.

If Natasha attempted to describe tonight to Anna, she might not understand how such deeply sexual activity was also fundamentally innocent. When it came to matters of sex, Anna refused to believe any man could behave innocently. Anna would make a terrible juror.

When Natasha had begun her periods, aged twelve, her mother sat her down to give her a level-headed talk about sex. There was nothing included in this lesson which might make Natasha anticipate that sex, for a woman, could be pleasurable and that she had every right to desire and pursue such pleasure. Thinking back to this now, Natasha wondered whether her mother had never enjoyed sex. This might go some way to explaining her acrimonious relationship with her husband. Her early practical lessons in sex had done little, either, to make Natasha believe sex could be enjoyable. As her experience grew, however, so did her enjoyment, culminating in tonight, when – she told herself – she had practically stripped and lain spread-eagled for him. She wondered what he thought of her. She looked at the sleeping Geoffrey. She would have liked to ask him if he had changed his mind, and would now like to end the night by making love properly, naked, like adults. But she didn't wake him.

Natasha had once gone home with a boy she knew from the *Apollo*. From the moment the question had been asked to the moment they were on his couch and he first kissed her, she knew that she was there for sex and had been in the mood for the adventure simply for a more thrilling end to an otherwise miserable week. Except that she had changed her mind. She did not fancy him less, nor was she even less aroused; all that had changed was – and she realised this only afterwards, on her own, in the taxi back to her flat – that he had never expected her to refuse, and a substantial part of the thrill of sex under these circumstances was surprising the man with your eager complicity.

Although she had happily told him of her change of heart, she had arrived home wearing her first smile of the evening.

She thought about stripping, then waking Geoffrey. Then thought, What if he's shocked? He might scream.

Natasha had once gone home with a boy and they talked and kissed until he asked if they were going to make love; by this time Natasha was too involved in his intelligence. Two months passed before they met again, another Saturday night, the *Apollo*, his second visit. He was with two other lads whom he had coaxed into the place – they were soon eagerly involved in the delights of other girls while he sought out and spoke to Natasha. After having a too typical night in the *Apollo*, seeing him delighted her. This was the first time she had abandoned Anna to her own company. An hour later, he asked Natasha back to his house and she agreed. They made love, which was tender, passionate, reckless. Laughs were more common than endearments. They fell asleep holding each other, woke up in the morning, made love again and parted without recriminations or any need for lies.

Sex might be that same full experience again – if she persuaded Geoffrey to make love to her. She didn't wake him. He slept with his mouth slightly open, which made him look rather dopey.

She moved around so that Geoffrey would wake up. He looked at her for a moment as if surprised, or remembering something.

'Tell me about sex,' she asked Geoffrey.

In his head he answered, '*Boy are you asking the wrong person!*', but aloud he said: 'What do you mean?'

'Tell me about your past sex life.'

He cleared his throat and rubbed his eyes, waking.

'Do you know how we are now, *this*: we met tonight and you

came home with me? Well, I've only ever been in a similar situation twice before, you know – meeting a girl, asking her home, her accepting. Both times, the girl told me beforehand that sex was not going to happen. In fact, the first girl repeated her "No" as many as twenty times on the journey to her flat; the second even went so far as to demand I repeat the word back so there could be no confusion.'

He was thinking to himself that tonight, with Natasha, might be his first ever one-night stand. That is, if he never saw her again, and if sex took place. Two monumentally large 'if's. Though this was his first ever real chance, he knew that plenty of things could still go wrong. More crucially, he knew that if anything did go wrong, there was no one more certain to make a mistake than him: he would bore her, annoy her, repulse her.

'Who did you lose your virginity to?' Natasha asked.

'Julie Hanson. I was nineteen. She was seventeen, small, short hair, vivacious and had long since lost her virginity. I asked her out; we went for pizza, I went back to her house with her. Her parents were already in bed. I asked her to bed – then had a near heart attack when she said yes. I asked her what she meant, like I'd never heard the word "Yes" before. I even explained, so that there could be no misunderstanding, that I meant for us to go to bed for sex. So anyway, we went to bed, made love, then she broke my heart by never wanting to see me again – informing me of this by sending a message via her sister. The message was "Julie says to tell you you're dumped." After Julie, I met and asked out a girl called Linda. Pizza, back to her house, I asked if we could go to bed, thinking this was all too familiar. She slapped me and told me to leave. After Linda, I went out with Debbie for three months. I never made the attempt to persuade her into bed so she thought I had no interest in sex. Her best mate later told me that Debbie would have been prepared to sleep with me after three hours.'

More than ever, Natasha wanted to ask him, straight, outright, up front, to have sex with her. She didn't. She thought of Michelle Whitaker.

'Was there a girl at your school everyone thought of as the school slut?'

'Not really. And I asked everyone, regularly,' Geoffrey answered. 'Why do you ask?'

'No reason.'

Natasha and Anna had been working in the shoe shop for a couple of months when an old schoolmate of theirs, Michelle Whitaker, came in, hesitating for one moment when she saw the girls, then being brave enough to stay and be served.

To their shame, both Anna and Natasha had been in the confederacy of bullies Michelle had endured through school. There was never any incident of actual violence, yet the three-year campaign of abuse, jokes and graffiti had been equally vile. She had been seen by a whole class having sex with a boy against the giant bins behind the school canteen. She had also been caught having sex with a boy on the school playing fields. The spectacle had ruined Sports Day. Michelle had never denied being the reason that Mr Mathews, the economics teacher, had been dismissed. Her answer to her bullies, her tormentors, to all girls, was always the same: 'You're jealous because the boys like me.'

The sickening reality was that the boys despised her even more than the girls. Any boy who received the benefit of her sexual generosity immediately used this experience to ingratiate himself with other girls, supplying them with more ammunition for their bullying.

Anna served Michelle, neither of them acknowledging the other. Michelle had apparently passed through this potentially destructive phase and had emerged having learnt the lessons every woman learns. Sex makes men like you; sex doesn't always last long.

'Do you know who that was?' Natasha had asked Anna. They looked at her cheque. Her account was in the name of Mrs Michelle Mathews.

Clearly Geoffrey liked Natasha and was attracted to her. Natasha felt insecure because he was so obviously well-off, with a lovely house and a car – why would he even be interested in her?

Once they had finally fallen asleep, both slept so solidly that when Natasha woke in the morning, then saw the video clock, she quickly realised she had less than an hour and half to return home, wash, change and arrive at her parents' for the Sunday ritual of torment. Her frenzied activity woke Geoffrey. She explained her rush and declined his offer of a lift. A hurried exit suited her: his lasting memory would be the fun of last night.

She phoned for a taxi, and as they waited Geoffrey knew he was expected to ask to see her again, or offer her his phone number.

He wanted to be honest. He liked her lack of pretension, her acceptance of his lack of confidence. He liked the way she had been forward yet not forceful or tarty. He had spent a night of fun and intimacy which had not been ruined with recollections of ex-husbands. Best of all, she had listened when he told her of his previous failings with women and had chosen to think better of him for these failings. Geoffrey was more accustomed to being pitied.

'I think there's something I should explain about the house and the car and everything.'

In her enthusiasm she needed no explanation.

'I cannot believe your house! It's fantastic! If it was me, I wouldn't change a thing about it, you've got it perfect. And, all right, I admit I was impressed by the car, but I really like you, too. I like the reserve you have. Reserve and . . . not scared to be direct, either. I like it.'

The taxi pulled up, and she scribbled down her phone number. He waved her goodbye, wishing she was staying in spite of hoping he would have the good sense to forget her.

'I'm really glad last night happened,' Natasha told herself as she waved back through the taxi window to Geoffrey. Through the ride back to her flat, she subjected every word he had spoken, every gesture he had made, every slight facial expression, to the most careful analysis. By this method she realised that he had never asked to see her again, nor offered her his phone number. The thought hit her like the deciphering of an ingenious insult.

'Oh God,' she said, humiliated.

'What's that?' the taxi driver asked.

'Nothing. Sorry. I was . . . The next left, please.'

Natasha and Anna had mastered the art of turning down pests: they used humour, honesty, lies. They knew every technique possible for holding back on giving out their phone number, even to the most persistent. If push came to shove, Natasha would tell them Anna was her lover. Even this wasn't a deterrent to some – for these she had HIV or seven children. Or, in extreme cases, Natasha would give out a phoney number – but only when the bloke had become a real nuisance who deserved such treatment.

In the three-yard walk to her home, Natasha's thoughts were transformed from despair into jubilation as she remembered further back into the night, remembering how she had virtually offered herself to him, without condition. If he had regarded her casually, as a quick lay, then he would have slept with her. She remembered Geoffrey's nervousness, his shyness, his caution not to take advantage of her. He had not given her his phone number simply because of these distractions.

ELEVEN

If anyone else had been in her bedroom that morning they would have seen Anna lying there asleep with a smile on her face, pushed precariously close to one side of the bed so as to give her guest plenty of room. When she woke up her first thought was of Richard, and her smile broadened. She put her hand out behind her to test whether she could roll safely onto her back without colliding with him, but her hand found only sheets and she sat bolt upright, covering her breasts, now fully awake. She looked around her room. In the first half-hearted shadows of morning she saw her clothes scattered around the floor. Her clothes only, not his. He had got dressed, so he clearly couldn't have just got up to go to the toilet.

'The fucker!' she screamed.

She had been thoroughly conned; she had permitted her guard to drop, which had enabled her to fall into deep sleep, otherwise she would have been alerted by the first significant noise he had made.

She looked around her bedroom and saw the tatty furniture, the untidiness, the old carpet, the neglected decorations. Not having given them a thought last night, she now saw the room through his eyes. He didn't belong here.

For want of anything more constructive to scream, she repeated, with nastier emphasis: '*The fuck-er!*'

The room was a mess, she had to admit. For the first time since they'd lived together, Anna had to concede that Natasha was right – she was a messy cow. She wished now that she had listened to

Natasha's nagging and made some effort to clean up. She began to count how many times she had hoovered her room in the last year, embarrassed to realise that she never had. Richard didn't belong here; the council fumigation unit did. Maybe he had fled on health grounds; maybe he suffered allergies, or asthma. She had met Richard, allowed him to buy her one drink, then gone to bed with him barely an hour later. That wasn't good – no wonder he had fled. Yet this behaviour had seemed appropriate last night, he had genuinely liked her and . . .

. . . she had been thoroughly conned. They *always* say they like you.

Anna thought back to the times in her past when she had sneaked out of men's homes the morning after, waking up hungover and regretful. On the occasions they caught her, she told tactful, thought-through lies. *I have a suspicion that I left my front door unlocked; I have children to pick up; my husband will be wondering where I am.*

Whenever she had confronted men who had tried to sneak away from her, even though she might be happy never to see them again, she would never – she refused as an act of principle – pretend to accept their lies as truth. If she ever caught up with Richard she would batter the truth from him: she needed to hear his explanation for leaving.

Then she remembered his wife.

No man is different from any other. Richard was no different from her father. She had diminishing memories of her dad. He always had unsuitably long hair, not a fashion statement, just a lack of care. His hair was black, streaked with white, no grey half-measures. Though his face had always remained gaunt, slim as if young, in later years he was a mesh of wrinkles. He was always stubbly, giving Anna 'chin pies' when she was a toddler, rubbing her flesh with his sandpaper bristles. And always, the red, watery eyes, the red, blotchy complexion – the mementoes of a habitual drinker.

The many times her parents split up, always after her dad had got involved with another woman, there was a ritual of suitcase packing, then abuse, followed by pleading. For days, her mother would parade a false, happy front of going out and drinking every night. This would be followed by days of staying at home, drinking, with morbid predictions for her lonely future. She once told Anna, 'Women only cheat when men have made them miserable. Men only cheat when they are given the chance. Remember that.'

Finally, there was always a reconciliation sealed with his vows of strict, devoted fidelity. Anna and her brothers always saw through this nonsense, even though their father seemed to make these vows sincerely every single time. Only Anna managed to preserve a disdain for infidelity into her own adulthood. Her brothers now cheated on their girlfriends as a matter of course. Richard had deceived his wife by sleeping with Anna, then deceived Anna by leaving without even talking to her.

'*THE FUCKER!*'

To establish a sensibility which would not torment her, Anna forced out a more rational thought. If Richard had left without comment, this was, in fact, preferable. He would not be forced to lie to her, she would not have to break with precedent and act as if she believed such lies.

They had met, had enjoyable sex, then he had left. This way Anna did not have to consider his wife, did not have to dwell upon guilt, did not have think through the consequences if Richard had liked her as much as she liked him. This way they remained strangers.

Richard crept into the room, being extra quiet in case Anna hadn't yet woken up. He was carrying a tube of Pringles. She was sitting up in bed chewing her nails.

'Oh. You haven't gone?' she asked, wide-eyed.

'I wouldn't leave without . . . I wouldn't leave you without speaking.'

Anna grinned with relief, all rational thoughts forgotten. He held up the Pringles, by way of explanation.

'I went to a service station. For these. I thought you might like them. Last night was . . . for me, anyway.'

'Yeah. Me too. Crisps?'

'I wanted to get you flowers, but they didn't sell them.'

'I get hay fever.'

'I have a lot to learn about you,' he told her.

'Come here then, for the advanced course.'

He sat next to her and they began to eat the crisps, while explaining to each other how they usually spent their Sundays.

When Richard eventually did leave she wanted to phone him. Immediately. She thought about dialling, then waiting for him to answer. Then she thought about the possibility of hearing a woman's voice. Her instinct would be to talk to her, even perhaps to tell his wife of his infidelity. She wondered what Richard's wife looked like, and the type of person she might be. 'I'll bet she's really nice. Why would Richard marry anyone who wasn't nice? And good-looking, too. I'd probably hate her guts.'

Natasha broke her stride and jogged upstairs to the flat; excited at the prospect of telling Anna about last night. As she thought this through she realised that she wouldn't get away with telling Anna only selective details. Anna would demand to know everything. Even now, when their friendship was at its most vulnerable, Natasha rarely kept a secret from Anna. This was a measure of how Natasha already regarded Geoffrey. As a worthy secret. Natasha decided she would not take the risk of saying anything. Maybe Geoffrey was using her. She dismissed this thought immediately. Maybe he was taking the piss. Natasha would certainly not mention him to her family. They would think that her mission to find a rich man had been successful, and Geoffrey did not deserve to be introduced like that – as Natasha's rich catch. And maybe, quite possibly, she hadn't yet caught him.

Once inside, Natasha expected that she'd have to go into Anna's bedroom and wake her. Instead she found her on the settee, in jeans and a T-shirt and still – noticeably – wearing last night's make-up. And last night's smile. When Natasha walked in, Anna began a routine of mock-outrage.

'So you're just coming home? I can't believe that you slept with that guy on the first night!'

'Just because we spent the night together doesn't mean we had sex,' Natasha replied. By insinuating that they *hadn't* slept together she would make Anna convinced they had – a deception Natasha didn't mind.

'And anyway,' Natasha continued, 'are you going to try and pretend that guy you met didn't spend the night here? Since when were you ever up at this time on a Sunday?'

Without really thinking about it, Anna told Natasha about Richard, and explained – though there was no need – why she had invited him back last night. 'Maybe, in the past, maybe I have rushed into sex with men . . . But – *unlike some* – my reasons have never been mercenary.'

Natasha was genuinely angry with Anna for bringing up the original reason for their trip to *Bartok's.* The quest for a man with money no longer seemed completely relevant.

Before Anna had any opportunity to ask about Geoffrey, Natasha asked her about her night. 'So cough up – did he come back here, this Richard?'

'You're jumping to conclusions.'

Natasha saw a man's watch on the coffee table.

'Whose is that?'

'OK, he did come back. But we only talked.'

'And that required him to take his watch off?'

'Oh shut up, you slut.'

'No, *you* shut up, you tart.'

With this, and in spite of being pressed for time, Natasha collapsed on the settee next to her friend, so they could both spend a few moments with each other's happiness, enjoying the mutual ease this brought to the atmosphere of the house. Moments like these were sparse these days. Natasha didn't ask the usual question of 'Are you going to see him again?'

'When are you seeing him again?' she asked instead.

'Tonight,' Anna told Natasha. 'I think the fifteen quid to get into *Bartok's* was the wisest money I've ever spent. Except perhaps for that three quid I spent on those black tights I bought five years ago and can still wear.'

'Sometimes in life, just occasionally, things go well, don't they?' Natasha asked before she had, moments later, to ruin her day by preparing to go to her parents'.

TWELVE

If the real attractions for Natasha were not the Jag and the big house, then they must actually be his looks, his charm and his personality. This idea was so absurd that Geoffrey cringed at even thinking it. He knew he should destroy the slip of paper bearing Natasha's phone number. If he had done the same thing a few years ago, made sure he could not contact Janette, his ex, before their relationship really began, he would have avoided all his subsequent unhappiness. He would ride out the next few weeks here in this house, enjoying all this luxury, trying to write in comfortable surroundings, sleep well, eat well, watch cable TV. Alone.

Geoffrey was determined not to repeat the same mistake of being with a woman who didn't truly want to be with him, he thought, as he committed the number to memory.

Natasha didn't speculate on which DIY project her father might be engaged in; nor did she envisage how the inevitable argument between Keith and Brenda might begin; least of all was she interested in the scandals and conflicts of the *EastEnders* omnibus. She tolerated these people, their food, their choice of TV programmes, each and every Sunday simply because they were her family. Here was a loyalty greater than to country or ideals. No sane person would sign a contract as binding as this, with such concrete commitments yet no get-out clause or benefits.

As she entered the house, her main concern was that she would have to endure the weekly cross-examining about her love life without being tempted to tell all. She had learnt her lesson with Derek and others before him: saying her love life might be improving always cursed it. She wanted no such curse on Geoffrey.

Brenda and Keith had not yet arrived. Natasha found her father alone in the kitchen, mashing potatoes.

'Hello, love,' he greeted her.

'Am I early? Where's Mum?'

'Keith's driven her and Brenda to Tradco, they should be back soon.'

Tradco was a discount warehouse Brenda and her mother regularly visited, always returning empty-handed. They went in order to complain.

'Do you need a hand with anything, Dad?'

'Turn the oven off, will you? And you can drain the carrots.'

For a while father and daughter did their chores in silence, Natasha draining the carrots and her father banging the masher against the side of the pan to dislodge stubborn lumps.

'Did you go out last night?' he eventually asked.

'Me and Anna, we went . . . We had a change.'

'You enjoyed yourself?'

'Very much.'

'Then I take it you didn't go to the *Apollo*?' he joked. Natasha was a little surprised to hear her father mention the *Apollo*; she was never certain how much notice he took of conversations held around him.

'I met someone,' she said, then was relieved that he did not respond. 'Don't you and Mum ever go out?' she asked, surprising herself.

'All the time. Just not together.' He went to the oven, with his back to his daughter.

'Ow. Shit. I've burnt my hand,' he told her. The medicine cabinet was in the bathroom. He left the room. Natasha went to the oven. It was warm, but not hot.

He returned minutes later, with an unnecessary plaster on his hand. She dared not tell her father that she sided with him, that her mother was ungrateful and rude. Neither did she dare to ask her father if he was happy.

'You're a good cook, Dad,' she said.

'Practice,' he said, and winked at her. She grinned back as if they were sharing a joke. Then she heard the rest of her family return. Her mother entered the kitchen.

'Oh for crying out loud, is it too much to ask that you open a window? It's like a sauna in here.'

Natasha kept her eyes on her father, who made no response to his wife. As Natasha's mother opened the outside kitchen door, her father rolled his eyes at Natasha, and she understood the joke better now.

After Brenda had moved in with Keith, Natasha had remained with her mum and dad for just four more months. The conversation she had just enjoyed with her dad was longer than any she had held with him during that time. With her mother, Natasha listened, speaking only when a response was needed to show she was still conscious. Between her parents, conversation was as doubtful a concept as levitation.

Throughout dinner, Natasha, her father and Keith ate in silence. Natasha's mother and Brenda talked amongst themselves – holding the conversation as if talking to everyone else, mostly about how appalling Tradco was and what a waste of time every one of their visits there had been.

'You say this every time we go. If it's such rubbish, why do you drag me there every month or so?' Keith mumbled to his fiancée. Natasha presumed this would be the start of their argument, so permitted herself to drift off into happier reflections, remembering being with Geoffrey last night and speculating upon how he might be spending his time now, wondering if he might be thinking of her.

'Why are you grinning?' Brenda asked the silent Natasha. Brenda had apparently avoided Keith's search for an argument. 'Are you grinning because of something that happened last night? I'll bet you didn't go, did you? Did you go to *Bartok's*?'

The interrogation was about to begin. Keith, Brenda and her

mum all held their knives and forks, without touching their food, waiting. Even Natasha's dad looked at her.

'Why is everyone so keen to know what goes on in my social life? All that proves is what crap lives you lot must lead.'

No one disagreed.

Brenda sneered. 'You're always saying you're going to do things you never do. Saying you were going to find yourself a man with money is just another thing forgotten later.'

This was a reference to Natasha's previously expressed ambition of saving to go to America. She saved seventy pounds, then spent it on a watch. Or the other time, when Natasha had once made the mistake of telling her family she planned on going to college, in the hope of one day having a career not related to other people's foul feet. She had phoned up Bradford College to find out the details of courses she was interested in: how much they would cost and the nights and locations they were held at. Natasha made careful notes of the details, then settled back into the routine of her work, letting the day for enrolment pass and thinking she could always begin the escape some other year. For months afterwards Brenda teased her with feeble jokes like: 'So how's the degree coming along, Natasha?'

Natasha had told Anna about Brenda's taunts.

'Tell her – tell the bitch that the only reason she did so well at school is because she had no social life to distract her. Are you going to tell her?'

'I can't be bothered. She isn't worth it.'

The following Sunday Brenda had tried to arrange a night out with her sister, and Natasha – as she always did – made excuses. On this occasion she made such flimsy excuses that Brenda knew her company was being avoided on purpose. There was no taunting that day.

Brenda's worst taunts had followed Natasha's abandoned bid to start her own business. One of the courses she had considered at college was Business Studies. In anticipation of this she had researched the possibility of starting her own shoe retail business. She had looked into acquiring premises and stock and had made a detailed estimate of the capital needed. She had even visited the library to type out a proposition.

'What's the next step?' Anna had asked.

'Work on Monday,' Natasha had answered, and the project was dropped.

'How's the business empire going?' Brenda had taunted the following Sunday.

Natasha remembered all this, yet was determined not to rise to Brenda's taunts as her sister again asked: 'So, come on, admit it, you didn't even get to *Bartok's,* did you?'

Natasha kept silent, shaking her head deliberately.

'I knew it!' Brenda cheered.

The family resumed their dinner, making comments which never fully developed into conversation and passing remarks which were commonplace and dull and designed only to prevent silence. Natasha said nothing, burning with an anger she knew was dangerous to succumb to.

'Try to arrange a night out with me,' she willed Brenda. She wanted the attempt made so she could turn her sister down. 'What a fucking hypocrite you are,' Natasha would have loved to say to her sister. 'You take the piss out of me because I go to the *Apollo*, and because sometimes I make plans I don't follow up on, but you won't fart without first seeking Keith's approval.' She was tempted to tell Brenda about Geoffrey so that she could boast about his house and his car and how he had so much money he needn't work. More importantly, Geoffrey had a quality which would make Brenda really envious. He wasn't Keith.

'So how was the *Apollo*? Fun?'

'I went to *Bartok's*!' she retorted, emphasising the point by holding her fork like a gun. 'And I did meet someone. He owns a Jag and a beautiful house and he's so well-off he doesn't even need to work! I'll be seeing him again sometime this week.'

Natasha was disappointed at her lack of restraint, like a liberal parent who had spanked a child.

'If he's got money he'll be dull or he'll fancy himself,' Brenda answered, spiteful in revenge for being attacked. 'And if he isn't dull then you'll have got it wrong somewhere – he'll be broke. Now *that* I can see working.'

'If he was broke then he'd be history. I told you last week and I meant it – I've had enough of that type. But Geoffrey has money. And he's genuinely nice.'

Embarrassed to be the centre of attention now, Natasha asked Keith if he had any new thoughts about moving house. This subject always provoked an argument.

'We should move,' Keith said. He was answering Natasha, but talking to his wife.

Brenda bit. 'Why? Because it makes *economic* sense?'

'The mortgage on our home is too affordable. The way house prices are going, even in Bradford, we can't go wrong buying property. I have capital I'm not using. If we had a much larger mortgage then that would be the soundest investment we could make.'

'But who wants to move just for the sake of moving?'

This was the beginning. While Keith and Brenda had the same argument they had held countless times before, Brenda's parents sat consumed by their own thoughts, and Natasha anticipated going home. Because Anna would not have left the flat all day it would be messy, warm, cosy. She would be ligged out on the settee with an anecdote to tell about how she had done nothing all day, then tease Natasha for not having the freedom to do the same thing. In spite of how messy Anna was, and how untidy she kept the flat, Natasha did enjoy returning home to her after her Sunday visits to her parents'. For a moment she wondered if Brenda and Keith thought the same way, if their return home came with a sense of relief or was filled with dread. Being alone, away from witnesses, maybe their arguments took on an acrimony and volume not demonstrated in front of others. If true, this was a terrible life for Brenda to be leading, lacking in love and happiness. The thought cheered her up. Maybe living with Anna, and all her faults, was a better option for the future after all.

'Drop it can't you, Keith? God!' Brenda exclaimed. Natasha hoped that, as some compensation, the sex between Keith and Brenda was spectacular.

THIRTEEN

Natasha left her parents' immediately after dinner, excusing herself by saying she had stomach pains. Her mother made great efforts to persuade her to stay, desperate for more information about Geoffrey.

How foolish she had been not to ask for his number; how foolish she had been to succumb to the taunts and tell her family of his existence. She was putting too much trust in a man she barely knew.

Returning home, Natasha anticipated every problem that might prevent Geoffrey phoning. This morning, in her haste to write out her number, she might have written one or more of the figures illegibly. Her fours too often looked like nines while her fives looked like sixes: at work she had been taken off the task of re-stocking when the shop was sent too few shoes in a mixture of sizes, too large and too tiny.

What if Geoffrey had phoned already, and Anna answered? Anna had a habit of being abrupt when the call wasn't for her, especially abrupt when she was waiting for a call herself; and today she would be waiting for a call from Richard. If she answered and was disappointed she might hang up without explaining to him that she was not Natasha.

Natasha entered and found Anna on the phone. She stood in front of her, trying to look stern. Anna didn't take the hint; she kept talking, gave Natasha a thumbs-up and excitedly mouthed 'Richard', her head tilted to the receiver as if she were resting against his shoulders. She had bare feet, a plain blue T-shirt, old jeans, dishevelled hair and free time. Natasha wanted to shout abuse.

Natasha calmed herself by digging out a scrap of sense from her brain, a tiny segment of rationality which reminded her that Anna had a right to be excited, and had a perfect right to use the phone whenever and for as long as she wished. If Geoffrey phoned and found the phone was engaged, he would call back if he was interested enough. Satisfied by these self-assurances, Natasha took off her jacket, mouthed the question 'Coffee?' to Anna, and then, after receiving only a dismissive shake of the head, went into the kitchen. In there, she tried to think of a song to cheer herself up and appear carefree.

Natasha tidied up, drinking her coffee, waiting to hear the receiver being replaced. She even washed the dishes Anna had dirtied during the day. Without ever making a substantial meal, Anna had the gift of creating huge amounts of washing-up. Natasha then reorganised the cupboard where the tinned food was kept, undoing the random system Anna preferred.

Thirty minutes later, with the coffee drunk and the cup washed, Natasha's bad temper finally resurfaced and she crashed into the living room, turning on the TV and using the remote to edge up the volume until Anna was forced to put her hand over the receiver.

'Natasha!'

'What? Oh. Was putting the TV up too loud *inconsiderate*?' Natasha asked sarcastically. 'I hate it when people are inconsiderate, don't you?'

'I'd better go,' Anna told Richard. 'Yeah, I look forward to it.' She hung up. Then, to Natasha, 'What the fuck is wrong with you? If you've had another shitty day at your mum's, don't come back here and take it out on me.'

Natasha, not wanting any distraction from the argument, turned off the TV.

'How long were you on the phone?'

'What? I don't know. Since when have we had time restrictions? I pay half the bill, but you use it far more than me.'

'That's not what I mean. I'm not bothered about the bill. But it's my phone as much as it is yours, and if someone's been trying to get through to me –'

'Oh, right, I get it. This guy from last night –'

'He's called Geoff! I told you his name. But not necessarily just him. Anyone could be trying to get through.'

'I'd never have thought to see you like this – dashing home, panicking in case you've missed a phone call from some bloke.'

'I'm not panicking.'

'Then why are you sweating?'

Natasha hadn't realised she had been sweating. She brushed her index finger along the top of her lip, then dabbed her forehead.

'Because I ate too much.'

'Panic,' Anna taunted. 'I didn't phone Richard, he phoned me. And if the conversation's going well, what am I supposed to do? Hang up on him just on the off chance your boyfriend decides to call? I like Richard.'

'Well so long as you're happy, that's the only important thing.'

'Oh, for fuck's sake don't talk like a –' Anna couldn't think of a suitable simile for someone who was being a melodramatic martyr, so simply said '– twat. If he wants to see you again, he'll get in touch.'

If Natasha pursued this argument she risked sounding pathetic, so she instead complained about the filthy state of the flat. Anna had no intention of being drawn into this.

'Not this again! If it's untidy,' Anna replied, as she picked up a magazine and sprawled out on the settee, 'then clean it. I refuse to clean on Sundays.'

'Not just Sundays!'

'You're arguing with me because some guy hasn't phoned? You're letting a man you've only known for a day take precedence over me?'

'Of course not. You're twisting it.'

'Then put me right. How is it?'

'You spend too much time on the phone!' Natasha shouted, weakly. Anna grinned at the stupidity. Natasha was so infuriated she began to clean as an act of vengeance, hoping the flicking of the duster, then the Hoover banging into the settee, would provoke Anna into a fight.

Twice the vibrations of the Hoover rattled glasses displayed in a cabinet. Both times Natasha switched off the Hoover, believing the sound was the phone ringing. The living room was hoovered thoroughly, with special attention given to the square yard around the telephone.

On Sundays, after returning from her parents', Natasha didn't normally eat anything for the rest of the day. Today she made some sandwiches, with the intention of eating them selfishly. Anna never looked up from her magazine.

Natasha realised that Anna was right – prolonging this argument would increase its significance, making Geoffrey, this man from nowhere, suddenly far more important than Anna.

Natasha had nibbled the crust off one of the sandwiches, and one remained.

'You can have this, if you want,' she told Anna cautiously.

'What's in it?'

'Tuna and sweetcorn.'

'Oh, lovely, cheers,' Anna said, leaning over and taking the plate from Natasha. Natasha prevented herself from reminding Anna to keep the plate under her chin as she ate, to catch the crumbs.

'He'll phone you,' Anna told her. 'It's simple: if he doesn't phone he's a prick, with no taste in women, so you're well rid.'

'So what did Richard have to say?'

'We're going out tomorrow night.'

'Oh? Anywhere good?'

'The theatre,' Anna answered, making the word rhyme with *later* and laughing for reasons she knew Natasha would immediately understand. As Anna laughed, bits of tuna sprang from her mouth.

Natasha said, 'Maybe he doesn't mean the theatre like in plays, but the theatre as in a show, a musical . . . If it's a play, try and behave yourself.'

'I can be cultured, if I have to be. It's OK to heckle during a play, right?'

'Of course. The actors expect it.'

'We went to see a play with school once – do you remember? It was just after we'd got our test scores back. What was it called?'

'Punishment.'

The two girls laughed with a sense of relief that their friendship had been repaired, the minor damage was already forgotten.

'I'm right, aren't I, you're wondering why he hasn't phoned you?'

Natasha shrugged her shoulders as if she didn't care, though knowing she was fooling neither herself nor Anna. Anna wanted to help.

She said, 'You didn't expect him to phone tonight, did you? Guys always like to play it cool, you know that. Richard only phoned because I forced a promise from him this morning.'

'Did you use violence?'

'The worse kind of violence – I shagged a promise out of him. Look, just relax. Geoffrey, I'll bet you anything, will be at home now desperately wanting to phone you but resisting because he'll want you to think he's not keen.'

'You're probably right, but I didn't think he'd be like that.'

The phone rang.

'Spooky.'

'How should I play it?'

'Cool,' Anna advised.

'I always play it cool.'

'And it always works.'

'Cool it is. Detached?' Natasha wondered.

'Don't overdo it. After all, you do actually like this guy. You don't know how to deal with his type, so take it easy.'

'Whatever happens, I won't tell him I like him.' Natasha was now standing over the phone.

Anna added, 'Let him know you like him without actually saying it.'

Natasha answered the phone. It was her mother, phoning to extract information about Geoffrey – whom Natasha feared she would never see again if he was phoning now and failing to get through. She attempted to dismiss her mum with lies.

'I'm just having my tea, Mum.'

Then, after this had failed: 'I have guests here, Mum.'

Another failure; her mum still talked on. For Natasha her mother's voice could not now be deciphered into individual words; she heard only an irksome hubbub.

'Mum, me and Anna are going out and we're already late. I have to go.'

Five minutes later her mum was still talking. A sentence was cut short with: 'Bye, Mum,' then Natasha hung up.

'I'm going to have a bath,' she told Anna. She ran a shallow bath, then washed quickly. She had purposely not washed her hair so that she wouldn't have to use the hair-dryer. The phone rang. It was Anna's aunt and uncle. While Anna talked to them, Natasha had a reprieve, and so went into her room to prepare her clothes for work tomorrow. The thought of Monday elbowed every other thought from her mind so that later, even though the call had been uppermost in her thoughts all day, she was caught off guard when Geoffrey phoned. Replies she had carefully constructed, her rehearsed coolness and friendly indifference, all vanished.

'Hi, Geoff. God, I'm glad you phoned.'

Anna, listening to this, pretended to vomit and Natasha closed her eyes and shook her head, an indictment of how pathetic she was. Anna then went into the kitchen to make coffee, to pretend to give her friend privacy. She carefully left the door open and put the kettle on the simmer ring so as to make the least amount of distracting noise. In spite of all this effort, she heard nothing that would help her understand the conversation. When she heard a final, 'OK, I'll look forward to hearing from you then. Lovely. Bye,' she quickly put the kettle onto a higher ring and busied herself with coffee before Natasha came into the kitchen. Natasha smiled. She stirred the dry coffee granules and sugar in a cup, mixing them. Anna spoke first.

'So he phones you the next day? He's obviously not cool.'

'I don't care if he's not cool. That's the reason I like him.' After a thought she added, 'The thing is, I don't want to be so keen on him. Women who are so keen on a bloke this quickly are dummies.'

'You mean like the way I'm keen on Richard?'

Natasha side-tracked the embarrassment of this. 'Geoffrey's phoning me again tomorrow night – when you're out – so we can have a proper talk.'

'Hey – dial one four seven one! You'll hear his phone number!'

For a moment Natasha almost refused on the grounds that to do so lacked dignity and trust; the next moment she was heading back to the phone; she reached for the receiver just as the phone rang. She answered.

'Natasha, you hung up before I finished speaking,' her mother said. 'Please don't ever be that rude again – it's not how we brought you up.'

FOURTEEN

The girls plodded through Monday barely speaking to each other. When Anna went to the bank at dinnertime she was relieved to see that her wages had been paid in and she was be able to shop for a new skirt for the evening.

On the bus home, Anna showed Natasha the skirt she'd bought. Now they began to talk. Anna had two hours to prepare herself, although she didn't have to concern herself with making something to eat: she had been promised a meal.

She told Natasha, 'Sounds like he's taking me to a proper restaurant, you know, where you don't hold the food you're eating. Do you see how *Bartok's* has already improved my life?'

If Anna continued to see Richard, and everything went well, Natasha would have to accept that she would become less important to her. For Natasha, no one had ever come close to rivalling Anna in her affections. Except for once, when she was sixteen.

Natasha had accompanied her parents and her sister on their last family holiday. She had begged them to allow Anna to come but they had refused, and Natasha went on the holiday demonstrating a degree of resentment that only a teenager can.

'God, I'm so bored! I just want to go home!' she moaned five minutes into the journey there.

The holiday was in a caravan park near Cleethorpes. On the first night, Natasha phoned her friend.

'They're making me go to this crap kids' disco because they don't want Brenda to go on her own.'

'Is there anything for you to do?' Anna asked.

'Nothing. This holiday is the worst holiday imaginable. It's boring and dull and just shit. I wish you'd come. I'll phone you tomorrow night.'

Sixteen is the perfect age to feel completely alien from those only a year or two younger than you, so while Brenda danced relentlessly, Natasha stood on the sidelines sneering in disdain at every kid in the room. Then she saw someone like her: older, bored, detached, a boy constantly pestered by the quibbles of a younger girl. He exercised this responsibility by glaring at the girl in loathing. He kept this evil glare as he caught Natasha's eye. Startled, she turned away. He walked over to her.

'Sorry,' he began. 'I didn't mean to look at you like that. I'm watching my parents' friends' daughter. She's getting on my nerves.'

'Tell me about it,' Natasha said, transforming from a cocky, knowing adult into a petrified, vulnerable child. Recovering quickly, she pointed towards Brenda. 'Sister.'

He laughed. 'They should at least have a bar.'

'Tell me about it,' Natasha said, cursing herself for not taking a moment or two longer to think of a different answer. 'But we might as well be here as anywhere else on this camp,' she added quickly. 'Let's face it – we might as well be in prison.'

'Have you ever been in prison?' he asked as a joke. She laughed, to please him. He introduced himself – Michael – then she accepted his offer of a drink. While he was away she took the opportunity to ask herself if she fancied him. He was very skinny, with a smile which made him appear rather dopey. Not only that, but he walked clumsily, as if having to remind himself constantly how to.

When he returned with their Dr Peppers – the nearest to a stimulant in the place – she forgot all his flaws. His eyes were black with depth and mystery. She needed to talk to him to find out how he worked.

Refusing to dance, they had to spend the remainder of that first evening talking about their home towns and their friends, Natasha telling him all about Anna. Neither had ever spent such a prolonged period simply talking to a fanciable member of the opposite sex.

At nine-thirty the lights came on full, like a police raid, and Natasha was relieved to see, in this clearer light, that he suffered from no major blemishes. As their young wards returned, sweating and panting, they felt especially cool and sophisticated. They gave a civilised goodbye to each other, secure in the knowledge that they had already made binding arrangements to meet in the morning.

'I couldn't sleep for thinking about you last night,' were the first words he spoke when they met up at the camp gates at ten a.m., as arranged. He kissed her as if they were established lovers, then took her hand as they passed through the gates.

'Did your parents give you any grief, ask you what you were planning on doing this morning?' he asked as they walked towards Cleethorpes front.

'Brenda – that's my little sister – told them I'd been talking to a guy last night, so I guess they know. I don't care, it's not up to them.'

He smiled and winked, as if they were in some great conspiracy, as if they were eloping.

For the rest of the week she spent every morning with Michael, the afternoon with her family, then the evening until nine-thirty at the disco, the two of them separate from the rest of the world. Natasha forgot to phone Anna. And when she eventually remembered, she still didn't phone.

On their morning walks around Cleethorpes, sometimes in the arcades, sometimes along the shore, eating junk and devouring time, they built up a small repertoire of anecdotes; and in the evening at the disco, fighting against the noise of the music and the attention of their dependants, they told each other every detail of their lives so that their time together always passed faster than they could tolerate. That they would be returning to their usual lives and this week would cease to exist occurred to neither of them until they met on the last night, Friday.

'I won't forget you,' he told her, 'but is there something you have which you could give me so that I have a specific memory?'

She acted on her first instinct, took him outside, away from the disco, and out towards the changing rooms of the deserted outdoor swimming pool. They made love and then returned to the club at nine o'clock. They spent their last thirty minutes together knowing that from now on they were inseparable, even though they would never see each other again.

When they got home from work Anna took a bath. Later, Natasha went into Anna's bedroom while she was getting dressed. A space on the floor had been cleared by her shovelling everything to one side – the closest she'd ever come to tidying up. She had still not made her bed.

'I know what you think about me,' Anna said to Natasha, who was standing at her side as she looked into the full-length mirror wearing the new skirt. 'You think I meet someone who's reasonably OK, and the next minute, I fall for them.'

'Have you ever been in love?' Natasha asked. She had been thinking about Michael, from Cleethorpes. 'I mean, come on, really? Looking back over all those men you've had – and it's hundreds, maybe thousands now, right?' she joked, 'is there any particular one you think, um, maybe I should have tried harder with him, or that you still think of fondly?'

Anna thought. She looked sad. Then grinned. 'No.'

'Maybe this one, eh?' Natasha asked.

'I don't know. I don't know enough about him; all I can think is, if he's as great as he seemed on Saturday night . . . he's my best chance yet. But we'll see. That's the difference between me and you, Natasha, I like them too easily. You never like any of them. Ever.'

Anna's knowledge of Natasha's behaviour had been built up over many years, almost their entire lives, so she believed Natasha's story that she had never met anyone she liked further than superficial attraction and a basic compatibility. Natasha had told Anna about Michael, though not that it was love: she was able to think of Michael in terms of 'love' because since him no experience had come close; and also because she had known him for only a week, in unreal circumstances, without the contamination of real life. How he was for that week was how she imagined he would always have been. No one is that flawless, she now knew.

'More than anything else I want our friendship to continue,' Natasha suddenly told Anna.

'It will,' she answered, without even wondering why Natasha had ever doubted it. 'We've always said that nothing will stop us from being friends.'

'But all great friends say that, then, eventually, love raises its ugly head – and of course it *isn't* ugly – and the friend is pushed into second place.'

Anna said, 'I know as well as you do that that's how it usually works. But you know as well as me that *we* aren't the same as most friends. Even if living with you means you sometimes get on my tits, still . . . our friendship started at such an early age I have no memories of my life without you. So that's the difference – just as the past is there, so will be the future.'

'What will Richard have to say about that?'

'I haven't thought about it,' Anna lied. She had thought about *everything*. 'I've never imagined it as an actual conversation we will have. I just imagine that he'll realise. If he doesn't, then he'll have to be told.'

Anna was deliberately holding back the truth from Natasha – that Richard was married – in order to perpetuate the happiness she was indulging herself in. If Natasha continued to believe that Anna was in a straightforward relationship, that made the illusion just a little more real.

When Anna was finally ready, and permitted herself to be the subject of a critical inspection by Natasha, Natasha remembered how she had been after that Cleethorpes holiday, returning to Bradford having lost a friend whom she could have envisaged one day as someone she would always want to be with. There followed a two-week period of depression: a punishment double the length of time of the joy she had experienced. When she finally began to recover, she realised that the joy had not been worth the misery, and so promised herself to be more careful of love in the future. And so she had been, though her will had never been seriously tested: the *Apollo* had no supply of loveable men, only an abundance of jailable men.

Anna was looking out of the living-room window, searching for Richard even though he was not due for another ten minutes. Natasha joined her.

'You've been with me when we've gone into the toilets of the *Apollo* and there's been some girl consoling her mate, who's in tears over some lad. Me and you have always laughed at them, thinking how stupid they were. And that's how I want it to stay. I don't ever want to have to console you because Richard has hurt you.'

'He won't,' Anna said, immediately thinking how Richard must be hurting his wife.

'Here's what we should do, Anna. We've never had to do it before because neither of us has met men as promising as these two. But let's face up to it, let's be honest, when it comes to this type – *decent* men – both of us are virgins. All I'm saying is, promise me and I'll promise you – let's take it easy, let's be careful. Let's give them the benefit of the doubt, let's be trusting but let's still never forget – they're men. Men hurt women. Even good men – they can hurt the worst.'

'OK,' Anna told her, 'we'll take it easy. But, I don't know, the thing is, I'm already really happy. That's good, isn't it?'

Before Natasha could reply, and she would only have said yes, Anna spotted Richard parking his car.

'He's here! He's here!' she screamed like the first Christian spotting the return of Jesus, though this analogy wouldn't hold up after she added, 'He looks gorgeous, maybe we should just stay in and screw!'

Anna had a short, panicky debate as to whether she should wait for him to come to the door or whether she should dash out to him, as she wanted, which would betray her eagerness. The debate was won by her true self, and she ran. Natasha watched her outside as Richard embraced her. Anna didn't look back to wave at Natasha; she was thinking only of Richard.

The phone rang. It was Geoffrey. Natasha put on a lazy, uninterested voice as if she had not been waiting for his call. The conversation wasn't immediately successful: they struggled after saying hello, a silence which in real life could have been filled with a gesture or smile, but on the phone languished like an illness. Geoffrey panicked.

'So do you go to *Bartok's* often?'

'We talked about this on Saturday,' Natasha answered impatiently. 'Don't you remember?'

'I do remember. I don't know why I asked. It was your first time,' he added to illustrate he had been listening. Then he tried too hard: 'You normally go to . . . er . . . something to do with mythology.'

'The *Apollo*,' she reminded him, careful this time not to sound impatient. 'It's not that we normally go there, we *always* go there.' She told him that those days were ending with the imminent closure of the club. She told him that the only times they hadn't gone in the past had been when they were broke, or once when they had instead attended Corrine Slater's wedding.

'What would be your ideal wedding?' Geoffrey asked, only to avoid silence. He recovered enough to make a joke: 'This isn't a proposal, I'm just interested.'

She already had an answer of sorts. 'All I can tell you is the type of wedding I wouldn't want, and that's the type – the only type – I've ever gone to. Local church, local pub. Instantly forgettable. What would be yours?'

Geoffrey went straight into his answer, giving Natasha the same answer he'd given to Janette when they had had this same conversation.

'Las Vegas. An Elvis impersonator presiding over the service. No friends or family attending, just me and the woman I'm marrying. Then a pizza afterwards and a honeymoon in a cheesy motel.'

Natasha wasn't laughing, though there was a smile in her voice in appreciation of Geoffrey's opinion.

'Have you ever been to America?' she asked. 'Don't answer! I'll bet you have. Am I right?'

Geoffrey answered truthfully, as always, only worrying that he was perpetuating the false idea she had about him.

'Yes.'

'I don't even know why I asked. It's somewhere I've always wanted to go to.'

They talked about America for a while, Geoffrey destroying some of her incorrect assumptions, then building up her desire again by telling her why he liked the country so much. She told him some of her badly informed opinions about reactionary American politics, and he answered with his admiration for the American constitution – Britain had nothing comparable. They agreed on a repulsion against American gun culture, then agreed on their preference for American TV shows to British. Natasha, however, preferred English bands predominantly, while Geoffrey preferred American ones. His love of country music provoked the latest silence as Natasha struggled to think of a more intelligent response than '*country music is shite*'. He redeemed himself by mentioning other artists, The White Stripes, Red Hot Chilli Peppers, The Strokes, which she also liked. Heat and sweat forced Natasha to move the telephone from one ear to another, quickly, so as not to miss a word he said. They talked about their preferred type of songs, and they both named their favourite ballads. This turned the conversation towards love, and Geoffrey asked her questions to prevent him thinking of Janette. Natasha didn't think about Anna until she was half-way through telling Geoffrey about Michael, the boy from Cleethorpes. She even told Geoffrey about having sex with him on their last night.

'The difference between then and now is that I was much younger then – I would be old and wise enough now to avoid feeling like that.'

'Age has nothing to do with love, or feeling, thinking you're in love,' Geoffrey said. He lapsed: 'This time last year I was obsessed by a woman who made me miserable, yet I knew in my head, in that second, lower level of thought, the one which doesn't dictate how we behave but is still our true voice – I knew I didn't genuinely love her, nor could I ever. Yet on the day she told me she intended to re-marry her ex-husband – although she'd spent the last three years repeatedly boring me with his faults – I'd never felt so depressed. Nothing in my life had prepared me for how I felt.' There was a silence. Geoffrey had his eyes shut, waiting for her to hang up. Or maybe she was asleep.

Natasha was listening, thinking: 'I'm going to tell him I like him. I might even tell him exactly how much I like him.' He had not wished to sound cool, he had not refrained from an honest account of a failed love affair.

'What do you think of her now?' Natasha asked.

Out of relief that he had been given this opportunity, he gushed: 'I think nothing of her. Sometimes it makes me angry, but I'm just angry with myself for acting like I did about someone I really knew wasn't right for me. I behaved like a kid.'

She reassured Geoffrey that the mistakes he had made with his ex-girlfriend did not make him foolish, or naive. Everything she said made her aware that she sounded like one of those women she hated, afraid of asserting herself or voicing a strong opinion for fear of offending her boyfriend. Part of her thought Geoffrey was a wimp for putting up with this Jannette.

'Could a woman make you act like that again?'

'She'd have to be someone' – he had a sudden inspiration – 'who I talked to on the phone for nearly two hours.'

Natasha looked at her clock. They had been speaking for nearly two hours. The longest conversation she'd ever had previously with a man on the phone – disregarding the time her bank had overcharged her for an overdraft – was seven minutes. And that wasn't a conversation – she barely spoke. The only other person she had ever spoken to on the phone for this length of time was Anna.

As he listened to Natasha, Geoffrey hoped the call would not register on the bill. The telephone conversation ended then, with

Geoffrey promising to phone her again, tomorrow night, at the same time.

Geoffrey went to make himself a drink, running through some of the subjects they had discussed, some of her comments which had made him laugh or he had disagreed with – and her readiness to do battle in defence of her opinions. A woman with strong opinions, ready to argue for them. He was tempted to call her back and ask if she wanted to come over now, in spite of the fact that most of the evening had already passed. He had not asked her out and had still not given her his phone number.

Natasha dialled one four seven one. The number had been withheld.

FIFTEEN

Anna and Richard's first real date began promisingly. He flattered her by immediately making sure she could contact him again.

'Here's my work number. And my mobile,' he told her. 'You can fax me if you want – on this number. And my e-mail address is –'

'I don't have a computer. Or a fax machine. I wouldn't know how to work one either – I have trouble figuring out how my bedside lamp works.' She gave him her mobile number, without asking the question she would have liked to ask, namely – 'What if I phone you when you're with your wife?'

Immediately they were settled in his car he told her that after finding somewhere to eat they were going to see a touring production of *Anthony and Cleopatra.* Anna's smile froze on her face, in case there was a punch-line. While Richard summarised the plot of Shakespeare's tragic love story, her only thought was, 'Shakespeare? Shit, it'll be like having homework.'

Richard asked if she had ever seen a production. Anna answered an honest 'No' rather than an equally honest yet potentially shaming, 'No, but I've seen *Carry On Cleo*, if that's any help.'

They went to a Chinese restaurant which served a running buffet; you paid a fixed price then ate as much as you liked.

Growing up the children of two alcoholic parents, Anna and her brothers often had to make their own meals. Her brothers were masters at opening tins and warming their contents. If Anna cooked, she would have to fend off her brothers as they tried to steal her food. If she ever went to the trouble of something as luxurious as chips, she ate out in the yard.

Richard watched Anna with her third helping, eating as if the food was in danger of being stolen.

'This is frightening,' he told her. 'Are you as insatiable in all your appetites?'

'I think you already know the answer to that.'

When she finished this third plate and Richard looked at his watch, she suggested that they skip the theatre and instead just go to a bar.

'I've got the tickets,' he protested, concerned by her expression. 'You'll love it, I promise.'

In the theatre, while Anna sat waiting for the curtain to rise, every unsolicited thought she had, persistent though she despised them, told her she did not belong with someone who believed the theatre was a good first date. Least of all a first date with a man who was married. She tried not to care: the predominant reason she liked this man was that he was so different from all the others.

She caught sight of Richard's profile as he read through the programme. She kept her face forward, with her eyes to the side so she could look at him without him noticing. She wanted to keep looking at his face in profile; handsome, strong, a perfectly shaped nose and the darkness around the jaw where hair growth was persistent. He was worth the effort of Shakespeare, she thought.

The play started and she worked hard, making a strained effort to follow the plot and understand the language. During a scene change, Richard excused himself to use the loo. Her main concern now was the play, getting the drift. There had been a battle and the guy fancied the woman.

A quarter of an hour later, worrying about his absence, she turned on her mobile and tapped out – to the annoyance of her stuffy neighbours – the text message, WHERE R U? At the first interval, when she turned her mobile back on, she received the reply, BAR. 3RD DRINK. WHERE R U?

She controlled her temper on the way from the circle to the bar.

'You're missing the play,' she remonstrated. She didn't add, 'You lucky bastard.'

'I don't understand you,' he told her. 'Why would you want to see a play – *they serve alcohol here.*'

So she stayed in the bar with him, pleased that she had been duped. They spent the rest of the night drinking and laughing about how uncultured they both were.

'My perfect evening is sprawled out on the settee watching a good video,' he told her.

A woman passed by, dressed sexily, full-on make-up, the figure, the blonde hair.

'Hell-o,' Richard said as if he had been speaking to her, grinning wickedly to antagonise Anna. She punched him on his knee.

'She's a tart,' Anna told him.

'You say that as if it's a bad thing.'

Free to tease her in this manner, Richard knew Anna was right for him.

Anna told him anecdotes she might only, normally, have told Natasha, or held in reserve for men she knew far better. Stories of being drunk, of mischief, of sex and boyfriends. She exercised caution only so he wouldn't be *too* appalled, but on the whole she felt free to tell him most details. Anna knew, she already knew, there was no retreat. They made each other laugh, and there is no more powerful aphrodisiac. They held nothing in reserve, confident enough to show each other their best and their worst. The only caution Anna held on to was of the inherent hope in such a sentiment; she would wish for more in the future. Who ever wants less happiness? But she knew she would be denied.

Richard liked the way Anna told an anecdote, speaking faster as her excitement grew until he was forced to slow her down so he could understand. He liked the way she had begun the evening careful not to swear, but now each story was littered with expletives.

He left his car in the theatre car park, and in the taxi to Anna's home they had a kiss before she was dropped off. Richard didn't tell her how much he had enjoyed himself, how much he hoped to see her again, and how much he liked her. He had only ever said these things previously when he had not meant them.

Natasha was still awake.

'How did it go?'

'Did Geoff phone?'

Richard returned home wondering what might happen now. This was unknown territory for him; Anna was a mystery. Richard already knew there was no reserve. Without great experience of her, without previous testing, without a catalogue of shared tales, without bickering, fall-outs or recriminations – he already knew. Richard's only reservation was fear. He had sought Anna out for the change, to take out a girl who wasn't obsessed with her looks, her clothes, her weight. He wanted pretty, naturally, but was willing to trade off startling beauty for a girl who wasn't such hard work: a woman who could begin and bolster a conversation, someone who could give him smart answers, who would respond intelligently, even humorously. Knowing this had still not prepared him for how amazing these attributes would be: the interest, the excitement, even the sexuality of being with a girl where sex wasn't the exclusive attraction. Again, he felt scared. He had no plans to end this relationship. So if he never finished with her, this held the frightening prospect of him, at some future date, being ditched by her. Or, more scary yet, if she didn't ditch him, he had met a girl whom he would never ditch and might never be ditched by.

In six months Geoffrey had written precisely twenty pages of his proposed novel. The maths were not promising. At this rate a reasonable sized novel would take seven years. He marvelled at how Anthony Burgess, believing he didn't have long to live, wrote three novels in a year so as to leave his wife a legacy. Or Dostoyevsky, who wrote a novel in two weeks in order to meet a publisher's deadline. And by now Geoffrey had learnt that his talent was no match for Burgess or Dostoyevsky. He couldn't hope to live long enough to write a novel matching their brilliance. In their situation Geoffrey would have had either a lawsuit or a starving widow.

The price for Geoffrey of pursuing his desire to be an author was to live in a room where neighbours outnumbered friends, home was a cell and cold dominated even on warm days. Living there was a necessity caused by having no income. Living in such a fashion was also a pretension. Rather than having a real desire to write, Geoffrey merely liked the romantic idea of being a writer living in squalor, smoking Gitanes, drinking too much, hoping wretchedness in life might manifest itself in his art. This was why the words came slowly; they had to be thought up rather than recorded.

Geoffrey was temporarily staying in his friends' home. To have Geoffrey guard their house while they were away had been Stuart's idea. The last two times Melanie had accompanied him to a tournament their home had been burgled. Geoffrey had happily agreed. Their house had heating more sophisticated than the two-bar electric fire Geoffrey owned, which severely burnt you if you were closer than three inches to it, yet if you stood more than four inches away, the fire might as well have been off. The bed in their spare room was firm and comfortable, while the mattress Geoffrey usually slept on was as flat and listless as a slice of bread. They had a freezer full of food, while in his bedsit Geoffrey had a half-eaten packet of crisps sealed shut for freshness with an elastic band. He also hoped that working on the PC might, with the different approach to writing, help him progress to a new chapter. In his bedsit he owned a manual typewriter, an Olympia Traveller Deluxe. He enjoyed the noise it made when he tapped at it, but had soon learnt that a pleasing noise contributed little to the writing process.

Geoffrey's real genius was his ability to avoid writing. He sat in front of Stuart's PC, looking through the different programmes. He found a voice-recognition programme, fitted the headset and microphone and began to talk.

'It doesn't matter how I *feel* about Natasha. If I ever really want progress there has to be a time when I make the confession or she makes the discovery that I'm not this rich guy she thinks I am. And even if my assumption is incorrect, and she isn't interested in me mainly because of this house and their car, I can only imagine she will still be so outraged that I misled her that she'll have no choice but to finish with me. And the worst part of knowing this is the paradox that if she didn't dump me because of this, then I would like her less for having no self-respect.'

He continued to talk into the microphone.

'And how do I live with that? How do I let this one slip through my hands without putting up a fight for her? It's not as if I've had streams of women in my life. I've had barely a handful, and none that I really liked. And even those I liked being with, like Janette, even then I've always had the living, subconscious knowledge that I was fooling myself, that we weren't really compatible. Yet with Natasha, though I have doubts about her motives for being with me, I have no doubts about her. I want to see how she and I would be if we were alone, carefree, responsible for nothing else but the two of us together. I *could* hope that she goes out with me for long enough and is so overwhelmed by my charm and personality that when she finally understands that this house and this car and this lifestyle aren't mine, and aren't me, she won't care, she'll have fallen in love with me. Except that I'm not the type to inspire love in women. I usually inspire boredom. They like me, they think I'm sweet, but they don't love me. It would be nice to have her and have her trust me. Some trust has already been established. I told her many things about Janette and she listened and made the right responses. She didn't laugh or think I was stupid.'

This was all he had to say. He printed the document off. Perhaps he had not used the programme correctly or had not spoken clearly enough. Some words were decipherable, but never enough to make a comprehensible sentence. The whole page was gobbledegook. Nonsense. He shut down the PC and ripped up the page.

He had thrown her number into the kitchen pedal bin, then later – with a second flush of determination – he had emptied the bin outside. He had then returned inside to attempt – once again – to write.

He took the torn pieces of paper outside to the bin where he then rummaged in search of the paper with her phone number on it. It was so badly creased and stained that some of the numbers were illegible and some had run, so if he was weak enough to phone her – and he knew he was – any failure would be fate. He would confess that he had so little money he could not take her out.

He phoned. She answered. They talked. Every negative thought he had had during the day vanished as if it had never existed. The vibration of her voice in his ear, the ease of their carefree conversation, made for an intimacy which was premature, yet robust and sensual.

SIXTEEN

Natasha answered her friend's question; yes Geoffrey had phoned. She then began questioning Anna about her theatre date, not sure how best to tell Anna that Geoffrey was all she could have hoped for, even though she feared that he did not care for her to the same degree.

'Just tell me about the theatre. Was it a play?'

Anna needed no further prompting. Though it was nearly one o'clock in the morning, she spared no details in describing the night she had had: the early scare when she worried that Richard was dull, then her delight when she discovered his behaviour had been a hoax. She told Natasha about the Chinese restaurant and how Richard pulled her leg about her enormous appetite. For Anna the greatest joy was the ease she felt in his company, the way they drank and talked as if they had known each other for years.

'He's more down to earth than I first thought.'

'Which is a good thing,' Natasha said. 'Otherwise you'd have scared him off.'

'Are you saying I'm rough compared to Richard?'

'I'm saying you're rough compared to gravel.'

Ignoring this, her face lit with happiness, Anna continued: 'The time flew by, I never stopped laughing. And if you ask me now what we talked about, I'll bet I couldn't tell you. All I know is that I'm seeing him again tomorrow night. I should get some sleep, really, otherwise I'm going to be knackered tomorrow. You're seeing Geoff again, I take it?'

'He's phoning again, tomorrow night.'

As Natasha said this she became more reconciled to her decision not to see him again. The intimacy was lovely. At this early stage, less intimacy and more fun would have been healthier. Anna and Richard – as all *other* couples do – had the balance right. To make sure Anna did not get the wrong impression, to make certain she understood that while she liked Geoffrey there was nothing serious expected, Natasha told her: 'There have been other blokes I've liked. And there are some now.'

'Yeah? Who?'

'There are some I like certain things about. There's a guy who goes to the *Apollo*, I've never spoken to him, but I've seen him loads of times. I like the way he dresses. He wears short-sleeved shirts, they have a fifties look about them.'

Anna told Natasha, 'There's a guy who walks past the shop regularly. He must work nearby, and he always smiles at me and raises his eyebrows. I've never spoken to him but I like him.'

'Do you remember Luke Collins?'

'You went out with him for a while . . . Years ago.'

'I liked the way he kissed,' Natasha said.

'Sam Collins, his older brother – do you remember him? – I had a snog with him once. I loved the way he used to touch my face and neck as we kissed. It must be a family thing.'

'And there've been other men who've all had one quality, or maybe a couple of qualities I've liked. But none that . . .'

'Together added up to . . .' Anna did not finish, not knowing what too many good qualities might add up to. 'Like Richard and –'

'Geoffrey,' Natasha confessed.

They went to bed.

In spite of the late hour, Natasha lay in bed not immediately able to sleep.

On Saturday nights Natasha occasionally saw a man around town she knew only as Ken. For as long as she had been old enough to go drinking she had known him. When she saw him, the time since she had last seen him lost significance; he would immediately be at her, chatting to her, telling her nonsense. Though they kissed and Ken made the suggestion, they had never slept together nor arranged to go out. When she saw him she was transformed, her previous mood irrelevant. Whenever Natasha was in a bad mood, Anna used to joke that she wished Ken would show up. He knew instinctively, without any effort or contrivance, how to make her laugh. Thank God Geoffrey hadn't yet made her laugh like Ken, otherwise Natasha knew she would have no chance of maintaining her resolution not to see him again. Only by thinking about this could she sleep.

Anna, on the other hand, went to sleep straight away, untroubled.

Anna's elder brother had a mate, Gary, who had joined the army immediately after his last day of school. On a massive drinking binge, Anna had been one of those out to see him off. Later, when both of them had drunk enough, he asked her for a kiss, to see him on his way. She refused, then deliberately qualified the refusal so he would persist.

'I wouldn't kiss you here, too many people,' said the girl who had once enjoyed a snog on a packed bus. With the driver.

He whispered, 'I'll see you outside in five minutes,' as if the matter was settled. She didn't argue; they were only going to kiss.

She slept with him that night. She could never honestly say she liked him or was even interested in him, yet whenever she knew he was on leave she hoped to see him. She had sex with him as if fucking a soldier was her civic duty. She relished the way he set about her, making no show of interest in anything other than sex; then, when sex was over, leaving as rapidly as he could.

Anna doubted she could ever fall in love with someone she did not enjoy sex with. Richard wanted to be with her, wanted them to fall asleep holding each other; and he enjoyed talking with her; and he made her laugh. Thank God he wasn't all these things as well as being a lover like Gary. She would not have been able to part from him as easily as she had tonight.

The next morning Anna shouted at Natasha for taking too long in the bathroom, then in turn Natasha shouted at Anna for not having made her a coffee as she had promised.

'What's up with you?' Anna bellowed. 'What's the hardship in making coffee for yourself? Do you want me to write out the recipe?'

'The hardship is it's too late to have one now, and you know what I'm like without a cup of coffee first thing.'

'Yeah, you're like this,' Anna told her, 'a real bitch.'

Anna made amends for this by making a coffee for her friend, cool enough to drink immediately. They both dressed and fixed their hair in a rush, applied the barest minimum of make-up, yet still had to hurry to catch the bus. Anna's knickers were twisted; her constant fidgeting on the ride to work gave Natasha enough of a clue to understand her friend's problem, and the minute they were off the bus she sheltered Anna from onlookers as she adjusted herself.

'See?' Natasha said as if they had held a discussion. 'Richard wouldn't do this for you.'

Anna recovered her good humour sooner than Natasha, and at work reprised the same conversation they had held last night, recounting the evening she had enjoyed with Richard. Just in case Natasha had not heard, Anna repeated this again at regular intervals throughout the day.

As the workday ended, Natasha told herself that it would be such a waste if she didn't see Geoffrey again. *After all, he expects to be seeing me and might arrange to do so when he next phones.* Natasha looked out from the door of the stock room, watching Anna serve her last customer, and imagined asking her what she thought about this. Anna approached and walked past Natasha. She did not return the smile Natasha gave her.

On the bus home she asked Anna, for the sake of a conversation she hoped would divert her thoughts, where Richard was taking her tonight.

'He hasn't said. The truth is, I don't really want to go out. At the pictures we can't talk, I don't fancy another meal, and I had enough alcohol last night. If he hasn't planned anywhere specific then I'll tell him we should just stay in.'

'He might think you're hinting at a night of nothing but sex.'

'You think so? Oh good.'

Before she could be asked if she and Geoffrey had made plans, Natasha asked Anna, carefully wording the question so she wouldn't know she meant Geoffrey:

'Have you ever been out with someone who wouldn't give you his phone number?'

'*Wouldn't?*'

'Hasn't. Didn't. Someone who didn't immediately, you know.'

'Is this about Geoffrey? He still hasn't –'

'It's not about him,' she lied, then tried to recover. 'I haven't asked for it. It's not important. Have you got Richard's?'

'He gave me his home, work and mobile.' This was a lie: she did not have his home telephone number. Anna wanted to confess this, to lead into a further confession that Richard was married. Both girls had long since stated their opposition to relationships with married men.

Anna had only once before been out with a man who was in a committed relationship. To gauge Natasha's reaction, she reminded her.

'I've only ever had one man who refused outright to give me his phone number. It was Phil, Philip – don't you remember him? Very tall, always nicely dressed.'

'Oh – the married man,' Natasha said.

'Well, he wasn't married, he only seemed married because he was so fucking miserable. He just lived with someone. That's what I found out – and that's why he wouldn't give me his phone number. He didn't want me phoning and speaking to her.'

Natasha's reaction was silence. For the rest of the journey she began to picture a life for Geoffrey where he was married yet still able to have the house to himself. He might be separated. His wife worked away. She was on holiday with friends. His wife was in hospital – *the bastard.*

By the time Natasha arrived home she hated him so much she would agree to go out with him just so as to use him: he deserved to be tortured for using her and betraying his wife.

While Anna was preparing herself for Richard, Natasha sat down to watch the Tuesday edition of *Emmerdale*, answering the phone casually under the assumption the call would be Richard with a message for Anna.

Geoffrey said hello. Natasha immediately disliked herself for her chirpy reply, an admission she was pleased he had called.

Anna came out of the bathroom.

'Is that for me?'

'Geoffrey,' Natasha told her.

When Anna arrived home that night, more reluctant than ever to think about the day she and Richard would break up, she immediately went to bed in the hope that she would fall asleep straight away. Natasha ruined this plan. She had heard her friend return and came into Anna's room, hoping that Anna might ask about her phone call from Geoffrey. They had talked from seven till nine-thirty. Again he had not given his phone number, nor had he asked her out. He had only promised he would phone again tomorrow night. Through tonight's phone call they had discovered they had the same opinions on child-rearing – they were both in favour of being disciplinarians; car ownership – small cars and feeling guilty; serial killers – against them, naturally, but both fascinated by them. They also discovered they violently disagreed on anchovies and Frank Skinner – Natasha liked them both, Geoffrey hated them both.

'Did you go anywhere nice?' Natasha asked Anna.

'His flat,' Anna lied, hoping Natasha would not ask any awkward questions. The flat they had gone to belonged to a friend of Richard's who had lent them the key.

Anna told Natasha, 'Do you know how we were talking about other boys we've known, who had small things we liked – to express it really badly – but not enough things put together? But that I thought Richard was different. He is different. But he's not perfect.' Anna had said this as a precursor to telling Natasha that Richard was married. Natasha said nothing for so long that Anna couldn't add anything further, the momentum lost.

After Natasha had returned to bed, Anna turned off her bedroom light. She wouldn't have minded fewer things to like about Richard – in exchange for him not being married. This was the difference for her. In every other one of her relationships she had always hoped for, but never received, consistency. The difference now was that she wanted change. She wanted progress, to which Richard being married was a fairly big obstacle.

SEVENTEEN

On Wednesday night Geoffrey phoned at the same time again, seven o'clock. Anna had already left to go out with Richard. Natasha had made herself a cup of coffee in preparation and had brought the coffee table up to the armchair so she could spread out. She had decided to enjoy the talking simply for its own sake, rather than in any expectation that he should ask her out. However, she found herself thinking all through their conversation, *He won't give me his phone number. That can't mean anything other than he doesn't like me at all – worst-case scenario. Or he has doubts – still not good. I mean, I'm not saying I'm lovely, or he should be glad to have me, but . . . What's his problem?*

Geoffrey began by telling Natasha he intended not to talk any longer than an hour, as there was a documentary he was determined to watch on Channel Five which started at eight.

'What's the documentary about?' Natasha asked. *Give me your phone number.*

'Tanks,' he told her, like a bloke.

'Oh,' she responded, like a girl. There was a pause here before the two separate species redirected their efforts towards common territory. They talked about the Second World War, politics, foreigners, Europe, sex, porn films, boxing, assassinated historical figures and their favourite rock bands whose lead singers were now dead. Geoffrey chose Joy Division, Natasha erroneously chose Pulp. At eight forty-five Natasha told Geoffrey he had missed his documentary. He told her he didn't care.

The phone call ended. Thirty minutes later he phoned her

again, confessing that he had nothing particular to say. They talked for a further fifty minutes before she insisted the call ended.

'Phone again tomorrow night,' she told him. Then added, deliberately: 'Or I'll phone you, if you want?'

'That's OK. I'll phone at seven.'

On Tuesday, to test him by his response, Anna had asked Richard to pick her up at six-thirty, then changed this to eight before finally telling him to come for her at seven. On Wednesday she had named several places she would like to go, all highly public, before finally admitting she was happy simply to spend another evening at his friend's flat. She had made all these decisions in the expectation that he would have to decline, make excuses, tell her the hurtful truth – he had to see his wife, go home and placate her. To Anna's delight he only ever made the most modest of amendments to accommodate his work or give him time to go home to wash and change first. Anna wondered how he excused himself to his wife, though she never asked him about this. She was content to believe his marriage was unhappy – though he never said so – or that he was so afraid of losing Anna he never dared refuse her anything.

Through her disorganised, hectic Thursday, Anna texted Richard to remind him he was collecting her after work, not from home. This was her third such reminder. His text message back – 'I KNOW!' – was abrupt, even though by necessity all text messages are abrupt. She gave this little consideration until the time they were supposed to meet passed. Even though he was late only by a matter of minutes, Anna began to speculate on whether he had decided not to show. She would never see him again. She even began to compose a text message in which she accepted this was the end and wished him well. She stood outside the shop, locked, with its blinds down. The precinct was emptying and the sky was overcast with weather and the dying day. Her coat was inadequate for the breeze and she thought about the meal she could make for tea, not immediately fancying anything. There was nothing much on TV, either. To be filled, this evening would need more than food and entertainment. The thought of returning to the flat, to Natasha, and staying in with nothing to do – once the routine – was now abhorrent to her.

Then Richard arrived.

'Sorry I'm late, love. I had to stop for petrol, and the tyres needed air.'

She was so grateful to see him that she embraced him.

'And I'm sorry for all those reminders I sent you.' Anna knew her behaviour – this profuse apologising and eagerness to please – was out of character, and if her old self had taken a moment to step back to examine this new self, she would have been appalled. *Silly cow*, she thought to herself.

Anna wasn't instinctively a tactile person, neither was she inclined to romanticism or romantic gestures. With Richard, however, she often took his hand as they were walking along and sometimes she would stop him mid-sentence with a spontaneous kiss. They embraced frequently, touched tenderly. Initially Anna had touched and kissed him as an act of provocation, expecting him to glance furtively around for witnesses, or even hold her off. This never happened. Instead he always treated her as if the two of them together was the only thing that mattered. When testing him was no longer the incentive, Anna still found herself happily – and now routinely – taking his hand, kissing him, holding him. Through his influence, Anna found herself transformed in an extraordinarily short space of time. *Sloppy cow*, she thought to herself.

As Richard drove to the flat, she was happy to listen to him tell her about his day. His peculiar phrases were becoming familiar to her. He said, 'You know,' on its own, as an exclamation of frustration and Anna, she now realised, had been doing the same all week. Not only this, she had been telling other people his opinions, imitating his gestures and idioms, acting as if this new behaviour was her own. All that prevented Anna becoming thoroughly sickened by herself was her directness, the way she often confronted Richard and ridiculed his pretensions and faults.

He pretended to be outraged by her abrupt frankness – in reality he took joy in such refreshing openness.

'No-one has ever been as rude to me as you are.'

'The sad part is,' she replied, 'you think I'm being rude when in fact this is me on my best behaviour.'

'Jesus.'

At the flat they did not make coffee, they did not light the fire, they did not turn on the TV. She showered. Richard, also coming straight from work, had intended to shower after her – until she called him beneath the stream. They washed each other, paying tender attention to areas they usually only washed functionally. After the shower they sat wrapped up in towels eating a pizza they had phoned out for, and flicking through the TV channels.

Then bed. In the bedroom they pulled shut the curtains to close off the daylight, then held each other for several minutes, their flesh providing that moderate, perfect warmth which no other form of heating can, warming their skin, muscle and soul.

'How can it get better than this?' she asked.

'Pizza followed by sex – perfect.'

In that vacant few moments immediately after sex, when there is an amnesty on anything which might be said simply because, for those few seconds, the outside world doesn't exist, Anna asked a question which had been on her mind since she first met Richard. The question now came out as accidentally and as disastrously as if she had called him by the name of a previous lover.

'Would you ever leave your wife?'

By nothing more than the slightest change in his hold of her, the tiniest tension in the muscles, the atmosphere in the room altered.

'God, forget that, Richard. Pretend I never asked it.'

By virtue of him not giving an answer, she had her answer. It was as if she had farted a rendition of *I Should Be So Lucky* in front of him: he could never think of her in the same way again.

'What are you doing on Saturday night?' he asked.

Anna and Natasha had not lived together for long when chance conspired that both of them had dates on a Saturday night, each agreeing only after clearing it with the other. The novelty, the change from an average Saturday night, appealed to the girls. They imagined that change would add to the enjoyment, even though neither girl particularly liked the boy she had agreed to go out with.

At the end of the night both girls brought their boy back to the flat, then the next morning dispensed with them quickly so they could compare notes.

'We went to Halifax,' Anna told Natasha.

'Any good?'

'It was *Halifax*,' was Anna's negative answer. 'But us two should go – it would be a laugh. We could go on the train, and catch the last one back, in time to get to the *Apollo*.'

'OK. We went out to Bingley.'

'Why?'

Natasha answered with an expression she knew Anna would read accurately, another negative. 'There weren't that many pubs, and he knew people there, so he was talking to them all night with me just stood around, bored.'

'My bloke bored me too.'

'So you're not seeing him again?' Natasha asked.

'Maybe. He was good in bed.'

'Good . . . ?'

'Stamina.'

Natasha repeated the same expression as before: disappointment.

Anna asked, 'So yours was crap?'

'*Stamina*. Had none. And he sweated in his sleep.'

'Without sex,' Anna wondered, 'would we even bother with men?'

'We'd bother with them because we enjoy tormenting them.'

After that night, dates with boys were made for Fridays or Sundays, but usually confined to mid-week. They kept Saturday nights free for each other. It remained the only night of the week their friendship was as secure as it had always been.

Anna could not, now, ask Richard if he did not have a similar arrangement with his wife.

'I'm not doing anything,' she said instead.

'Then we'll go to *Bartok's* again. OK?'

'OK,' she had to answer.

Anna tried hard not to think of the future. When this failed, and the denial always failed, she could only think of futures which contained him. She then realised that this might mean that Natasha would not be part of her future.

Anna also tried not to think of Richard's wife, but she was always there.

EIGHTEEN

At seven o'clock, Natasha positioned herself in her chair and waited. As a joke she picked up the phone before the first ring was even complete, and spoke before he had a chance.

'Hello, Geoff.'

'Am I getting so predictable?'

'No. I mean, I have no idea what we're going to talk about tonight.'

'You say that as if I choose subjects, as if I have a list written down,' he answered, glancing down at his Post-it note.

Two hours passed, and Geoffrey had not once referred to these notes. Tonight they talked more personally: each dared to describe – keeping it within the safety of the hypothetical – their ideal partner and their ideal relationships. When they agreed, they agreed with enthusiasm, and when they disagreed they searched around for a compromise until agreement could be reached. Both wanted to be happy, and they were compatible enough to know that there was no need to say this, nor comment on how they knew that this desire was rarer than commonly supposed.

In spite of Natasha coming off the phone with a smile on her face, she realised that she had misled herself. The conversation had seemed intimate, even erotic, when she had been speaking but now, on reflection, she remembered that she had held similar conversations with Anna. So she and Geoffrey had talked as friends rather than as girlfriend to boyfriend? Natasha went to bed worrying whether this might be all Geoffrey wanted from her. People from his class had female friends who were nothing other than friends. In this respect Natasha was fundamentally working-class; she wanted only female friends. Only Anna. She wanted Geoffrey as her boyfriend, a proper boyfriend she actually saw every now and again. Twice she had asked him if he would prefer her to phone him, and both times he had said he liked phoning her. These weren't hints she was dropping, these were accusations. He stood accused, refusing to plead either guilty or innocent.

Natasha did not wait up for Anna. In the morning she received a text asking her to bring a clean uniform to work, so Anna could change there.

At work Natasha watched as Anna changed into the clean clothes.

'Do you think we're falling in love? I can't stop thinking about Richard. I make no effort to stop thinking about him.'

'I think about Geoffrey a lot too. Not all the thoughts are happy thoughts.'

'That doesn't sound like love,' Anna said, her smile never diminishing.

'I've always assumed love would be unequivocal happiness.'

'If that's what love is, then I'm not in love,' Anna confessed. She saw Natasha digest this and get ready to ask her to elaborate.

Anna blurted out: 'You'll be seeing Geoffrey won't you, tomorrow night? Only Richard's asked if I fancy going to *Bartok's*. I've said yes, but I can tell him no if you want *us* to go out instead. We can't afford *Bartok's*, so I suppose we'll end up at the *Apollo*. Who knows, now it's closing maybe it won't be so crap.'

'Closing or not, it'll be crap. You go out with Richard,' Natasha told her. Maybe Geoffrey would ask her out. 'I hope you have a good time.' If Geoffrey didn't ask her out, she hoped Anna would have a miserable time.

They did not speak to each other for the rest of the day. In the evening, Anna left the flat with little comment and avoided eye contact. She was out by six thirty.

Natasha picked up the *Radio Times*, and flicked through the whole magazine with no article catching her eye. She stood up to turn the TV on, then immediately sat down, bewildered, as she noticed that it was already on. At seven o'clock, Natasha again positioned herself in her chair and waited.

The phone did not ring all night. Natasha began dreading spending tomorrow night in again, doing nothing again, praying for a phone call. Anna had barely been gone for an hour when Natasha wondered if she had ever felt this lonely in the whole time she had lived with Anna.

Each girl had had their reason for wanting to move out of their old homes. Natasha's main reason had been sex. At home she found it too embarrassing to stay out all night, even though her parents made no comment the next morning, asked no questions. Anna had never felt comfortable staying out, simply because her naive aunt and uncle asked too many questions. When they had made their announcement that they were selling up to move to Scarborough and wondered if Anna wanted to go with them, Anna knew Natasha would want to stay in Bradford.

Having agreed to find a place together, Anna bought a *Telegraph and Argus* every night, to circle the flats that looked promising. The idea of sharing so immediately excited them that no spare moment in the following week was wasted on anything other than looking at flats and writing to Housing Associations. They even optimistically applied to the Council. The flat the Council offered them was appalling, yet they were asked to give assurances that they did not own pets.

'We don't,' Natasha told the Council. 'And besides, we wouldn't keep a dog in those conditions.'

As soon as they were offered a two-bedroomed flat which was suitable, they took it. It was unfurnished, but neither took any time to consider the problems this might cause. They looked around the empty rooms that were going to be their new home and discussed fantastic concepts of how their future here might be. They were fortunate to have much of their new furniture donated by Anna's aunt and uncle, who were moving into a cottage. They adapted carpets and curtains, and were given wardrobes, beds, and a fridge. Anna's brothers and Natasha's dad helped with the move. Their first night at home, the girls sat up until past midnight, excited by this new beginning.

Even the hardships of having their own bills, and buying food, and saving for an oven, became part of the fun. They knew each other's income, each other's strengths and shortcomings, and for those territories to which both were strangers, like wallpapering, they worked together and found compromises. Visitors with acute vision would see that the very top of the wallpaper in the living room was held to the wall with staples.

Corinne Slater's hen night had cost them far more than they could afford. They debated whether to go to her wedding as well, deciding in favour because it was at a Working Men's Club and bitter was £1.20 a pint. So the girls went along and drank pints. Soon drunk, and desperate for entertainment, they concentrated on watching a woman in her forties, but dressed like a teenager, dancing.

'How big does that arse look in those trousers? It looks like she's smuggling a settee.' They were appalled at her inappropriate clothes, her clumsy dancing, her sordid attempts to get men to dance with her.

The woman noticed Anna and Natasha staring and confronted them.

'Do you think I'm too old to be having a good time, is that it? I'm only forty-three. My ex-husband's fifty and he's fucked off with a twenty-eight-year-old. How old are you two?'

By a tragic coincidence, Anna and Natasha were then twenty-eight. They didn't answer.

'So am I just supposed to rot now? Am I supposed to stay at home and prepare myself for old age and death without ever having a good time again? I want to meet someone else, have a relationship, maybe even get married again. Is that what you find funny?'

When she had finally gone the girls finished their drinks and were suddenly plunged into a dark mood.

'How can you be so scared of being alone that you're prepared to behave like her?'

'Let's swear to each other that if we ever get a man we want to live with, or marry, our real special relationship will still be with each other. Me with you, you with me. That way men can be disposed of if they become a nuisance.'

'Do we have to make a vow on that? I'd always taken it for granted.'

NINETEEN

Geoffrey had decided that he would spend Saturday writing. By teatime he hadn't written anything. He was watching TV when Stuart phoned from Canada.

'Geoff? Stuart here. How's the house?'

'It's fine. Do you want me to say it's missing you?'

'We're still in Canada.'

Geoffrey made a guess. 'But you're coming back tomorrow because you've been knocked out in the first round. Am I right?' Stuart was a tennis player, ranked seven in Britain but with no ranking in world tournaments.

'No, not even remotely. I'm phoning to tell you we're staying longer. It's lovely here and everything's paid for another week.'

Geoffrey cruelly persisted. 'But you've been knocked out?'

After a significant pause, Stuart conceded: 'Yes. Wasn't it on the news?'

'I've been writing, I haven't been watching TV,' Geoffrey lied, glad he had the *Cartoon Network* on mute.

'So you're OK to stay on in the house for another week?'

They had left him without saying how long they would be gone, and Geoffrey had nothing else to do, so staying here rather than returning to his own bedsit was like being granted parole.

'Another week here suits me fine. It'll give a chance for the smoke to clear and the water to drain.'

'That's not funny, Geoff.'

At seven thirty – so he wasn't being too predictable – he

phoned Natasha. Wanting to see her again without having to spend any money, he asked if she would like to come over and he would cook for her.

Natasha didn't hesitate to accept.

She added, lying, 'By the way, did you phone last night? I was out, you see.'

'No, I didn't phone. Was I supposed to?'

'I was just asking.'

She had already showered, so she got dressed in a rush. She looked through the window. Two cars passed each other: one was Richard taking Anna away, and the other Geoffrey, coming to collect Natasha. As soon as she saw the Jag she went to clean her teeth again, unnecessarily, just to keep him waiting.

Geoffrey drove Natasha back to the house at high speed, worried in case the lasagne he had cooking might spoil. She was happy to believe he was keen for their evening together to begin.

'Where did you go last night?' Geoffrey asked.

'Oh. Er. Just out,' Natasha lied.

'Sounds nice,' Geoffrey said. She was learning that she couldn't always tell if his comments were jokes, sarcasm, or sincere but stupid.

In Richard's car, Anna deliberately caught Richard off guard.

'Remember when I asked you on Thursday night "Would you ever leave your wife?" then asked you to forget I'd said it? Well, have you? I mean, is it possible you could wipe it from your memory, act as if the question had never been spoken? I ask because since it was said, it feels – I don't know – the question is still hanging over us, and I don't want it to be.'

Many years ago, some time between Anna leaving school and starting work at the shoe shop, a friend had tried to set her up with her brother. Anna made excuses, but the friend persisted so frequently and forcefully, saying how compatible the two would be, that she eventually agreed.

'It might be a laugh,' Anna told Natasha. 'I was just worried because of it being a blind date.'

'But then again, what have you got to be worried about?'

Natasha told her. 'He can't be any uglier than some of the monsters you've been out with.'

Anna's date went well enough. He didn't pester her, he was a good listener and didn't inflict any dull stories on her, and best of all he was quick to catch on that, although she liked him, she wasn't attracted to him. The evening was ended by him, not her – he expressed regret and apologised.

'The worst part of this,' he told Anna, 'will be explaining to my sister why it didn't work out.'

To Anna's bemusment, the next time she saw her friend she received the cold shoulder. The girl was abrupt and tried avoiding her. So eventually Anna confronted her. 'This is all because of your brother, right?'

'I don't know what you're talking about,' the girl insisted. Yet her odd behaviour continued. Whenever Anna approached her, the girl made excuses and backed off, or killed dead any attempt at conversation.

Anna phoned the girl's brother, arranged to meet him, and told him how his sister was behaving. Together they confronted his sister and she was forced to admit that she'd been wrong, and so was reconciled with Anna.

This was how Anna had always been, she didn't like to see disputes unresolved. If a problem was causing friction, then in her opinion a full-blown row was the best way to clear the air.

Since she had uttered those immortal words, *Would you ever leave your wife?* Anna had been determined to clear the air with Richard. Already becoming accustomed to her headstrong ways, Richard considered how best to answer.

'I haven't forgotten the question.'

'I knew it!'

'How could I? But you had a right to ask it. I like being with you, Anna; I want to be with you. As yet, I don't know if this is going to end or if it's going to continue. All I know is that I do *want* it to continue, and that it won't be *me* who ends it.'

Anna nearly spoke her first thought, which was that she would never finish with him, but she managed to stop herself. She still had no way of telling if he would ever leave his wife.

But to avert any future misery, she had to give him an ultimatum: he must leave his wife or else she could never see him again. Yet for a woman he had known for such a short time to issue such an ultimatum was madness. His answer would be that he would stay with his wife. Then he would think that he had had a lucky escape. He would think that Anna was a nutter to give such an ultimatum.

So the planned confrontation never happened, and Anna remained attached to a man who was not hers, might never be hers, might never wish to be hers; and yet she no longer knew how to behave as she once had, could not free herself from this flawed man, because he was now too much a part of her. And because each reaction was equally irrational, Anna had no way of separating her two opinions of Richard's wife, whom she had never met. Anna hated her, yet pitied her. She would never again ask Richard if he would leave his wife, in fear of either answer.

Once in the house, Natasha finished setting the table, following Geoffrey's specific instructions, while he finished the salad then served the food.

'You know, I wasn't too sure whether you would phone tonight, either,' Natasha admitted as they began eating. She continued before he could comment. She told him about her day at work, and then all about Anna and Richard – this was followed by their first kiss of the evening and Natasha wiping tomato off Geoffrey's mouth.

'I love cooking,' Geoffrey told her. 'I don't get much chance these days. Not to cook for someone else, I mean.'

'So that's why you invited me over? Just so you'd have an excuse to cook?'

'I wanted to see you. To be honest, I wasn't sure if I was going to phone you either. You see, my worry is that I'm not all that you might hope for.'

'I don't know what that means,' she told him, a little angrily.

'But I can tell you that I know my own mind, and that if I didn't want to see you I'd tell you.' This wasn't strictly true. Natasha had regularly been out with men for longer than she wanted, reluctant to finish with them for fear of offending them. Anna predicted that one day Natasha would end up marrying someone she simply didn't have the guts to dump.

'I'm glad I did phone now,' Geoffrey told her.

The meal had ended and coffee had been drunk. Natasha observed that when Geoffrey was thinking, he had a tendency to stick out his lower jaw.

'No I don't,' he insisted when she pointed this out.

Natasha did an impersonation of him to illustrate his behaviour, then began laughing at his hurt expression. Then she asked him if he could curl the sides of his tongue up. He could.

'Do you know what I could never do?' he asked. 'Make bubbles with bubble gum.'

'I was an expert at that,' she told him proudly. 'You can't do it so much with the bubble gum they sell these days, but do you remember those round, pink bubble gums they sold, about the size of a two pence piece? I'd blow bubbles bigger than my head. My mum was always having to cut it out of my hair when it exploded. For about three years of my life I had the worst haircut on the estate.'

They held hands across the table, exchanged kisses and looked into each other's eyes. There were some silences and she knew enough from last time to know that he would be hesitant, so she took the lead.

'Last Saturday night,' she began, 'was fun. I enjoyed it.'

'I've never been in there before,' he answered, believing she was talking about *Bartok's*.

'Actually I meant back here – you know? Us on the settee.'

'Yes, that was fun. Better than fun.'

'I'm glad we didn't just, you know, jump into bed.'

'So, shall we . . .' he began. 'Shall we sit down?'

'We are sitting down.'

'I meant –'

She silenced him. 'Don't tell me what you mean, tell me what you want. Be brave and you'll be rewarded.'

In the bedroom, in darkness, they stood and kissed, slowly, tenderly. Then Geoffrey began to undress Natasha, knocking her hands away when she began to undress him. He did not kiss her again until she was in her bra and knickers.

'Let me undress you,' she told him.

'Wait.'

He turned her around so he was standing behind her. He undid her bra without removing it, moving his hands up over her stomach then cupping her breasts, just failing to keep the slightest of gaps between his hands and her skin. He kissed around her neck till he reached her chin, when she turned to face him, desperate for the full kiss. He removed her bra and stroked her breasts as they kissed, the tips of his fingers very gently circling her aureoles. She held his head, pulling him closer and harder so that their lips were squashed. He stood back from her, smoothing her arms down to her sides as he lowered himself to his knees. He kissed and licked her stomach, his fingers stroking down from her breasts to her stomach, around her hips, onto her bum, then along and inside her knickers until each hand held a cheek. He kissed down from her stomach to the top of one thigh, then jumped to the other, using his hands at her back to separate her legs slightly. He licked up along the edge of her knickers, then brought one hand around to pull them to one side. When she was open to him he made her think he had abandoned the idea and again returned to kissing her stomach, then, quickly, to catch her unaware, he licked her so that she gasped and pulled a little away from him. He eased her knickers down and off her legs. He licked and caressed her, working his way back up her body as he stood up.

'Now undress me,' he told her. Though short of breath, she still had to kiss him.

Throughout the sex the doubt was still there, probably nothing to be concerned about but nevertheless hard to ignore. How did he really regard her? He commanded sex in a manner that disturbed and flattered her, and both these thoughts added to her pleasure.

After sex, when they were exhausted and lay there facing each other, staring into the blackness where they guessed the other's eyes were, Geoffrey had to fight off sleep so she would not think him a typical man. Natasha fought off sleep out of fear that she might never want to wake. Sex ought not to be that great, not with someone you actually liked.

'I hate to say this,' she eventually said, 'I could just stay here for ever . . . But I have to go. I go to my parents' on Sundays, if you remember.'

'I know. How hard is it going to be to move from this position, get up, get dressed and leave each other?' He kissed her.

She said, with a grin he could not detect, 'You surprised me. You were quite rough.'

'Oh.'

'I'm not complaining, it's not necessarily a bad thing. In fact . . . well.'

In that second, they both knew that they were lying next to their futures; that nothing else mattered and for the first time ever – for both of them – being with someone else was so simple, and joyous, that it was an absolute. Then it was broad daylight and they had to put on their clothes.

They said little on the drive home; they knew that any word spoken would rescind perfection. Every second that passed added complications of history and of other people, so that when they parted, even though Geoffrey had arranged to meet her again in the evening, neither was entirely confident that they really would ever see each other again.

Natasha heard the voices coming from Anna's room. Only minutes after leaving her boyfriend and only minutes away from seeing her family, she wanted to talk. Or at least be asked questions she could pretend to avoid.

She made toast and coffee and consumed them alone. She would now have to take the bus to her parents' house. She dunked the toast in her coffee, a habit she believed she had grown out of. The margarine formed a slick on top of the coffee. She threw the drink away.

TWENTY

After *Bartok's* Richard had come home with Anna, like last Saturday, and stayed the night. Anna was awake before him. She had watched Geoffrey drop Natasha off, moving away from the window as they exchanged looks that were not designed for anyone else to see. Anna returned to bed and pretended Richard's movements had woken her.

'Are you going home?' she asked.

'Not yet.' This made her happy enough to stop her asking how he explained his nights away. Anna guessed he would tell his wife he had to work late, or away; he might tell her that he had a sick friend he was taking care of. Relations might be so poor between them – Anna hoped – that he never offered any explanation and his wife never asked. She wondered how their lives were, and if they were getting along badly. She could not imagine that it could be anything but bliss to be with Richard.

Richard drifted back to sleep. Anna had her arm under his head. By individual inches, which she coincided with his breathing, she retrieved her arm.

She found Natasha in the kitchen.

'Last night,' Anna began, grinning, 'what happened? Did you go to bed again?'

Natasha didn't answer quickly enough, always coy confirmation of an allegation. During sex Geoffrey was the opposite of the way he behaved the rest of the time. There was no reserve, no shyness, no need for coaxing. He was happy to ask her desires and had a natural, pleasant authority when making a request.

'Why won't you tell me more details?' Anna demanded. Natasha was usually more forthcoming. 'It must be because he's crap at it.'

Anna saw that this man's effect on Natasha was so precious to her that she would never confide in her. In return, she did not tell Natasha about Richard, or how their love-making had that same sense of consummation. Neither spoke. Silence had never happened before at a time when there had been so much to discuss. They merely exchanged smiles because neither of them wanted a rift, and then Anna returned to Richard and Natasha set off to her parents.

'I fucking love Sundays,' Natasha said with sarcasm.

'And I love fucking *on* Sundays,' Anna grinned.

The erratic Sunday bus service made Natasha early. Willing to do anything rather than be at her parents' home sooner than she needed, she killed time by walking around the estate, past houses full of ornaments and decorations that had not changed since she was a child, up cul-de-sacs familiar from her adolescence, where she and Anna would hang around waiting for nothing to happen. The estate had changed so little it was as if it had been abandoned. She passed houses she recognised as formerly belonging to a friend, a family friend, or an acquaintance. In her memory, the estate was chaotic and lively, full of intrigues and activity. This Sunday morning, except for passing cars, she saw no one.

'Hello!' she dared to shout out. There was no answer.

She thought about returning home to tell Anna all about Geoffrey. Everything: her worries about his restraint, her joy in his company, and his surprising physicality. There was so much to tell. Instead she was obliged to go to her parents'. Today, she vowed to herself, *'If I hear any nonsense, I'll retaliate. I'll pretend I know the climax to EastEnders and reveal it.'*

She walked towards the house, each step tiring her into a dread of her mother insulting her father, her father's silence and the petty arguments between her sister and her future brother-in-law.

It was Brenda she most dreaded speaking to. Yet Brenda never understood this: to her they were sisters and by definition should be close. Brenda still wanted Natasha to confide in her, shop with her, socialise with her; have a relationship now that they had never had when they were younger. No matter how many times the proposition had been made and Natasha had declined, Brenda still made fresh attempts. Natasha had never actively sought Brenda's company, and when circumstances had forced them together, they had never been comfortable.

Natasha stopped. She took out her phone. She would phone Anna and tell her to ring her parents and fake an illness on Natasha's behalf, as if she was taking time off work. Except that her mother might use the illness as an excuse to visit. She put the phone away.

Genuinely ill now – bloated, exhausted and with a thumping head – Natasha entered the house through the kitchen, through the steam, nodding to her father and not hesitating before she entered the living room. To hesitate would be to anticipate the next few hours and the anticipation was agony.

During dinner, Brenda asked about Geoffrey. With the perfect intonation that warned Brenda that if she probed further Natasha would retaliate, Natasha answered that she was, happily, still seeing him.

A mortuary silence.

Keith never looked up from his food; he sat constructing a castle out of his mash, with a moat of gravy, squashing each pea viciously, as if it was his girlfriend's head. Brenda watched every movement. Her eyes closed slowly, and she shook her head. There was a sigh. In empathy, Natasha's mother and father looked at each other: they recognised the same sadness embalmed in each other's passive expression.

Natasha looked at them all, without them noticing. Each was too preoccupied with their own misery. Natasha ate healthily, thinking, *One way or the other, my life will change. If I continue to see Geoffrey, I will stop coming here on Sundays. I will never allow our relationship to deteriorate like this. If we stop seeing each other, that's OK too – at least I can be certain I won't have a life like Mum and Dad or Brenda and Keith.*

'Is there a pudding, Dad?' Natasha asked. None of the others were anywhere near finished. And there was never pudding.

'We have some ice cream in the freezer,' he suggested.

Natasha stood, grinning like a kid. 'Anyone else?'

She ate the ice cream alone. It had been in the freezer too long, and splinters of ice cracked in her mouth.

'The Queen Vic burns down,' she lied. Things livened up.

Geoffrey worried that if he simply invited Natasha to the house again, instead of taking her out, she would think he was ashamed of her – which could not be further from the truth. If she asked why he didn't spend any money on her, he would admit to her that he had no money.

He phoned her in the early evening.

'We're seeing each other tonight, right?'

'Yes,' she answered, not able to judge how cautious she sounded.

He attempted to sound as natural as possible. 'I thought we could just come back here again. Watch TV. Talk. Is that all right?'

'Um, yeah, that's fine,' she told him. In that slight pause, Geoffrey read the hesitation and the lack of enthusiasm in her response; she seemed disappointed that he was not taking her out somewhere expensive.

Her hesitation was only a manifestation of her confusion. *He wanted her at his house.* If he were married and his wife was not there owing to work, holiday, illness, he still wouldn't want to have another woman in the house so regularly, in case a relative or friend of his wife should call.

'Where's he taking you?' Anna asked.

'Just his house.'

'Really? What's the special occasion?' Anna asked sarcastically.

Natasha washed and changed into a T-shirt and jeans. Though

the T-shirt was new and the jeans were her most expensive, as she thought about her appearance her previous paranoia was replaced by another.

She asked Anna, 'Do you remember Pants?'

'God, yeah. What the hell was his real name?'

During the last year at school, Natasha and Anna began to go swimming regularly in a mixed group. Girls coupled up with boys, leaving one girl, Natasha, and one boy, Victor Weller, on their own. Victor's nickname was Pants, a hangover from years ago when his mother had made him wear short trousers long after other boys had stopped. Pants was very short for his age, and he grinned like someone five years younger. After swimming they would go to a café for coffee, slices of pizza or chip butties. Natasha thought Pants was sweet and let him sit with her. Yet when anyone else from their school saw them, without knowing they were not a couple, Natasha felt ashamed. She began to avoid Pants, but he persisted. The more Pants spoke to her, the ruder she became; her responses became briefer, and she eventually began to bark expletives at him.

This was Natasha's new paranoia. Geoffrey liked her. He just didn't want to be seen out with her.

Natasha was ferociously silent for the first two minutes of the Jag ride to Geoffrey's home. Then she snapped.

'Look, just because I work in a shoe shop doesn't mean I'm thick. You know what I mean?' She flinched at having said 'You know what I mean'; the phrase made her sound thick. 'It means I'm badly educated – and there's a big difference. Just because I was brought up on a council estate doesn't mean I don't know how to behave respectably. I've never had money and I've never had a real chance to get ahead in life – but I'm not stupid and I'm a good person.'

Geoffrey waited until he could be certain she had finished.

'OK,' was all he could think of to say.

The silence resumed and continued for the rest of the journey.

Geoffrey stole two bottles of Melanie and Stuart's wine to help them recover from Natasha's outburst. They talked over the sound of TV.

'My earliest memory is playing on a bomb site,' Geoffrey told her. 'But today I watched *Passport to Pimlico* and now I think that all I'm doing is remembering that film.'

'Where were you brought up?'

'Cheshire.'

'Was Cheshire bombed?'

'I don't know, but even if it was – how old do you think I am? . . . So, I can't think what my real earliest memory is.'

'Mine is watching Anna climbing up a tree at junior school. She climbed so high that I could hardly see her. Then we were surrounded by teachers.'

'I can't imagine still having a friend I'd known all my life. Most of my friendships have barely lasted a handshake.'

Natasha asked him more about his friends, until he was forced to confess that Stuart was his only one. For anyone else there might have been shame in this, but he already knew that Natasha regarded Anna as her only friend.

'We became good friends by accident,' he told Natasha about Stuart. 'He was going out on his first date with Melanie, who he's married to now, and she had been a bit nervous – which, if you knew her, you'd know was not like her – so she wanted to make it a double date. She said she'd bring a friend and told Stuart to bring a single man. I was the only man he knew who didn't have a girlfriend. It was a bit of a disaster. I got there late and arrived without my wallet. Apparently, I bored everyone by telling them why I was late and how I had forgotten my wallet. Stuart lent me some money, so I met him the next day to pay him back. He was pleased to meet me because he wanted to tell someone all about Melanie. So we went for a drink and that's how we became mates. Which suited me. I've never made friends easily. And, come to think of it, Stuart is the only one I've made in adulthood.'

'What about you and the girl they fixed you up with?'

'She left an hour after I arrived. Melanie tells me she's never spoken to her again since.'

'You're not that bad,' Natasha joked.

'I make a bad first impression. But prolonged exposure really puts people off.'

'Now you're just feeling sorry for yourself,' Natasha told him. 'I like you, don't I? And the more I see you, the more I like you. So shut up.'

After this there were some more minor kissing skirmishes when they remembered that the evening would soon have to end, yet sex never seemed likely to happen. Geoffrey had to phone a taxi for Natasha, and asked if she was OK for money, knowing that if he worded the question this way she would simply answer that she was fine.

For him, the evening confirmed everything he had suspected all along. He liked her, he enjoyed her company, she understood him and knew how to take him, yet she remained too impressed by how he lived, and this was still the main attraction for her. She had complimented him on the decor of the house, the choice of furniture and some of the ornaments. When the taxi arrived, he told her he would phone her again, though he knew he would not.

For Natasha, the night confirmed that she had met someone who was genuinely interested in her. He asked her questions which were not designed solely – as was common practice with men – for her to return the question and permit him to talk about himself. Geoffrey was someone who would naturally make her happy, but would also make an effort. She knew she would grow to like him more the longer she knew him. Yet he hadn't made a move on her all night, never suggested they went to bed, or had spontaneous sex on the settee. There hadn't been any fervour or urgency to see her again – otherwise he would have forced his phone number upon her. If there was no urgency at this early stage, then she couldn't see how their passion would ever thrive.

When her taxi arrived and they kissed goodbye, she knew

he would be puzzled by how sad she sounded in her final words.

'Goodbye, Geoffrey. I enjoyed this evening.'

TWENTY-ONE

On Monday, Anna couldn't stop telling Natasha how amazing Richard was. She explained why: his personality, his charm, his character, his ability to make her laugh. Natasha reacted like a nodding dog, pretending she was listening. She was preoccupied with preparing a speech for when Geoffrey phoned later that night. She would try telling him honestly that she didn't want to see him again because she suspected he had not been entirely open with her. Then she considered being sentimental, telling him how much she genuinely liked him and that he would always be a fond memory.

Then she considered telling him none of this. She had never talked to any man as often and for as long as she had with Geoffrey. Here was a guy she genuinely liked, with few, and then only minor, flaws. What was so wrong with her that she had to manufacture flaws?

'Am I too cautious?' she asked Anna, knowing the answer.

'I remember you once running across a busy road with your bra around your eyes.'

'When I'm sober, am I too cautious?'

When they were kids, she would refuse to meet Anna after school until her homework was completed. Even if the deadline for the work was a week away, Natasha would do it the night the homework had been set, while Anna would do it on the morning of the last day. If it was English, Natasha would hand in a neat, four-page completed essay, and Anna would hand in half a page of scrawl, written with the book balanced on her knee during the bus ride to school. Mr Burnett, their English teacher, described her writing as a spider's scrawl. A spider with a limp. A drunk spider with a limp. A drunk spider with a limp that had suddenly, inexplicably terminated its journey, sometimes in mid-sentence.

After school, they would usually eat at each other's houses. Natasha preferred it if they stayed in, in one of their bedrooms, listening to records, chatting, flicking through magazines. Anna preferred to be out on the estate, hanging around, seeing what others were up to. Even if it was a freezing cold night, Anna was happiest outside, trying to find a place to shelter along with whoever else was hanging around. This was how they both had their first taste of alcohol, from a two-litre bottle of cider shared between seven teenagers, handed around at the bus stop. Then they had their first cigarette. As more and more of their gang began to smoke, someone would say 'Two's up,' then someone else would add, 'Three's up,' and so on, till often one cigarette was shared between as many as eight people.

There was no doubt in anyone's mind that it was Anna's disruptive influence on Natasha that prevented her doing better at school. Anna was the reason behind the increasing number of schooldays lost through slamming. They would enter school to take registration, then sneak out behind the gym.

On their hardest days at work, when the customers were constant and troublesome, or the shop was so quiet that the day dragged to twice its usual length, Natasha wondered how her life might have worked out without Anna's negative influence. She might have studied hard, passed exams and gained qualifications, taken up a career which interested her and paid her enough to escape. But these thoughts were rare and far outnumbered by the only happy memories she had from her life as a whole – which all involved Anna.

The girls had gone through a short phase of taking acid tabs on Saturday nights, and would stand in the *Apollo* talking, oblivious to anyone else: the music, the people, the lights. They would remind each other of their opinions and the anecdotes from their shared lives, incomprehensibly short sentences to anyone listening in, because the girls knew the secret language of each other's abbreviations. They would laugh so much their jaws would ache. All Natasha knew was that such laughter was rare in adults and she had Anna to thank for this. Without Anna in her life, Natasha knew she would rarely have had fun, acted recklessly, been foolish. The lack of caution in her life, taught to her by Anna, had worked.

So she had no need to be cautious with Geoffrey.

Disregarding everything else – she actually liked him. She would see him again and try to make it work, let events take their course. She might not be exactly certain how she felt, but there was no other way to discover than to go out with him.

'You're far too cautious,' Anna told her.

'No I'm not,' Natasha protested.

'What about that time you wanted us to set up our own shoe stall? You spent weeks researching the problems, you even typed out a business plan and everything. You told me all about it, how you thought we could get it started and make it work, got me all excited – then just binned the plans because there were some risks involved. You're far too cautious.'

'I didn't bin them. I still have them – I put them in a ring-binder I bought specially.'

'Then I take it back – you are born to be wild!'

That evening, Anna went out with Richard. Natasha sat by the phone, ready, not ready. Her waned resolve returned and she gathered the courage to ditch the most instantly compatible man she had ever known. She remained determined to tell him this when he phoned.

When Anna returned, only minutes short of midnight, she began recounting the evening she had spent with Richard.

'What did you and Geoffrey talk about?' she eventually asked.

'He didn't phone.' Natasha didn't have the TV on. She was sitting holding a book, still – since eight thirty – open at page forty-three.

'That doesn't necessarily mean anything. Does it?'

'It means he didn't phone. That's all. No big deal. I'm going to bed.' She went to bed carrying the book, so she could hold it open at the same page, not reading, until she fell asleep.

Geoffrey had said he would phone. And he hadn't. As far as Anna was concerned, the opposite sex had attacked her friend, and Anna declared war. On Tuesday night Richard was picking Anna up to take her to the cinema. Natasha had insisted she went.

'I should really stay at home with you and be supportive,' Anna said.

'What would be the point in that? There's nothing you can say.'

'We could talk about how awful men are, and warn each other off them, remind ourselves that we have each other and that we'll always have each other. Men are vermin.'

She heard Richard's car horn and had to leave.

Anna didn't greet Richard with a kiss; she gave short answers to his questions about her history of cinema-going, how often she went, her favourite films and actors. She found herself incapable of following the plot, conscious only of the explosions and the shouting. Sitting next to Richard for two hours without comment or physical contact, she decided that the only possible result of her continuing bad temper was that they would split up and never see each other again. Though a split was inevitable one day, she had no desire to hasten the end.

'So what's happening?' she whispered to him at last.

'Well –' he said, just as the end credits began to roll.

Anna realised that Geoffrey was an excuse for her bad behaviour; she was really angry with Richard for being so ideal for her, so fun, so sexy, so smart – and so not single.

As they made their way out of the cinema Richard asked her directly why she had been so silent.

'Is something wrong?'

'Nothing's wrong,' she told him, smiling and taking his hand. 'Nothing's ever wrong when I'm with you.'

'I'm glad you think that,' he told her as they walked to his car. 'Do you know what's surprised me most about you? I've never felt so strongly about someone so quickly.'

She told him she felt the same. To explain her earlier behaviour she told him about Natasha and Geoffrey, and how he had not phoned her.

They went for a drink, then back to his flat to make love. Before they parted she asked Richard several questions about his wife. She was trying to be casual, hoping to fool him into believing that she now regarded their relationship as a bit of fun; sweet and intimate, yes, but nevertheless only transitory.

'How long have you been married?'

'I can't say exactly, not off the top of my head. What's the longest relationship you've had?'

'A year and a week.'

'What happened?'

'I met him a week before Christmas and he bought me a beautiful necklace. The next Christmas he bought me wellingtons.' She asked, 'Where did you meet your wife?'

'Oh, uh, you know – I can't remember.' Anna knew this to be untrue, a lie designed to save her feelings. Maybe they had met at *Bartok's*.

'Where does your wife think you are tonight?'

'Out. Why are you so interested? It's nothing, it's irrelevant to *us*.' Richard tried to remain good-humoured. 'What I mean is, when I'm with you I don't want to think about *anything* else.'

All the time he was saying this, even though he was moving closer, gripping both her hands tighter when he wanted to emphasise a word, he never made eye contact. Even when Anna had freed one of her hands and held his chin to force his eyes onto hers, he didn't hold the look.

Guilt.

She could have reassured him that he had no reason to feel guilty. But it wasn't true. And she was guilty, too. Guilty of ruining the life of someone she did not know; guilty of knowing this, and yet still persisting.

He embraced her, saying, 'When I'm with you, Anna, I don't want to be anywhere else, with anyone else, and when I'm not with you I'm thinking only of the next time we'll be together. I don't know if it's this exciting because it's so new or whether it's always going to be this good. But if you trust me, I'll never hurt you.'

The third and worst part of Anna's guilt was her belief that it was wrong to be this happy.

At home, Natasha tried to forge a similar imagined conversation with the absent Geoffrey that she regularly imagined with Anna. Her inability to do this demonstrated how little she really knew him. She could only guess his responses, not imagine them.

'Why didn't you phone me?' she imagined asking.

'I didn't think it would be such a big deal. Why are you obsessing about it?'

Natasha immediately dismissed this answer. It didn't sound like him; it was too confrontational, too aggressive.

'Why didn't you phone me?' she repeated. This time he made no reply. She could envisage his face, even his voice, but no words he might actually have to say.

When Anna returned, Natasha was sitting in silence, in the living room, pretending to read a magazine. She tried to be interested in the details of Anna's night with Richard, but as she spoke her concentration drifted. She kept a strained grin on her face; her eyes focused into the distance past Anna's head, the distance where her future was. She didn't hear Anna, but though Anna was aware of this, she continued talking. To stop would mean silence, and silence would remind Natasha of how unhappy she was. Besides, Anna was happy to talk about Richard, even if no one was listening.

During the night, woken by the sound of the TV, Anna went into the living room and found Natasha watching a terrible, sloppy TV movie on Channel 5. Anna sat down next to her and they watched the rest of the film together. Someone old was crying, probably lonely; someone young was bald, probably dying. Neither of them spoke till the end of the film, when Natasha turned the TV off and said to Anna, without having to explain who she was talking about:

'Bastard.'

'I know,' Anna answered. 'Good night.'

The time was four thirty a.m.; Anna prayed that Richard wouldn't have his mobile near his bed, she didn't want to wake him. She wanted him to wake up in the morning to the message: 'I'M SO HAPPY TO BE WITH YOU.'

At breakfast – to avoid silence, or worse, talking – Anna switched on the TV. They ate toast and drank coffee, sharing the settee. They kept the curtains drawn. On the breakfast programme there was a review of the tabloid newspapers, most of which led with the story of a married soap star who had been caught kissing one of her co-actors off-screen.

'Her husband would be a fool not to divorce her now,' Natasha told Anna. 'And I hope she gets sacked from her job.'

The ferocity with which Natasha spoke alarmed Anna. When Natasha found out – as she inevitably would – that Richard was married, she might hold Anna in the same contempt that she held the soap actress.

The two of them had briefly worked with a woman who was separated from her husband and never stopped talking about it.

'I'll never care about anyone so much that it affects me like that,' Anna had told Natasha. 'If he was such a dick, why is she bothered about losing him? That's like complaining that your headache has gone.'

Anna was aware that, frighteningly soon, she would fall in love with Richard; and the only possible conclusion to this was that Richard would finish with her. A prelude to months of unanswered questions, regret and gut-wrenching misery. If *she* finished with him, however, she would keep her dignity – but would also have deliberately stopped seeing the first man who intrigued her, made an effort to understand her, and rejoiced in those aspects of her he did not understand. She would be intentionally sabotaging her happiness.

She knew then that she would continue lying to Natasha. She couldn't risk revealing Richard's marital status. She justified this by telling herself that Natasha would only want her to be happy, and by keeping silent in this way, she did remain happy. No one, not even Natasha, had made her this happy before.

TWENTY-TWO

The drudgery of work displaced Natasha's anger. She had been angry with Geoffrey for not phoning. She had been angry at her own foolishness in being angry. By not phoning, he had confirmed all her own paranoias about how he must regard her: she was not good enough for him, she didn't dress well enough, was not intelligent or amusing enough. If he had phoned, her resolve would have failed her and she would now have a boyfriend she genuinely liked. Imagine the future. A car, a nice house, holidays, well brought-up children. Friendship, companionship, sex, love; someone who was equipped with the desire to make your life easier.

She had Anna, she remembered. How had she forgotten? Remembering Anna, her misery vanished. Then it returned just as suddenly: Geoffrey had not phoned her and Anna had changed. Natasha remembered Geoffrey again; then her parents, then her job.

'I need to get drunk.'

On several occasions throughout the day Anna kept having to nudge Natasha out of her daydreams, and remind her that she was at work, with a shop full of waiting customers. Natasha became so distracted at one point that she attempted to sell a customer his own shoes.

'It was you who said we should be careful not to let them hurt us,' Anna said to her friend, only too aware of the cause of Natasha's persistent trance.

'It's not him. I don't care. I'm glad he didn't ring,' she said, defiant as a child caught out in a lie.

Later, when the shop was a little less busy, Natasha grabbed her friend, attempting to strengthen her argument.

'It's not as if I cared about him. How could I? I've only known him a short while. And he'd have turned out to be a prat, like they all do.'

As if to illustrate her indifference further, Natasha made a point of deliberately changing the subject.

'So *Bartok's* is out of bounds. Where do you fancy going this Saturday?'

A while ago, Natasha had gone out with Peter Flannaghan for exactly a month, starting one Saturday and ending three Saturdays later. He had very black hair, very dark eyes, was tall, well-built and had a smile that Natasha found impossible to turn down. He would call her only when the mood took him. He would not call when she asked him to, whatever he promised. He refused to argue, walking away or hanging up if she began a dispute. One row, on their fourth Saturday night together, caused her to tell him to go to Hell, and add that this time she meant it. Later she wished, for the first time in the four weeks she had known him, that he was there with her. She began to attribute qualities to him that he did not deserve, and had never demonstrated. She vowed that if she saw him the following Saturday she would tell him she wanted to try again.

She saw him. She saw him with someone else. Natasha felt as if she had been winded. Then, free of him, remembering Anna, and with a fresh drink, she forgot all about Peter and for the rest of the night simply concentrated on having a good time. She never gave him another significant thought, until now, when she felt equally depressed about Geoffrey. All she needed to forget about Geoffrey was a really good night out.

'Well I . . . Saturday? I'll be seeing Richard again, I think,' Anna answered. 'We haven't made definite plans, but we have talked about Saturday.'

Natasha became flustered, as if she had just wet herself. 'That's, er, all right. To be honest, I'm happy to have a quiet Saturday night in. I'll catch up on reading, or watch a good video. I'll maybe have an early night.'

For the rest of the day, she said nothing, forcing herself to concentrate on keeping the customers happy and not think about her depression: its source, its inexplicability, its pointlessness. The friend she had known all her life, whom she had always been able to depend on and who was the only person able to show her a fun time, had chosen to desert her because she now had a boyfriend she preferred.

Anna slept badly that night. It was only Wednesday, and she had already made plans with Richard for Saturday. She had ignored the only rule of her friendship with Natasha. She blamed herself. Then she blamed Natasha. Natasha should not have expected anything less. Just because her own boyfriend had let her down, she couldn't take Anna's availability for granted.

She eventually fell asleep, and the morning brought coherence. The only person Anna hated was Geoffrey, for making Natasha lose hope.

Before they set off to work, even though they were late, Anna made Natasha sit down at the dining table. They didn't have much time so she began talking straightaway.

'Geoffrey's a twat, right?' she asked her friend, making the question rhetorical by not giving Natasha chance to agree. 'And so, to a degree, in a way, is Richard. Because he's married. But don't hate him, hate me. He told me straightaway he was married.'

Natasha didn't say anything. This was a better response than Anna had dared to dream of.

'But I'm not going to stop seeing him, Natasha. I'm not used to this sort of happiness with a man. I don't know how to behave but I'm determined to enjoy it. Tell me what you think, Nat. Tell me.'

Natasha stood and nodded towards the door; they had to set off.

'You're an idiot, Anna. But you know you're an idiot. If you know you're going to get hurt, then I suppose all I can say to you is . . . there's precious little happiness about, so take what you can get. If it's morally wrong . . . Well, fuck it, that's probably the only way to be happy.'

Anna didn't dare smile. A smile would be insulting in the face of Natasha's obvious misery.

They set off to work to earn their money.

Proud of his strength thus far, Geoffrey remained determined not to phone Natasha. Determined, until he began to wonder whether she deserved this form of respect. After all, he told himself, contriving the most spurious of arguments, *if she is under the illusion that I have money and is prepared to go out with me for that reason alone, and use me in that way, then don't I have the right to use her in return? She doesn't deserve decency. So phone her, see her, have fun with her, sleep with her.*

To fulfil the role of Lothario, Geoffrey began to try on Stuart's clothes: the suits initially, then his jeans and casual tops; trying on various pairs of sunglasses, and smoothing his hair flat to give him a vaguely Mediterranean appearance. At best, he looked like a Latino with no appetite who rarely left the house. Looking into the mirror, he attempted smarmy charm; he tried to smile as if he was knowing and wise; he tried to stand confidently and appear sophisticated. But the clothes didn't fit him well, and no matter how he stood or posed he just looked awkward, like amateur dramatics.

He took his ATM card, drove to the nearest machine and withdrew one hundred and fifty pounds. The soundest financial advice he could give himself at this moment was not to look at his remaining balance. If these machines were programmed with responsive personalities, this one would be sniggering.

Back at the house he phoned Natasha, with a substantial part of him praying she would refuse to talk.

Anna answered the phone. Natasha knew who she was talking to when her expression transformed from one of surprise into cautious pleasure. Though Anna held her hand over the receiver, it was inadequate to stifle her shout.

'It's him. Geoffrey!' Then, not immediately reading Natasha's expression – which was both dazed and elated, like a victorious boxer regaining consciousness – she asked, 'Are you going to speak to him?'

As she took the receiver, Natasha prepared her response. Should she be delighted or offhand?

'It's me,' Geoffrey said needlessly.

'You were supposed to ring on Monday.'

'Are you angry with me?'

'Not angry,' she said, then hesitated as she considered whether this could be revoked. She then conceded a conciliatory, 'All it is, if someone says they're going to phone, it's annoying when they don't.'

Anna was on the settee, digging dirt out from under her fingernails, pretending not to listen.

'I was thinking,' Geoffrey continued, 'I was thinking on Monday . . . even though I haven't phoned I've still been thinking about you . . .' He stalled for a split second, ashamed of the half-lie. He was thinking about her, he just hadn't been thinking this. 'I was thinking we could go to Blackpool tomorrow. Is that possible?'

Natasha hadn't had a day off sick in eighteen months. Anna ridiculed her for having so few days off – she said it made the rest of the staff look bad.

'I'll get Anna to tell them I have some disease. Or something.'

Anna dug too hard and sucked on her finger. She wanted the call to end, eager to hear why Natasha needed a fake disease. She stood up and hovered around Natasha.

Natasha made the arrangements for her trip the next day.

His final words to her were, 'I'm sorry I didn't phone you on Monday.'

Having been sullen and abrupt all day, Natasha now had a clown smile, and eagerly told her friend about her trip. This was the metamorphosis that single people missed: the unexpected, instant transformation of their fortunes, from absolute misery into unmitigated happiness.

'You've really got it bad for this guy, haven't you?' Anna asked.

Natasha's grinning denial failed as spectacularly as an amputee trapeze act.

As she lay in bed that night, unable to sleep for excitement, Natasha carefully planned how she would act on their trip together. Though determined to end the day by giving Geoffrey an ultimatum, she thought she might as well be relaxed and enjoy the fun. If he could not make the simple gesture of giving her his phone number, then she would not see him again.

For Geoffrey, the journey to Blackpool was marred only by the scare of having to dent his finances by stopping for petrol. He had some trouble navigating the route. Natasha mocked him for this and took over the navigating.

They headed straight for the Pleasure Beach, reverting to childhood as they bought wristbands and dashed from ride to ride. Instead of wasting time in a restaurant they ate hot dogs and then waffles as they walked along the front, bobbing into joke and souvenir shops. They spent handfuls of coppers on the slot machines, then played each other at arcade games.

'You're useless!' Natasha taunted when she thrashed Geoffrey at Air Hockey. 'Shall I give you a two-points start in the next game?' When Geoffrey beat her at pool she made elaborate excuses; her cue wasn't straight, the table sloped, the noise was distracting.

When the sky began darkening, they walked back to the car hand in hand, not breaking stride when they kissed, too content in their pleasure.

Natasha sat on the bonnet of the Jag, Geoffrey standing in front of her. They kissed passionately. People passed, muted in the sunset. The sea was audible above the sound of traffic. They heard and saw only each other.

Natasha slept for some of the drive home, during which Geoffrey hated himself for malicious thoughts he'd had about her in the past. While sleeping she had an innocent grace. When they reached home he didn't wake her immediately, daring to hope that this girl, this beauty, could be his.

'Wake up. We're here.'

'Where?'

'Home,' he told her, not deliberately lying.

She laid her head on his shoulder as they entered the house, then took his hand and pulled him towards the bedroom, not pausing to turn on the lights or to speak. They undressed. In bed they held each other, kissed, made love easily. The first words spoken, an inappropriate reminder, were when Natasha asked Geoffrey to set the alarm for seven, so he could drive her home and she would still have time to shower and get to work.

'Don't go to work. Spend the day with me. Another day sick won't matter so much, will it?'

'It's sweet of you to say that, but you don't get it.' She kissed him. 'If', *kiss*, 'I', *kiss*, 'don't', *kiss*, 'work', *kiss*, 'I', *kiss*, 'don't', *kiss*, 'get', *kiss*, 'paid.'

TWENTY-THREE

When she arrived home, Natasha had to wake Anna. With time running short they had to get ready in a hurry, and their hair was still damp when they caught the bus.

'How was Blackpool?'

'Fun,' Natasha answered. 'What did you do last night?'

'Richard.' They laughed, too loudly for public transport, elevating themselves above the humdrum of this ordinary working day.

Gerard Peters reprimanded Natasha for her day off. He took note of her continuous smile. She took note of his continuous snarl. No one this young should be this miserable, she thought to herself. *Whatever they're paying him isn't compensation enough. He's old before his time.*

Natasha didn't say anything about Geoffrey, not daring to risk Anna's condemnation. She would undoubtedly tell her she was rushing in, and letting her emotions dominate.

But Natasha had overlooked one vital new aspect to Anna's life that had mellowed her from a caustic cynic to a rank romantic – Richard.

'I tell you,' Anna said at dinner time, when they queued for a hot dog at the stand on the bottom of Darley Street, 'I feel like I'm falling in love. Does that sound stupid? I can't stop thinking about him. I keep having little laughs to myself, as I'm serving customers, when I remember something he's said or something we've done. And I know what you're thinking, I know what you're going to say. I'm an idiot. Or, be careful. But I don't want to be careful. I want to . . .'

Anna had no idea how to finish this sentence. All she knew was that telling anyone of her hopes might jinx them. All she knew was that she wanted Richard. Less and less did she consider her hopes to be misplaced.

After taking Natasha to her flat, Geoffrey had returned to the house and gone back to bed. Exhausted yet content, he slept through till midday, when he was woken by the telephone.

'Yuygh?' was his unhelpful answer.

'Is that you, Geoff?' Stuart asked. 'What time is it over there?'

'It's me. I wasn't sleeping,' Geoffrey lied needlessly.

'We're flying back tomorrow.'

'I've met a girl,' Geoffrey blurted out. As soon as he'd said this he didn't understand why he had done so. If Stuart and Melanie were returning home tomorrow, then Natasha would find out who really owned this house. He wanted Stuart to ask him about Natasha, who she was, how they'd met and – most importantly – how he felt about her. If he'd only recently met her, Stuart should ask what was so significant that Geoffrey should mention her during a long-distance phone call. Geoffrey would tell his friend that his most inveterate thought about her was that he wanted to know her for the rest of his life.

'So we'll be back at five o'clock tomorrow morning – your time,' Stuart answered, as if he'd not heard. 'Get the place tidied up, Geoff. Melanie's worried.'

'Is that why you're coming home? You don't trust me?'

Stuart ignored this, telling Geoffrey to make certain he was at the airport waiting to pick them up. Geoffrey gave his promise.

'See you later then,' Stuart said as he hung up. Geoffrey wondered if there was a fault on the line which had prevented Stuart hearing anything he had said.

Before he washed or dressed, Geoffrey toured the house, returning all Melanie's possessions to their rightful places. With the deadline set, he had no choice. He would have to meet Natasha that night and tell her everything.

Geoffrey phoned her and they arranged to meet at a pub

approximately halfway between her flat and Melanie and Stuart's house. If she asked why he hadn't brought the Jag he would tell her that the Jag only had enough petrol in it for the journey to the airport tomorrow. If the evening went well, he would tell Natasha they should go back to her flat as he had tidied and cleaned the house he had been staying in, which belonged to friends of his. If the evening went badly he might bring her back to the house and let her discover for herself that it wasn't his.

He drank fast while he was waiting for her, looking over at the door every time anyone entered, and checking his watch every few seconds. Within a short time from now she might never want to see him again.

When she arrived he stood up.

'Are you OK?' she asked.

'I'm fine,' he said, then repeated it an octave lower, in his normal voice. 'I'm fine.'

After he had bought her a drink, and they were settled at a table, she began to tell him about her day, as if they were a settled couple, familiar with each other's lives and routines. He listened attentively as she became more comfortable, looping one leg of hers over one of his, holding his hands with her face only inches from his. Now nearer, he paid even closer attention.

'. . . idiots, every one of them. All hopeless. My mother goes on about how I should find someone decent, by which she means someone with a good job; someone with money, really. So I hope she doesn't think I'm with you just to make her happy. But I guess she has a point. The hopeless cases I've been out with before you . . . I go to my parents' tomorrow, I go every Sunday. Mum will love you! We'll go in the Jag! I'd love that!'

She gripped his hand, grinning as she thought of the delight on her mother's face and at her own pride in showing off Geoffrey.

'I can't bring the car tomorrow.'

'It doesn't matter. But I can't wait for them to meet you.'

He had never liked her as much as he did right then.

'Have you come in the Jag tonight?'

Now was the time for the truth.

'I don't like to drive when I've had a drink.'

She was going home on her own to have an early night so that she would be clear-headed for tomorrow, when she introduced Geoffrey to her family.

He wrote some numbers down on a slip of paper. He had finally given her his phone number. She was sober yet happy on Saturday night. A first. It occurred to her that not so long ago she would have thought this pathetic, but she brushed the thought aside. If this change made her happy, then it was clearly a change for the better.

Geoffrey also went home on his own, miserable.

Anna had not yet returned when Natasha arrived home. She was already certain that she would sleep badly, so she didn't make herself a coffee. She watched TV for a while, not able to concentrate. She decided to phone Geoffrey.

She phoned again. Then again.

As Anna came through the door she had just finished dialling Geoffrey's number for the eighth time.

'*The number you have dialled has not been recognised. Please check and try again*,' Natasha heard again.

'Did you have a good night?' Anna asked, beaming as usual. 'Who are you phoning at this time?'

Unable to answer, Natasha dialled the numbers again, scrutinising each number on the paper and dialling carefully.

'*The number you have dialled –*'

TWENTY-FOUR

Though names were changed to protect not only the innocent but also that guilty bitch Janette, Geoffrey's novel was – loosely – going to be based on the years he had squandered with her. He would fabricate some incidents to give credibility to his over-reactions and jealousy; her treachery would be elaborated to give rationality to his mammoth depression. Her character would have to be written as nicer; there was no other way for the narrative to pardon his continuing affection. Some of the changes from reality to fiction lacked much effort on his part: in the book Janette was called Janet.

Back at Stuart and Melanie's house, Geoffrey made coffee and turned on the PC. He wasted no time in beginning to construct a rough synopsis for his novel, written as if for a prospective publisher.

He began with the title in bold text, then his name. Childish vanities, as if the synopsis itself was the finished work.

ALL THIS AND MORE

a novel by

Geoffrey Barker

When George first meets Janet she has only recently divorced and confesses that the divorce is the smartest move she has ever made, yet nevertheless it will not be easy for her to forget her ex-husband.

After several dates, George's misgivings about her vanish.

She is interesting, independent and spirited – qualities he always looks for yet has never found combined in one person.

However, it annoys him that she speaks so frequently about her ex-husband. When he mentions his concern she reacts aggressively. They have a furious row, their first, which comes very close to splitting them up.

After this, George is less certain how he feels, yet paradoxically finds himself telling her how greatly he loves her and imagines their future together.

One day Janet tells him that her ex-husband has asked her out for a meal. She insists her feelings for him are only those of a friend, and that George should trust her.

His reply is that if she cared about George at all, she wouldn't want to go. Her sudden reaction to this is that he is over-possessive and is smothering her. She tells him she no longer wishes to see him, that it is over.

Nothing in his life so far has prepared George for the depression and misery he now suffers.

He remembers making love with her, and imagines how sex might have been in the future. He misses being with her, and it rips him apart to think of her making love with someone else. He hates her for her arrogance, for knowing that she has this power over him. He hates himself for feeling so distraught over a woman he knows to be far from ideal for him.

He thinks about the time they have spent together, never dull, sometimes passionate, sometimes intimate.

He contrives a meeting. She tells him she has missed him and is sorry if she hurt him.

He accepts that they will not get back together. Ultimately he could not be happy with her, so friendship should be a satisfactory stopgap until he recovers from the habit of being with her.

As friends, they later go out for a drink: she confides in him, as they become drunk together, that she is back with her ex-husband but that she is already beginning to remember all the faults which persuaded her to divorce him in the first place.

She tells George she is pleased she can confide these things in him, then kisses him in gratitude.

They make love, but in the morning she thinks only of her ex-husband, how she might explain her absence should he have called at her house the previous night.

When she has gone, George asks himself unanswerable questions about why she prefers her ex to him, why he can do nothing to win her permanently; why he has these thoughts when he knows she would not make him happy and he feels no real, sustainable love for her.

He has answers for these questions – all sensible and mature, true to his real character. All forgotten instantly – he wants to be with her. It destroys him every time he thinks about her not being his.

Nearly three years have passed since their first meeting.

The next time he sees her she tells him she is re-marrying her ex-husband. He feels shell-shocked. He tells Janet he loves only her and will never be happy without her. He knows this is not true yet the passion in his tone, the choke in his voice, are both natural and sincere. A sentiment beyond rational or reasonable thought *does* love her and makes him believe he couldn't be happy without her. Her response to this confession is so cold he has no choice but to run away from her.

He does not tell her where he is going – so he can fool himself into thinking that the reason she never contacts him is because she doesn't know where he is.

When he has gone his obsession carries on – sadder now because not only does he know he does not ultimately want her, but he also knows he could never ultimately have her.

Geoffrey had been convinced he could channel this new wave of depression into creative writing, and delighted by having written so much, he prepared to continue his novel in earnest – chapter two.

He wrote nothing. He wrote then spell-checked the word

'FUCK'. The alternative word was 'FUCOID'. He wrote 'TWAT'; the spell-check suggested 'TWANG'.

Writing the synopsis had re-ignited too many smouldering stupidities. He turned the PC off and watched cable TV channels, fifty-eight of them in five-second bursts, all rubbish. He marvelled at how uncomfortable, cold and gloomy this luxurious home was. He would have preferred his crap bedsit if Natasha was there with him. Here was a girl like Janette, but without the selfishness; less erratic, braver, ruder, more honest and with no ex-husband.

He watched cable repeats of *Ballykissangel*, *The Cosby Show*, *LA Law*. Every show had a theme or incident Geoffrey could distort into relating to him and Natasha, whether the story was doomed love, gold-digging women, couples unsuitably matched, or someone wallowing in melancholy for someone they'd lost and were too proud to pursue.

Janette was now of no interest to him. He would have to write about Natasha: but the beginning was too extraordinary, the middle too overwhelming, the end too sudden. These failings kept him away from the PC; these and the growing conviction that he simply lacked the ability to write.

Meeting Natasha had been superb in terms of helping him get over Janette, and was one of the reasons he had liked her so much and so rapidly. She had freed him of those persistent thoughts of Janette.

He had been aware that he would feel bad about this act. Nevertheless, he knew that giving Natasha a false phone number was the smartest thing he could have done.

Geoffrey was in the house of an absent friend who owned a well-stocked drinks cabinet. His plan was not to drown his sorrows, only to wade in a little, enough to help him sleep.

If he had had any money he would have sent Natasha flowers anonymously; if he had had any courage he would have written a long letter of sorrow and explanation; if he had had infinite powers he would have found her a wealthy boyfriend to make her happy.

As he acquired the taste for alcohol, he found a pamphlet on exotic cocktails and really began to enjoy himself. Giving Natasha a false phone number had been a shitty, cowardly way to act, which she had not deserved. She should not have had to suffer this. She had believed that she had met the man of her dreams. Instead she had met *him*: the lying, cowardly wanker. These thoughts kept Geoffrey drinking until three a.m., when he fell into a sleep as heavy as a coma.

'. . . cowardly wanker . . .' he muttered through his sleep. '. . . wanker . . .'

'Wanker! Wanker! Wanker!' Stuart bellowed. It was five thirty a.m. 'Have you completely forgotten our existence? Who's fucking house are you in? Who is it you're supposed to be picking up from the airport – half an hour ago?!'

After Stuart had rung off Geoffrey attributed his disorientation and slight queasiness to exhaustion and the shock of the sudden waking. Only when he attempted to stand did he remember how much he had drunk and how drunk he remained. Being unable to negotiate the turn from the living room into the downstairs bathroom without colliding with both door-frames undeniably meant he was in no fit state to drive Stuart's very expensive car. But he had no choice. As he stood looking down at the water in the toilet bowl, Geoffrey was not sure whether to pee or be sick first. There was risk involved in attempting to do both simultaneously.

Geoffrey collected up his possessions. He made repeated attempts to insert the key into the lock of the boot, succeeding on the fifth attempt, but scratching the paint in the process.

He then sat in the car trying to think how to start the engine. He had left the keys dangling in the car door.

'Focus!' he shouted at himself as he retrieved the keys. He tensed, flexed his hands, then started the car. The early hour and the darkness gave him some hope that the sporadic traffic would minimise the chances of hitting another car. He carefully pulled out of Melanie and Stuart's driveway, edged his way onto the street and cautiously gained speed as he headed for the motorway. At one dangerous point he topped twenty-five miles an hour.

TWENTY-FIVE

Even after Natasha had accepted that she had been given a false phone number, she had still kept re-dialling. To stop would have been to acknowledge the fact that she had been duped. Finally, she had made Anna dial, in case she had been making a stupid mistake. Anna received the same pre-recorded BT message.

'He's given me a fake number?' Natasha asked her friend.

With the calibre of comfort that sends suicidal people leaping off bridges, Anna replied: 'Well . . . I mean, come on, let's be honest. You've given fake phone numbers to men before now.'

Now Natasha felt humiliated.

'To think he sees me the same way I thought of them!'

Anna had to find a way of better comforting her friend. Before this, when Natasha lost boyfriends, Anna had only been expected to congratulate, never commiserate.

'You'll meet someone else, Nat. It's not as if you'd known him all that long.' Anna flinched as she said this; she had meant to say, 'It's not as if you knew him all that well.' Anna had known Richard for only the same length of time, yet she genuinely believed she fully understood and knew how wonderful Richard was.

'I'm not going to say he was different,' Natasha began. 'He's probably no different from thousands of other men. But he was different from the men I'm used to.'

'The money part?' Anna asked, flinching again. Anna now saw how genuinely sad her friend was, looking forlornly at the phone.

'Not the money. He seemed so nice, so sincere; we got along so well. Perhaps if I'd been dumped by him face to face I could have . . . Well, I could have hit him – got the anger out of my system. But this way, to be given a false phone number!'

Anna, from lack of inspiration, clutched at the most obvious straw. 'He might have made a mistake. Look in the telephone book.'

Natasha shook her head.

'I'm not going to humiliate myself by chasing him! . . . I've looked. He's not in the telephone book. I wouldn't be surprised if he'd given me a false name as well.'

'You know where he lives,' Anna tried again. 'Write to him.'

'Do you really imagine I'd want to write to a man who's treated me so badly?'

Anna's last words on the matter had been, 'Write something vicious, get all your hate out of your system.'

Natasha's sense of loss was felt in her lungs, in her stomach; real physical pain.

At six o' clock, she finally conceded that she would have no sleep, and got dressed. *Write something vicious, get all your hate out of your system.* She searched the flat for a red pen. Red for danger. Red for anger. Red for blood. She had to throw away the first draft, because she had pressed too hard with the pen and the paper had torn. In the letter Natasha asked Geoffrey why he had given her a false phone number. His imagined face stared back, silent, as expressionless as a death mask.

Dear . . .

I will not use your real name because it's probably as false as the phone number you gave me. The only reason I'm taking the trouble to write this is to let you know what I think about you. It's pathetic that you were forced to put on such an act just to get someone into bed. You should be embarrassed and ashamed of yourself. That's if you know what shame is. I'll admit, you had me fooled. I genuinely liked you, I thought that you were a nice person. Which shows what an idiot I was. Anyone who can lie as well as you can – well, it wouldn't surprise me if you were married. If you are then your poor wife has my sympathy.

Goodbye and good riddance,

Natasha

Natasha sealed the envelope shut. If she hadn't she would have re-read the letter a hundred times on the way to Geoffrey's house. The envelope was blank, though she had considered addressing it to *The Rat*, or *The Prat* or even *The Twat.*

His house was even more imposing now that she wasn't supposed to be there. On the driveway she quickened her pace to demonstrate her confidence. She could not see his Jag, which made her think that he might already be up and about. In case she was mistaken she carefully rehearsed her response should he have the guts to come out. She would walk away and say nothing: he was invisible. Better still, he no longer existed.

She put the letter through the letterbox, making as much noise as she could in case he was at home. She waited as long as she dared, then slowly walked away from the house.

At Stuart's insistence they had taken their luggage outside the terminal, where they continued to wait for another hour and a half.

'Wanker,' Melanie said to alert Stuart. She had spotted their car. The Jag was being driven too slowly, Geoffrey's face pressed up close to the windscreen, his eyes squinting in concentration. 'Why is he driving like he's having his first lesson?'

'I think he's seen us,' Stuart said when he saw Geoffrey wave – with both hands. The Jag came to a sudden halt.

Before they reached him, Geoffrey clambered onto the rear seat. He was concentrating very hard on appearing sober while Stuart put their luggage into the boot. Melanie spoke to him.

'Why didn't you . . . ? You've been drinking!'

'I have not! . . . How can you tell?'

'Drunk? He's drunk?' Stuart screamed. He came to join his wife at the car door. Geoffrey forgot to be apologetic. He grinned.

'You've been driving my Jag fucking-well drunk?'

'It needs some petrol as well.'

'We left it with a full tank! You – Melanie, he's been driving the Jag while we were away!'

Melanie ordered Stuart into the car. None of them said anything until they were driving away from the petrol station. Stuart was still dangerously smouldering.

'Look,' Melanie began, 'the car's OK and the house is OK – right? Well that's all that's important.'

'They're OK,' Geoffrey confirmed. Though Melanie was sitting with him in the back seat he spoke loudly, so Stuart could hear.

'What did you get up to while we were away?'

'I've abandoned the novel,' Geoffrey told her, even though he was not sure he had.

'You shouldn't give up, Geoff.'

'I'm probably not going to give up . . . Maybe I'll give up on *this* novel. I've had the inspiration for another story . . . maybe.'

'Oh?'

Stupid-tired from drink, Geoffrey spilt his guts about Natasha, describing her as perfect. She was pretty, she was easy to talk to, she was down to earth in a good way, she was sexy without falling into the trap of being tarty, she made him laugh, she did not understand him yet knew this was no drawback . . . Then:

'It's over, though.'

'Why?' Melanie asked. Geoffrey was forced to explain that Natasha had thought their car and house were his.

'Sounds like you're well rid,' Stuart heckled when Geoffrey's story came to its end.

'Why is he well rid?'

The debate Melanie and Stuart had then was a repeat of the one Geoffrey had already had with himself. He knew Stuart's hard-headedness was sensible, yet silently hoped Melanie would win: he preferred her more open-minded arguments. Stuart said that clearly Natasha was only interested in the money, which Geoffrey did not believe to be true; Melanie said that Natasha might be attracted to a man with money – *what's wrong with that?* – but that now she knew Geoffrey she must genuinely like him. Geoffrey thought this unlikely.

'Will you drop me at my flat, please?' Geoffrey asked when he saw that they had begun on the route to their own home.

When they stopped at his flat, Stuart – his mate again – climbed out of the car with Geoffrey, seizing the chance to pass on advice.

'If you like this girl, then – well, you have no choice – go for it. Sometimes you have to persevere with women. You can never fully hope to give them what they want, because half the time they don't know themselves what they want.'

'I heard that!' Melanie shouted from inside the car.

'So you think I should have another go at cracking Natasha?' Geoffrey asked.

'It's not a code you're trying to break,' Stuart said. 'Try something romantic.'

'I thought of that. Like?'

'Persistence.'

Persistence was Geoffrey's specialist subject. He didn't need any advice on this. But it had never brought him any success. This time he had been smart. She had been in the wrong, not him. He had been strong, he had been determined not to invest years of his life in yet another relationship that was doomed before it even began.

TWENTY-SIX

After Stuart and Melanie had driven away, Geoffrey stayed on the street outside his flat watching until the Jag was completely out of sight. Then he turned in a deliberate, slow movement to examine the building where he lived. He walked inside, in one hand a carrier bag of the clothes he had taken with him on his brief holiday in luxury, the other clutching the tatty pages that were the single chapter he had yet managed to complete.

His fatigue was caused by waking early, and drinking too much. He instead chose to attribute his exhaustion to his way of life. The joke had worn thin.

He had learnt there is no glory in destitution, there is no glamour in poverty. Having no money means being colder than is comfortable, eating food you would not normally choose to eat, not always being comfortable in the clothes you wear, and having to work against the rest of the world as you learn that it's designed to accommodate only those with money. Being poor is only ever fun when you are very young, and no-one expects you to have any money. Being poor is like having acne: acceptable only up to a certain age, after which people suspect you've brought the condition upon yourself. Being poor is only glamorous when you can then walk off the set; or when it's a distant memory.

The house was silent when he entered. Each step up to his flat was hard work; he noticed a cold which might be there, or might be imagined, a come-down from the alcohol. The building smelt of emptiness.

Inside his room, for want of anything sensible to do, he got out his manual typewriter and began to write. Having grown accustomed to keys requiring just the lightest of touches, he had to retype the first sentence so that the keys would impress upon the ribbon. His cold fingers hurt from the impact.

He kept the same title. As before, it still had little relevance.

ALL THIS AND MORE
a novel by
Geoffrey Barker

Natalie was looking for a wealthy man. She was a straightforward, traditional-style gold-digger. The circumstance had arisen that George was looking after a flash car and taking care of an impressively large house, which Natalie believed to be his. It was this belief which attracted her to him.

George, having just enough experience of women, should have obeyed his initial warning instincts.

After they had made love for the first time he was convinced that his initial conceptions about her were wrong, though he was still cautious enough not to tell her the whole truth about himself.

The deception continued, until Natalie also developed genuine feelings for George. When he finally felt secure enough to reveal the truth about his financial circumstances, Natalie finished with him. She told him this was not because he was poor, but because he had lied to her.

He decided to give her the benefit of the doubt and pursue her. He sent her flowers and called at her house.

Eventually she was won over and they began seeing each other again. But though everything was now out in the open, the initial falsehood always tainted their relationship. As he discovered more about her character, and she did the same about him, they became convinced that if they had been honest with each other from the beginning, there would never have been . . .

Geoffrey immediately tore this up, all too aware of how its development might haunt him. He was writing an ending based on his experience of another woman, Janette, not Natasha. He had decided to ignore Stuart's advice, believing he *knew* where pursuing her might lead. Now he understood that he had been judging her by his past experiences, and love doesn't always work like that. Pursuing Janette had been a mistake, pursuing Natasha might not be.

Their first year living together had been the girls' first real test of their friendship. They had passed the test only inasmuch as they had survived. Now, Anna's growing affection for Richard set a harder test. Natasha's trouble was that her friendship with Anna had been too extraordinary. She was beginning to understand the mistake she had made in becoming too dependent on Anna. She had no other real friends, her sister was awful, and the other girls she worked with, whenever she had been out with them, only talked about work, until they became drunk – which they did very easily – when all they talked about was boys. Natasha was only slightly older than them, but old enough for the difference to matter. Only Anna could understand Natasha's attitude to men, the mistrust and caution yet also the willingness to play along. At least the pre-Richard Anna thought this; the new Anna might not be so readily cynical.

It wasn't until the shop was closing on Tuesday that Natasha told Anna that instead of going home with her she would be going to her parents' house.

'You're going to your parents' *midweek*? Is something wrong?'

'Why should there be anything wrong?'

'Because you hate going to your parents' house when you're obliged to, so why go of your own free will? Has there been a car accident? Are they divorcing?'

'I'm visiting my parents so I have something to look forward to – going home afterwards.'

Anna didn't respond.

'What?' Natasha asked, wondering what she was thinking.

'Shall we go to the *Apollo* again, on Saturday night? For old times' sake?'

The expression *for old time's sake* so shocked Natasha she was unable to answer.

'What?' Anna asked.

'You'll be going out with Richard,' Natasha said coldly.

'You're going to see your mother, midweek?' Anna needlessly repeated. 'You're going without her having asked you to come?'

Natasha, from nowhere, shouted, 'What am I supposed to do, stay in on my own?' What she didn't say, but Anna heard anyway, was '*You'll be out with your boyfriend – who you think more of than me!*'

'Are you still pissed off because of Geoffrey?'

Natasha sighed wearily: at first she intended this to show Anna that she was bored by the question, but halfway, and accidentally, the sigh became one of piteous depression.

On the bus home Anna sent a text message to Richard, telling him there was a change of plan and that, if he wanted to, they could spend an evening in, at her flat. He immediately texted his reply back: 'Yes'.

He had a confession to make, and making it at her home would eliminate the risk of her walking out.

Though she had plenty to occupy her, and time passed quickly, Anna had a sense of how different the flat was when she was there alone.

On the way to Anna's flat Richard followed the orders she had given him and stopped for a Kentucky Fried Chicken. They ate quickly so that the rest of the evening could begin. Anna made Richard a coffee he never drank. They agreed to abandon watching the video Anna had hastily selected from her meagre collection, and were in bed together within an hour of him arriving; and this record time included the twenty minutes they had spent together in the shower.

He didn't dare make his confession before sex in case there followed an argument that wouldn't be resolved, which might mean that sex would be off the agenda. After sex he dared not confess from fear of destroying their joy. There was nothing either of them found that remarkable about their sex life except that they had retained the enthusiasm of their first time, and it showed no signs of diminishing.

She freed herself from his embrace.

'Where are you going?' he pleaded.

'Window.' She opened her bedroom window slightly, to let a breeze in, to clean and cool the air. A street light illuminated her body in yellow. She was about to close the curtain again.

'Don't,' he told her.

'Why?' she asked. As soon as she saw his expression she understood. She stood with the curtains still open so that he could look at her; yellow, warm, naked.

'Can I come back to bed yet?' she asked pointedly.

'What are you thinking about?'

'Natasha. I wish she was as happy as me. I even wish she was happy instead of me.'

Back in bed she was wise enough not to speak again. He, on the other hand, had thought of everything he wanted to say and how best to say it without sounding clichéd or sentimental. He wanted to tell her about his amazement, about how he had been unable to recognise himself since he had met her.

'Let's try not to go to sleep.'

'All right.'

She asked him if he had made any plans for them for Saturday night.

'Nothing specific,' he answered.

'I'm going out with Natasha,' she blurted out, unsure of any other, more diplomatic way she could have phrased this. When Anna explained about Natasha going to her mother's, and the implication of this, Richard made no objections.

They persevered with attempts at conversation, asking each other to name the quality they most admired in the other.

'I like your openness best,' Richard told her.

'I most like your honesty,' Anna said. He couldn't bring himself to shatter this belief. Anna slept soundly.

TWENTY-SEVEN

Natasha didn't phone before she set off, in case she changed her mind on the way. She had nothing to tell her mother and no way of anticipating the warmth or chill of the reception she might receive.

The front door was locked; she had to knock.

She heard her dad's voice. 'Oh – fuck!' There was real violence in the way the key was turned and the door pulled open.

'Oh. Natasha. Hello, love. I was just putting my feet up. I'd slung *High Plains Drifter* in the video, heated up a curry, poured a beer. Your mum's gone out with Brenda.'

'Brenda? Out?'

'I know. What are the odds on you both showing up on a Tuesday night? They've gone to Bingo, at St Martin's. You've got seven minutes to get there if you fancy a game. That's unless you want to come in and ruin the first night I've had in alone for a month.'

So Natasha went to St Martin's.

St Martin's was built at the same time as the rest of the estate in the optimistic hope that some of its residents might wish to visit a church, if not for weddings or christenings, then possibly at Christmas and certainly for funerals.

Father Regan conducted the bingo sessions in good humour, resisting the temptation to ask why his Sunday sermons, promising the reward of eternal redemption, never attracted congregations as large as the possibility of a hundred-pound cash win.

Natasha found her mother and Brenda among the chaotic

hubbub of the crowd, predominantly women, who were settling themselves at the tables having bought their cards, drinks and pens. Once Natasha had bought her cards she sat down opposite them and simply said 'hello'. Then the Bingo began and the noise ended, like a class of obedient kids beneath a tyrannical teacher.

Father Regan's code for the numbers was unique to himself and confusing for the newcomer: *The Waffen SS – 55*, *Hurry Up Harry – 69*, *Laurel And Hardy – 18*, *Lambert And Butler – 20*. After Natasha settled into the rhythm, however, she became lost in each game, caught up in the thrill of the near misses, the tense anticipation of waiting for the elusive final number, and the inevitable disappointment when someone else called 'HOUSE!'

The last game ended at ten o'clock. Brenda offered Natasha a lift home. 'How come you're at mum's midweek?' she asked after they had dropped off their mother.

Natasha had no lie prepared so told the semi-truth, that she was making the flat available for Anna and her boyfriend.

'What about *your* boyfriend?' Brenda asked. 'What's he doing tonight?'

Natasha answered truthfully, in a way. 'I don't know.' Nor could she guess.

Although the reason could only be that Brenda had had a row with Keith, Natasha asked her sister why she had also called at her parents'.

'I just fancied a game of Bingo,' Brenda lied. The reason was never important. Keith and Brenda's latest war had continued every night for several days. They both finished work at five, and the deal was that whoever had the clearest drive home would make the tea.

Brenda complained that Keith often rushed home so he could make spicy curries or chilli con carne, foods whose quality he measured by how much his eyes watered. Keith complained that Brenda dawdled on her way home so as to avoid cooking.

Eventually Brenda had told Keith not to bother cooking for her – she found his food inedible.

On Monday night, when Brenda had arrived home before

Keith, she thought it only reasonable – seeing he had not cooked for her last Thursday and Friday – not to cook for him. When he arrived home, Keith disagreed. The argument ended only when Keith left the house to buy his own food. Tonight, Tuesday, they had both cooked and eaten separately, without speaking.

They would always avoid speaking through these battles. Worse, they would begin to whistle or sing when the other was around. The whistling was designed to hurt each other, and they were both hurt. When he was alone Keith's hatred manifested itself in frustrated anger, so that he found himself punching at walls and screaming at the ceiling, all to prevent his anger turning into violence directed at Brenda.

Tonight, after eating, Keith went out. So that she would not be at home when he returned and he would be left guessing where she had gone, Brenda also went out. There was nowhere she could think of to go to. So she went to her mother's and persuaded her to go to Bingo.

On Wednesday evening Natasha began to cook the evening meal to allow her friend more time to prepare herself for her nightly date with Richard. Natasha listened patiently, feigning interest, whenever Anna gave details of her previous dates.

In the past there had always been odd nights that Natasha had been alone in the flat when Anna had gone out on a date. The difference now was that Natasha and Anna had met these men on the same night: Anna had struck lucky, while Natasha had only met another idiot – even if he was the most convincing idiot yet. This one had made her genuinely like him. Now he was gone, and Anna's Richard was still around. The more Anna eulogised Richard, the more Natasha disliked him.

Natasha hoped that she had worded her letter well enough to insult Geoffrey yet still oblige him to respond.

He did not respond.

Natasha answered the phone while Anna was still getting ready.

'Hello?' she said. Silence. Straightaway, instinctively, Natasha knew the call was Geoffrey wanting to make contact. Faced with the reality of having to speak, he was lost for words. Then the line went dead as he hung up.

By this one silent phone call Natasha understood that she could not have been entirely irrelevant to him; he also had been hurt. She felt a little better now. As she picked up the *Radio Times*, this time, unlike when she had glanced through thirty minutes earlier, she found plenty of programmes that she wouldn't mind watching. She decided to make herself a coffee so that as soon as Anna had left, she could sprawl out in peace, and relax for the first time in days.

The phone rang again. Richard asked Natasha to tell Anna that he would be a little delayed in picking her up, he was stuck in a tailback. Their conversation was clumsy and strained, punctuated by crackling silences as Richard's mobile flickered between life and death. He ended the conversation by apologising to Natasha.

'Sorry about the – Hello? . . . to get it repaired . . . can you hear . . . not sure . . . Natasha? . . . I phoned a few minutes ago – hello? – you answered but you couldn't hear me speak . . .'

Natasha slammed the phone down.

With a cotton-wool ball soaked in Dettol, Melanie dabbed at Stuart's persistent bleeding.

'I udd nedder de undaithful do do,' he had muttered through his broken nose.

'I'm so sorry, love,' she told him. After returning from the airport Stuart had been in an uncharacteristically active mood, so as soon as they had entered the house he had decided to expend his energy on cleaning out the Jag. Meanwhile, Melanie had begun to sift through the backlog of junk mail and bills that had accumulated during their time away. Finally she came to a plain, unaddressed white envelope which she opened and, disorientated by jet lag, read the enclosed letter. Melanie took one of Stuart's tennis rackets out to the driveway. She tapped him on the shoulder, then landed him a back-handed whack. Her aim was perfect, breaking his nose and giving him two black eyes with a single blow. It wasn't until he was screaming in agony that her brain kicked into gear and she realised whom the letter must have been intended for.

Twenty minutes later his nose wouldn't stop bleeding.

'*We're happy, aren't we?*' Stuart protested. Or at least this was what he was trying to say. '*It was Geoffrey. That woman he talked about.*'

The letter had clearly been intended for Geoffrey: obviously there was more to the story of him and this girl than he had been prepared to admit. Secure in a happy and successful marriage, Melanie was greatly intrigued by Geoffrey's behaviour. Over the next few days she bombarded her husband with hundreds of questions.

'If it means I get some peace,' he eventually conceded, 'then I'll phone him and ask if he fancies a pint. I'll get him to talk about her.'

TWENTY-EIGHT

Instead of writing productively, Geoffrey wrote a letter to Natasha, the letter he would have sent her if he had not been so gutless.

Dear Natasha,

The most amazing thing about you is that so many of the characteristics I recognised in you when I first saw you, before I had ever spoken to you or could have any way of knowing what you were really like, were true. I hoped that you would be smart, and funny; I hoped you would lack pretension but have passions and idiosyncracies to mark you out as different. You had all of these things, plus other qualities I had not even dreamed of. You are open, impulsive, sexy, considerate and interesting.

But I can't see you again.

I wish we could have met under different circumstances, where you could have seen me as I really am. That way I would have known that any attraction you feel towards me was based on the real picture. You see, the truth is that the Jag is not mine, neither is the house. I am currently living in a bedsit I would have been ashamed to bring you to. My worry is that you would have refused to come. I have no way of knowing this for certain, of course, but I do know that the doubt would always have prevented me from trusting you as explicitly as I would have desired.

It might also have been true that if you had met me knowing

nothing about me, you might still have been attracted to me and

He wrote no more. He picked up the completed chapter of his novel. He read the first sentence, which was so familiar to him. He tore each page up, into smaller and smaller pieces, so he wouldn't be tempted to try to use this chapter again. His novel was no longer simply stalling. He could not write about Janette because he no longer cared about her, and he could not write about Natasha, as he knew less about her; there were fewer incidents to call upon, he had a less complete picture of her character. Worse, there was no acceptable ending. Editors, agents, the reading public – they all demanded a happy ending, and real life only ends miserably or, at best, inconclusively. Any happy ending for *All This And More* would require a feat of imagination beyond the reasonable.

He tore up the letter he had begun, then tore up the synopsis for the novel. He took the tiny pieces of paper down to the communal loo and flushed them away.

Using the only number he had for Geoffrey, Stuart made two attempts to phone. The first time, when Stuart asked if he could speak to Geoffrey, the answer had been an abrupt 'FUCK OFF,' then the phone had been hung up. The second time, whoever answered had been more courteous, telling Stuart they would bring Geoffrey to the phone. After twenty minutes of silence Stuart decided that it would be quicker for him to go round there himself. Having slouched around for several days, and not daring to risk taking the Jag to Geoffrey's neighbourhood, he decided to walk.

Stuart knocked politely on the door to the main building, and waited. No one came. He knocked harder, waited longer, and then entered. The house had a smell that reminded him of Play-Doh and old watchstraps.

'You woke me up,' Geoffrey told Stuart after he had answered the door.

'Pub?' Stuart asked. Geoffrey walked out of his flat without even stopping to collect his coat.

'You're paying, right?'

At the pub Stuart explained to Geoffrey his reason for visiting. 'I've got permission to stay out and get drunk. Melanie owes me. Besides, she wants me to find out about this girl you were seeing.'

'What happened to your nose?' Geoffrey asked when Stuart returned from the bar with the drinks. Stuart gave him Natasha's letter and explained Melanie's misinterpretation of it.

'Basically the letter says you're a bastard.'

'Couldn't you have told me about this sooner?'

'What would you have done – got in contact with her? After reading this, I think that might have been a mistake.'

'Yeah I know, but . . .'

Stuart waited, knowing Geoffrey had nothing more to say and letting the silence emphasise this. He took a substantial gulp of his pint, emptying the glass by a quarter, before he spoke.

'Me, I'm lucky. I know I'm lucky. I managed to find a woman who suits me. You should ask yourself, could being with this woman have suited you?'

'There's nothing you can say that I haven't already thought,' Geoffrey replied sadly. 'You are lucky to have Melanie,' he added, abstractedly, with a sentimentality several pints ahead of schedule.

'I need some details – just a few – about this woman you were seeing, just so that I can pass them on to Melanie, to keep her happy.'

To loosen Geoffrey's tongue, Stuart spent a few minutes celebrating his wife, and as he did so he reminded himself of the natural perpetuation that kept his marriage flourishing without struggle. He became so gratified by describing her, her behaviour, her peculiarities, her joys, that he paid little attention to Geoffrey, who had progressed into his story only as far as the night when he first met Natasha.

'. . . But she couldn't see past the house and the Jag and

everything associated with it. She was with me because she saw how I lived. Do you see?'

'You know what? In the very beginning Melanie liked me mainly because of the money, because I was an up-and-coming tennis star, of sorts. She told me about it once, but we've never mentioned it since. What did Natasha say when you asked her if she was only interested in you for your money?'

This was the moment of clarity many drinkers enjoy, a tumble into a truth. For Geoffrey the revelation was his own stupidity – he had let Natasha go, dismissed her, made assumptions about her, and given her no chance to deny or rationalise them. He had never directly asked her if she was only interested in him for his money.

'If I go and see her again I run the risk of looking like an idiot.'

'So what?' Stuart demanded. 'Anyone who ever says hello to someone they don't know runs the risk of making an idiot of themselves. Anyone who moves in for a kiss, or asks someone to spend the night, runs that risk. But really, what's the risk? You go to talk to her – she might be happy to see you. You go to talk to her and she isn't interested. Fine, OK, move on – at least you know where you stand then. What I'm trying to say is, you had instincts about Janette which you told me you didn't follow and three years later regretted not following. What are your instincts about Natasha?'

Geoffrey lifted the lager up to his mouth and paused for effect, staring straight into the eyes of his friend to emphasise his certainty.

'We belong together.'

'Really?' Stuart smiled, then grinned, then laughed. 'Fucking hell! Really? That strong, so soon?'

Geoffrey drank from the lager, finishing his fourth pint. 'Just instincts. Flimsy evidence.'

Stuart finished his pint now, taking several gulps to help catch up with his more desperate friend. He grabbed the two empty glasses but didn't get up.

'I'll bet if you take the risk, approach her, speak to her, she won't reject you. She'll give you another chance.'

When Stuart returned with more drinks he noticed that Geoffrey was now sitting straighter. As they talked he made large demonstrative gestures, speaking without giving Stuart the chance to contribute or reply.

'When I put my mind to it I can write a pretty effective letter. Maybe I should write to Natasha explaining everything?'

'Not a letter,' Stuart advised. 'You run the risk of being too formal: you know, you're putting it all in writing as if there are conditions you expect both of you to adhere to. It's not a legally binding contract you're drawing up. You're just asking a girl out. No, the best thing you can do – in my opinion – is go and see her. Even if she doesn't give you chance to speak, the gesture of going might be enough to make her see that you're sorry you judged her without giving her chance to explain. But don't tell her she has to explain anything. And don't tell her you're there to give her a second chance. And for God's sake don't be too apologetic, you'll make her think –'

'OK!' exclaimed Geoffrey. 'I'm not totally inexperienced with women, you know. Give me some credit.' He immediately began thinking up a new plan of approach now that the option of being too apologetic was ruled out.

Stuart excused himself and from the toilet used his mobile phone to tell Melanie to phone the pub and make up an emergency, so that he could leave and return to his wife, where he was always happiest. Geoffrey wouldn't mind. He had new, happy thoughts.

When Geoffrey left the pub he had drunk enough to feel sufficiently brave to walk to Natasha's flat. The long walk sobered him up. He remembered the day Janette had told him that she was remarrying her husband, and his inability to keep control over how he felt, even though he knew his hurt was unwarranted, and at odds with his true emotions. For all the songs, novels, and films, for all the experiences which everyone who ever breathed has had, love was still an indecipherable puzzle.

When he reached Natasha's house he knew he no longer had anything comprehensible to say. He stared at the house for a while, watching as its features faded into silhouette; in the darkness his will weakened and he finally turned and walked away.

TWENTY-NINE

On Saturday night the girls paid their entrance fee, and exchanged nods and smiles of recognition with the bouncers. Natasha went to the bar while Anna found a regular spot to sit. If all this was too familiar, it was at least made unusual in that neither of them asked the other why they had come to the *Apollo*.

Natasha began to hope that someone, any old drunk, would approach them and try to chat them up. She wanted to demonstrate how unchanged she was by Geoffrey.

They nodded along to the music, pretending that it held their attention.

A very tall, thin man, only in his early twenties, weaved his way towards them, so drunk that he was spilling his beer everywhere, even though he was drinking from a bottle.

'I like that dress you're wearing,' he announced. He stood between the girls, and pointed randomly, his eyes not focusing on either of them.

'Hello? Which of us are you talking to?' Natasha asked. Neither of the girls wore a dress. Her tone was so threatening he was deterred from answering her. He positioned his body so he was facing Anna, and prepared himself to speak.

'Fuck. Off,' she barked. He fucked off. More than ever, Anna was happy that she had Richard, and she wished he were here with her now.

Anna went to the bar, the short expedition being a distraction from the vapidity of the club.

Natasha began to smile at every half-decent man she could see, desperate to avoid Anna. For the first time ever it seemed that neither of them dared to begin a conversation – their pre-occupations were just so different.

Every fault the *Apollo* had – the shabby decor, the aggressive bouncers, the desperate clientele – was far worse than they remembered: rotten, violent, despondent. Natasha could see now that its closing down was inevitable: it would either close or collapse.

She tried to think positively. If the relationship had carried on – she told herself – if Geoffrey had strung her along for longer, she knew that she would have fallen in love with him. At least now her recovery would come sooner.

She saw Derek. Selfish, smug, stupid Derek. He was looking over at her. Remembering the last time she had seen him, the night she had conned some thug into hitting him over the head, he had good cause to hate her. She held his gaze, permitting him to smile. He approached.

'I came last week but you weren't here. Were you avoiding me?'

'Why would I be avoiding you?' she answered, making him understand he was too inconsequential for her even to think of it.

'You were angry at me for . . . because you thought I'd been seeing some other girl.'

He had been kissing another girl, of that there was no doubt. Natasha didn't want this argument. She just wanted to talk. The alternative was to sit in a silence that would continue when Anna returned with the drinks.

'I've been thinking about you,' Derek continued. Natasha waited. Anna returned; she handed Natasha a bottle of clear WKD.

'What are you letting this little shit talk to you for?' Anna asked Natasha, looking directly at Derek.

'She can talk to who she wants, what's it got to do with you?'

'I'll tell you what it's got to do with me,' Anna began. She put her own bottle down so her hands would be free. 'I'm her friend –

right? And she doesn't want to talk to you or to any of the other fuck-heads that come in here. Do you think she's forgotten what you were doing last time she saw you?'

'Bleeding?' Derek asked provocatively. Natasha laughed, which minutes earlier she had not expected to do tonight.

'Tell him to go away, Nat,' Anna said. 'Come on – you don't want anything to do with him or anyone like him, do you? Tell him.'

In the three weeks Natasha had officially gone out with Derek every one of her thoughts had ended with the rhetorical question: How can I get rid of him? To revert back to Derek's type now would be a retrograde step as stupid as a liposuction patient asking for the fat to be pumped back.

'Fuck off, Derek,' Natasha told him. Derek fucked off, glaring hatred at Anna.

And now, at long last, good sense returned.

'Why have we come here?' Natasha asked.

Anna laughed. 'You know what? We tolerated it before because we were on the look-out for men. And men come here. Men of a sort. But if we just forget that, just drink and dance, then maybe we can have real fun. There're too many things we daren't talk about. What do you reckon?'

Anna took a long drink from her bottle and took Natasha's hand, pulling her onto the dance floor.

'Come on then, let's get a sweat on.'

Finding himself unexpectedly free this Saturday night, Richard was pleased when Malcolm phoned.

'I don't suppose you're out tonight, are you? You'll be out with that bird again, won't you?' Malcolm taunted.

'Not tonight. So where are we meeting?' Richard asked, needlessly. He knew the lads would be meeting in the usual pub at the usual time.

'Has she blown you out, then?' Malcolm asked.

'No.'

'Then you've blown her out?'

'No. *No*,' Richard emphasised. 'I'm just going to have a night out with my mates, what's so unusual about that?'

Malcolm teased, 'Yeah, well, maybe we don't want you out with us. Maybe now you're *in love* you can't be one of the lads.'

'Who said I was in love?' he challenged, immediately regretting it. Whichever inadequate epithet was used, all he knew for certain was that he liked being with Anna, wanted to be with her as often and for as long as possible, and that any denial of this was treachery.

In a break from dancing, Anna went to the bar and Natasha found a place to stand. A man approached her. His face was skeletal, pale and grinning.

'Would you like to take a walk on the wild side?'

Natasha laughed in spite of herself.

'You are the ugliest fucker I've ever seen in my life,' she told him.

'This is true,' he admitted. 'And I'll fight any bastard who says different.'

Anna brought their drinks.

'Jesus,' she exclaimed when the skull man smiled at her.

'Not nice, is it?' he smirked. When he had gone Natasha and Anna began laughing, not really sure why. Another man approached.

'What's Brazil famous for?' he asked Anna.

This was an old gag, a cheap set-up. Anna played along.

'Footballers.'

He looked disappointed. 'No. What's *Brazil* famous for?'

'Nuts?'

'No! Think about it. You drink it. What's Brazil famous for?'

'Coffee?'

'OK,' he told her, pleased with himself. 'Your place or mine?'

Anna and Natasha had begun laughing; now they stared at him blankly until he understood he had failed.

'I didn't fancy you anyway,' he said as he walked off.

Close by, another man caught their eye. Anna stared back, aggressively.

'Am I wearing something of yours?' she yelled. He scampered away. They danced again, staying on the floor through each track, flirting with men who danced near them, until the man was about to speak, when they would turn away and concentrate upon each other. Exhausted from dancing and desperate to pee, Anna again dragged her friend off the dance floor. Their drinks had been stolen.

'Don't get another drink,' Anna said. 'I'm off to the loo. When I get back we'll just dance again.'

The experience was unchanged – Richard rang for a taxi that dropped him off outside the Queen's, near the Interchange, at seven thirty. The sun was making its descent to mark the commencement of an evening full of booze and laughs, and girls. In the past, the fun had been mostly in the pursuit of women, any conquest a bonus. He now wanted neither pursuit nor conquest.

He knew where his mates would be standing – and there they were. He knew the drinks they would have ordered – and so they had. He knew how they would greet him – and so they did.

All the lads – Malcolm, Raymond and Daniel – pretended to detect a fundamental change in Richard. When he was slow to join in with their ogling of women, they attributed this to Anna having castrated him; when he refused to join in with approaching and pestering women, he was clearly afraid of Anna, under the thumb, a cuckold, pussy-whipped.

Richard began to drink double vodkas and Red Bulls, determined to enjoy himself. He had to transform his mood. As the night progressed he marvelled at his new ability to drink without getting drunk. Even by the time they had arrived at *Bartok's* he remained clear-sighted: every girl the lads pointed out looked the same, make-up, hair, clothes. He could predict every response they would make to jokes and suggestions; he knew every mediocre, second-hand, small-minded opinion they had and knew all their expectations and fears. He found none of them attractive enough to risk losing Anna for.

Waiting for Anna to buy the drinks, Natasha stood away from the dance floor, against a far wall lined with stools. She stood among the crowd there, away from the main glare of the lights. She caught her breath, cooled down a little and had time to look out over the main body of the club.

Then she saw Geoffrey, his eyes darting as he walked. He would inevitably see her.

She found a free stool that she pushed back against the wall, and sat down, hoping not to be seen.

'Hello, Natasha.'

He tapped her on her shoulder, her bare shoulder, and she turned sharply, as if she was being accosted.

'Your letter . . .' Geoffrey began. He was silenced by people jostling past him. 'I thought I should find you and explain. I remembered you telling me about this place, so . . . I thought if I explained then maybe there'd be a chance you might not hate me.'

Natasha did a half-spin on the stool, looking around, but not at him. She waved to someone – no one there really – behind Geoffrey's back, smiling broadly. He turned to see who she had waved to. He was in the way.

'You got the letter then?'

'Eventually.'

'I'm interested to hear your explanation for giving me a false phone number,' she told him, 'but whatever you say won't matter.'

'Well that's OK,' he joked, 'so long as you give me a fair hearing – that's all I can ask for.'

'All I've been able to think about is what I'd like to say to you if I saw you face to face. I had it honed down to perfection, but now I actually see you, all the insults seem inadequate. And not worth the trouble.' She remembered dismissing Derek. 'Fuck off,' she told Geoffrey, immediately regretting it. She waved to another invisible person, so as to distract him while she recovered. She did not want him to fuck off. She needed to hear him explain.

He tried harder, 'OK. Listen. I didn't give you the right telephone number for that house because . . . well, it's not my house. The truth is, I live in a bedsit and I don't have my own phone.'

Natasha's hard stare dissolved into confusion. She had to grip the stool so that she would not fall off.

'Bedsit?'

'You managed to make that sound like "refugee camp".'

In spite of herself, he now had her full attention. Having established that Geoffrey didn't own the house, Natasha tried to work out the rest for herself. He was clearly well educated: he spoke well and knew plenty of trivial nonsense, typical of those who read a great deal. She couldn't understand why someone would live in a bedsit yet own such a beautiful and expensive car.

'It's not your car either!' she deduced, clearly outraged that he dared to be poor. 'It's not that I care about those things,' she said, sincerely, before she remembered that in fact this was a lie. She lied again. 'All I care about is the fact that you lied to me.'

'When did I lie to you?'

'You knew what I thought. You misled me.'

Geoffrey continued, moving closer to let people through, and not stepping back once they had passed. 'My friend and his wife went to Canada. He's a professional tennis player and every time they're away they get burgled. I was looking after . . . You see, what I thought was . . . you met me in that expensive club, talked to me because you'd seen my car. One of the first questions you asked me was what I did for a living. I'm surprised I wasn't asked to produce a recent bank statement. At first I thought – well, I knew I liked you, and so I wanted to see if I could find out why you were interested in me. I didn't find out anything to contradict my worst assumptions. So I decided that I had to give you a false phone number . . . so that it would end. If I've been wrong about you, then I really do apologise. We can start seeing each other properly, if you're willing to take me for what I am.'

'Unemployed?'

'See! You managed to make that sound like "leper". Things like that shouldn't matter – not if you were interested in me as a person.'

Geoffrey had come to see her, to explain. Recently she had thought of nothing but him. And here he was, being honest, obviously really wanting to be with her.

As she came out of the toilet, Anna saw Natasha talking to Geoffrey. Her usual instinct would have been to join Natasha to give moral support; instead she went to the bar and ordered more drinks to give her friend the chance to talk to him alone. They might only resolve any differences alone.

THIRTY

Richard knew that if inclined, his smile and non-threatening perseverance would persuade any of these girls onto their backs. Then, afterwards, he could walk away happily knowing that he would never want to see them again.

He was full of contempt for his old self, amazed at what a sordid fool he had been in the past, being so self-congratulatory about such easy conquests, and never wanting to find someone special like Anna. As he watched Malcolm, Ray and Daniel try and chat the girls up, he knew that he no longer had anything to say to them, nor did he care if they despised or pitied him.

He wanted to text Anna; he wished that she were with him. He would phone her and ask her if he could come round later. He missed her; and he wanted to talk to the lads about her, prepared to tolerate their ridicule.

He told Daniel, 'This girl I'm seeing, Anna – she's amazing.'

'You mean in bed?'

'No, no, not that. She's so easy to be around. It's like being able to kiss your best friend –'

'Eh!'

'I mean, it's like being able to laugh with then hold someone who wants nothing more than to laugh with you and hold you too.'

Daniel informed him, 'Warren Beatty said "Love is the mistaken belief that one woman is any different from another".'

'I'm not saying it's love . . . I'm saying I've met someone who might actually be *it*, you know, the thing I've been telling girls they are for years, the things they want to hear about themselves, that you find them interesting and sexy and fun . . . you don't get it, do you?' Daniel's expression was blank.

'I don't want to get it. Shut up and have a laugh. You're not out with her, you're out with us.'

Ray joined them, pointing at a girl as he approached. 'Fuck me, look at the arse on that.'

Malcolm came over, finally breaking away from some girl he had been kissing. He relished being the centre of attention as Richard recounted the events of the last night they were all out together, when he had been drenched in red wine.

Ray asked Malcolm, 'Why do you even bother telling them you're married? Just tell them the truth, that you're single but you don't want anything serious.'

The three others – including Richard – laughed at Ray's naiveté. They reminded him again why they always told the girls they picked up that they were married.

'If they think you're married,' Daniel began, 'you never have to take them out, because you have to be "discreet". So you save a lot of time. No dates: you just go over to their place, and – boom – straight to bed, with a ready-made excuse for why you have to leave straight after. "My wife's expecting me home".'

Malcolm continued: 'Straightforward, unconditional sex. And they don't nag you about the future, and they don't pester you with phone calls. And how can you phone them? It's really awkward – you're married. And if they ever do catch you with another woman they're more than likely to say nothing, just in case she's your wife!'

Ray had been successfully reminded. 'We are fucking geniuses.'

Richard, though listening attentively and grinning, had made no contribution to the reaffirmation of their confederacy.

'What have you been up to, mate?' Daniel asked Richard. 'This bird you got off with last time we were out – did you tell her the usual, that you're married?'

'I told her,' Richard confessed, making sure he had no smile on his face this time – so they would see the difference. 'I've seen her . . . a few times. I like her.'

'Uh, for fuck's sake! Don't let's be hearing this bollocks from you, Rick!' Malcolm told him. 'What's to like? She's a lass – they're only likeable when they're new.'

Ray added, 'Warren Beatty said "Love is the mistaken belief that one woman is any different from another".'

Richard was exhausted by this repetition, like an anecdote repeated for the millionth time by a deranged uncle.

'You've got that shit from Daniel. And Warren Beatty is now happily married. All I'm saying is that this one is . . .' Then he made no attempt to conclude his explanation. There was no description he could give that would sum her up, and a longer description was not appropriate here and now.

'All I'm saying is that . . . Well, let me put it this way – I've been thinking about telling her I'm not married. I can't think how I'll do it, I've been waiting for the right time, but I am gonna tell her.'

His mates buried any real disappointment beneath derision, taking great joy at having new material to take the piss out of him.

Every attempt Richard had made to blow his cover had failed. No matter how frequently he took Anna out or spent the entire night with her, she never once questioned how a married man could have such liberty. She had trained herself not to ask.

Like a declaration of love, the most compelling time to make a stark confession was after sex, when resistance was lowered through exhaustion and intimacy. Yet he never succumbed, out of a dread of permanently exploding the foundations upon which they had prepared their future. If there was one thing that Richard knew for certain, it was that he wanted his future to include Anna.

'Let's go somewhere else,' Richard told his mates. They didn't hear. Richard left them, pretending only to go to the loo. Instead he walked straight out of the door.

He wasn't inarticulate, nor were his friends hopelessly insensitive. Love is impossible to explain to onlookers, especially as those without direct experience of it are too often bemused.

*

Natasha stood up. Anna would be returning shortly and she didn't want her to see her talking to Geoffrey, even though Natasha had more questions to ask him and more anger to vent. He had challenged her to accept him for how he was – poor.

'Grow up, Geoffrey. And goodbye.'

She was delighted at how she walked away, dignified, head held high. She felt like Anne Boleyn, though she hoped for a better fate.

She soon realised that she had nowhere to walk to. She looked for Anna but couldn't see her. She headed for the toilets and by some miracle there was a cubicle free. She put the lid down and sat on the toilet. While dancing she had begun to enjoy herself. She had never thought about there being a last Saturday night at the *Apollo*, but perhaps this might be it. Tonight could have been tolerable if it had been just another ordinary Saturday night. As it was, it was dreadful because it was so very different. Anna had changed. And she, she realised, had changed too. She wanted someone other than Anna, someone she might be happy with, someone whom she had just said goodbye to. The contradictions were too complicated for rational, sober thought, let alone half-drunk, emotional thought. She tried to think how a conversation with Anna might begin, but could only think of Anna talking to Richard. In spite of being soothed by its welcome chill, Natasha left the toilet.

The coast was clear, Geoffrey had gone. Natasha returned to her stool, without a drink. Derek came back. He began asking about Geoffrey. Who was he? Did she know him? What had he said? When this failed to receive any response Derek resorted to his familiar routine of charm and apologies. Natasha was aware of his presence yet did not acknowledge him, though he was useful to have around at this moment. She was lonely. Where was Anna?

It had taken Anna ages to get served. She had been unable to make eye contact with any of the bar staff because she had not been able to concentrate. She had been thinking of Richard, out somewhere with his mates – maybe he would remember how much that life appealed to him and wonder why he was tying himself down to another girl when he already had a wife.

Anna was aware of Richard's distraction each time they'd finished making love. He had a habit, afterwards, of staring, and struggled to begin a sentence that never came. She was happy to interpret this as him wanting to tell her he had fallen in love with her, yet was too afraid to ask in case the words sounded foolish, in view of the relatively short time they had been together. She wondered now if perhaps he was only gathering the courage to finish with her.

'I'll get these,' Richard told the barman, sneaking up behind Anna. He handed over a twenty-pound note. 'And a Jack Daniels with Coke, please.'

The affection of the joke – a repeat of their first meeting – and her delight at seeing him, compelled Anna to embrace him.

He told her. 'If you tell me to go, that's fine. I understand. You've come out with Natasha, this is women out together, they don't want boyfriends interfering. So tell me and I'll go.'

'It doesn't matter. Natasha's boyfriend – well, her ex, you know, who I told you about? – well he's turned up, so I would only have been in the way and . . . oh, sod it, I wouldn't have cared anyway. I'm just so glad to see you. I haven't enjoyed myself at all tonight, I've been thinking about you.'

'Cheers!'

'You know what I mean. I can't believe you came to this shit-hole just to find me! Well, what do you reckon to the place?'

'It's . . .' Richard searched too long for an encouraging word until his failure caused them both to laugh.

'I know it is,' Anna told him. They got their drinks.

Richard noticed that his glass was dirty and asked for another. He then had to ask for ice. His twenty-pound note was written on, picked at, held up to the light.

Looking past Derek, who still appeared to be talking to her, Natasha finally saw Anna and Richard. The couple seemed oblivious to everything. From a distance she saw how comfortable they were together, how they couldn't help smiling.

They moved away from the bar although they didn't immediately go over to Natasha. Anna wanted to enjoy Richard's undiluted attention. They punctuated every remark with a kiss. He told her about his evening so far, how little he had enjoyed himself when only a very short time ago – before Anna was in his life – those nights out with his mates were all he cared about. He couldn't enjoy their humour: he thought their jokes were vicious; he couldn't involve himself in the pursuit of girls; he was no longer interested.

'Even alcohol has no effect on me,' he told Anna. 'You've made me permanently sober! I don't know if I'll be able to forgive you!'

In here, this club, crowded and suspicious, he was now – finally – experiencing some of the disorientating effects of drink. He had to check himself in mid-sentence to remember the question he had been asked, then judge whether his response was relevant. He was determined now, tonight, here, when she could have no misconception about how he felt, to confess the lie. He wanted to tell her that there wasn't any wife. He was single and wanted to be with her. Anna looked eager and gorgeous, made all the more beautiful by eyes which never looked away from his. She finished her drink – which reminded her she still held Natasha's full bottle. She guided Richard towards Natasha, then stopped some distance away.

'What?' he said, asking why they had halted.

Geoffrey was gone. Natasha was now back with Derek, who seemed to be speaking relentlessly even though Natasha didn't register a word.

Anna asked Richard to buy her a fresh drink while she took Natasha hers. She scowled at Derek. 'Didn't she tell you to fuck off?' Anna reminded him. 'Surely even you, dense as you are, couldn't have misunderstood that.'

'Why don't *you* fuck off?' Derek answered back. 'We were doing all right till you interfered.'

'How were we doing all right?' Natasha asked. 'I do not like you, Derek. I do not want to talk to you.'

Derek pleaded, 'All I ask is that you hear me out –'

'Bye-bye,' Anna told him.

'I'm fucking warning you –' Derek began. He stopped when Richard arrived next to Anna. Richard gave Anna her fresh drink.

'What's going on?'

Derek did a quick survey of Richard: well-groomed hair, smart suit, unblemished face. A push-over; some office boy he could pagger in a breath.

'Who the fuck are you? If this is your bird I think you'd better tell her to keep quiet, else I'm going to pick you up and knock her out using you. Got it?'

Three bouncers halted any further aggression. Surveying Richard as quickly and as dismissively as Derek had, they concluded that he must be the victim, and began to throw Derek out. Richard explained that they were going to leave anyway.

Outside, Derek chose to focus his aggression on Richard, who started to walk away. Richard kept silent while Natasha and Anna shouted abuse.

'Don't fucking turn your back on me, you stuck-up twat,' Derek shouted, pushing Richard in the shoulder. Richard stopped. He turned. He grabbed Derek's hand, twisting the wrist until Derek was on his knees, his face contorted in agony.

'Look, just leave us alone –' Richard began to reason. Anna and Natasha had different reasoning. Anna stomped on the back of Derek's calf, Natasha smashed down on his twisted, outstretched arm. Richard had to let go. The three of them left Derek curled up on the pavement in agony, fearful of more attacks.

'I've seen a violent side to you tonight,' Richard told Anna, grinning, as they walked towards a taxi stand.

'Yeah, so watch yourself,' she grinned back. 'Where did you learn to do that, you know, with his wrist?'

'I took five Judo lessons when I was eleven. That's the one move I remember. Handy, isn't it?'

The three of them took a taxi back to Anna and Natasha's flat. Though Richard was paying the fare, Natasha sat in the front so that the couple could sit together. They tried to engage her in conversation. Though she kept her replies light-hearted she also kept them short – and so they soon only had eyes for each other. Anna held onto Richard's arm, smiling as if her face had never known any other expression. Drunk and too happy, Richard no longer remembered that he had intended to confess to his lie.

Back at the flat, Natasha dreaded being kept awake by the sounds of Anna and Richard having sex. Fortunately she had drunk enough to make her fall asleep quickly, and she slept soundly.

In the morning she was out of bed, showered and on her way to her parents' a full hour sooner than was necessary.

At her parents' door she thought to herself, 'My life has turned to shit.'

Richard and Anna stayed in bed all morning. Once again having failed to confess, he had decided to hold a party to demonstrate to Anna how happy and relaxed he was about being seen with her in front of people who knew him well. From this she could only deduce that he was not, after all, married.

'I'm going to have a party. I want you to come,' he told her. She would have to ask how this was possible – wasn't she his secret?

She said, 'OK, that sounds like fun.'

'Couples only,' he added, to illustrate the point that he and she were the only couple in his life.

'Why?'

Richard had no real answer. 'To make it even. So that there's an equal number of men and women. And a good excuse not to have to invite my idiot mates.'

'Then I won't be able to invite Natasha.'

'She'll survive,' Richard said. And for a moment, for the first time, Anna was genuinely mad at him. But she made no protest.

THIRTY-ONE

It became a mantra, repeated ad nauseam. *My life has turned to shit.* Anna would have denied this. She would have tried to sound positive, complimenting Natasha on all the great things she had going for her: being young, smart and pretty.

But the imagined Anna in Natasha's mind was very different.

'It's not that your life's turned to shit, it's that it's always been shit. You've always been too dependent on me, so you've had no time for other friends, or for boyfriends, or for your family. And time's running out. I've found someone who will free me. You're going to be on your own, matey.' In spite of the 'matey', a word Anna often used when she was being belligerent, Natasha now knew she was not imagining hearing Anna's voice, but Brenda, her sister, sat opposite her at the dining table.

'It doesn't work out the way you seem to believe it will, Natasha. You don't just go to a different club and meet Prince-fucking-Charming. That's not how it is. The best you can hope for is that you meet someone whose worst characteristics you can tolerate and whose best ones make your life easier.'

'That's not true,' Natasha told her. 'You're sad and pathetic. You're marrying a man you actively dislike because you have such low self-esteem that you think he's the best you can get.'

'I –' Brenda began. Natasha interrupted these imagined thoughts with her own real thoughts.

'I don't care about losing Geoffrey,' she surmised. 'I care about losing Anna.'

Dinner was finished. Natasha's father began to clear away the dishes. He refused the offered help, wanting to be alone. After dinner he would always take a walk around the garden, to clear his head.

Natasha began to wonder if the imagined conversation she had held with Brenda had, in fact, really happened.

Keith hadn't come with Brenda today, their argument now in its sixth day – which was by no means a record for them. In the living room the three women had several minutes to fill before *EastEnders* began. Preferring to stomach a lecture rather than weather this awkwardness, Natasha announced that she was no longer seeing Geoffrey. Her mother was especially sympathetic.

'He lied to me, Mum. I thought he was well-off and it turns out he isn't.'

On hearing this, she told her daughter, 'In that case you're well out of it, love.'

'Money isn't everything,' Brenda offered.

Her mother remonstrated, 'Only people with money say that.'

'Me and Keith might be better off than some, but I'd rather be in love than wealthy.'

'Don't you listen to her, Natasha!' her mother said, moving next to her elder daughter and putting an arm around her shoulders, even though Natasha was showing no signs of distress. She pointed towards the kitchen door, towards her husband. 'That's what marrying for love gets you – you end up tied and bound to a pillock like that. Stuck for the rest of your fucking life. Love fades, money is for ever.'

Brenda sat at the other side of Natasha. 'Marry for love, Natasha – just make certain it is love.'

Natasha leant forward to break contact with both her sister and mother, then dared to ask Brenda the question which had intruded through the day because until then no one had had the courage to banish it by asking.

'So how come Keith isn't with you? Are you having trouble again?'

Their mother moved away from Natasha to sit next to Brenda.

'He just annoys me. Constantly. Even when I'm alone in the

house I find him annoying me to death. Perhaps I shouldn't marry him if I don't love him?'

Her mother responded to this before Natasha could answer. 'There's a word for women who wait for love before they marry. *Spinsters!*'

The *EastEnders* theme tune ended any further discussion. After a few moments Brenda excused herself, saying she had a slight headache and would take a walk around the back garden for the fresh air.

'I don't think it's a headache, I think she's upset.' Natasha stood up, pleased to escape from the room. 'I'll see if she's all right, Mum.'

'I'll come with you.'

'Best not to. She'll think we're ganging up.'

In the garden Brenda was standing over their father. He was poking at the grass with a gardening fork, digging for any reason to stay out of the house. Neither of them spoke.

The back garden was rimmed with short hedges. There were no flowers. A flagstone path divided a well-groomed lawn. At the far end of the lawn there were two relics from the girls' childhood: a metal swing, recently painted to avoid becoming derelict, and a tall wooden Wendy house with a small veranda and window-boxes. When their father had first built the house the girls had spent whole days playing inside. During their adolescent years the house had fallen into disuse. Natasha guessed the swing and Wendy house were kept in good repair in readiness for future grandchildren, or were being preserved as reminders of a time when their home was a little happier.

'Has your mother sent you out?' Natasha's father asked her.

'No.'

'Is she watching *EastEnders* alone?'

'Yes.'

'Uh, she won't like that,' he said, grinning.

Natasha looked at the kitchen window. Her mother was standing there, but ducked out of view as Natasha looked over.

'I used to ask if I could play in there,' Brenda said, pointing at the Wendy house. 'But whenever Anna was here, you never let me.'

'Didn't I?' Natasha asked, though she remembered clearly enough.

Brenda looked back towards the house, as if considering going back inside. To her mother. She stayed.

'You're better off – the way you are,' Brenda told her sister. 'You're better off without a man.'

'Do you really think that's true?' Natasha wondered.

'I feel as if I've wasted most of my life pursuing things before I'd questioned whether they were worth chasing. I'm with Keith and I don't know if I want to be with him.'

'I can't help thinking, then, that if you're not happy with him you shouldn't marry him. Don't listen to Mum.'

'It isn't that simple.'

'It's exactly that simple, isn't it? You work, so you have money. You don't have kids.'

Brenda stood on the veranda of the Wendy house.

'You mean walk out and leave everything behind?'

'So you leave him and start again . . . You're still young enough to start again. Christ, you're younger than me, Brenda. It wouldn't take you long to get everything I've got. A week, tops.'

For a while Brenda said nothing.

'Start *what* again? And if I don't marry Keith – *what*? I remember what the *Apollo* was like. I don't want to go back to that life of . . . looking for someone. It's fun when you're young, but as you get older it becomes . . . I don't know. Undignified. I'm sorry, Nat, but you know what I mean. There's an increasing desperation to people as they get older. Everyone over a certain age has a story to tell, and I can't ever imagine being interested.'

'Then be alone. It's better to be on your own than to be with someone and be unhappy. It is.'

'No it isn't.' Brenda turned and looked directly – for the first time – at her sister. 'But things are going to be different from now on. I've had enough of his sulks and pettiness. From now on I'm going to assert myself.'

The sense of relief that suddenly filled Natasha was so overpowering that she smiled before she could stop herself. Brenda didn't see the smile. Natasha thought about her sister leaving Keith, and realised that her relief was not on Brenda's behalf.

They left the house and began to walk slowly back along the garden path.

Natasha had reached no new conclusions. She had always known that all relationships are riddled with faults. Few people are truly happy. No love is unconditional. She would not allow the first disastrous experience of finding a wealthy man to deter her.

But she no longer had Anna to go out with.

'How do you fancy going out next weekend, me and you?' she asked her sister. They had not been out drinking together since Corinne Slater's hen night, and Brenda was always suggesting that they should.

'I can't. Keith wouldn't like it.'

That evening, Natasha returned to an empty flat. She watched TV until she began to doze, and then went to bed.

By morning, she began to presume that Anna was still with Richard. She became angry that her friend had not even bothered to contact her, keep her informed so that she wouldn't worry.

Natasha arrived at work and Gerard, their manager, asked about Anna's absence. He found her explanation implausible.

'Are you trying to tell me you've no idea where she is or whether or not she'll be coming into work?'

No sooner had he said this than Anna walked in. She was wearing her store uniform. The shop already had customers, some of whom were waiting to be served, so Gerard kept his rebuke quick and moderate.

'What use are you?'

'Wow, Richard this morning!' Anna giggled to Natasha as they later passed each other.

'I told him we'd be late for work, but . . . he had a stiffy, and I was horny as hell. So . . . but what a rush!'

Natasha wanted to say nothing. But couldn't resist.

'The sex?'

'No! Afterwards was a rush!' Anna exclaimed, still smirking. 'He drove me to the flat, then waited till I was dressed, then drove me here. I need a shower! He's picking me up tonight at seven, so that'll be another rush!'

Anna's make-up had been patched up rather than freshly applied; her hair was tidy at the front and top though dishevelled at the back.

Anna casually told Natasha about Richard's party.

'I would never think of going to a house party without you,' Natasha reprimanded.

'It isn't a house party. It's a party . . . in a house, that's all.'

'Explain the difference.'

'It's not like the house parties we've been to. This is dinner, and wine and . . .'

'So I can't come because it'll be good food and drink and maybe some eligible well-off men there? Sounds like a nightmare.'

'Not eligible men. Men in couples.'

Natasha made no answer, but didn't look away.

For the rest of the day Natasha contrived things so the two girls had little chance to talk again. She kept herself busy, pouncing on every customer the minute they walked into the shop, being extremely helpful, suggesting different styles and insisting that they tried each style in different sizes to ensure a comfortable fit. At five o'clock Gerard congratulated Natasha on her day's individual sales figure. Anna bit her top lip; Natasha blushed with embarrassment. Until this day, as a point of principle, the two girls had always done everything possible to avoid Gerard's praise.

'What about my day's individual sales figures, Gerard?' Anna taunted.

'What use are you?'

On the bus home Natasha deliberately sat stony-faced as Anna talked about Richard. Anna did not notice Natasha's silence.

THIRTY-TWO

Anna continued to talk about Richard all week: at breakfast, on the way to work, at work, and for the few minutes they had together in the evening. She was oblivious to everything else, including Natasha's total lack of response.

At work, Natasha made every effort to be wherever Anna was not. If Anna was on the shop floor serving, then Natasha would be in the store room. If Anna was pricing shoes, Natasha would be altering the displays.

In the evenings, should they have tea together, Anna always rushed, eager to begin her preparations for meeting Richard. When they didn't eat together, Anna would run straight into the bathroom, and then get dressed and leave the house without exchanging more than a few perfunctory words with Natasha.

It got to the stage where Natasha could only relax after Anna had left. The phone seldom rang. She dreaded that sound. It was never Geoffrey, and Natasha hated herself for wanting it to be. She consoled herself by thinking that she really only wanted him for company, now that she had lost Anna.

To fill the time, Natasha tried to read. Between them, the girls had acquired an eclectic mixture of books: self-help, romances, Reader's Digest compilations and other popular novels. Natasha never progressed far with any of them, tossing them aside within pages. She found reading in silence too oppressive, but if she read with music on, she found this too distracting. She watched TV, but when the telly was turned off at the end of the night, and Anna still wasn't home, the silence before she fell asleep haunted her.

'I am so lonely,' she told the room. Then, 'I'm so lonely that I'm even *talking to myself*!'

She had prepared a spiteful yet dignified speech in case Geoffrey had phoned on Monday, re-emphasising how she had set herself on a definite course, and any deviation from it would be a betrayal of her aspirations. To conclude, she would add that any attempt to win her back was futile. If he had phoned on Tuesday, she would have told him that she was willing to give him another chance. On Wednesday, she would have told him to go to hell. On Thursday, she might have told him that she could only explain these contradictions by admitting that she had begun to fall in love with him.

Geoffrey didn't phone.

On Friday morning, Natasha read through the *Radio Times* in anticipation of a Saturday night at home. Nothing appealed to her.

'My mistake,' she told an absent Anna, 'has been to concentrate on one friend. You've now met a man you genuinely like and so, naturally, want to spend as much time with him as possible. That's fine, but . . .'

She decided that she would go out the next night with Stephanie and Nicola. They were always asking her out, on the one condition that they would not go to the *Apollo*.

She went to bed early, staying awake long enough to hear Anna and Richard come home.

Natasha tried to work out what she would wear tomorrow night; then anticipated the journey into town, alone. She thought about what they might talk about, and how she might feel about the nightclub they took her to, which was bound to be full of people far younger than herself. She decided to bow to the inevitable and stay in.

At breakfast, Natasha sat at the table with Anna and Richard. Anna was dressed and ready for work, while Richard was still in the clothes he had worn last night. The couple made a point of involving Natasha in their conversation. When they were in Richard's car, they discussed how they might spend the evening. Richard asked Natasha about her plans.

She told him she was going out.

Anna made no comment.

As soon as she arrived at work, Natasha asked the two friends if they were going out that night. She also asked if they would be going out with their boyfriends.

'We're out on our own tonight,' Stephanie answered. 'So we can enjoy ourselves.'

'Will you be going to a nightclub?'

'Of course!'

'Which one?' Natasha's enquiry was definitely sounding less casual now.

'We usually just see what happens,' Nicola told her.

Natasha worded her next response cautiously. 'I only ever go to the *Apollo* with Anna, but she's out with her boyfriend tonight.'

They asked Natasha out with them.

For the rest of the day Natasha hoped Anna would ask her about her plans for that night. Anna had seen Natasha talking to Stephanie and Nicola. Annoyingly, though they were usually so chatty, they didn't mention their plans for the evening to Anna. Natasha became even more convinced there was hardly any point in going out.

Back home, Natasha and Anna avoided each other. The nearest they came to conversation was when they each turned up the music in their rooms, trying to drown out the sound of the other's.

After Richard picked Anna up at seven, Natasha had a bit of time in the house alone, so she sat there, dressed up, make-up on, and wished she could just stay in, if only she could guarantee that staying in tonight would not be a prelude to a new life of Saturday nights spent in watching TV.

'Why didn't you even say goodbye?' Natasha asked aloud. She heard no response from the imagined Anna.

As she was about to order a taxi there was a knock on the door.

*

By replacing her, Natasha had cleansed Geoffrey of his Janette fixation. He felt as if he had replaced measles with chicken pox.

He had begun to accept that he would never meet someone he could love who would return that love equally, but he still clung to some hope. There was still some fight left in him.

Geoffrey considered all Natasha's possible reactions when she opened the door to find him standing before her. For a while these thoughts distracted him, but when he knocked he was flooded with fear, paralysing him so that he could not turn and run – which was suddenly his dearest wish.

'It's taken me a week to summon up the courage to come and see you. All I've thought about is you,' Geoffrey began.

'That's not my problem,' Natasha snarled at him. 'I'm not going to tell you anything different from what I told you in the *Apollo*.'

'You don't think that maybe you should give me another chance?'

Natasha took a deep breath and then took a moment to speak, as if her reply was only now occurring to her.

'I have thought about it, but then again I've had so many thoughts, there's nothing that hasn't crossed my mind. Geoffrey, I do like you. I've set myself on a certain course and I'm determined to see it through. Too often in my life I've been determined to do something but then let my resolve slip. If I do that again I'm betraying myself, and I don't want that to happen. Look, anyway, as you can see I'm going out, and I don't want to be late.'

'But –' he began. She interrupted him and he was glad to be interrupted: the 'but' was spoken with beaten despondency, the complete opposite of the attitude he had hoped to strike.

'No! I don't want either of us to say any more. You'd better go now. You're going to end up putting me in a gloomy mood and I don't want that. I've been miserable enough lately, and tonight I want to enjoy myself.'

Geoffrey said goodbye and walked away. Natasha phoned

for a taxi. As she waited she became appalled at herself for having enjoyed the hurt she had clearly caused him. Minutes later she was glad of this hurt; he deserved it for not persevering hard enough.

THIRTY-THREE

Natasha had expected to see both Stephanie and Nicola dressed causally in trousers and flat shoes, intending only to get drunk and have a dance. When they both arrived in very short skirts, and a top that was backless in the case of Nicola and armless in the case of Stephanie, Natasha immediately knew that the girls were clearly on the look out for new men. Both were in high heels, completely unsuitable for dancing. Natasha had not discussed clothes with them beforehand, and was dressed in trousers and a plain white cardigan. She felt like a supervising teacher at a school disco.

Nothing about the night surprised Natasha. When she talked, she felt like a pensioner boring the milkman. Though the girls politely feigned interest, nodding and responding where appropriate, their eyes were constantly roving around the room, searching for men.

Natasha marvelled at how accepting the girls were of compliments they were paid, how inexperienced they were in dealing with idiots and how eager they were to be chatted up. These girls were no substitute for Anna. She had never really expected them to be, but had hoped that together they would at least have fun. Perhaps the young no longer know how to have fun, she thought, and heard Anna's voice in her head, 'I can't believe you said that. *You old bag.*' Though Natasha smiled at Anna's imagined response, every acquaintance she spoke to who was her own age confirmed her feelings. She bumped into a woman she had gone to school with. Natasha was shocked at how old she appeared, and worried in case the woman thought the same about her.

The queue for the club was the first indication she might not enjoy the place she was being taken to. Even before they entered, the music was deafening. In Natasha's old bag mentality, all those tunes and beats sounded similar, and the words were clichéd and repetitive.

To her relief, she gradually realised that the club was not the house/jungle/garage nightmare she had dreaded. There were three floors, the ground floor being the youngest, loudest, busiest; the middle floor was quieter, and the top floor had tunes with decipherable lyrics, a greater cross-section of customers, and few enough people to allow speedy service at the bar. Nicola and Stephanie wanted to stay on the ground floor, but Natasha, in mother mode, dragged them upstairs. The girls used this time to discuss their opinions on how the evening had passed so far and how they hoped the night would continue. They bitched about other girls, even those they had spoken to pleasantly: how fat they were, how badly dressed, and how they had failed to find boyfriends.

'I wish we hadn't come here,' Nicola said.

'I know what you mean,' Stephanie added. 'It's like we come here every week now, I'm bored of it. It never changes.'

'How many times have you come?' Natasha asked.

'Four or five times now – easily that many.'

Natasha squirmed.

Anna and Natasha's nights out at the *Apollo* had become so frequent that for Natasha the memory had become generic: hamburgers after work, Anna's last-minute choice of clothes, the familiar route of pubs, the anticipation of heading towards the *Apollo*, then the disappointment. So there was nothing else to do but drink more, take the piss out of the idiots who tried to chat them up, or instead just stay on the dance floor, getting hotter, into a frenzy of heat and beat. On some nights they just talked to each other, or to those few lads who were fun to talk to. Saturday night was always a necessary reminder for them both of why they were friends. Like good health, Natasha had once taken the joys of Saturday nights out with Anna for granted, but now it was gone she missed the experience – not only of going to the *Apollo* with her best friend, but also of knowing that that was how the week would end. Now there was no such certainty.

When Nicola and Stephanie had succeeded in persuading Natasha to go down to the ground floor she was relieved to discover that, in the dark and the crowds, she did not stand out as alarmingly as she had feared. *I am an old bag. I think bad lighting is more flattering.* Natasha saw that beneath the younger, prettier faces, the better, smarter, more fashionable clothes, the more discreet encounters between the sexes, and the fact that none of these youngsters acted drunk, the real glaring difference between this club and the *Apollo* was that at the *Apollo* people had fun: they laughed and smiled and joked. In this club everyone was too damned preoccupied with being unblemished. Consequently they all acted bored. Natasha was glad she didn't fit in. At least she understood that the object of going out was to have a laugh. The transforming effect of her improved humour was immediate: she bought another round, out of turn, then began to try and have some fun, bitching about people to make them laugh. When Nicola pointed out a boy who had taken her fancy, Natasha alarmed her by offering to talk to the boy on her behalf. She assured her she had only been teasing, but when Nicola turned her back Natasha was at the boy in seconds.

'Hello,' she said. 'Don't look behind me, but I'm out with two friends. See them? Look over slowly, very casually.'

He span around as if a brick had hit him on the back of the head.

'They're staring at us,' he told Natasha.

'They're wondering what I'm saying to you. The fact is, one of them fancies you and I'm here to find out if you fancy her back. See the girl with the bare arms – not her, but the other one. She's called Nicola.'

'She's nice,' the boy said.

'But you don't fancy her? If you do, and bearing in mind what I've just told you – why are you still listening to me? Why aren't you over there talking to her?'

'Well, I . . . Because I . . . The thing is, I don't know what to say. Can't I go back with you and you can introduce me? I'm Gary.'

'I'm Dave,' called another lad, one of Gary's friends. He'd been listening in. 'I always have something to say – and I fancy her with the bare arms. What's she called?'

Gary and Dave had come out with a gang of several other lads, who now followed, flocking around Nicola, Stephanie and Natasha. The three girls enjoyed the fuss made of them by a crowd of boys competing with each other for their attention.

The lad who was trying his best to charm Natasha – talking about his job and the car he had just bought – was perhaps only three or four years her junior, yet she felt so little threat from him, and so little interest in him, it was as if he were her son's best friend, trying to impress her with boasts of doing well at soccer and maths. She hoped for his sake that he read her smile as attraction rather than what it really was, condescension.

At one o'clock, Stephanie, Nicola and the gang of lads decided they were heading off to another club, one that stayed open until three. In the toilet, Natasha told the girls she wouldn't be coming with them.

'Come on, Nat,' Nicola pleaded. 'Come with us. I've had a brilliant night so far.'

'I'm going to hang around here for a while, go up to the top floor, sit down and chill out,' she answered. They didn't believe Natasha was staying on her own, and thought she must have arranged to meet a man.

She waited for them to leave and then went upstairs and found a vacant buffet on the fringes of a large group of people, where she could sit without encroaching on them, yet close enough so that anyone who saw her would think she wasn't on her own.

Her first thought was of Geoffrey. She thought back to the night they'd first met and the things they'd talked about that evening. She dreaded that he would stay in her thoughts all through the night, and that consequently she wouldn't be able to sleep.

'You don't look as if you're enjoying yourself.' His face was less than a foot from hers. He was bending down so he could stare directly at her. Lost in thought, it took her a moment to work out that he was speaking to her and expected a reply.

'What do you mean?' she asked. She began to assess him: his appearance, his manner, his possible intentions.

'You look sad, that's all.'

She smiled to contradict him, which he took as encouragement to pull up a buffet and sit next to her.

To fend off further thoughts of Geoffrey she indulged this stranger. Like her, he had never been in this club before, had come out with younger work colleagues who bored him, and now felt out of place. He had spotted her and chosen to speak to her because she stood out by being wisely bored.

'I figured that anyone who was bored in here must have the right idea, which is when I decided that you might be interesting to talk to.'

She knew he was flattering her, but she chose to give him the benefit of the doubt.

'I wasn't bored, just reflective. So I don't know if I'll be interesting to talk to, but you're welcome to try.'

He introduced himself and bought her a drink. They talked for about forty minutes, until the bouncers began sweeping up the customers, urging them to finish their drinks and leave.

'There's nothing to it,' Natasha imagined telling Anna. 'We thought smarter blokes were scarce when really they were only scarce at the *Apollo*. This is easy.'

'What's so fucking smart about him?'

'He's charming.'

'And that's such a rare commodity in men who are trying to fuck you!' Natasha shut out Anna's critical voice. This guy was nice, pleasant, smart, she told herself. She left with him and went back to his home.

On his couch, as they kissed, Natasha knew that she had been entirely passive, letting him hail a taxi, guide her into it, and then tell the driver the destination without once consulting her. She hadn't told him at any time that sex was not going to happen.

As he tentatively touched her breast, sex became inevitable, simply because stopping him now, explaining, going home, was all too much trouble. To go home and go to bed alone, to think of Geoffrey . . . How much easier to stay, have her sadness deflected. Casual sex was a more certain device than watching TV, reading a book or waiting for another man she genuinely liked. It had taken her the best part of three decades to find even one bloke she liked.

As he became more passionate, and one of his hands worked its way down her body, from her waist down to her knee, Natasha had to concentrate both on kissing with equal passion, and on expelling the stupid thought which had manifested itself in her head without warning. She wondered how she might regard Geoffrey after she had slept with this man; then she wondered what Geoffrey might think about her should he ever find out. His fingers gripped the toggle of her trousers' zip.

In the taxi home she began to calm down. He had reacted as she had known he would, accusing her of being a tease and of leading him on.

She had moved his hand; then pushed him off her and stood up. He had been insulting and abusive as she tidied herself to leave. He had even scared her when she began to retaliate – and she became worried that he was going to hit her. He had grabbed her arms and tried to force her down, but she had been agile enough to avoid him. She dodged past him and ran out of the house. As she began to run down his street, he had continued to shout abuse from the front door.

'Do you still want my phone number?' she yelled back, mocking herself more than him.

She'd taken her shoes off to run home and with freezing feet she entered the flat. She heard the energetic sounds of Richard and Anna having sex: Richard's grunts, Anna's moans, the bed's creaking protests. Hearing the same sound from her parents' room when she was very young, Natasha had thought her parents were trying to lift the bed.

Instead of going to her room, where Anna and Richard's athletic/asthmatic noises would be even louder, Natasha sat on the couch. She had not turned the lights on in the living room. The darkness made their noises more prominent; the headboard battered against the wall like they were trying for an open-plan living room. Natasha massaged her feet then lay down. She considered shouting to them to shut up. The noises sickened her, but she continued to listen. Anna's voice grew less and less recognisable, as she approached either ecstasy or asphyxiation. Richard's groans were constant, but gained speed, interspersed with an irregular curse.

Natasha fell into an uneasy sleep accompanied by the sound of other people making love. She wished she could contact Geoffrey.

Natasha was woken the following morning by sounds she had never heard before. *Anna was making breakfast!* She created an even greater racket than the night before. She made washing dishes sound like a suit of armour falling down a fire escape. Natasha walked into the kitchen scratching and yawning. Then remembered.

'Richard isn't still here, is he?'

'He's gone. I asked him to go. You look like shit, did you have a good night?'

Natasha was still in last night's clothes, creased and dishevelled. She had dragged herself off the couch and into her bedroom only hours earlier. To perpetuate the image of recovering from a good night out, she sat down and rubbed her eyes, yawned and sighed heavily. She told Anna that Geoffrey had called but that she had been able to expel him from her mind.

Anna served Natasha breakfast. Toast and tea, serving the tea in a pot and cutting the toast diagonally to give the breakfast more substance. To complete the illusion she put margarine, a jar of jam and a jar of marmalade out on the table.

'It's weird to see you like this,' Anna said as she sat down alongside her friend. In Natasha's eyes was a remote sadness, a glaze which was not tiredness or pain. 'You know, so bothered about a man. What was so wonderful about him?'

Natasha answered, 'Nothing. He wasn't so good-looking, he didn't split my sides with laughter, he wasn't tall or . . . And, he was exactly what I have said I'm *not* looking for. He's a complete bum. He's unemployed – which is even worse than . . .' She wanted to continue listing his bad points, but she had exhausted them. 'All it is, *he gets it*. The shorthand is there, you know? One of those guys that don't judge or pretend to judge you harshly if you're crude or pretend to be crude, or if you pretend to be violent or if you pretend to boss them around. I was instantly, within minutes, relaxed around him, not having to think through everything I said first because I knew if I said something fucking stupid he'd tell me, then the joke would become me admitting it, or defending myself, or even threatening to batter him for calling me stupid. He had no pretensions I couldn't laugh at without knowing he wouldn't mind me laughing. That was what it was like straight away, then it got better. Very quickly. God, thanks, Anna! You've got me thinking about him again! Tell me about Richard, for fuck's sake. What's so wonderful about *him*?'

Anna was eating toast. Eager to answer, she began her reply before she had swallowed. Crumbs gathered around her lips.

Soon bored of all this, Natasha asked: 'Yeah, yeah, OK, so if he's so wonderful, why can't I come to his goddamn party?'

THIRTY-FOUR

Natasha went to her parents' house as usual. She had a terrible Sunday.

Richard returned for Anna and took her out. She had a wonderful Sunday. The two girls didn't meet up again until Monday morning. They had breakfast in virtual silence, then said nothing at all on the journey to work.

They didn't speak to each other until Natasha was replacing shoes on their appropriate shelves on the outside racks and Anna came out to intercept a delivery which could surely only be for her. The delivery woman struggled beneath a large display of flowers, checking an address she had written down on a card against the shop sign. Natasha and Anna followed her inside.

'I'll bet they're from Richard,' Anna announced. Gerard Peters, the shop manager, intercepted the flowers and read the card. Anna stood in front of him, arms outstretched.

Gerard handed the flowers to Natasha.

'Are they from a customer?'

'How likely is that?' Gerard handed her the accompanying card, which simply said, FROM GEOFFREY. Anna failed to keep the expression of dismay, even humiliation, from her face.

On the bus home Natasha hugged the flowers like a new mother would her child. Anna watched, not speaking, not being spoken to. She watched in disbelief as Natasha even stroked the flowers. Though being sent flowers was a cliché, like receiving grapes when in hospital, Natasha had still been delighted. The flowers knocked Anna's smug smile out of joint.

At home Anna's hay fever began in earnest. Natasha acted as if she was oblivious to her friend's sneezing and watering eyes. Anna dared not point out the obvious cause of her affliction in case Natasha might think her whinging was a symptom of jealousy rather than hay fever. Natasha spent twenty minutes arranging the flowers in empty coffee jars. (Anna's condition had made owning a vase pointless.) Watching for as long as she could bear, Anna – her nose reddening – could not contain her anger any longer. She had Richard's party coming up, and she was determined to look her best.

'Can't you put those flowers in your room, Nat?'

'I want to be able to look at them.'

'What do you want to look at them for? They're not going to do anything.'

'I don't ask you to put Richard's presents in your room.'

Richard had bought Anna a CD and a watch, neither of which were offensive enough to warrant isolation.

Anna feared her nose would make her look like an alcoholic. She dared not mention the party again to Natasha.

'Why has Geoffrey sent you flowers if you've told him you don't want to see him again? Why would he persevere if he thinks you're just a mercenary bitch, only interested in men with money?'

'Because he likes me! He obviously doesn't think that! He's smart enough to have realised –'

Natasha was silenced by the telephone ringing. She had expected this call, yet hadn't prepared herself for it. With no idea of what she was going to say, she still had to be sure that whatever answer she gave was the one she truly meant.

'Did you get the flowers?' Geoffrey asked.

'Why did you send them?' Natasha demanded. 'And why are you phoning me?'

'I'm going to call at your flat. Tonight. Seven o'clock.' He waited, expecting her to protest. Anna glared at Natasha, which kept them both silent. Geoffrey continued: 'I'll be there at seven exactly. I'll knock once. If you don't answer, then I know I'm wasting my time and I'll never bother you again.'

He hung up. *I'll never bother you again.* Even though this was only an echo of the desire she had expressed, the finality was a shock for Natasha.

'What time are you going out?' she asked Anna.

'Richard's calling for me at seven thirty.'

Natasha told her about Geoffrey and asked if she would answer the door on her behalf.

'Only if you agree to keep those flowers in your room.'

'All right. Tell him . . . Tell him . . . You'll think of something to say,' Natasha said, not really believing Anna would tell him anything suitable.

The girls ate a meal together, an event which now happened rarely. Immediately after they had finished eating Anna began – to Natasha's amazement – washing up the dishes.

'My God, being in love is turning you into a woman.'

When Natasha did the washing-up she had the water scalding hot and used rubber gloves. Anna had the water scalding hot and plunged her bare hands into it, grabbing a dish then pulling it free to clean in the cooler air. Natasha would construct a carefully-thought out structure of dishes, to let them dry quickly and evenly. Anna filled the rack hastily, making a ramshackle construction which tottered and slid. Two glasses slipped, but fortunately they both fell into the bowl. Anna shouted 'Fuck'. Natasha laughed. Anna joined in the laughter.

'Move,' Natasha said. 'I'll wash up.'

'Nothing's changed, you know. It might not seem like it – but you're still more important to me than anyone else in the world, including Richard.'

'I know nothing's changed. You're still useless around the house.'

The washing-up done, Anna took a shower and Natasha was left alone to fondle again the flowers Geoffrey had sent. She began to think, as she heard Anna happily singing 'Like A Virgin', that she could tell Geoffrey that they could be friends *only*. If he accepted this then he could accompany her to the party. She would explain that she wanted to meet some of the men Richard knew, those like him, in well-paid jobs. She gambled that even under these cruel conditions Geoffrey would still want to go to the party in the hope of reminding her of how well matched they were.

Natasha heard the shower stop at three minutes to seven.

She looked out of the living room window. She saw Geoffrey. He was getting out of an old Mini; then he approached the house.

Anna came out of the bathroom. She had a towel wrapped around her hair and another around her body.

'Is he here yet?'

'No,' Natasha lied, ashamed of her broken resolve. 'Your nose is even redder – the best thing you can do is put Vaseline on it straight away.'

'Fuck!' Anna exclaimed. The noise of her slamming the bathroom door shut coincided exactly with Geoffrey's single knock on the front door.

Natasha did a silent whistle, squeezed her eyes shut and walked decisively, startling Geoffrey with the speed with which she opened the door. He was about to speak; he was smiling.

'Tell me that isn't your car,' she demanded.

'The Mini? I'm afraid it is. Sort of.'

'How can you "sort of" own a car?'

He explained, 'The "sort of" wasn't about ownership, it was referring to the term "car". It's seen better days, that's the best way I can think to put it.'

'Yeah, the sixties, I should guess. On Saturday we're going to a party –'

'*We?*'

'Please don't interrupt or else I'll change my mind. It's a party held by Richard, Anna's boyfriend. We're going as *friends*, Geoffrey. That's clear – right? Friends – nothing else.' He nodded, trying not to smile. 'Pick me up at eight. *But not in that Mini.* Do you think you'll be able to borrow that Jag again, by any chance?'

Geoffrey nodded yes, without thinking – just like any condemned man would when granted a re-trial. Natasha nodded goodbye and closed the door.

When Natasha turned away from the door, Anna had taken the towel off her hair and was smoothing the strands out. She couldn't have made a greater effort not to speak if she had stuffed the towel into her mouth.

'I told him we could go to Richard's party together, but I made a point of telling him it was only as friends, so there can't be any misunderstanding.'

'Friends!'

'Have you ever had a male friend?' Natasha asked Anna. Anna spun the damp towel she was holding around into a rope then flicked the end at Natasha.

'Don't be so fucking stupid!' Anna yelled.

'What do you mean?'

'Men don't understand what a female friend is. To them it's like *apprentice* girlfriend.'

Anna flicked Natasha again. Natasha anticipated the attack and dodged.

Anna continued, 'He bought you flowers. He fancies you, wants to go out with you. And are you so sure you can definitely say you only want him as a friend? Honestly?'

'I'm still determined to stick to my plan. I want to go to Richard's party to meet someone in a good job. If that means taking Geoffrey, leading him on . . . But I'm not leading him on. I've told him. We're only going to be friends.'

'Good luck,' Anna said in a mock-earnest voice which then gave way to laughter as she went into her room to get ready for her evening with Richard.

'I'm glad you're coming, though,' Anna called back. 'It would have been crap without you.'

Geoffrey called at Melanie and Stuart's house during the following week to tell them about his date with Natasha and to borrow a suit. He did not mention borrowing the Jag.

On Saturday night Geoffrey waited until the very last minute before he knocked on their door. He had considered running all the way to their house, so he would be sweating when he arrived, as if he was panic-stricken. Instead, the tightness of the shirt collar had made him sweat naturally. Only when he heard the front door being unlocked did he have his first real anticipation of disaster: the Jag was not in their driveway. This worry appeared groundless when both Melanie and Stuart came to the door.

'Geoff?' Melanie said. 'You're going out with Natasha, aren't you? You're going to be late.'

He told the well-rehearsed lie. 'You'll never guess what's happened! My bloody Mini! Whatever I do it's useless – I just can't get it to start.'

Stuart was suspiciously quick to mention the Jag.

'We'd only be too happy to let you use the Jag, mate.'

'Great!'

'But we put it in for servicing this morning. We don't get it back till Tuesday.'

'Servicing? Tuesday?' Geoffrey stammered.

Melanie told him, 'If you'd have asked earlier in the week . . . That suit looks really good on you though, Geoff.'

'Fantastic. We'll be the best-dressed couple on the bus.'

Faced with diminishing options, Geoffrey had to return to his flat. He would have to take the Mini, and he would now be very late. He had no reason to believe she would wait.

THIRTY-FIVE

Natasha was hogging the mirror over the bathroom sink, checking her teeth and her make-up. Anna forced her aside so she would have space to do the same. The girls began to play-fight, vying for position.

They dressed, as usual, in Natasha's room. Natasha was aware, though she made no comment on this change, of the greater care Anna now took in dressing, making certain no underwear lines were visible through the cloth; she made several adjustments to make sure her bra strap was hidden. Her eyebrows were plucked individually rather than in tufts; mascara was applied with cautious, faint strokes rather than daubed on in gluey clumps; each hair out of place was a personal affront she ruthlessly disciplined into obedience.

'Are we ready?' Natasha asked. 'It's going to be a good night.'

'You think so?'

'Don't you?'

A pause. Then a very unconvincing 'Yes.'

'I hope Geoffrey's made an effort with his appearance. I don't want him to look out of place. But I don't know if I have the right – as a friend rather than girlfriend – to criticise him. There's a whole new set of rules to this that I know nothing about.'

'It won't work. You can't do it.'

'Yes I can,' Natasha said. 'I'm too cynical to really fall for him – not if I set my mind against it.'

'You? Too cynical? You weep buckets during *Animal Hospital*.'

Natasha knew that Anna was wrong. Geoffrey wasn't stupid,

and he wasn't immature. If he did adhere to the conditions then she had a good chance of forming a friendship with someone she genuinely enjoyed being with. With Anna increasingly less likely to be around, Natasha would need a friend.

Natasha had only once ever had a male friend. This was when she was fourteen and, for a short while, had a paper round. On her very first day one of the regular lads, Mark, completed his round and came to help her finish hers. He was aware of obstacles like dogs and difficult-to-find addresses. He carried the bag for Natasha while she delivered the rest of the newspapers.

He came to help her again the next day, and then the day after that. After work they would then walk some of the way home together. Natasha was not yet aware of the concept of a platonic friendship; she only knew that she liked Mark, but not in a sexual way. She presumed he felt the same way and told him her thoughts. In response he made a different confession, telling her that he had never felt as strongly about a girl as he did about her and that he really wanted to go out with her.

She explained that she liked him, he was funny and bitchy and teased her as viciously as she teased him and she could see no problem in being friends with him; but only friends.

Mark never delivered another newspaper from that shop again, leaving without giving notice and without taking the time to explain to Natasha. She never saw him again. Anna jokingly suggested that he might have killed himself rather than face up to life without her.

Geoffrey started his dilapidated white Mini. Lately the car had been as temperamental as a self-neutered cat, and tonight the engine shook so violently that an oblong of rust debris marked the spot where it had been parked. As he drove along his street, blue smoke clouded behind him, and a fanfare of car alarms bade him farewell, activated by the force of the car's vibrations.

Richard immediately knew something was wrong when he saw Anna standing at her door looking out for his car. When he went to kiss her she stopped him.

'You'll smudge my lipstick.'

The butterflies in his stomach went berserk with activity, settling only when she went on to explain that Geoffrey had let Natasha down. Immensely relieved, Richard agreed that Natasha could come on her own. He had learnt how desperately Anna needed an ally against the small army of his friends.

Even though Natasha had got dressed up for a party, in the end she told Anna that she didn't want to draw attention to herself as being the only unaccompanied person there, so Richard and Anna left on their own.

Natasha took off her make-up, and relaxed into some scruffy clothes. If Geoffrey did arrive now he would realise just how much he had ruined her night. In her own mind she would be justified in stabbing him. The Geoffrey who had sent her flowers, and who later came to the house to plead his case, was still the same Geoffrey who had given her a fake phone number. She had forgotten this and been an idiot. Again.

Fifteen minutes later Anna phoned Natasha from Richard's flat. Before she had even asked the question, Natasha told her that Geoffrey had still not turned up but that she was not concerned.

'I don't care, I'm not bothered – really I'm not,' Natasha kept insisting even though Anna had not contradicted her. 'All I think is what an idiot I must have been to think we could have been friends. He's clearly a *FUCKING WANKER!* . . . but I'm not bothered.'

Natasha told Anna to have a good time, then hung up. Less than an hour later, she phoned Anna back. Richard smoothly hid his annoyance as he handed the receiver to his girlfriend.

Natasha began speaking before Anna could: 'You know what? Even if he did show up now, I wouldn't come.' Natasha regretted saying this. If he turned up now with a great explanation, she really would want to go out.

'Natasha – you have to come. I need a friend here.'

Natasha was pleased to hear Anna say this.

'Well – I'll come, but I'm going to beat him up a bit.'

'Oh, no danger,' Anna agreed. 'I'll give him a smack or two myself.'

After she came off the phone Natasha turned off the living-room light and went to the curtain. She watched out for him, wanting the room to be in darkness so he would not see her looking out.

After a few minutes, though it felt like hours, Natasha was ashamed to realise that she was praying for him to arrive; she knew if he did she would not be angry, but grateful.

Natasha was disturbed by the sound of Geoffrey's car. The whole of her street was disturbed by its sound. Within ninety seconds of realising it was him she had brushed her hair, sprayed on some perfume and applied some lipstick. She calmed herself down enough to fake astonishment successfully when she opened the door. She did not let him speak before she launched into her attack. She was determined to abuse, then dismiss him.

'You don't think I'm going anywhere in that old wreck, do you? And look at the time! Why the hell did you chase after me if you were going to let me down like this? I hate it when I've set my mind on going out and then for some reason I can't. It's really frustrating.'

'I'm sorry,' he told her. 'We can still go out, can't we?'

'No! No chance! Not a hope in hell now.'

While Natasha was getting changed, Geoffrey used her phone to call Stuart. Stuart took a long time to answer, and when he did he sounded out of breath.

'Have you been practising?' Geoffrey asked, imagining Stuart in his tennis clothes having just returned from the courts.

Stuart was in bed; Melanie was clawing at his back.

'Sort of,' Stuart answered. 'What is it you want, Geoffrey?'

'I'm phoning from Natasha's. We're not going to the party now. But we're still going out.'

'*And?*' Stuart demanded.

Geoffrey was frustrated by his friend's sarcasm, so asked to speak to Melanie, whom he expected to be more sympathetic. Melanie took the phone from her husband, listened to Geoffrey repeat the same information, to which she answered, 'Good for you', and then hung up.

‘She was out of breath, too,’ Geoffrey said to himself. Then immediately understood that he had interrupted sex.

Natasha came back into the living room.

‘So have you decided where you want to go?’ he asked her.

A childish, yet also evil, grin grew on her face.

THIRTY-SIX

Natasha had last gone skating – the only time she had gone without Anna – when she was sixteen, on a date with Simon Jones. They held hands as they skated, then kissed in the middle of the rink as everyone circled around them.

Geoffrey had never skated in his life.

On the journey to the rink, Geoffrey didn't confess that he couldn't skate. On the contrary, he actually boasted that he could skate well.

The secret was soon known to the world: Natasha glided on to the ice, turning and skating in reverse so she could see where Geoffrey was. Geoffrey had glided two feet out onto the ice, and then stopped. He sat down, turned around, pushed himself back, then clung onto the rail which circled the rink. He made another attempt to move out – his knees touched and his feet bent in on each other so his blades were at an acute angle to the ice.

'I'm a little rusty too, I haven't been skating in years,' Natasha told him, trying to be encouraging as she supported him on the way back to the rail. There, Geoffrey pushed himself off again, straight back towards Natasha. She caught him, turned him and pushed him back – he came close to colliding with a bunch of twelve-year-old girls who, fortunately, were dextrous enough to dodge him. As they skated away they pointed back, giggling.

'I think I'm over-dressed for this,' Geoffrey told Natasha.

'I don't think they were laughing at the way you're dressed,' Natasha told him, smirking and twirling.

More people passed. Geoffrey didn't want to spoil her fun. 'You go ahead, I'll catch up.'

Without hesitation she was off, and every time she skated past him she taunted him, 'Come on! Catch me up!' Then, 'How many times have I lapped you now?' Eventually she stopped beside him. He hadn't moved in fifteen minutes, but miraculously he had remained upright. 'Something tells me you can't skate.'

'I can!' he protested. 'Yes I can, I just can't do those bits where you turn or stop.'

They took a short break. Geoffrey, like an adult, had a coffee; Natasha had a Pepsi, blowing bubbles with the straw, watching the skaters all the time, eager to return to the rink.

They both went back on the ice, though Geoffrey would have preferred to stay sitting down, watching her. She had a compelling grace as she skated, while on the ice all his most feared attributes – his clumsiness, his awkwardness, his susceptibility to embarrassment – became demonstrably worse. He carried on skating only because she found it funny and her laughter added to her fun. He was sacrificing his dignity to make her happy.

When Natasha had finally had enough, they left the rink, comparing their experiences. On one of the occasions Geoffrey had fallen he had caused a collision of other skaters, creating a pile-up of bodies. Natasha had laughed so hysterically that no actual noise came out: she had had to rest against the rail, unable to move, contorted, eyes shut, hand to mouth.

'I nearly broke my neck and you thought it was funny!' Geoffrey reminded her. Straight away, as the memory of him on his back returned, she again began laughing. Geoffrey blamed another skater for his fall, someone who had cut in front of him.

'You're such a baby!' Natasha laughed as he complained.

'He pushed me. I've a good mind to wait around until he comes out then thump him.'

'He was about nine years old, wasn't he?'

Neither wanted the evening to end. Natasha did not fancy the town-centre pubs. He suggested they bought fish and chips and simply walked around. On the way to the fish shop Natasha linked arms with him, realising too late the signal this might give out. She kept her arm there anyway. Walking from the fish shop they discussed some of the kids they had seen at the skating rink. Geoffrey believed the way they dressed and their behaviour towards each other was too adult: they were aware of sex at a much earlier age than he could remember.

'I was fifteen, maybe sixteen when I got my first crush. I guess that's ancient by today's standards.'

'Who was your crush on?' she asked.

'Anna Ford. I still hold out hope.'

Natasha confessed, 'I had so many I don't really remember one specific crush. All I can remember for certain is that when my friends were into boy bands or soap actors I used to think there was something very desirable about Harpo Marx. He was funny and he could take care of himself; he was in complete control of every situation he was in. Yet he seemed vulnerable because he couldn't speak.'

'Wow, a woman who likes Marx Brothers films. This should be where I ask you to marry me.'

'Do you remember your first kiss?'

'Not any more. All I remember is our first kiss.'

She threw a chip, which hit him on his cheek. Relaxed in each other's company, neither had noticed that they were walking along City Road, where the city's prostitutes worked.

'No food tastes better than fish and chips in the open air,' she told him. A raindrop clapped against the newspaper, and she leaned her head forward to stop rain falling on the food. 'It's only drizzle. Do you think it'll get worse?'

They both looked towards the sky.

'Nah,' Geoffrey reassured her.

Within seconds the rain came down like a toilet flush, and continued to fall heavily. Natasha was preoccupied with listening to a prostitute leaning into the window of a car that had pulled up alongside her.

'Why should it be cheaper now it's started raining?' she asked the man in the car.

He answered, 'Because I'm giving you the chance to get out of the rain. I'm doing you a favour.'

She shouted to him, as she walked around to the passenger side, 'Why can't I get perverts, why do I always get tight bastards?'

Geoffrey and Natasha threw away the wet remains of their food and Geoffrey took a moment to calculate the shortest route to the parked Mini.

Being in Geoffrey's Mini was often an ordeal. Sitting there in damp clothes was even worse.

The car was dead. The engine did not even have the decency to attempt a sound.

'What do we do now?' she asked. His flat was far nearer than hers.

They ran, Natasha holding her coat above them like a cape, with Geoffrey's arm around her waist to keep her close. The rain was too forceful for the coat to offer real protection, so by the time they reached Geoffrey's home they were drenched. Their rapid breaths merged with their inexplicable laughter.

Sleeked-back hair, moistened skin, smiles – they'd never seen each other look sexier. They kissed, less than passionately because of the cold.

'I knew it!' Anna would have said. Natasha couldn't imagine how she would reply.

Geoffrey, happy now, fumbled with the key, the delay made all the longer because of his awkwardness and his cold-numbed fingers.

'I need to get dry. Which is your room?'

He knew how the inside of his room looked: the bare bulb, the grey-green wallpaper, the sparse, scrappy furniture. The contradiction of emptiness and congestion. The police would not confine a prisoner to a room in this condition. Natasha was certain to question his affection for her when he led her in.

He hesitated. 'Do you know, we haven't talked about money or work all night. I knew it was possible.'

For want of a reply, she smiled – but this wasn't a reflection of her thoughts. Then he let her into the room.

He immediately put the electric fire on full. She took off her coat; she wiped her hair back; she looked around for anywhere to sit. She was colder.

'This is where you live?' This wasn't a question, so she didn't give him the opportunity to respond. 'You can't want to live like this for ever though. Money brings freedom, it brings comfort, the absence of worry.'

He put the kettle on. He used his last two tea bags. The inside of his cups were dark grey.

'I'm not denying that,' he replied. 'But all I've ever wanted was to be content. To find a way of life which makes me happy and to stay happy.'

He watched the kettle for a while, even though it had just been plugged in. She watched the fire.

'Is that on, Geoff?' She leaned forward, her hands held out to the fire, bringing them closer till they almost touched: warm.

'It takes a while to get going,' he told her.

She stood close to him, behind him. He was still watching the kettle, not daring to face her.

'It's freezing in here. You can't tell me your standard of living doesn't contribute to how happy or unhappy you are.'

Geoffrey answered by shivering. Not just from cold. He knew she was backing away.

'I'm going to have to go home.'

'Don't.' His eyes were scrunched shut.

Natasha's hand was on the door handle. 'I can't catch a cold. I can't afford to take time off work. Go downstairs and phone me a taxi.'

He turned to face her, his eyes watering from being closed so tight; rain still trickled down his cheek.

She told him, 'Don't look so unhappy. If you knew the thoughts I was having about you, you'd be flattered.'

'You never want to see me again?'

'I can't. I've had a really great time tonight. You are exactly everything I've ever looked for. Before. I think you're . . . I really . . . This is useless.'

'What's useless? You rattle off reasons why we should be together – *but you don't want us to be together.* I don't understand. Do you know how rare this chance is?'

She forced herself not to turn away from him.

'I'll bet I understand better than you. But romance is a luxury I prefer to sacrifice in favour of more practical needs.'

'I don't think romance is a *luxury.*' As he said this he knew he had lost. Cold. Wet. Hopeless. Squalid.

She opened the door.

'Phone me a taxi.'

'I'd like you to stay.'

She walked out of the door, telling him: 'I can't. I'm being sensible for once in my life.'

As soon as she arrived home Natasha phoned Anna at Richard's. Anna answered the phone. Natasha explained about Geoffrey's flat.

'I couldn't live like that, or with anyone who could. I had to escape.'

'You've surprised me.'

'Really?' Natasha asked. Then she thought about this. 'I know. How's the party?'

'You should be here,' Anna said with a revealing tone of desperation and panic.

Natasha took a shower. She changed and settled in front of the fire with a cup of coffee, carefully remembering the enjoyable part of her evening with Geoffrey.

She went to bed before she was tired, not wishing to be up when Anna came home. Natasha knew she would hear enough about Richard's party tomorrow. Expecting to sleep badly, she appreciated the warmth and comfort of her duvet and slept soundly.

THIRTY-SEVEN

Throughout the party Anna kept her eye on Richard, and noticed him doing the same with her. He winked. She smiled. He blew her kisses; she – secretly – gave him the finger, jokingly attempting to faze him. She wasn't nervous of the other guests, but was careful of how she spoke. She did not dive into the food as she would normally. Her most enduring concern was to make sure that she did not speak her mind. Her bluntness was the quality that strangers most often complimented her on, but the reality was that it was the attribute that most often caused friction, or awkwardness, or even open hostility. When people told her, 'Well, at least you're honest,' they really meant 'Bitch'. Even if she knew that she was saying something foolish, the knowledge would not prevent her speaking, making comments which were often impossible to respond to: 'You're very tall,' 'That's a Scouse accent,' 'That dress is a very bright colour.' At this party the possibilities of accidentally insulting someone were endless; she knew no one and was desperate to be liked. When she was spoken to she took so long to analyse her reply that no reply emerged, so every conversation stalled. She saw that Richard's friends thought her dull or even slow. He had not dared invite anyone who knew him – or his wife – too well. Some were work colleagues, others were friends he saw rarely.

Anna spent as much time as she could standing next to Richard as he talked to his guests. He included her in conversations by addressing his comments to her, but without expecting her to participate.

Anna wanted Natasha to be there. She needed the prop of someone she could relax around, have a laugh with, so that everyone would see how amusing she was, how fun, how lively. This way they might understand why Richard was interested in her.

She noticed that one woman kept going up to Richard whenever she was not by his side and talking to him – even if she was interrupting a conversation. There could be little doubt from her expression, her eyes, and her smile, that she fancied Richard.

Anna's instinct was to attack her. To launch at her with a smack then to swing her around the room by her hair. To suppress this instinct was even harder than guarding her words, but she feared that such an outrage would permanently alienate Richard from her.

She nibbled at a cracker topped with a pink cream that was tepid and vaguely fishy. She wanted to spew. That would really turn heads.

The party had put Richard's affections for Anna into another context. He was able to compare her directly with other women he knew. None of them came close. They all concentrated their energies on their appearance, and as a result had nothing worthwhile to contribute to conversations, debates – to anything. They were happy to have no opinions and happy that no one cared enough to hear them even if they did. They feared age and ugliness so much that every look in a mirror fuelled their paranoia, magnifying flaws few others would even notice.

Richard saw that Anna was struggling. Her smiles were fake, flashing on and off like a Belisha beacon. She had been cornered by one of his work colleagues, Jake, who had the ability to talk about *any* subject and still be boring. When Richard interrupted Jake, Anna whispered to him:

'Thank fuck you're here. Who is this guy?'

Jake was there with his sister. Richard told Anna about Jake's job, and that he was a genuinely nice guy and maybe Natasha would like to meet him.

Anna considered this idea, which led to her wondering how these people acted when they were in couples. She was thinking so hard that she was unaware she was unnerving Richard. The detached stare alarmed him.

'What's up?' he asked.

'There are plenty of attractive women here.'

'Plenty. Some of them are gorgeous.'

Anna thumped him in the chest.

'Why are you even going out with me?' she asked him. She made this into a joke, though she could not entirely disguise the concern in her voice. 'Most of the women here are far prettier than me. Some are genuinely beautiful.'

'Do you think it's natural beauty, though?' he asked. 'You're a woman – you should know. They dedicate their lives to looking like this. They have nothing else to do.'

'I get you. So you're saying I might be ugly but I'm more interesting?'

Richard laughed.

'I'm saying you're the most interesting and most naturally beautiful woman here.'

'You're full of shit,' she told him, then kissed him. 'But I feel better now.'

She didn't ask, though she considered it, whether his wife was beautiful.

In the morning the girls had a hurried breakfast, with Anna complaining of a mild hangover. Anna didn't say anything about the party. She was ashamed of her own happiness. Natasha risked telling her more about her evening with Geoffrey.

'I can't be friends with him – I like him too much. I'd end up wanting to be with him, and that wouldn't work.'

'Forget about him.' Anna grinned mischievously. 'There was someone at this party last night . . .' Anna looked vague for a moment before she remembered the name. 'Jake! That's right. Richard didn't say as much, but I think he was lining you up for him all along. This Jake has a good job and he's single.'

'Who was he at the party with, then?'

'His sister. Which sounds sad, but wasn't really. She copped off with someone! He's not bad-looking, as well. I mean, it's not a big deal, but if you want, we thought you might want us to fix you up with him? I talked to him, I told him all about you. He sounded keen on the idea.'

'OK,' Natasha said.

'As easy as that? You don't want to know anything more?'

'I'll meet him. What have I got to lose?'

'Are you really that depressed?'

'It's just about to get so much worse,' Natasha said. She stood up, ready to make the weekly trip to her parents'.

'You know what, I've often thought that if you hate it so much, why do you insist on going week after week?'

'Going makes me unique. I'm the only person I know for whom Monday isn't the worst day of the week.'

'You only go because you're scared of upsetting your mum.'

'Not at all. Upsetting her is the incentive to go.'

On Monday morning Anna recognised her first customer, but she couldn't remember where she knew her from. She brought the girl the shoes she had requested, all the time frustrated by not being able to place her. Only as the girl tried on the shoes did Anna remember that this was the girl she had seen in *Bartok's*, pouring a glass of red wine over Richard's friend Malcolm.

'I hope you don't mind me asking this,' she began cautiously, 'but you used to go out with a lad called Malcolm, didn't you?'

'Malcolm? I did, yes. How do you know him?' There was antagonism in her voice, and Anna immediately realised she could not openly tell her how she knew Malcolm, that she was seeing Richard, in case this girl knew Richard's wife.

'I just know him through a friend,' she mumbled; then said more confidently, smiling: 'I was in *Bartok's* that night you poured wine over him.'

Reassured by Anna's smile, the girl confided: 'You know, I

never drink red wine. I knew beforehand what I was going to do, so I bought it especially.'

'I was a distance away, but I could see you were angry. Am I right in thinking you'd found out he was married?'

'Well, no. Is that what people think?' Her smile dropped. 'I'd been seeing him just a couple of weeks. He'd *told* me he was married, but that night I found out he'd been lying, he isn't married at all.'

'I don't get you,' Anna said. She was conscious that Gerard was hovering around, checking that Anna wasn't simply chatting. This didn't stop her. 'Are you saying you poured wine over your boyfriend's head because you found out that he *wasn't* married?'

'Apparently they all do it – him and his mates. They meet girls and tell them they're married so that the relationship stays casual: the girls don't bother them, they don't expect to be taken out, there's no pressure – just sex.'

'When you say they *all* do it . . . do you know Richard?'

The girl was now back in her own shoes. She stood and searched through her purse for money, handing the notes to Anna so as to try and hide a smile.

'So Richard's told you he's married? I'm sorry. They're bastards – all of them. No exceptions. Bastards.'

With the truth revealed beyond doubt, Anna's only surprise was how willingly she had ignored her suspicions. Like a loving mother with a delinquent child, every excuse and lie, no matter how implausible, had been readily accepted.

She had accepted with relief how easily they had been able to flaunt their supposedly illicit relationship. She had shied from openly questioning his blatant freedom. She had suppressed her contempt for adultery by pardoning Richard's simply by favourably comparing him to the likes of her father. Richard wasn't simply with Anna as a diversion from his marriage; he genuinely liked her.

Now the truth was revealed too starkly for her to ignore. Richard was with her, and had told her he was married, simply because he thought of her casually. She was for sex, not for ever.

'Are you OK?' Natasha asked when she discovered Anna in the stock room kicking shoe-boxes.

'Fine.' She kicked another box. Natasha ducked just in time.

THIRTY-EIGHT

Several years ago a man named Dominic Hall had told Anna that he was a squaddie. Five weeks after she had begun seeing him, Natasha asked Anna to ask why his Marines regiment never left Bradford. Dominic confessed the lie: although he had served in the Marines, hence the plentiful supply of anecdotes, he was unemployed at the moment. Natasha told Anna that for once she should forgive a lie, as after all it was told out of genuine shame. Anna reconciled with Dominic and set out to demonstrate that she was not as superficial as he might think. At first she always insisted on paying her way, buying her own drinks and cinema tickets, and paying half the bill in restaurants. As Dominic increasingly put off his dates with her because of shortage of money, she began to take him out, buy his drinks, pay his entrance fee into clubs.

Another five weeks passed. In the *Apollo*, Dominic met up with an old comrade from his regiment. He went to the bar, with money Anna had given him at the beginning of the night. His friend spoke to Anna, defending his own choice of expensive drink.

'Dom won't mind, not with his money.'

'His money? What do you mean?'

'He'll have spent some by now – but not most of it. He can't have.' When Anna said nothing, still puzzling this through, he continued: 'Has Dom never told you how much he got? He lost three toes from his left foot under a tank. Fucking idiot.'

'He told me he'd been born like that! It did seem odd, the Marines taking someone with toes missing.'

'The regiment paid him off – just short of two hundred grand.'

The relationship between Dominic and Anna ended that very night, three minutes later. Anna said farewell to Dominic by punching him in the balls while he was unable to defend himself, as he was carrying the three drinks.

Even though she had asked for clarity to make certain there could be no misunderstanding, Anna kept repeating the girl's words back to herself, turning them over and over in her mind, analysing them in the hope of a loophole. *'They meet girls and tell them they're married so that it always stays casual.'*

So saying he was married had been a calculated lie, with only one devious, nasty intent.

Richard wasn't like this. Richard wouldn't do that to her.

Not only was he not married, but he had made no attempt to disguise his bachelor status, clearly in the belief that Anna was too stupid to put two and two together. And she had to concede he was right, she never had. Her suspicions, instincts and past experience had been ignored – that was how very stupid she had been.

Natasha began to interrupt her thoughts about Richard by boasting about how strong she had been, in spite of genuinely liking Geoffrey, in telling him straight out that they had no future together.

Anna in turn began to tell Natasha more details about Richard's party, without mentioning that she had now discovered that Richard was single. Even though the *only* thoughts Anna was having about Richard were bad, she did not want Natasha to think badly of him.

Anna texted Richard: I HAVE JUST FOUND OUT YOU'RE NOT MARRIED. YOU LIED AND I KNOW WHY. KEEP AWAY FROM ME. I HATE YOU.

Anna pre-wrote her replies to messages she anticipated she might receive from Richard. She thought of vicious, nasty ways to tell him, in text shorthand, that she wished he was dead and she had never really cared for him. When Richard did not text her back she read each of the answers she had prepared and was horrified to think that she had intended sending them. She erased them all; each time, as her thoughts circled back to how he had lied, she wrote new, nastier messages. She had no experience of how to behave in this situation.

At tea Anna and Natasha had a slight row after Anna had sworn at Natasha, shouting to her, 'For the fiftieth fucking time – *THERE'S NOTHING WRONG WITH ME!* So stop asking, please.'

Natasha made a guess. Richard had not phoned. Anna was staying in. Anna went to bed early. Anna *never* went to bed early. Anna could lose her legs in a car accident but wouldn't get into bed until she was obliged to.

Anna sat up in bed, not able to understand why she dared not tell Natasha the truth; and why she still wanted Natasha to think well of Richard. Natasha knew how much Anna despised liars. She could forgive almost anything else – stupidity, stealing, poverty – so long as she was not lied to. But never to see him again meant reverting back to her old life of plodding through the week here with Natasha, waiting for weekends that inevitably disappointed.

Anna wanted Richard. She tried to sleep in the lonely exaggeration of her bed, remembering how Richard would always sleep close to her, often with a heavy arm or leg around her, making her sweat; and if she shuffled away he would shuffle back. Afraid to wake him, she would end up perched on the very edge of the bed. She now regretted ever uttering any word of complaint.

When they arrived home from work the next evening, Natasha noted that Anna again simply collapsed on the settee instead of either heading straight for the bathroom, to shower, or to the kitchen, to eat.

'Aren't you seeing Richard tonight?'

'Not tonight,' Anna replied, pleased with her nonchalance. She didn't want to say anything because she clung to the senseless hope that Richard might have fallen so deeply in love that he bitterly regretted the lie and would, any minute, phone her and apologise, beg forgiveness and explain that his dishonesty somehow had plausible, honourable intent.

Anna ran through the many conversations she had held with him, this time playing her role by catching him out in the lie, then finishing with him.

She hoped he would ring. He didn't.

She had a shower. When she came out of the bathroom Natasha was preparing ravioli on toast for both of them. If Richard had phoned, Natasha would have said so. If Anna asked Natasha if he had phoned, then Natasha would know that there was a problem.

As they ate, to give the impression that all was fine with her and Richard, she talked more about his party. Anna told Natasha about a woman she'd met there who'd been a real bitch. The woman had asked about Anna's work. When she had told her what she did, the woman had reacted snobbishly, surprised by Anna's lowly job.

She remembered Richard telling her that he had dated women like her all his life. None of them had ever been blessed with Anna's spirit, humour or lack of pretension. These qualities, he had told her, made him certain that he was happy to be with her, and he would not exchange her for any woman he had ever known.

'You seem unhappy,' Natasha ventured.

'The shop was busy today, I'm fucked.'

Natasha knew this was not the reason, but played along.

'I hate that place,' she said to her friend.

'How many years have we been there now? It stopped being fun after day one.'

Natasha sighed. 'The things we do for money.'

Anna joked, 'You mean Geoffrey?'

Natasha laughed in order to cheer Anna up. Then asked: 'Have you ever wondered what we would do if we were sacked, or if the shop went out of business?'

'I have a whole dance routine prepared!'

'But seriously?'

'Seriously? Easy. We carry out your grand plan, and set up our own shoe stall in the market.'

'I factored everything into my plan except the risk.'

'If we had no other choice, where would be the risk? We'd need money to start with, though.'

After tea Anna began ruthlessly to clear out her wardrobe. Throwing clothes out was difficult for Anna; she liked to own a large reserve. Now they were spilling out all over the place, and she had to be strong. The pile of dispensable clothes was growing until Natasha entered the room, and began rummaging through, championing virtually everything. Listening to Natasha, Anna began to change her mind about most of the clothes, and soon the trend was reversed: most of the pile was returned to the wardrobe. To divert Natasha, Anna told her more about Jake. Previously, whenever lining Natasha up with a man, Anna would have begun by describing his looks, or his personality, even his height. This time she was operating under a new set of guidelines.

'He has a good job. Which means money. Have you changed your mind or are you still going to meet him?'

Before Natasha could answer, the phone began ringing. Anna did not immediately pounce; she even turned away from the phone. This gave Natasha further proof that Anna had fallen out with Richard.

'If it's Richard, what are you going to do?'

Anna examined the blouse she was holding. She remembered buying it. Its colours were lurid and its style was a little more flamboyant than she was used to. The price had been far higher than she would normally have paid. She had hoped the blouse might make her appear elegant and sophisticated. At home, though, she saw that it was out of place on her, ill-fitting, as if borrowed from someone more stylish. The blouse had cost her a lot of money and had never been worn. She threw the mistake onto the pile of unwanted clothes.

'Tell him I'm out. No! Tell him I can't come to the phone.'

Natasha answered the phone. Richard. Not by accident, Natasha told him, 'She *won't* come to the phone.'

Anna nearly cried out the correction, then changed her mind. Better if he knew they were finished permanently.

Natasha asked Richard to make the arrangements for her date with Jake. After hanging up, she helped Anna continue to sort out her wardrobe.

'He sounded upset.'

'Suicidal?'

'No.'

'Pity.'

'What happened?' Natasha dared to ask.

'He lied to me.'

'Maybe he's sorry.'

'I'm sorry about a lot of these clothes. That's why they're being binned.'

With this, Anna suddenly became ruthless, and three bin-liners were filled with unwanted clothes.

The next day the girls were five minutes late for work. Gerard brought them into his office to warn them that they were keeping their jobs just by the skin of their teeth, they were skating on thin ice and sailing close to the wind, etc. etc. They managed to keep a straight face until they were back on the shop floor.

'It's getting so that I want him to sack us,' Natasha said.

'Then we could set up our own stall.'

'Do you know what I thought we could do? Buy stock from those massive discount stores we go to, put our own mark-up on them, and make a comfortable profit. That way we wouldn't need too much money for stock; we could re-stock in small amounts each day until the stall took off.'

Anna was impressed. 'You've been thinking about it? Me too. Last night. It stopped me thinking about Richard.' Their break-up was now an open secret.

They began work. Neither of them spoke again that day about their continuing dream of owning their own shoe stall, or about Richard and Geoffrey.

They left work with Anna expecting Natasha to change her mind and cancel the date with Jake. Natasha had agreed too readily, and since accepting the invitation had asked no further questions. When Anna had tried to raise some enthusiasm, as they walked from the bus towards their home, Natasha still made no comment. She did not even answer Anna's direct question: 'Have you changed your mind about seeing Jake?'

Natasha lacked the courage to say one word, 'Yes'. That would be reverting to the misguided and immature opinion that boyfriends should be fun and desirable.

Anna was prevented from repeating the question when she saw Derek, waiting by their door.

'Let me,' she told Natasha, walking ahead. 'It'll cheer me up.'

'What is it with men?' Anna asked Derek.

'Natasha,' Derek called over her, 'I have to talk to you.'

Anna continued, 'Why are you incapable of acting like straightforward, normal human beings? You think you can behave any damn way you want because you're so special, so wonderful, we'll take you back. No matter what you've done –'

'I haven't done anything!' Derek protested. 'I want to talk to Natasha, not you.'

Derek then spoke directly to Natasha, though only Derek and Anna heard what he said. Natasha was instead remembering the *Apollo*, and the only other men that were available to her, the only other type she had ever met. All those other Dereks.

Natasha walked away from Derek without saying a word to him. Stupid as he was, even he understood.

'Why were you so angry at him?' Natasha asked Anna.

'Fucking men!' Anna spat.

THIRTY-NINE

She had made her position unequivocal; she wanted a man with money. A part of Geoffrey admired Natasha for this determination. But only a very small part of him, perhaps some insignificant, useless part – like an earlobe. Nothing had ever been expected of her throughout her entire life, and now she was intent on defying that lack of expectations. If she was not able to make a life on her own, he could hardly blame her for wanting someone who would provide the comforts she wanted.

Geoffrey wanted honesty, a woman who would see his personality and character regardless of circumstances such as money, job, lifestyle.

The pursuit of such a woman, he had to concede, had been a disaster. Like everything else he had *wanted* in his life, he had failed. Any achievements he had made, he had carelessly drifted into.

As a final act in defiance of fate, he again began to type.

ALL THIS AND MORE
a novel by
Geoffrey Barker

I have spent all my adult life in a career Fate destined for me when I was as young as twelve: I received a good mark in chemistry, just as my parents were looking for a present to buy for my birthday. They bought me a chemistry set and from then on chemistry was the subject I excelled in. I took it at university, sailing through exam questions that confounded others. I was happy to have one aspect of my life where people admired my understanding, and sought my advice. After university, every career move I made was born out of convenience. My specialities were learnt from having been assigned unpopular projects, and this is how I found myself working on liquid fuels. This led to working in America, for American Chemical Industries, and through them I found myself working for NASA, working with the liquid oxygen and liquid hydrogen fuelling systems that power the space shuttle. I can say with pride that the next time you see one of those billion-dollar beauties engulfed in flames, it's partially down to me.

Imagine, then, if the things I wanted in life – being a writer, meeting a woman who interested me and who somehow liked me – had somehow happened with the same ease as my career.

I cannot be a writer because I lack substantial talent and have been unable to master the craft; and besides, I am never sure what it is, ultimately, that I wish to say. I don't have the patience, the discipline, the stamina to complete a novel. Finishing a second chapter appears to be nearly impossible. Even as I write this, using the first person for the first time, being direct and honest, even in this I know I will not succeed. It sounds less like an interesting confession and more like a prolonged whine.

But in this part of my life, from now on, I will at least be able to say that I made a valid attempt. I had saved enough money to take a sabbatical for a year. That time is barely halfway through; and the money's nearly spent. The experiment has only succeeded in demonstrating to me that even a sabbatical of ten years could easily prove not to be enough.

I came to Bradford to write for two reasons. The first was that Stuart – who lives here – is my friend. I use the singular advisedly. Also, I had seen Les Dawson – of all people! – talking about his youthful ambition to write a novel and go to Paris, but he had failed, there had been too many distractions. It would have been smarter, he said, to go to Bradford.

I am writing this, I think, to try and concentrate my thoughts, in a detached way, on my failings so I can understand why I mess up with women.

I know why Natasha will not see me. This alone, this knowledge, should give me the instant sense to forget her and move on. Yet I cannot help thinking it is luck again, it is bad timing. I met her at the wrong time. At any other time we would

Geoffrey reached the end of a page. He counted out his money. If he returned to America, his home, work would make him think of the things he was a success at. At least now he knew that should he meet Janette he would regard her with astonishment. *How could I ever have been so stupid?*

He now fully accepted the person he was. He would only ever know romance in his own speculations. He began on a new sheet of paper.

When I was growing up and began to understand that girls were different from us and that this was something that we liked not hated, my approach was immediately flawed. While my friends teased and tormented them – resulting in physical contact – I would confide in them and listen to their complaints. I always believed women were better than us, that they acted more decently, their thoughts were purer and they were more likely to be honest.

Geoffrey sat back in the chair and slapped his palm against his forehead in acknowledgement of his one revelation, his mistaken belief that women were better than men.

He read the last sentence he had written. He would return home – to America. He would first go and see Natasha and tell her: *'I always believed women were better than us, that they acted more decently, their thoughts were purer and they were more likely to be honest.'*

The next morning Geoffrey read through the few new pages he

had written. He began to guess how Natasha might react if he told her the truth.

'What do you mean,' she might ask, 'you've got money after all?'

'Not money as in not-needing-to-work money. I took a year off from my job to try and write, but that hasn't succeeded. But I have a well-paid job and a good lifestyle. So all the things you hoped about me are true, to a degree. So I'm here to say, if you want to try and make a go of it between us, I'm still willing.'

He would go and see her without planning ahead. He would go tonight, when she returned from work.

> After Janette and now Natasha, I have to accept that it's not enough to believe that I have simply been unlucky. Women are no different from men. We have the same secret, selfish, nasty thoughts. The difference is only that each sex is trained to respond to the same instincts differently.
>
> Woman are no better or worse than men. I want Natasha to be perfect when I am offering, in return, myself, and I'm far from perfect. A woman who looks like Natasha, with her intelligence and wit, brings more to this than I do. I am privileged to have this chance, and an idiot if I let it pass simply because of my tired old reactionary belief that she should want me in spite of my circumstances. I will go and see her, tell her honestly how I feel and that I hope – pray! – that I can convince her.

Geoffrey thought about his long, abysmal relationship with Janette and about the countless, relentless thoughts he had had about Natasha, and how he was again – *again* – again thinking about her now. Writing had provided no exorcism. He tore the new writing into confetti, flinging the pieces into the air, and then stormed out of his room and out of the house with the hard-faced determination of a boxer entering a ring, telling himself repeatedly, so the fervour spilled out and he shouted aloud, that he would tell

Natasha that if she didn't want him he would be leaving Britain for good.

'You will never see me again!'

The only person to hear this was a young lad at a bus stop, to whom it was excellent news.

FORTY

With the eager assistance of Anna, Natasha took first-date care about getting ready. She began about an hour and a half before Jake was due to arrive.

'I want to look sensational,' Natasha said.

'Shall I phone and tell him to come much later then?' Anna teased. 'How about tomorrow?'

Though Natasha looked to be having fun getting ready, she was performing a post-mortem on how life might have been if she had continued to see Geoffrey. The chance of happiness, of fun, the experience of being with a lover who you know wants to be nowhere else . . . She didn't even think about whether their happiness would depend on how much money they might have.

'You look lovely,' Anna told Natasha when she was ready, 'but cheer up.'

The doorbell rang.

'He's eager,' Anna said. 'He probably hasn't had sex in ages,' she added, to torment her friend. Natasha pushed Anna away and had one last look at herself in the mirror. She smiled, in spite of herself. She was dressed to make the best possible first impression. She breathed in, raised her head, orchestrated a suitable smile, then opened the door.

To Geoffrey. Whose own smile dropped.

He had been working out an appropriate opening line, a self-effacing remark, witty and charming. 'I . . . Puh,' was all that came out now. From the way she was dressed and how her expression changed when she saw him, he immediately knew that she was expecting someone else. He was pleased.

'You look nice,' he said weakly.

Natasha thanked him.

He was pleased because he could relax, he had lost – which was a condition he knew how to handle. He could now retreat and never think about attempting to see her again. Nothing he could say would return her to him, so it didn't matter if he only said foolish things. He didn't walk away immediately. He would soon be leaving this country, and abandoning his dreams of becoming a writer. This would all begin as soon as he left. So he stayed. Her natural prettiness was enhanced by her clothes and make-up to produce a real effect of elegance and intelligence for which he was no match.

He held some flowers out to her. She hesitated before taking them. She regretted the hesitation.

'Flowers seemed to do the trick last time, so . . .' he told her.

She picked off a dead petal as she mumbled: 'You shouldn't be here, Geoffrey.'

'Shouldn't I?' he asked. 'I wouldn't feel sensible being anywhere else. This is a last-ditch attempt to persuade you that we could be good together. Funny, but it seems that everything we've done has been a last-ditch attempt.'

Now she looked at him. She was determined that he would see the stubbornness in her eyes and know that she could not be convinced. She pretended her unhappiness was viciousness.

'It's not going to succeed. We're not going to start seeing each other again.'

'That would be easier to take if you didn't look so good.' Geoffrey smiled. 'Skating was fun, wasn't it? I know my bedsit, the place I'm living now, is a dump –'

'It doesn't matter.'

'Of course it matters. Listen –'

She continued as if she had not heard him.

'I'm going out. On a date.'

His shock was not at the news but at her determination to shock him.

'Date?'

'Date.'

'In that case I think the smartest thing I can say is – *oh shit.*'

He kept his smile. She stepped back.

'I do like you. And we did have fun the other night. But so what? It's easy to find someone to have fun with.'

He stepped forward. 'That's true. And I hope you have fun on your date tonight. But I'll just say this – you're right, finding someone to have fun with is easy. But when you meet someone you just fall into sync with, like you're both reading from the same script, speaking the same language, and it's a language that up till then you'd never spoken and weren't aware existed . . . that's different. Because you belong with me, it's redundant me telling you so – *you already know it.* I'd only known you for a day when I began to forget how I was before I knew you. Between us, Natasha – I'm simply reminding you – there's this natural instinct where the gear changes are automatic, where we both know when the other is making a hash of something, or we're trying to avoid something, or scrambling to impress or amuse. You get when I'm being sarcastic or ironic or when I'm being dishonest. And I get that – no matter how much you're trying to prove otherwise – you know that we're both alike. We have exactly the same attitude and outlook.'

Natasha grabbed the door handle, standing behind the door.

'It seems to me it was a mistake thinking we could ever be friends. It's best if I just say that I don't ever want to see you again. There's no point. I don't want any of the things you're hinting at.'

She knew, he knew, they both knew, she was saying this just to test him. Geoffrey knew he had to say something similarly significant.

'I know I love you, Natasha.'

'No you don't,' she told him. She moved the door so that it touched his leg.

He told her, 'Maybe it's not love yet. But certainly there are the early signals, the uneven mixture of elation and misery, the buzz and the exhaustion. The real thing is so rare as to be worth pursuing in spite of the odds against it.'

'Love is stupid,' she answered.

He saw now, clearer than ever, that she was forcing herself against her nature, spiting herself.

'That's the fun in it. Why so cynical, Natasha?'

'I am cynical now – it's the only effective prevention of misery.'

'It's the cause.'

There was such a long silence that Anna, who had been listening in, presumed Geoffrey had left and came out to Natasha. Natasha smiled at her, like an apology.

'You have to go now,' Anna told Geoffrey, gently, like she would to a widower draped over a coffin. Without another word, he turned away. He didn't look back, and if he had done Natasha would not have seen him anyway, since Anna had closed the door.

'Don't look so miserable,' Anna told her friend. 'It ruins the effect.'

Natasha said absently, 'What if we never go to the *Apollo* again, Anna, before it closes? It might happen. All those times we went, all the things that happened there, all the laughs we had and all the things we saw . . . We had a last night, an end to it all, and we didn't even realise it. Our last night there was so crap, it might be how we always remember the *Apollo* from now on.'

Anna was too confused to respond. Natasha offered no explanation. She walked back into the living room to fetch her coat, ready to meet Jake.

Natasha feared that the last image she had of Geoffrey's face might be her most enduring memory of him, now she was never going to see him again.

Walking as slowly as a pall-bearer, Geoffrey passed a smartly dressed man on the stairs. He knew the man was there for Natasha and so hated him irrationally. This man was unaware of Geoffrey's existence in Natasha's life, and this ignorance made Geoffrey want to push him down the stairs.

Though aware of the lunatic staring at him, Jake was wise enough to say nothing. He knocked on Natasha's door. When she answered he was sure that the smile on her face dropped slightly when she saw him.

'You!' Geoffrey muttered from the foot of the stairs. He had never been very good at aggression.

On Geoffrey's death-row walk back home he passed through every psychotic, deranged, and then rational and sensible emotion known to man. He was simultaneously happy, relieved, furious, depressed, amused. Twice he missed the correct turning and had to retrace his steps; several times he had to stop himself shouting out his internal dialogue. *I should not be this miserable!* Then: *I cannot imagine being anything other than miserable ever again!*

When he saw the slum which was his home he could only bear the thought of entering it in the knowledge, the unquestionable belief, that he no longer lived there.

After years of dreaming, of hesitating, of backing down and then acting impulsively, when he had written the final, seven-thousandth draft of the letter asking for this sabbatical, everything else seemed to fall into place as if to validate his decision.

He packed as if in a race, throwing his clothes and his few possessions into a suitcase. In less than three minutes he was ready to leave, even though he would have to stay longer. He would sell his Mini. The typewriter would stay here, a gift to whatever sad soul inherited this room.

FORTY-ONE

Under scrutiny Natasha thought that Jake, while not unattractive, had such an unremarkable face she could forget it even when she was looking at him: his features simply existed.

'Are you taking her somewhere exciting?' Anna asked Jake.

'A restaurant.'

'Somewhere flash?' Natasha asked. 'Are you going to spend a lot of cash in an attempt to impress me?' To make certain he would understand she was making a joke she gave a broad, cheeky smile and raised her eyebrows quickly, suggestively.

'Ha, I see I shall have to watch myself with you,' he said. He smiled as well, to demonstrate he was being light-hearted.

Natasha put down her coat and excused herself. She took Anna into the kitchen.

'I don't think this is going to work.'

'What do you mean?' Anna asked. 'Give him a chance, you've barely said hello to each other.'

'He's . . . He's just . . . It's . . .'

'What? What is it? What's wrong with him?' Anna asked, suddenly losing her temper. Taken aback, Natasha had even less to say to explain her change of heart.

'Don't you think he looks a bit like Keith?'

'Keith who? Keith, your sister's boyfriend? In what way?'

'He . . . I don't know.'

'Just go out with the guy, for fuck's sake,' Anna hissed. 'Just . . . try and have a good time.'

Each girl touched the other, both sorry.

As Jake led her out to his car Natasha was already bored. She looked around to see if Geoffrey was still nearby, ready to make one last attempt.

'It's going to be a chilly night, I think,' Jake commented. She hadn't noticed the temperature until she sat in his car. She shivered, then.

When Richard had received Anna's text message he was in a meeting and could not answer immediately. All his powers of concentration were used to keep his mind focused on the agenda of the meeting and not refer to everyone present as Anna.

Richard read the message over and over again, considering how best to answer. Then he decided against answering too quickly on impulse. He had no succinct explanation for her. He would take time to consider how best to talk to her about his deception. When he eventually phoned and she refused to speak to him, this was a relief. Throughout Wednesday, as he continued to think about her and how much he had hurt her, he understood that he had to make her speak to him, to give her the opportunity to insult him in the way he deserved. Ideally, she would slap him.

Anna wanted to go back in time to the night she had met Richard at *Bartok's,* and tell him, when he told her he was married, that she knew he wasn't. Then they could begin again, with everything happening in exactly the same way, except with complete honesty.

Richard did not phone while Natasha was out, yet the phone didn't stop ringing. Anna's aunt called from Scarborough, then Brenda phoned. Three times. After Brenda's third phone call, Anna – to prevent her phoning again – told her to come over. Brenda sounded upset – Anna hoped she was; she needed someone else's misery to distract her from her own.

As she waited for Brenda to arrive, Anna hoped that Natasha would abort her date with Jake and return home. She hated herself for wanting Natasha's date to be a failure, but wanted Natasha on her own again, the way things were before – just the two of them and no one else, an enduring, exclusive friendship which puzzled the world outside while being the aspect of her life that she herself questioned least. If she came home now they could sit down and discuss frankly the differences that had emerged between them, which had made living together less than the joy they had once anticipated.

When the phone rang again Anna expected it to be Brenda, changing her mind. So, having not thought about Richard for several seconds, Anna was pleased that she had answered the phone casually, nonchalantly. She was determined to maintain this same tone throughout their conversation. In the event she said one sentence.

Richard wasted no time: 'You think I lied to you, Anna, but I didn't. I lied to someone I didn't know, some girl in a nightclub I fancied and hoped to get into bed. At that point – that night – it wasn't you. And you know what? It wasn't *me* lying. You've changed me so much, in such a short space of time, that the person who I was that night, who I've been all my life, has gone. I want to be with you, Anna. I did lie, and I'm sorry. But I think if you say you can't forgive me and that you don't want us to be together – that'll be a lie too. A far bigger lie.'

'I can't forgive you and I don't want us to be together,' she answered. There was a silence after this which, if Richard had held it for one moment longer, Anna would have ended by screaming to him that she did forgive him, loved him even, and wanted his mistake to be forgotten so they could be together again, and be happy.

Instead Richard ended the silence.

'I understand. I can't blame you. I . . . Erm . . . All right, then. Goodbye, Anna.'

Then there was the purr of the receiver.

'I cannot believe I said that!' she screamed, punching her head as if she was punching her brain.

Anna sat on the armchair with her mobile phone, trying to compose a text message which would repeat her assertion that she never wanted to see him again, yet one which he would also be compelled to answer. She could then reply, and this dialogue would lead to another phone call, then a proper conversation, which would conclude with a happy reconciliation.

Twenty minutes later Brenda – red and puffy-eyed from crying – arrived, and Anna had not typed in one letter.

It had been another row. Another falling-out. She had left Keith again. To make a distinction, to impress upon him that this time was *different*, was *serious* and *final*, Brenda had phoned Natasha instead of her mother. Brenda knew that Anna's invitation to call around, even though Natasha was out, was only politeness, but she had accepted nevertheless.

At the door Anna explained to Brenda that Natasha was still on her date, and when this did not immediately send Brenda away, she begrudgingly invited her in.

'Do you know something?' Brenda asked as she was shown into the living room. 'In all the time you and Natasha have lived here, this is only the second time I've been inside.'

'Is it?' Anna asked, for want of anything else to say. She could not remember the first time. If asked, she would struggle to remember Brenda's name. All she could think about was Richard. She kept her mobile in her hand, as if inspiration might strike at any time and require immediate action.

'I came here with Keith once,' Brenda explained. 'We were giving you a table we were throwing out.'

Hoping Brenda would decline, Anna offered her coffee. Brenda accepted, using the opportunity of Anna being out of the room to take off her coat and sit down. To make conversation, Anna told Brenda about Jake.

Brenda made no response, only hoping that Anna might ask why she was here, which would give her the opportunity to talk about Keith, how much she hated him and how determined she was that this time she had left him for good.

The meal was the only successful part of Jake and Natasha's evening. At least while the food was in front of them they had something to talk about, and any silences could be excused by full mouths. Silence had persisted on the car journey. At the restaurant, though she had chosen more or less the moment the waiter had handed her the menu, Natasha continued to ask Jake questions about each dish. This, at least, was almost like a conversation.

Jake didn't stand a chance. With every remark he made, every attempt to amuse her, Natasha compared him with Geoffrey.

She tried to have fun. She asked him questions and showed an interest, then when he replied she made comments as feeds for obvious jokes – none of which he made, not understanding that they were feeds.

'This restaurant is expensive, I'm glad I'm not paying.' He should have answered with something like, 'What makes you think you're not?' In actuality he replied, 'It's expensive but good quality. I find you get what you pay for.'

'I won't have a dessert, I'm watching my weight.' He should have replied with something like, 'Have a dessert, surely someone your size is past worrying?' Instead he said, 'I think you have a very nice figure.'

She made mild, playful insults, hoping he would criticise her in return. Instead he acted genuinely insulted, and she then had to explain that she had been joking. About his suit: 'Very conservative, does your dad know you've borrowed it?' He assured her it was his own. His shoes: 'How did you get a shine like that? That must be top quality vinyl.' He took one off to show her that they were leather. His hair: 'There's not a hair out of place, where did you buy it?' He was appalled in case she really thought he was wearing a wig.

When she asked about his job, he took twenty minutes to explain what he did and she was still no wiser. When she asked about his parents he was actually proud, and spoke affectionately about them both. She asked how he knew Richard and marvelled at how Jake could talk for so long without taking a breath or haemorrhaging from boredom.

She did not again insult, she did not again ask questions, she commented on nothing and showed no interest in anything he said. Anything he had already told her, she had already forgotten.

She knew she had no need to remember as she was certain she would never see him again. You don't revise for an exam you'll never take. Having made this decision, she began to tell him some of the stories from her and Anna's adventures at the *Apollo*. They were stories of drunken excess, lewd behaviour, threats and acts of violence. She had no reason to care if he was repulsed.

FORTY-TWO

Anna never asked Brenda why she had come, as asking would imply that she had no right to be there. She wanted Brenda to ask about Richard, as this would give her a chance to voice her most persistent thoughts. Hopefully, Brenda would advise Anna to take Richard back.

The two women made the tiniest of small talk, discussing the TV programmes scheduled for that night, reviewing the weather so far that year. The only thing they had in common was Natasha, so they were forced to discuss her. They soon found that they both had plenty to say.

'I used to hate you, not *hate* you, but resent you,' Brenda told Anna, smiling so she would know the resentment was gone.

'Resent me? Why?'

'I used to wonder why Natasha and me weren't as close as you and her. I used to think that it was me she should be going out drinking with, going shopping with.'

'I'd rather you went shopping with her than me. She's a nightmare. She takes a fortnight to make a decision, then two seconds to change her mind. If she ever has kids she won't settle a name on them till they're twelve.'

Brenda smiled out of politeness.

Anna went on, 'Me and Natasha have been friends for always. So neither of us ever made any other friends. And that's how it's always been.'

'But you're *still* friends, which is . . . odd. I don't know anyone else who's still best friends with the best friend they had at school. Do you?'

'It's not just friendship. It's like being friends and sisters and . . . everything.' Anna said this in the hope that she might get Brenda to understand something of Natasha and Anna's relationship. But this was unlikely when Anna herself did not understand its definition. Natasha was just there, in Anna's life as fundamentally important and necessary as her past and future, part of who she was.

'When I started seeing Keith I thought that might make Natasha jealous of me, like I've always been jealous of her.'

'You're jealous of her?' Anna asked, instead of asking the more obvious, but rude question, *'Why would Natasha be jealous of you seeing that obnoxious prick?'*

'Because she has you. But Keith didn't bother her. I think she's always thought of the two of us as doomed. Maybe I thought that if I met someone and went out with them for long enough I'd have the same closeness that you two have.'

'It's different between men and women from how it is between friends. Isn't it?'

'Is it?'

'Isn't it?' Anna replied. She knew, absolutely, that it was different. Anna and Natasha were mentally Siamese twins, inseparable now because their growing up, their development and influences, had been mutually inclusive. Separation now would not require surgery but might still be fatal; neither would know how to function without the other.

'Don't you have any female friends, Brenda? Don't you have a really good mate you can confide in, and gossip with and . . .'

Brenda stared at Anna, the stare drifting off around the room until it silenced Anna, and the silence continued into a death.

'You have a nice home, so Natasha tells me,' Anna said after several moments. This was the only compliment she could think of.

'I'd rather live here, like you two do.'

How could anyone live without such friendship? Anna glowed

with the joy of remembering how privileged she was, and how lucky she was to have Natasha. She could confide in Natasha about all her desires and fears. Without Natasha, Anna would have fewer expressions.

'I don't know why I'm marrying Keith,' Brenda said without warning.

'Because you love him,' Anna stated, then added a question mark only in her expression. Brenda's response was to close her eyes slowly.

Brenda began to talk about Keith. Her speech quickly accelerated as she listed his faults and added her frustrations. Anne watched Brenda's mouth move but did not listen; and if Brenda had not been so self-involved she would have noticed Anna's smile. Anna was thinking about Natasha returning home.

To Jake's dismay Natasha yawned on the drive home. She hoped he wouldn't ask to be invited in. To be certain, Natasha mentioned work tomorrow and told him that she had to get up early. Then she reminded him that Anna might still be up watching TV.

Even before Jake had stopped the car her hand was on the door, ready to escape in case he tried to kiss her.

The car stopped. Jake said nothing. Natasha, not sure how to react to this, didn't open the door.

'I would ask you in, but –'

'No, that's OK, I've got work in the morning, the same as you.'

As if she had not heard him she continued: 'You see, Anna will still be up, and I'm exhausted anyway.'

'Good night then. I enjoyed tonight.'

Out of the car, she planned on how best to tell Anna that the evening had been unsuccessful. Every argument she could make against seeing Jake again would contradict every previous argument she had made about finding a wealthy boyfriend.

Anna, alerted and relieved by the sound of the key in the lock, was out of her seat, and out of the room, whispering to her friend before Natasha had even closed the door.

'Your sister's here.'

'Brenda?' Natasha asked with incredulity, as if she had another. 'How come?'

'Keith?' Anna guessed.

'But she always goes to Mum's,' Natasha said as she entered the living room. She greeted her sister as if she was pleased to see her. The late hour permitted a degree of bluntness.

'Are you wanting to stay here because you've fallen out with Keith?'

A smile appeared on Brenda's face, startling Anna. Brenda was relieved that she wouldn't have to explain. She refused another coffee, explaining that the caffeine, on top of all the anxiety, would prevent her from sleeping.

The two sisters shared the same bed. Not having done this for twenty years, they also shared an openness that had been twenty years absent.

'Do you know how much I envy you?' Brenda asked.

'Sure you do. My terrific job, my terrific boyfriends, my terrific flat.'

'Yes, exactly. Yes! Your job gives you money and you don't have to thank anyone for it. And if your boyfriends have all been disasters – so what? They're adventures in themselves, and in the meantime you keep hope.'

'What good is hope?'

Brenda sat up in bed, as if Natasha could see her.

'Having hope is a far bigger deal than you might imagine. *You* take it for granted. And I do envy you living in this flat. You have true freedom here. How many girls from our estate ever lived away from their parents? They only ever do that when they move in with a bloke.'

Without leaving a pause suitable for a change of subject, Natasha asked: 'Do you love Keith?'

'No.'

Natasha was shocked at the ease, the suddenness, the casual way Brenda admitted this.

'God!' she exclaimed. 'Did you ever love him?'

Brenda struggled to answer. Her answer would always be an

absolute no, yet would need explaining, to give sense to her forthcoming marriage.

'I . . . sort of. I don't know. In the form of gratitude. In some ways he rescued me.'

'From?' Natasha asked.

Brenda didn't answer. There was a silence while she waited for the memory of the question to vanish.

'Instead I became a prisoner.'

'You mean he never lets you out?' With a shock Natasha realised how little she knew of the way her sister lived, how the relationship with Keith worked.

'It's not that,' Brenda explained. 'I never have to go after anything, it's all there for me. The house is lovely, it's just as I want it. Modern, luxurious, warm and comfortable. And if we need anything, we buy it. So what do we hope for? We hope for more of the same. And that's just *FUCK-ING* dull.'

'Have you told Keith any of this?' Natasha asked, as if she was an expert at relationships.

'It doesn't work like that,' Brenda answered, as if she was also an expert at relationships. Brenda knew Natasha still wouldn't understand her answer, so she attempted to clarify. 'There's never an occasion where we're talking in a way that . . . I could never tell him any of this.' She then added, mischievously, to shock her sister, 'But I have told him I don't love him.'

'Really? What did he say?'

'He said what I'd have said. That it doesn't matter.'

'Love doesn't matter?!' Natasha exclaimed, although she knew she was being a hypocrite.

'I never really thought it mattered, either, even when he asked me to marry him. Well, when I say *asked*, he didn't really ask. We just talked about it, and set a date. We put more thought into selecting the double glazing.'

Neither of them had heard the phone ring. Anna came into their room.

'For fuck's sake,' she said. 'Doesn't your mother possess a clock?'

'What's up?' Natasha asked.

'She's on the phone.'

Natasha sat up. Anna added, 'She wants to speak to Brenda.'

'Keith must have been on to her,' Brenda said as she climbed out of bed.

When Brenda left the room, Anna sat on the bed for a moment.

'Is listening to your sister putting you off men for life?'

'No,' Natasha answered. She concluded that anyone who married for anything other than love deserved their misery.

Natasha suggested they listen in to the conversation Brenda was having with her mother. Anna readily agreed, but Brenda was already storming back into the bedroom.

'My mum tricked me. My own mum! As soon as she heard my voice she put Keith on the line. Can you believe he's there, at this time of night? Christ knows what he's been telling them.'

'Did you speak to him?'

'Well, I listened to him for a bit. Then I told him to get stuffed and hung up. Before she passed me over to Keith, Mum said she thought I should go home.'

Brenda looked at Natasha. Natasha looked away, towards Anna: she knew her friend's conclusions would be the same as her own. Brenda had no hope of happiness with Keith.

Brenda saw the look that passed between them – despondency, resignation – and knew she did not belong here. She had nowhere else to be with dignity.

'I'm not going back to him tonight.'

'Don't,' Natasha said. Natasha was missing Geoffrey; and dreading hearing from Jake again.

'No, you're staying here,' Anna said. Anna was missing Richard. She wanted to go to sleep so that she could at least have the chance of dreaming about him.

Brenda also wanted to sleep. Sleep was her only real escape.

Before Natasha went back to bed, Anna called her out of the bedroom.

'How did it go with Jake?'

'He's not Geoffrey,' Natasha confessed.

'And I miss Richard.'

'What do we do now? Neither of us could go back to the type of men we meet at the *Apollo*, and maybe there are no other men like Richard and Geoffrey.'

Anna didn't smile. 'I guess we're lumbered with each other.'

The next morning Anna announced, 'My aunt and uncle have gone abroad. They live in Scarborough. I have a key. Their house is empty. Let's get away from this shitty city. Let's have a laugh! We need one.'

'But . . . work,' Natasha said, weakly. She had no great desire to go to Scarborough; she simply couldn't think of a convincing argument against it.

'Well, true, they won't be happy,' Anna said. 'Especially not if we both blob . . . But then again, what are they going to do about it? Sack us? They can't.'

Natasha told her sister that in the last year the shop had advertised for staff on three occasions. Twice the staff they recruited had left within weeks, the third time only three people applied, only one turned up for the interview, got the job, then never appeared on the day he was supposed to start. The shop now had a permanent vacancy notice in the *Telegraph & Argus*. In a much larger font the notice included the word *please*.

'So we're going to Scarborough?' Natasha asked. To Brenda, she said, 'We could have it as your hen night.'

'Keith doesn't want me to have one. Scarborough it is, then!'

Brenda phoned up the shop on their behalf and asked to speak to Gerard, their manager. She explained that she was Natasha's sister. She lied.

'Goodbye Hans,' Brenda said when she hung up.

'Hans?' Natasha asked.

'He said if you two were poorly he was a Dutchman.' Brenda had chosen to give them both food poisoning. Anna and Natasha had fun imagining how they might continue the lie on Monday, then decided to forget all about work.

They all turned off their mobile phones and agreed to leave them in Bradford.

‘And we’ll forget about men, too,’ Brenda added.

‘Well I don’t know about that!’ Natasha said.

‘Not men. Just the wankers we know,’ said Anna.

They packed hastily and caught the 10.35 for Scarborough.

FORTY-THREE

The further away they got from Bradford, the more their memories of the lives they led there seemed to fade away. Just for a while, they hoped to live a fantasy: be free, drink, laugh, no strings, no commitments, no faltering future. The journey reminded them of school trips, such an extraordinary change from their daily routine that the journey alone was thrilling. They planned their day: straight to Anna's aunt and uncle's home to freshen up, then return to the sea front, and the pubs; then food, back to the cottage, careful with make-up, best clothes, out again, down the main street, different pubs, drunker, louder. Then a club.

Once in Scarborough, they walked straight from the station into a taxi to take them to Anna's aunt and uncle's cottage.

The girls did not try to heat the house, and kept the taxi waiting to return them to town. They dropped their cases, sprayed on deodorant, combed their hair, and were driven back.

'I wonder what Keith thinks I'm up to?' Brenda asked. Natasha and Anna ignored the remark in the hope that it would be the last of its kind. It was as offensive as 'Where's the bar?' at an AA meeting.

They fixed up their make-up in the toilet of the first pub, and stayed in the same pub all afternoon. A karaoke machine and a coachload of women on a hen night from Glasgow provided the entertainment. To begin with the three girls were spectators, either enjoying the amateur renditions if the singer had a good voice, or mouthing along if the song was one they knew, or laughing at the singer if she sang badly. As they drank more they began to join in with the crowd, cheering and heckling as if they were all mates.

Several drinks later, Natasha said to Brenda, 'What was that song we used to sing together when we were kids? You know the one I mean, Brenda. It was from that film we loved, with Jennifer something and Patrick Swayze.'

'*Dirty Dancing*,' Brenda remembered. ' "I've Had the Time of My Life".'

'I'll go and see if they've got it,' Natasha said, making her way towards the karaoke machine as if Brenda had agreed.

'I can't sing,' Brenda, alarmed, told Anna.

'So what? It's just a laugh. We'll sing it together, the three of us, like Atomic Kitten.'

Natasha skipped back towards them, grinning, with both thumbs up.

'There's a queue, but our names are down.'

With alcohol now a necessity, they drank faster. Watching the next few singers, they swapped their derision for excuses: 'They were nervous; I don't think they could see the screen well; they were holding the mike too close.'

Then their turn came.

While Natasha and Anna's nerves disappeared on the first note, Brenda took until the chorus to warm up, then overtook the others, the shared mike being pulled closer to her mouth alone so that Anna and Natasha were demoted to backing singers. When their rendition ended, spontaneous applause broke out – Brenda clapping herself.

'What shall we sing next?' she bellowed as they returned to their drinks.

'All right, Britney, calm down,' her sister reproached her.

'Well, fuck it, I might as well make a fool of myself – I'm never going to see these people again. And there are no fanciable blokes here that I have to . . . Oh.'

Brenda saw a man, some years older than her, tidy, slim, short-haired and grinning. Anna and Natasha followed her stare. They saw the man and Anna waved. He smiled broadly.

'He's fucking gorgeous,' Brenda commented.

In turn the girls sang another five songs, Natasha and Anna duetting on 'Baby, Baby, Where Did Our Love Go?', Brenda duetting with Natasha on 'Angels', then Brenda going solo with 'Back For Good', Anna going solo with 'Have A Nice Day' and Natasha singing their final song, 'Girls Just Wanna Have Fun'.

The hours overtook them; Brenda surprised the others when she told them that it was six o'clock. Apart from chocolate bars bought in Bradford on the way, the girls had not eaten all day. They decided to grab a McDonald's, which they ate quickly before they went back to the cottage. Earlier in the day they had planned on being back out by seven; they now optimistically amended this to seven thirty, after each had showered, done her hair and make-up and then got dressed.

Though it was a sunny day, the cottage was cold when they entered it, and cramped and uncomfortable. They play-fought as each vied for the bathroom. They stripped down to their underwear without inhibitions.

'Today has been a good laugh,' Brenda said. 'It's been years since I've had one.'

'Years?'

'Before I took up with – *him*.' She stopped herself from spitting out her fiancé's name.

'It'll be even better tonight,' Anna assured her. 'We're going to get drunker, chat blokes up and dance –'

'Dance? Christ, I haven't done that in years either. What am I saying – I haven't flirted or done *anything* fun in years.'

'Not even been drunk?'

'Yeah, I've been that. But not happy drunk. Miserable drunk.'

'When was the last time you saw Natasha drunk?'

Brenda had to admit that the last time she had seen Natasha drunk was Corrine Slater's hen night.

Anna told her, 'She will talk you to death. And she flirts like crazy.'

Anna was taking her turn to shower when the phone rang. Brenda and Natasha were not sure whether to answer.

'It'll be all right,' Anna called to them. 'Just tell whoever it is that they're away.'

Brenda was taken aback to hear Natasha say: 'Hello? . . . Uh, Jesus! How the hell did you find out where we are?' She mouthed to her sister, 'It's our fucking mother!'

Brenda, in spite of everything she had told her sister, had texted Keith about the trip, and their mother had the phone number from when Natasha had stayed there before, a year ago.

'The thing is, Mum, we're getting ready to go out. We're in a rush.' Her mother was now asking to speak to Brenda. Natasha knew why.

'No,' Natasha answered. She knew she should add a reason, explain that Brenda had been enjoying herself and anything her mother would say to her would only spoil things. She heard her mother muffle the telephone, and speak in subdued tones. Someone else came on the line.

Keith demanded to speak to Brenda. Natasha grasped the phone in both hands. She looked at Brenda.

'What?' Brenda asked. 'Who is it?'

Natasha held the telephone tighter, and mouthed: 'It's Keith. He wants to speak to you. What shall I say?'

Brenda held out her hand. 'Give it here.'

'Are you sure?'

Brenda nodded. Natasha went into the bedroom, not wishing to hear what was said. She sat on the bed, knowing their plans for the night ahead were already ruined. Anna stepped out of the shower and began drying her hair.

'My sister is an imbecile,' she told Anna. Brenda wasn't escaping him; she would never leave Keith. She had enjoyed a few hours of fun and would now revert to type.

'Talking to him doesn't mean anything. Does it?' Anna asked. This was a question not requiring an answer.

'She needs him.'

'Why, what's so fucking special about Keith?'

'Nothing. He's not special, that's the whole point. She's

just so ordinary. Silly cow. We're smarter than her, aren't we, Anna?'

'Of course we are.'

'What are you doing in Scarborough?' Keith asked. Brenda knew he was trying to make the question sound casual, as if his only concern was that she hadn't given him adequate notice.

'Enjoying myself. I'd forgotten that I could.'

'I want you to come home. Tonight.'

'Not a chance. I'm coming back to Bradford tomorrow. And I won't be coming home to you.'

'Yes you will. This argument is no worse than any other we've had.'

'That's the point. We've had millions of similar arguments in the past and we'll have millions in the future – if we marry. So why get married?'

'So is that why you're in Scarborough, looking for someone else?'

'I'm bored of you now, Keith,' she told him. 'In fact, the truth is I've been bored of you for years. Ta ta.'

'Don't you dare hang up on me!' he yelled. 'If you don't tell me you're coming home right now I'll come up to Scarborough with Anna's boyfriend.'

Brenda was confused by this.

'What are you talking about? How do you know Anna's boyfriend?'

'I went to their flat. I met this bloke knocking on the door and asked him who he was, because – well, you know – because I was checking that he wasn't there for you. After he explained, I told him that you were going to Scarborough and so you must already have set off.'

'So her boyfriend's coming up for her?'

'I said I'd phone him, if you really were in Scarborough.'

Brenda liked the idea of having Keith travel all the way from Bradford to Scarborough, simply motivated by jealousy; she wanted him to come so he would talk to her with passion and pleading, emotions he had not demonstrated in years.

'I'm not coming home tonight, Keith, you can forget it. I'm going out and enjoying myself. I know you won't come to Scarborough looking for me,' she taunted. 'You haven't got the balls.'

She hung up. She took the receiver off the hook so he could not call back.

The account of the phone call that Brenda gave to Anna and Natasha was very different from what had actually happened. Keith had been completely unreasonable, she said, threatening to come up to Scarborough even though Brenda had assured him she was not going out.

'So what are you going to do?' Natasha asked.

Her reply was a simple, defeated, 'I'll have to stay in.'

Natasha was not surprised: she understood her sister.

'You haven't come all this way just to *stay in*,' Anna challenged. 'Are you really going to let him dictate how you behave even after you've left him?'

In the melodramatic tones of a martyr, Brenda moaned that she was sick of Keith's possessiveness, and that he had spoilt her day out with Natasha and Anna.

'He hasn't spoilt it if you come out!' Anna insisted.

'He's coming up with your boyfriend.'

'Richard . . . ?'

Natasha growled at Brenda, 'Don't say another word. If Keith's ruining today for you that's only because you're letting him ruin it. And the fact is . . . The fucking fact is, Brenda, that you want it ruined. You want him to come all this way just to beg you to come home. You're pathetic. You say you don't love him. Then it's simple. LEAVE HIM. Don't marry him. Come out with Anna and me and finish this day off. You can't even keep away from him for a day!'

The violence of Natasha's accusation propelled Brenda to respond angrily. *Natasha did not understand. She could not simply walk away from her years of investment. Natasha understood independence better than her; Natasha was less reliant on other people. Natasha was a bitch for not trying to be more sympathetic.*

Natasha asked Anna, 'And are you staying in waiting for Richard?'

'Am I fuck!'

FORTY-FOUR

By the time they had enjoyed their first drink and were heading towards the next pub, the sun had set. This crowd, the night-time drinkers, were younger and better dressed than those who had been out during the day. For Natasha there was a hardness to their expressions, casual and calculating. The girls made no contact with anyone else. They drank, talked, laughed, and later danced. The setting was different but the rest was habit. Anna's drunkenness had progressed steadily, continuing from where the afternoon drinking had left off; while Natasha had sobered up in the intervening hours – and no matter how much she drank she never managed to become drunk again. In the taxi home Natasha restrained herself from asking Anna if she expected Richard to be waiting for her, or if she had managed to forget about him.

'Have you enjoyed tonight?'

'Absolutely! Why do you ask?' Natasha had never asked this question before.

For Anna, the prospect that Richard might really have travelled there had preoccupied her through every minute of the evening. So she laughed particularly hard as they left the taxi, in case he might be listening, and would hear her enjoying herself.

In the darkness, after drinking so much and on this unfamiliar street, she had not noticed his car. When he saw the taxi pull up at the cottage he opened his car door and got out. He was nervous anyway, and Anna's laughter made his anxiety worse. He had come here to apologise, and she was clearly not in the mood.

'Anna,' he said from a distance. He hadn't approached, careful not to alarm her. The talk and laughter stopped abruptly.

'What do you want?' she demanded.

'Keith and Natasha's sister have made up and they've gone to spend the night in a hotel. That was about –' he looked at his watch '– three hours ago. I waited because . . . look, let me talk to you.'

'You're not coming in. Natasha, you go in. I'll talk to him in his car. I won't be long.'

Inside the unfamiliar cottage, alone, Natasha forgot about her friend. She was remembering the day she had spent with Geoffrey in Blackpool.

Though Natasha had switched on the cottage lights, she had neither turned on the fire nor got undressed. She had been inside for half an hour when Anna came in.

'Where's Richard?' was her first question.

Anna didn't answer. 'Do you know what I've been thinking about, Natasha? Brenda and Keith. Why is she so keen to be back with him? All this nonsense about coming here with us today was a lie. Really, all your sister wanted was a break. She wants to be with him. I'd be impressed if . . . I'd be *jealous* if she was like that because she was passionately in love, but it's not that. It's so sad. She's going to be with him . . . chances are, she's going to be with him for the rest of her life, even though she doesn't love him – well, not in any way that I consider to be love. I'm never going to be like that. I know everyone believes they feel things more accurately, more sensibly, than others, but . . . if it means swallowing pride, if it means loss of face, if it means foolishly forgiving someone – all that I'm prepared to do if I love that person. So . . .'

Anna deliberately paused here, expecting Natasha to reach her own conclusion.

'Where's Richard?'

'In his car. He's coming in in a minute. We'll drive back home tomorrow. Do you think I'm mad?'

'Barking,' Natasha smiled.

'Why haven't you got the fire on?'

'I don't know how it works.'

Anna turned the knob at the side of the gas fire.

'Yeah, tricky,' she continued. 'Richard explained to me about telling me he was married even when he wasn't. He's told me how he's never met anyone like me before and couldn't have imagined ever feeling the way he does. I know I might only believe him because I'm so eager to believe him . . . But I do believe him. He's told me he was determined not to blow it with me. Well, I didn't say much. We just kissed and . . .'

'I'm not going to warn you about anything, because the truth is I don't know if I'm anxious only because I'm worried that Richard will come between me and you.'

'Us? Never.'

'It's inevitable, so there's no use either of us complaining or worrying. And maybe if Geoffrey had somehow known I was here and pursued me, maybe I'd be so flattered, or afraid, I'd take him back.'

'Afraid?' Anna asked.

'Afraid like Brenda. But it's not only stupid people who are afraid of loneliness.'

Richard spent the night with Anna. Natasha was alone, sleeping on the couch, knowing how much she would have sacrificed to have had Geoffrey come to Scarborough and beg forgiveness. That way she could now be lying next to him. Or on top of him; the couch was very small.

The return journey to Bradford felt twice as long as it had done on the way out. Natasha sat in the rear seat of Richard's car, while Richard and Anna sat in the front, grinning at each other.

Natasha said nothing until they reached Bradford, driving through the filthy streets, passing its grotty shops, the squalor and destitution of a city which had lost its way years ago, wasted all its resources attempting to find its way back, then rolled over and given up the fight, happy to degenerate into divided worthlessness.

Natasha entered the flat alone. Anna had gone with Richard to his flat – which did not, after all, belong to a friend – to reconcile with him more completely.

Even though her last visit had been over a year ago, her mother visited, obviously egged on by Brenda. This was her sister's revenge.

'I need a bath, Mum, and I'm whacked out after the journey.'

'I'm not staying long,' her mother said, settling herself in the armchair. It was as if she felt compelled to explain why Brenda should be back with Keith, as if Natasha had never heard these arguments before. The repetitive drone allowed Natasha to indulge in her own memories of the only time she had ever been in love, during the holiday in Cleethorpes, when she had still been an adolescent. She knew now that the experience had not been love, not even close. Her emotions had just been a child's misinterpretation of love.

Geoffrey might be the nearest experience she would ever have to being genuinely in love, the adult version based on true compatibility. The cash equivalent of how she felt about him was incalculable. A rival could be wealthy in excess of all fantasy, but she would now choose Geoffrey.

Her mother had made herself a cup of coffee, then continued to talk about her youngest daughter's failed, unhappy relationship and why she must persevere with it. She asked a few probing questions about Natasha's love life, which Natasha expertly managed to avoid without giving any real reply.

'I won't be coming for dinner tomorrow, Mum,' Natasha said, trying to sound regretful.

'Why?' her mother asked.

'I don't want to see Keith or Brenda.'

'Why do you say it like that?'

'Well,' she started, 'it's just that,' she continued, very slowly, conceiving her own argument as she went along and thinking how best to cushion this in terms her mother would comprehend, 'she's barmy for getting back with him. And he's just as stupid for wanting her back. They don't make each other happy. I can't bear to watch it.'

When her mother had left Natasha immediately phoned Brenda.

'Why have you gone back to a man who makes you unhappy and a life you don't want?' she asked. This was the most stupid kind of question imaginable: a rhetorical question asked over the phone. Both sisters understood this, yet Natasha had been so passionate and expressive that an answer was compulsory.

Only when her sister answered with 'No one is with the person they want to be with. No one is that lucky,' did Natasha fully understand how terminally stupid her sister was, and that she deserved Keith, who was just as stupid. Natasha hoped they both would stay unhappy – such massive, deliberate stupidity deserves unhappiness.

Soaking in a very hot bath, Natasha forced herself to think about returning to work on Monday, to face the petulant complaints of their manager. Then she thought again about how she had lost Geoffrey, what he must think of her now and how she might have to wait this long all over again, and stomach an equal number of unsuitable boyfriends before she found someone else like him. Maybe she should go to see him, tell him of her change of heart, *embarrass* herself by explaining the mistake she had made. She had almost convinced herself of this until she was drying herself and saw the time. It was too late to go tonight.

Then Anna came home, accompanied by Richard, barely able to talk coherently because she was so deliriously happy. Anna said hello to Natasha, laughing as if this were the funniest remark she'd ever made. Natasha was spiteful enough to repeat everything her mother had said during her visit. This directly avoided acknowledging Anna's happiness, a deliberate attempt to caution her.

'She was telling me the usual stuff, you know? About why she thinks Brenda was right to go back with Keith. It doesn't matter to my mum that her daughter is miserable, just that she's secure.'

'Maybe Brenda's just naturally miserable,' Anna joked, refusing to have her good humour spoilt.

'Parents are bound to want their kids to be secure,' Richard added.

'If I ever have kids,' Anna began, hesitating slightly, 'you know – one day – I would never want them to be with someone just for the sake of being with someone. In fact, I would think I'd done a better job as a parent if they were happy on their own.' She turned to Richard. 'Do you know what I mean?'

'I suppose if I was in a happy marriage and I thought that's how it always was, then maybe I'd want my kids married too. But from what you tell me about Natasha's mum and dad . . .'

Before Anna could speak Natasha intervened. 'My mum and dad aren't the only ones that are unhappy. Most couples are. In fact – come on, Anna, isn't that true? Who do we know who's happily married, or happy in a long-term relationship?'

'So what?' Richard asked aggressively. 'What does that prove? I don't know anyone who's won the lottery, but I'm still happy to believe it's a desirable thing.'

'I'm not questioning its desirability, I'm questioning its probability. Yeah, I'll concede those odds.'

And with this the conversation ended abruptly. Anna and Richard went to bed. Natasha followed suit a few moments later, when she had calmed down. She knew but didn't care that she would take a long while to fall asleep. She lost hope that Geoffrey might be miserable too.

FORTY-FIVE

The next morning Natasha didn't get out of bed until Richard and Anna had left the house. She spent an enjoyable Sunday doing nothing, living through her thoughts without sinking into sadness. She went back to bed before Anna had returned home, though several hours passed before she fell asleep.

The following morning Anna woke her.

'We've got ten minutes before we have to set off for work. And there's someone here to see you.'

Natasha looked at herself in the mirror: her dishevelled hair could easily be brushed into a civilised shape; her complexion, however, was the yellow of a pub ceiling. She didn't want anyone to see her now, least of all Geoffrey.

But she had no choice, so she took the plunge and left her room.

But it wasn't Geoffrey who was there, it was Jake.

Natasha stayed silent, trying to take in the fact that it wasn't Geoffrey.

'I haven't been able to get in contact with you,' Jake began. 'But Anna explained that you've been away. I just wanted to tell you how much fun I had the other night, when we went out. And so I thought I'd pop round, in person, rather than phone, because we didn't make any arrangements, and I wanted to ask whether you might want to do it again. Go out.'

Already bored by him, Natasha wanted to tell him to fuck off, to explain that she could never spend any time with him, that he was too much like hard work; and regardless of any lucrative job, his money could never compensate for their chasm of incompatibility.

'The thing is,' she mumbled, 'I'm seeing someone else.'

Jake smiled weakly, at first. Then he hesitated, as if ready to be nasty. Instead he turned to Anna, puzzled.

'But you said . . .'

Anna stared at her friend. Natasha held Anna's gaze.

'I'm sorry, Jake. I must have got it wrong. She *was* seeing someone, but I thought it was over.' To spare his feelings, she added, 'I know how much fun she had with you the other night because she told me, and I made the presumption that she'd want to see you again. Sorry.'

Natasha and Jake managed to exchange a few pleasant words before he left. She thanked him for having taken her out, and he said that he hoped that whoever she was seeing made her happy.

'You're seeing Geoffrey again?' Anna asked immediately Jake was out of the door. 'When did this happen?'

'No, I'm not,' Natasha stated.

There was no time for Anna to be de-confused with an explanation; they had to leave and Natasha was not even dressed yet.

On the bus to town Natasha did little to help Anna understand. She told her that she hadn't had any further contact with Geoffrey, and didn't expect to have any in the future.

'And I specifically told you that I didn't want to see Jake again, Anna.'

'I know, but . . .' Anna didn't finish, unsure of her own motives for hoping Natasha might give Jake another try.

They arrived at work seventeen minutes late. Gerard Peters, furious at them for not turning up for work on either Friday or Saturday, the shop's busiest days, and angry that they were late this morning, took the girls into the office, even though he was conscious of the shop's staff shortages.

'You're sacked,' he told Anna, 'and you're on a final warning,' he told Natasha. They had not yet been in the shop for three minutes.

'I'm sacked?' Anna asked. 'Me?'

'Yes,' he answered, a big fat smug smile on his face. 'You.'

Anna began to think of the case she could make, the begging tactics she could employ. She knew that anything she might say would fall on deaf ears.

'You're a piece of shit,' she told him. This wasn't the plea he had anticipated, and his smile flickered away. Anna began to leave, and Natasha stopped her.

'You've sacked her?' Natasha asked. 'That's not fair! Be reasonable and sack me too. I also think you're a piece of shit.'

They both exited the office, with Natasha leading the way.

Anna stopped her at the shop doorway.

'Fuck. What just happened?'

'We're out of a job,' Natasha grinned.

'We're out of a job!' Anna yelped.

Natasha took her hand, smiling broadly. 'We're out of a shit job. We can walk into any shit job we want. All I care about right now is having the day off.'

'To do what?'

They were now out of the shop. The day was bright, and the sun startled them. Natasha shaded her face; as her eyes became accustomed to the brightness, she saw Derek.

'I need to see you,' he began. 'I like you, Natasha, and I want to go out with you. I think we'll be good together, once you've stopped being so jealous. Hear me out.'

Natasha reached out to the nearest rack, grabbed a shoe and swung it by its toes, striking Derek behind the ear. The shoe was a stiletto. He screamed in agony. Natasha and Anna ran away.

'Derek,' she called back, 'do you still not realise that our relationship is over? Every time I see you, you end up on the floor in agony. That's a clue.'

'What do we do now?'

'We start to think about the next move, about how we spend the rest of our lives.'

'Something we enjoy.'

'Something we enjoy – but for money? I can't think what.'

'The shoe stall in the market.'

'We need capital, which we don't have. We need premises, the stall fitting out, we need stock.'

'We need an investor.'

'We need a miracle.'

They returned home and talked extravagantly all day. Throughout the following week, flushed with growing excitement, the girls kept themselves busy, making enquiries, touring shoe markets, making calculations. Anna had only spoken to Richard on the phone, and until Saturday Natasha had not even mentioned Geoffrey. She was still planning to go and see him, explain that she no longer needed a man with money. Or something better, more revealing of her true thoughts. She needed him. Or something like that, though less desperate-sounding.

Though it was Saturday night, Anna insisted Richard went on a previously-planned night out with his mates. She would be staying in, alone, whilst Natasha went to see Geoffrey.

Natasha had finally settled on her choice of words. *Whatever you want, Geoffrey.* She would ask him what he wanted from her, and then she would agree. If he never wanted to see her again, so be it. If he told her he wanted her to move in with him, there in that shitty bedsit, she would. An act of extreme foolishness was called for; she needed to demonstrate the extent of her regret. Anna had Richard, and Natasha would have Geoffrey, at any cost.

She couldn't see his car but this did not worry her, perhaps believing it had finally faded into rust. She entered the building, mounted the stairs, knocked on his door. No answer. No noise. She left. She used her mobile to order a taxi, then counted the money she had in her purse. She had just enough to take her to the one place she could think he might be. Telling the taxi driver the address was like setting off in a barrel down Niagara; there was no return.

Natasha asked the taxi to wait, then ran towards the house, not nervous until she actually had to knock on the door and consider how she would explain who she was.

Melanie opened the door.

'I was seeing Geoffrey,' Natasha began. 'I know that you're friends of his. You see, I'm looking for him, I've been to his house –'

'You must be Natasha,' Melanie smiled. The smile vanished. 'He's gone. Do you want to come in?'

Natasha was still flushed with relief that Melanie knew who she was.

'I can't. Taxi waiting. He's gone where, though?'

'Back to America.'

'*America? . . . Back?*'

'Didn't you know he lived in America?' Melanie asked. Natasha glanced around, vacantly, as if she had made a mistake and come to the wrong house. Melanie continued. 'He took a sabbatical from work to write a novel.'

'*Novel? He's a novelist?*'

'No, he –'

The urgency forced Natasha to interrupt again; she was still trying to remain calm after being alarmed by the increasingly high-pitched voice she had used.

'Sabbatical? Is that something . . . Is he Jewish?

'No –'

'And sorry, but what work? He's unemployed.'

'He's a chemical engineer. He works in America, developing fuels for . . . Well, he's worked on the space-shuttle project.'

'Chemical . . . Space . . .' Natasha's confusion was diminishing her ability to complete a sentence.

Melanie was disappointed by Natasha's apparent lack of knowledge about Geoffrey.

'Didn't you two ever speak?'

'We spoke all the time, we talked loads. But . . . when did he go?'

'My husband's driven him to the airport.' Melanie bobbed back into her hallway, to look at the clock. 'You won't catch him, I shouldn't think.'

'I've got to try. Even though I don't – apparently – seem to know anything about him, I'm sure that I love him. Does that seem possible?'

'Sure.'

'I'd better apologise to you as well. I left a letter here . . .'

'There's no need to apologise for that. It gave Stuart an insight into how I'd react if he did ever stray.'

The taxi sounded its horn.

Though Natasha was embarrassed she still had to ask: 'I know you don't know me at all, but I have to get to the airport. You couldn't lend me any money, could you?'

At the airport Natasha had no clue where to go first. She looked on the departure board for the most recent flight to America. She went to the desk for that airline. The girl there refused to say whether Geoffrey was on the flight, though she did confirm that the plane was full.

There were no more questions Natasha could ask. Instead she went into the café and bought a coffee, then watched a plane – Geoffrey's possibly – taxi away, ready to take off. She wondered where he might be sitting, and if he might be looking out for her.

She watched the plane begin to gain speed and become airborne. In the sky, the plane turned, climbed, and disappeared from view. Forlornly, she waved at the disappearing plane; then turned to walk away.

Then she saw Geoffrey, slouched forward in a chair.

Natasha thought about Anna's reunion with Richard, their happiness and compatibility.

She saw Geoffrey sit up straight, and she flinched, looking away so he would not notice her. She couldn't speak to him until appropriate words were found. She wondered if he had changed his mind about leaving – wishing to see her now and be reconciled. Or maybe he was simply booked on a later flight.

She went home without speaking to him. As soon as she saw him she realised that everything she had intended to say had relied on him first seeing her and giving her an indication that he wanted to talk. Ideally, she had hoped to catch Geoffrey just moments before he got on his plane and he'd speak without her ever having to say a word.

She decided she would write to Geoffrey. A letter can be edited, reflected upon, worded carefully to avoid misinterpretation or ambiguity; or worded with deliberate ambiguity. She could ask questions which would demand answers, and tell him things without interruptions.

Only for a moment, as Natasha entered the flat, did Anna look unhappy. She saw Natasha and smiled, broadly.

'No Geoffrey?'

'He's gone to America.'

'Jesus, when blokes want to avoid you they take it really seriously.'

'Have you been thinking about Richard?'

'He texted me. He wants to come over later. I said no.'

'You said no to him? I'll bet the rich bastard has never been so insulted.'

The fire was turned on, lamps were lit, and the two girls turned on the TV, which they talked over until they were tired.

The flat was no longer their home, the fun had returned – they were camping out there, having a temporary adventure before heading on towards a more adult life.

'I don't think I'm in love with Richard any more. Now I just love him. Which is probably better.'

In the morning Anna found Natasha in the living room writing on a pad, with several sheets of paper already put aside, filled with tiny writing.

'What's this?' she asked, picking up one of the sheets. Natasha snatched it from her hand.

'Nothing. It's a letter. You can't read it. It's to Geoffrey.'

'Why are you writing so small?'

'Airmail.'

'Just write less.'

Natasha mocked her friend's ignorance, but then began to read the letter. Anna was right; there were far too many words. Natasha began again.

'I'll go with you to your parents' today,' Anna announced.

Natasha's pen slipped.

FORTY-SIX

When Billy Preston played the organ for the Beatles on their *Let It Be* sessions, the usually bickering band were on their best behaviour, partially to show a united front to an outsider but also to make him feel relaxed and welcome. So it also was when Anna went to Natasha's house for Sunday dinner. Natasha's mother avoided insulting her husband by not speaking to him at all, while he broke his usual silence by asking Anna polite questions: 'Can I take your coat?' and 'You'll tell us if there's anything you don't like?' No one wondered why Brenda and Keith, three weeks away from their wedding day, were not talking to each other. Or perhaps they were on speaking terms but simply had nothing to say – it was hard to tell. The meal was served to the accompaniment of Anna and Natasha's small talk – until Natasha, tired of beating about the bush, announced:

'We were sacked on Monday. But that's not the only piece of good news. We've had an idea we've been researching.'

Through silence, she explained how she and Anna intended to rent a stall on the market. She hoped her father would use his joinery skills to fit the stall with shelves – they would later reimburse him for the wood and his time; and they hoped that Keith would invest in their idea so that they had capital to buy stock. They also asked Brenda if she might be able to spare some Saturdays, helping them out on their busiest day, until they could employ someone permanently.

'Normally I would love to lend you money,' Keith began, the

first to recover from Natasha's announcement, 'but with the wedding coming up, all my spare cash is tied up.'

'That's bollocks,' Brenda said to Keith. 'And if it's true – let's postpone the wedding, then. This is more important. I like the idea of helping them out.'

'You'll have to give me an indication of the dimensions of the stall, love, so I can make rough designs,' Natasha's father told her. This was longest sentence he'd spoken for a week. He immediately had to take a drink of water.

'So are you going to lend them the money or not?' Brenda challenged. Keith looked around the table, too embarrassed to begin an argument here. 'Yes or no?' Brenda demanded. 'Because if the answer's no, then the wedding's off.'

'You say that as if it should bother me,' Keith told her. 'But I didn't say no. I said it would be difficult at the moment. I suppose if it's an investment, and there's a proper signed agreement, and it willl depend on how much you want to borrow –'

'We still have a lot of things to find out,' Anna told them.

There followed a livelier, happier meal than the family could remember, as Natasha and Anna were asked questions which they discovered they could not answer, increasingly aware that being entrepreneurs was not as straightforward as they had first hoped.

Their biggest obstacle in the first week was serving customers around the chaos of Natasha's father building their shelves and racks. They excused the small choice of styles and limited range of sizes by explaining that they did not yet have a big enough display area.

The stock of shoes they had bought was according to their own personal tastes, yet this limited stock turned over rapidly, so each morning Natasha served on the stall while Anna went out spending the previous day's takings on new stock. Each day the turnover went towards the next day's stock, the amount of stock growing daily.

Natasha's father had finished the rudimentary shop-fitting by

Friday teatime. They closed early to acquire more stock, their largest buy to date.

Natasha wrote to Geoffrey as regularly as every other day. She had sent the first letter to his friends' house, asking them to forward it to Geoffrey in America. Since receiving it, he had written back every other day. When she got home from work at the end of each day, the very first thing she did was check her mail.

Anna watched her friend on the settee, legs pulled up beneath her, her grinning teeth clipping at her fingernails as she read and re-read his letters.

'What's so fascinating about them?'

'They're fascinating to me.'

'Are they romantic?'

'Very. Are you jealous?'

'Of letters? Call me old-fashioned, but I think it's more romantic to have a boyfriend who actually lives in the same country as me.'

To Anna's frustration Natasha didn't respond. She kept on reading. She could phone Richard and talk to him, or see him any time she wished. That should be preferable.

On Saturday morning, when Anna and Natasha arrived, Brenda was already waiting outside their stall. She was eager to begin work.

'This beats staying at home,' she told her sister.

For the first hour business was slow, so they stocked the shelves and familiarised themselves with the different styles they had, just in case any selling patter was needed.

'Now that I'm working for myself,' Anna said to Natasha, 'does this mean I have to be polite to customers?'

'One step at a time,' Natasha told her. 'We can't expect miracles.'

The day progressed without the girls realising they had worked through lunch. An hour's lull preceded the market's closing time.

From under the counter, Natasha dug out the shoe-box which

they had filled during the day with overspill from the till. The shelves were decimated, they had worked non-stop, yet they felt elated. The shoe-box was full of notes, and the three women stared in awe.

'How much is there?' Anna asked. Natasha counted up. 'Wow,' Anna concluded.

'We mustn't get carried away, remember,' Natasha warned, desperately attempting to fight her elation. 'Think about our wages – we're at least going to pay ourselves the same wage we had before, right? – then there's the weekly amount we promised Keith, Brenda's wages, the money we'd said we'd give to Dad, the rent. And think about all the cash we'll need for new stock.'

'Yeah, but even so – wow!'

At last Natasha grinned. 'I know!'

'I hope you eventually get to earn more than Keith,' Brenda said about her husband-to-be. 'He'd hate that.'

The following week they took a risk and advertised for staff. They wanted only one assistant but gave two girls, who were friends, jobs. Sales reps called often, and the girls began to understand how they could further widen their profit margins. Two Saturdays after opening they had to entrust their fledgling business to the two new girls, as they took the day off to attend Brenda's wedding.

Natasha and Anna arrived together at Natasha's parents' house. Her mother was bustling around, still in curlers and a dressing-gown.

Natasha read through some of the cards of congratulations displayed on the room divider her father had made. She didn't know most of the names in the cards, and the comments were so bland that she didn't take the trouble to read any out to Anna. Astonishingly, the wishes for the couple to have a happy marriage were not spiked with sarcasm.

'Perhaps we should have sent our congratulations?' Natasha asked Anna.

'We'll save them for the divorce.'

'Aren't you going up to see your sister?' her mother asked.

'I'll only be in the way,' Natasha told her. Her mother left the room.

'I wonder what the dress is like,' Anna said, for want of anything else to say.

'Predictable, I should think.' The thought crossed Natasha's mind that one day she might have to choose a wedding dress. She'd never seen one she liked. Better never to put herself to the trouble.

'Have we ever been to a wedding we've enjoyed?' she asked Anna.

'We've usually enjoyed the receptions. Music. Booze. Blokes. People we know.'

'Today we need to get very, very drunk very, very quickly,' Natasha told her. 'Otherwise it's going to be a nightmare.'

'You're right. It's a shame we can't drink during the actual ceremony. Do you think your sister will be happy?'

'Not when she learns we're going to dock her wages for today.'

Keith and Brenda's registry office wedding had the atmosphere of a hostage negotiation, with every 'I do' conceded reluctantly, drenched in anxious sweat. The registrar rushed the proceedings, perhaps instinctively sensing that at any moment someone might have the wit to halt the pantomime.

Afterwards, family and friends gathered in a nearby Working Men's Club to take solace in alcohol. The wedding reception set the tone for the marriage: throughout the ordeal, everyone involved wished they were somewhere else.

'How long do we have to stay here?' Anna asked.

'We'll leave when Brenda starts looking happy.'

'So they're definitely serving afters?'

During the fourth hour of the reception the music became louder, though the dance floor stayed empty. No matter how hard he tried, nothing the DJ played enticed the guests onto their feet. Out of professional pride he considered setting off the fire alarm, but knew that once they were free to vacate the building nothing would be able to persuade them back.

Throughout the day, the gaps between each group of people

had widened. Those who had left to take their children home had not returned. Those guests who had arrived only for the evening do bought a drink in order to show their faces, then discreetly left. This was Saturday night – there were far more fun places to be.

At five o'clock Anna had phoned their employees. Their stall had enjoyed the highest takings of its existence.

She told Natasha, 'Sounds like the girls coped very well without us. The business isn't even a month old and we're redundant.'

Natasha and Anna had been cornered by Angela Watson, an old friend from the estate, who had spoken seamlessly for forty minutes about her boyfriend of four years, Tony, with whom she had two children, and who had repeatedly ditched her in the last four years, and had now, finally, gone for good. Except that he kept returning.

'I said to him,' she said to them, 'that he must think I'm stupid, he must think I don't know that the only reason he ever comes to see me is when he wants a fuck. It's every Saturday night. He goes out with his mates, gets pissed, gets horny, then knocks me up at three in the fucking morning. I'll bet you anything you like he'll be there tonight. I don't know what he takes me for. Then Sunday morning – *off.* He doesn't even hang around to say hello to the kids. When he lived with me and he'd been drinking *nothing* could get him out of bed. He says the same old shit to me every time he comes, "Can you look me in the eyes and tell me you don't still love me?"'

Lorraine Bates, Angela's closest friend, had been sitting with them, listening. She spoke to Anna, about Angela.

'I've told her, she's wrong in her head. What she wants to do is get herself done up, go out, meet someone and take him back to the house so that when Tony calls he gets a shock.'

'I won't do that,' Angela said, 'I wouldn't want Tony to think I'm a tart.'

There was a break in the music at seven thirty, when Keith and Brenda made their farewells. The DJ told everyone that the couple were going to have an early night, exhausted after their exciting day. 'No doubt they'll get home and jump straight into bed,' he joked suggestively. People clapped and made obscene catcalls as the couple left. Some of the more elderly guests were woken by the disruption.

The newly-weds put on a united happy face as they departed. But Natasha knew that they had not been speaking to each other all day. The silence continued on their way home and even when they went to bed. Their first and last words to each other that day had been their wedding vows.

After wangling herself free of Angela Watson, Natasha had gone to sit with her mother and father. The wedding had reminded her mother of her own wedding day. Reflecting upon the marriage which followed, she was in a foul mood. Talking to Natasha, her insults about her husband were relentless.

'Then divorce,' Natasha – grown weary of her mum's insults about her father – told her. Drink and exposure to the hypocritical sentiment of the day's proceedings had made her reckless, speaking aloud a thought she had held in for years. 'I wouldn't stay with someone just for sex, if that's what it is.'

'Sex? What makes you think we still have sex? The last time I had sex with your father you were still living at home.' Alcohol had also permitted Natasha's mum to be this candid. 'We're too old to divorce now,' Natasha's mother said, as if it was her epitaph.

Natasha wanted to explode. She wanted to shout at her mother. As she sat in silence, expressionless, she wished she was far drunker so that oblivion would free her.

'Let's get out of here,' Anna whispered to Natasha.

'How can you be too old to opt for happiness?' Natasha exclaimed.

'We have to get out of here,' Anna repeated. She stood, pulling her friend to her feet.

'We're off, Mum,' Natasha said. Her mother did not acknowledge her.

Anna continued, 'We're businesswomen. We're employers. We make good money. Let's celebrate with our type of people!'

*

The management had chosen to make the last night of the *Apollo* a celebration, of sorts. As customers entered they were given crackers to pull, the 'Happy Xmas' logo removed; saucers sprinkled with grains of salt were placed on the bar, so everyone would think they'd missed out on the free peanuts; three balloons were kicked around the dance floor, surviving from the dozen which had been dropped from the ceiling.

Natasha took care to look around the club, to familiarise herself with its set-up, so that in the future when she was reminiscing with her friend she could rely on having a definite picture in her mind.

'I hope there's a fight,' she said.

'Oh, there'll be a fight. It wouldn't be the *Apollo* without a fight.'

Coming here from Brenda's wedding reception, their mood could only improve. They continued to drink quickly, to take advantage, as if stocking up on the *Apollo*'s cheap drink. For the first time ever, no one tried to chat them up.

'Maybe we're getting old,' Anna suggested.

'Maybe men can somehow tell that we have boyfriends.'

'Yeah, like that would stop them trying to get off with us! . . . So, Geoffrey's your boyfriend?'

'I didn't expect him to be. What I mean is, I've never conducted a relationship by post, so when I wrote to him I didn't know what I expected his reply would be like. I thought we'd be like pen pals, but flirty. Or something.'

'Is it possible to flirt by letter?'

'Very possible.'

'When we get home tonight I want to read his letters.'

'Not a chance.'

'What does he say that you're too embarrassed to read to me?' Anna asked.

'It's private.'

'So it's something dirty? He's a fucking freak.'

'It's not dirty. He writes compliments.'

'Freak.'

'Maybe. But I really hope that if he ever returns and we stay together, he still writes to me.'

'I should imagine he'll want to. It'll be preferable to him actually having to talk to you. So do you think he'll come back?'

'He's never mentioned it and I've never asked him.'

'Would you want him to?'

'Yes.'

'That's good,' Anna said cautiously. 'I hope he does. I hope that you . . . Well, we both knew – didn't we? We knew that we wouldn't live together always?'

Natasha agreed, though she had never known this.

'And I've been thinking how much I'd like to buy a house,' Anna said.

'You mean you're moving out?'

'That's the idea. Are you shocked?'

'*You* buying a house, being a responsible adult? Of course I'm shocked. This is out of the blue, how come you've never mentioned it before?'

'Because before . . . I've told you all the dreams I had which had no way of coming true. This always seemed a possibility, even if remote. So we won't be living together any more.'

'I worked that out for myself, Anna.'

'Are you going to stay in the flat?'

Natasha knew the answer without even thinking about it: 'The flat is *our* home, it won't seem right on my own. I'll find somewhere else.'

'Maybe Geoff'll return and . . . No?'

'Maybe one day I'll live with him. Even if we're not living together, you and me, I still like the thought of being independent for a while, especially seeing as we're business women now.'

'I'm a businesswoman buying my own home!' Anna said, amazed.

'Maybe that's why we're not being chatted up,' Natasha suggested. 'We look too responsible.'

They drank Blue WKDs mixed with port, which one of the

girls they employed told them tasted like Vimto. It took a long time for Natasha to explain to the barmaid what she was asking for. They had two drinks then danced. They left before the very end, not forgetting – though neither mentioned this to the other – that they were walking out of the *Apollo* for ever.

FORTY-SEVEN

As their business settled into a routine, they began to recognise the qualities that made them good bosses, good managers and good workers. Anna hated serving customers. Unlike previously, Anna had to make a greater effort when serving. She had to be more patient when customers could not make a decision, more polite if they were difficult, more persuasive if they were hesitant. She had to learn that it was not good business practice to call customers awkward twats.

They had taken it in turns to shop for more stock, but this had gradually become solely Anna's job. Natasha had to concede that Anna's taste was more in line with public opinion. The only stock which remained from their opening days of trading were the styles that Natasha had chosen, while Anna's choices leapt off the shelf.

Even in spite of years of experience in shoe retailing, it was not until the responsibility became hers that Natasha discovered her natural gift for display. They had limited space, yet she managed to display all their choices without overwhelming their customers. On the days when stock was down, she would set out displays which made the few remaining styles look more exclusive, as if they were set out on their own because they were for the more discerning customers.

Contradicting both their assumptions, Anna proved to be the better with their accounts. Natasha knew how to make the sums add up, but Anna understood better how to juggle money around. They had opened accounts at several wholesale outlets, and had two different bank accounts. Anna always knew who required paying first, how little money their suppliers would accept without turning nasty, and which accounts to use on any particular date so that they always stayed in the black.

In less than three months they had put aside enough money to pay Keith back. Anna's instincts were to pay him only half the money back, and keep him waiting for the rest. On this occasion Natasha persuaded her of the virtues of clearing their debt.

'I want him off our backs,' Natasha said, though in truth Keith had not once mentioned the loan.

'Should we give him a present as a thank you?'

'Shoes.'

'Shoes?'

'No, you're right. Slippers. Let's not be too generous.'

'Yeah, and let's give him them in the wrong size, I've never liked him.'

Richard and Anna saw each other less frequently than in the early days of their relationship, often having several days apart. However, when Anna did go to Richard's flat, she regularly stayed for two or three nights without returning. Through this process she began to understand that it was not only Natasha who nagged when she was untidy. Richard nagged far more. What made this even more intolerable for Anna was that while she was at Richard's flat she made every effort to be tidy and clean – yet he didn't even seem to notice.

'You should be going out with Natasha, not me,' she told him. 'The way both of you nag me about being untidy, you'd be ideally suited.'

'Did your parents nag you about being untidy?'

'*My* parents? You've got to be kidding. After they died and the house had to be cleared, they found empty cider bottles dating back to the old currency. If they'd made their own funeral arrangements it would have been black bin-bags dumped in the quarry. Tidiness wasn't important to them. So long as they always knew where the bottle opener was, that's all they cared about.'

'And where was it?'

'It was usually in my room, I'd run down when they shouted.'

Richard and Anna's conversations unearthed more and more truths about each other, so that eventually Anna confessed her secret that living with Natasha had not been the joyful experience she had once hoped.

'Then live with me,' Richard told her.

'Smart idea, Richard. Perhaps you should think about that just a little bit harder.'

'Just because I said it casually, don't think that it's just occurred to me. I think we'd be happy.'

'Maybe,' she told him. 'I mean, maybe we'd be happy, not *maybe* I'll come and live with you.'

When Anna went to see the mortgage advisor, the most she hoped for was a mortgage of £35,000 so she could afford one of the ex-council houses on her old estate. To her delight, she was advised she could afford a much higher loan on her income.

'I've seen a house for sale near your sister's, think of that. That would really put Keith's nose out of joint.'

'He'd be gutted,' Natasha joked. 'If *you* moved into their neighbourhood the value of their house would plummet.'

Natasha showed interest in Anna's search for a home by accompanying her whenever she went to look at properties. Anna complained about Natasha's interventions, but retrospectively was always grateful for her more level-headed advice. Anna was often influenced by tasteful decor and stylish furniture, while Natasha looked at practicalities of structure and location.

Occasionally the girls looked at houses which could only be afforded if they took out a joint mortgage. They looked around each room, assigning it a function, discussing how it might be decorated or renovated. This was done without either of them directly suggesting that they should continue to live together.

Finally Anna found a house which suited all her needs and satisfied most of her desires. It was semi-detached, with three bedrooms and a beautiful fitted kitchen. When Natasha viewed the kitchen with Anna, after Anna had put in her offer, all she could say was: 'If you buy this house, what a terrible waste of a kitchen.'

Anna's offer was accepted and she was given a date to move in.

The success of their stall meant the girls began to make plans to move into a real shop in one of Bradford's many vacant premises. Consequently, they had little spare time. Anna saw Richard infrequently, and he did not again suggest that they should live together. Natasha's letters to Geoffrey now contained little personal detail; she was full of enthusiasm for the shop and told him about helping Anna decorate her new home.

Natasha collected Geoffrey's letters together, their growing number becoming an indication of how long he had been gone; the number of times she re-read them was an indication of her petrifying affection for him. When she replied to him she could not write fast enough to keep up with her thoughts. The things she found most annoying about his letters were his continual apologies in case he was boring her, and his over-use of modesty and self-deprecation. To boost his confidence and to guarantee the letters kept coming, she told him that she loved him. The first time she wrote this down she changed her mind and began the letter again. It took several more letters before she plucked up the courage to send the words, easing the confession by brutally insulting him for his continuing apologies.

He phoned the day he received the letter. This was the first time she had heard his voice since he had left the country.

'You love me?' he asked.

'Yes.'

'I'm coming back to England.'

'Good. But that's not why I wrote it.'

'It's still the reason I'm returning.'

She wrote a letter to him suggesting that instead of renting another grotty bedsit while he was considering job offers, he could take Anna's old room. In the meantime she would decorate and furnish it.

She had this letter in her pocket when she accompanied Anna

on one of her trips to look at the house she had bought. As they walked towards the house they passed another, just three doors down from Anna's, with a For Sale sign outside.

'Looks like the neighbours have already got wind that you're moving in,' Natasha joked. The two girls stopped outside the house, to view it in comparison to Anna's.

'It looks like it needs work.'

'Your dad could help you with that,' Anna said.

'Me? You think I should buy this house?'

'Don't you fancy the idea? Remember the name of the estate agents, and think about it.'

Nothing else was said about the house. Natasha did not post her letter.

FORTY-EIGHT

Two weeks later, and it was Anna and Natasha's last day living together. It was a Saturday.

The *Apollo* was shut, *Bartok's* was out of bounds because Richard was going out with the lads, and the two of them decided they would first go drinking around Shipley and see where the night led them.

Natasha showered first, then Anna knocked on the door to ask if she was done. By the time they ordered the taxi they were regretting the decision to go out.

After reprimanding each other for talking about their shoe stall too much, most of the conversations they held after this were full of nostalgia. Still, they were having a good time and agreed that they would do this again, maybe regularly.

Anna asked about Geoffrey, because she thought Natasha would want to talk about him. He was due back in England in a month, by which time Natasha would have begun the renovation in her new home.

Natasha asked about Richard, because she now accepted that he was the most important person in Anna's life. Each girl spoke briefly about her boyfriend, knowing the other was not really interested.

'It's a shame the *Apollo* isn't still open,' Anna said as last orders were called.

'So aren't we going to a nightclub?'

'Of course we are! But we need to loosen up. I don't want anyone as uptight as you as my neighbour.'

'It's you that's been uptight, not me. I'm celebrating. At last I get the flat to myself. I can have it tidy and clean!'

Having fun now, but not drunk, they took a taxi into Bradford and found a nightclub they had never been into before. They rushed their first three drinks and began to flirt. They were acting out their good humour, and reminiscing at the same time.

Soon Anna left Natasha. She had been asked to dance and was on the dance floor, feet hardly moving, dancing only from the waist up as the guy who had asked her held her elbow and talked into her ear. Her concentration, her pained expression, then the shake of her head, showed him that she could not hear a word he was saying.

Like a parent with her child, Natasha had been the closest witness to Anna's growth into womanhood, but she had seen her every day, so never had a period apart to scrutinise, on fresh inspection, any change. She saw change now, even through drunken eyes, even through erratic coloured lighting. Anna had developed all she was going to, she was a full adult woman articulate, confident, mature.

Seeing Natasha looking at her, Anna clutched her breasts, one in each hand, and moved them around in circles, to make Natasha laugh.

A man stood next to Natasha, pointing his glass to Anna.

'Let me guess. Your mate's single but you're married.'

Natasha looked at him, directly, forcefully, to discourage him He was too skinny, the glass he carried was almost as wide as him His hair was fuzzy. He had a slight squint, too – but Natash didn't hold this against him. She daren't; at this hour she migh also have a squint.

'What makes you think that?'

'She's dancing and you're not.'

'Someone asked her. No one's asked me.'

He put down his drink. 'Would you like to –'

'No,' she snapped at him, then smiled so he wouldn't walk of She wanted to talk, and wanted to pursue his guess that she wa married.

'I'm not married.'

'So you're single?'

She couldn't resist sarcasm, it was too obvious. 'Excellent detective work. Single, yes.'

'Engaged? Living with someone? Seeing someone?'

'None of those, at the moment.'

'Right. Good,' he grinned.

'But I do have someone,' Natasha said. Now that the epiphany had struck her, she did not wish to speak to this strange man. She realised, irrevocably, that she and Anna both had someone, someone *else*. She wanted Anna to dismiss the dancer and come and talk to her.

Having abandoned the idea of charming her with talk, the man had decided to impress Anna with his dance moves. He had even put his bottle down – this was serious. He danced as if he had practised a whole routine beforehand, and nothing like a different tune, beat or speed would alter his interpretation. His arms flew around; she held them down to avoid bruising. He misunderstood this contact as attraction, and winked at her.

Natasha knew she would always be Anna's friend. She knew, also, that she would always want Geoffrey, too.

'Are you still here?' Natasha sneered at the skinny man. He misunderstood the question as attraction, and pursed his lips.

'Don't worry, I'm still here.'

Anna caught Natasha's eye, and they shared the joke.